JENNA WOLFHART

**Kingdom in Exile**

Book Two of The Fallen Fae

Cover Design by Gene Mollica Studio

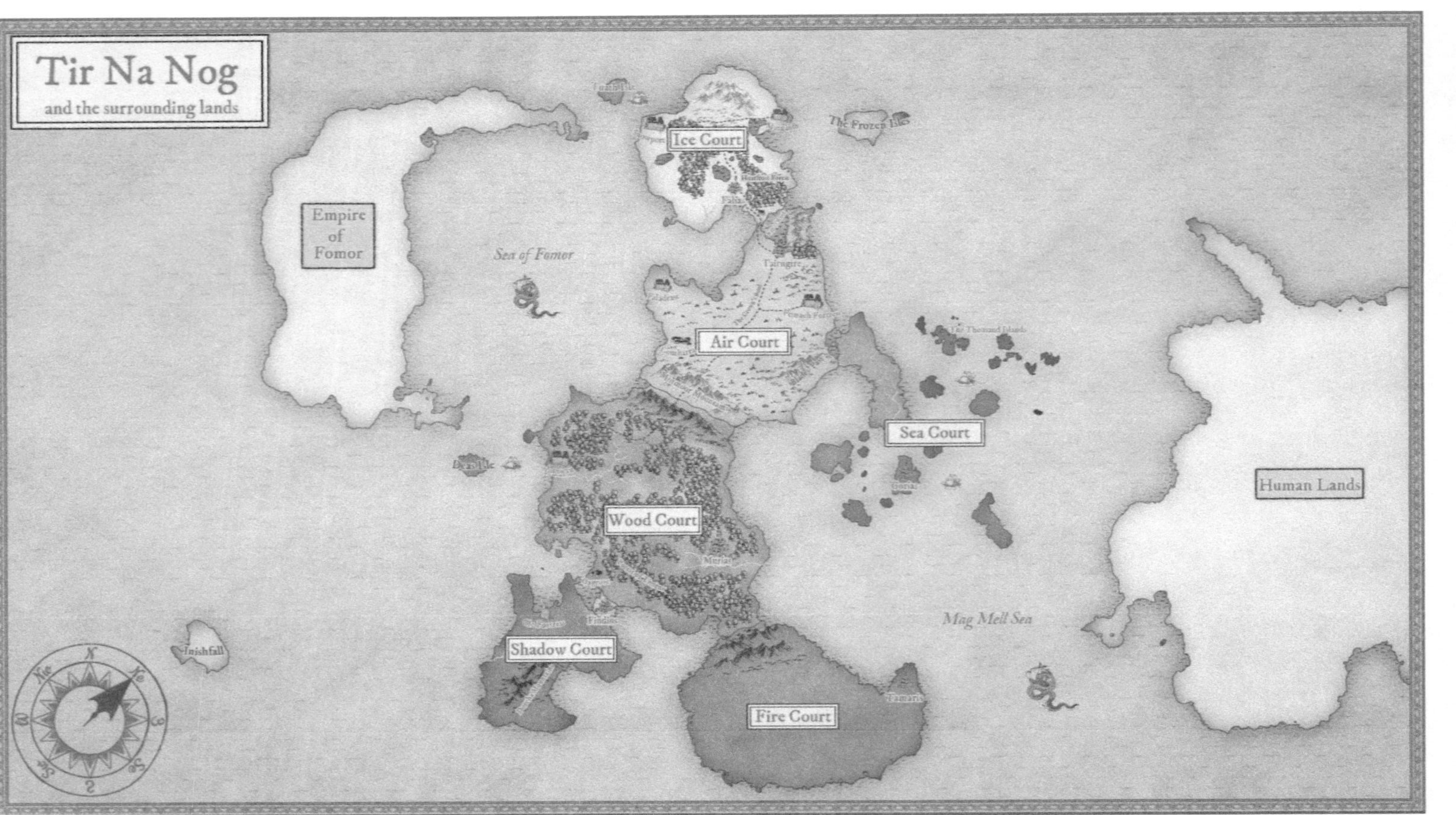
Tir Na Nog
and the surrounding lands
Empire of Fomor
Sea of Fomor
Ice Court
The Frozen Isles
Air Court
Sea Court
Wood Court
Human Lands
Mag Mell Sea
Shadow Court
Fire Court
Inishfall

# PROLOGUE

## IMOGEN

Darkness was everything, and everything was darkness until light finally speared the dusty floor outside of Imogen's cell. Eyes burning, she lifted her chin from her chest and peered toward the silhouette of the male striding down the corridor. He was tall and slim, and a thin rapier whispered by his armored thigh. Imogen's heart sank. It wasn't her Thane, her son returned from his mission down south.

It was that damn bastard. Her former lover.

Now her mortal enemy.

"Aengus," she hissed, pushing up onto her aching bare feet. Newfound energy coursed through her tired body, fuelled by anger and a thirst for vengeance. *He* was the one who had put her in this dungeon cell when once she had been the most powerful fae in all of Tir Na Nog. She had been the High Queen of the Air Court. The one who had commanded the mightiest kingdom of them all.

Aengus had stripped her of it all.

The ginger fae stopped just outside her iron-barred cell, flanked by two warriors donned in Air Court leather armor.

The infamous sigil was stamped into the center of their chests: a golden gleaming crown. She turned her glare on them both. They shifted uncomfortably on their feet. Traitors, the lot of them. They should be liberating her from this pitiful prison, not standing guard for the usurper who had put her here.

"Imogen." Aengus gave her a thin-lipped smile. Why had she ever thought him handsome? He was a rat. "I would say that you're looking absolutely ravishing this glorious day, but that would be a lie."

She narrowed her eyes. "Why are you here, Aengus? Has my son not yet returned to kick your traitorous arse off his throne?"

Her words were powered and her tone sharp, but inwardly, she felt as small as a hoarfrost worm. Thane had been missing for weeks. No one knew where he was, only that he'd narrowly escaped several attempts on his life. Of course, Imogen knew he was not dead. She could feel it in her bones, and the power of the throne had yet to transfer to Aengus. But that did not mean that her missing son was safe.

He was her only living child. Her three beautiful children before him had been brutally slaughtered by the shadow fae. Now, she worried they'd taken him away from her as well. And then there would be nothing left in this cruel world for her to fight for anymore.

"Ah. I'm afraid your cowardly spawn is still missing." Aengus, her former Grand Alderman, her former lover, took a step closer to the bars, almost close enough for her to reach through and wrap her fingers around his throat. "Unfortunately, it seems two others have gone missing as well. Princess Reyna Darragh and the warrior Lorcan."

Imogen smiled. The Darragh girl had pulled through, after all. Imogen had asked Reyna to sneak out of the city and find Thane. At least someone was on her side. Someone who

Imogen never would have counted on trusting. Only weeks ago, she had hated the girl. She almost laughed at the bitter irony of it all.

"I suppose you are none too pleased, Aengus."

"Grand Alderman," he replied crisply in his odd, foreign accent. "You will use my title."

"Hmm. Well, *Grand Alderman*. I don't quite understand what you wish for me to do about it. I'm in a prison of *your* making, as you can very well see. There is little I can do in here."

He arched a brow. "Is that truly so? Because some might believe that *you* were the one who asked the Princess to defy my command so that she might go in search of your son."

Imogen had expected this. She had known that Aengus would come for her eventually. As the de facto ruler of the realm, his command was ultimate above all else. Defying him was viewed as defying the Dagda, their god. To do so could have terrible consequences. It was treason.

But more than that, Imogen also knew that Aengus had been lurking in wait, hoping that she would do something that would give him the excuse to act with his full power.

Commanding Reyna to stand down might have been Aengus's way of trapping Imogen. He would know that she would do anything to save her son, even request the assistance of her former enemy. But it had been a trap that Imogen had gladly walked into. Because her son's life was far more important than her own.

"I can see why some might think that," Imogen said quietly, standing tall on her bruised and aching feet.

"And did you?" he asked. "Did you tell Reyna Darragh to defy my command?"

It was a yes or no question. Imogen never answered those. Most fae never would. In a world without lies, one had to be careful. But she saw no way to answer at all without giving the truth away. Imogen could not mince words where her son's life was concerned nor did she even want to try. Aengus had stolen the throne, her court, and her glorious life. And he would not hesitate to kill Thane if he got the chance.

For the first time in her life, she would proudly tell the truth in all its brutal glory.

"Yes," she said in a hiss, edging closer to the iron bars. "I most certainly did tell Reyna and the warrior to go find my son, the High King of this realm. *Your* High King. And when he returns, you will find your head on a spike."

Aengus stretched his thin lips wide as he smiled, flashing two rows of straight, sharp teeth that had never looked quite right in his face. "A command from me is a command from our god. You have now committed far worse treason than what put you in this cell. In the name of our great Dagda, I hereby sentence you to death. Guards."

Imogen gripped her stained dress in trembling fists as the cell door swung wide. The guards pushed inside, still avoiding her gaze. One grabbed her right arm; the other took the left. And then, slowly, they led the former High Queen toward her death.

Imogen stood on the gleaming, golden steps of the Adhradh, staring out at a crowd of silent low fae. The citizens of Tairngire had crowded into the outer courtyard of Dalais Castle to watch their former ruler face her fate. There were hundreds of them, their clothing a kaleidoscope of gold. Each and every one wore the official royal color of the Air Court, a symbol of their loyalty to the crown.

And yet, Imogen knew they would all gladly watch her die. They would do nothing to stop Aengus, even if he was a foreigner himself.

She had been born a sea fae. A royal match had been made with a Lord of the great Air Court when she had been a mere sixteen years of age. Lord Sloane Selkirk. His had been a powerful family, ruling over Feurach Fortress on the eastern coast of the realm. After they'd married, Sloane had become ambitious. He, his brother, and his two sisters had staged a coup against the reigning Dalais family. He gathered his army, stormed Tairngire, and murdered the High King and Queen.

At the time, Imogen had wanted nothing to do with the brutal slaughter. But her fate had been sealed. She had already married the male and there was little she could do. Not long after the coronation, Imogen had discovered that Sloane was half-human. His strength was nothing more than a lie until he sat his knobbly arse on the Seat of Power.

It had made sense to her then, his brutal quest for power. Only a pretender would commit atrocities for a throne. He'd never deserved to be king.

She closed her eyes and breathed in the scent of spring. There was only a hint of it in the air. The cold bite of the wind remained from the winter, but the pearly Hawthorn Blossoms pushed a sweeter, hopeful scent into the longer days. Soon, the snow and ice would melt, and the sun would warm the tired faces of this city.

Imogen would not be around to see it this year. Or any year thereafter.

She had made many mistakes in recent months, she knew. Perhaps her actions had caught up with her, and the Dagda had decided to punish her for her transgressions. But she had only tried to do her best in a cruel world, one so empty of the magic that had once brought hope and life to these lands.

Sloane's reign had needed to end. And Thane had not yet been ready.

She would not seek forgiveness, not when she'd had no

other choice. And now she would die in the shadow of her god's great bronze statue with his powerful wings flared wide.

"Citizens of Tairngire," Aengus shouted as he strode from one end of the wooden platform to the next, his voice clear and loud.

Fear twisted around her heart like a vine lined with thorns, each point stabbing deeper into her veins. A strange ringing filled her head, and sweat beaded on her brow. She had steeled herself for this moment, but that did not stop her fear. Imogen had expected to live another hundred years. She had been the High Queen, surrounded by a sturdy castle and guards. She was of noble blood. She wasn't a warrior or the captain of a sea-faring boat, lives that often ended far too soon due to the danger of their professions.

Her life could have stretched on for years.

But she could now see that queendom held far more danger than anything else, particularly in the realms of the fae.

Aengus came to a stop before her and smiled. "The Dagda has considered this fae standing before us, and he has judged her terrible and wicked and cruel. She has conspired against the crown. She has committed numerous treasons. And she has disobeyed direct commands from me, and therefore, our great god himself." He strode to the edge of the platform, the wood creaking beneath his leather boots. The crowd before her was a sea of blurred faces and golden hair. "Our laws are clear. Those who disobey the Dagda are to be punished. Harshly yet justly. And there is only one punishment for treason. Death, by hanging."

Imogen swallowed hard, the rough rope scraping the delicate skin at her neck. The ringing in her ears grew loud, drowning out the building murmur of the crowd. She squeezed her eyes shut and balled her fists.

"Imogen Selkirk of the Air Court." Aengus's voice was

suddenly loud, his lips brushing against her ear. Her balled fists tightened. "What words would you depart with?"

Her eyes flew open then, and her belly was lined with steel. His thin-lipped smile matched the sparkle in his eyes. The setting glare of the sun was a backdrop to his silhouette, his ever-present rapier whispering against his thigh.

Imogen drew all the remaining strength into her voice, and hissed, "I curse you, Aengus. May your life be long and full of misery. May your every ambition become true, and just when you think you've won, may it all bite you in your fucking arse."

Shock flickered in Aengus's narrow grey eyes, but he recovered quickly, even as excited whispers drifted through the crowd. Vicious anger rippled across his face. He raised his hand, signalling the guards behind her.

And then the world opened up beneath her feet.

# I

## REYNA

Reyna Darragh's skin itched. She could not say how many days had passed since she'd awoken trapped inside the Shadow Court, but it had been far more than one too many. Her bones throbbed; her mind raged. Reyna wasn't meant for captivity. She ached to do something, *anything* at all. If that something involved stabbing her way out of this dark and dreary castle, then all the better.

As it was, she had seen nothing but the black stone walls that surrounded her for days. Only one iron-barred window provided her with a view of the city. She sat on the cold stone ledge, Wingallock perching on her shoulder, and stared out at Findius.

It was a strange city. For one, it squatted beneath a very red sun that was shrouded in a thick impenetrable mist. The darkness of it almost seemed alive at times, twisting and whorling through the dirt-packed streets. Hundreds of lit windows dotted undulating land. The shadow fae had been pushed out of this city when they had been exiled. Now, some had returned to their former homes and many more were coming by the day. Still, even with the growing light, the streets were dark and dreary.

It looked like the kind of city that would easily swallow you whole.

Regardless, Reyna would have gladly jumped out the window to join the mist if it wasn't for the pesky iron bars blocking her way. She could not even touch them without getting burnt, let alone rip them out of the black stone walls.

"What do you reckon, Wingallock?" Reyna whispered quietly, all too aware of the guards at the door, always listening. "Any idea how we're going to get out of this castle?"

Even her owl familiar was stuck inside, and his frustration grew with every passing day. Wingallock was accustomed to sweeping through snow-blanketed forests each night, hunting for prey. He'd never enjoyed being fed scraps of even the most delicious castle food. He preferred to find his own. He enjoyed flying free. To be caged, to him, was a fate as cruel as death.

Wingallock hooted sadly, his sharp talons digging into her shoulder. With a sigh, Reyna nodded her agreement. There was no path out of this hellhole. She had attempted kicking the bars out of the way. She had tried to flee into the corridor when the guards brought her meals. She had even tried to steal their swords. But she was gravely outnumbered. Every time, they had bested her.

And Reyna did not like being bested any more than she enjoyed captivity.

A knock sounded on the door, but Reyna stayed right where she was. She knew who it was. The daily routine had been embedded into her soul, along with her misery.

The door swung wide and then shut quickly, revealing one of the strangest fae that Reyna had ever had the pleasure of meeting. Nollaig, a shadow fae female who insisted on hiding her face beneath a thick, black hood at all times. Her cloak stretched down to her feet, the ragged edges brushing against the stone floor. On her shoulder, a crow perched. Nollaig's familiar, Holas. Reyna had never actually seen Nollaig's face, but she'd been informed she had matching raven hair and eyes.

"Morning, Nollaig," Reyna said. "I don't suppose you've come here for your daily gossip, have you?"

Indeed, Reyna did not expect a response to her question. She only knew Nollaig's name from the first day they'd met. Tarrah, the High King's champion, had introduced them, but Nollaig had not uttered a single word in all the days she had visited Reyna.

All she did was hold up a dead mouse, toss it onto the floor, and then leave. At first, Wingallock had turned up his nose at the offering, but he had quickly caved. His hunger overrode his stubbornness.

Nollaig kept her hands tucked into her cloak. "The High King wishes to speak with you this morning."

Startled, Reyna jumped to her feet. Her mind raced as she stared at the shadow fae whose hidden face reflected everything about this strange realm. Shadows and darkness, cloaks and daggers, bitterness sharp and heavy like an axe.

The High King had only met once with Reyna during the long stretch of time that she had spent at the castle. On the day she had awoken from her poisonous slumber, he'd come to 'welcome' her to his court. A horrible stab of pain slammed into her gut at the thought of the poison that had spread through her veins, thick and full of nettles.

Lorcan had delivered that poison.

The flare of his name in her mind was like the unexpected slice of a broad sword that was then twisted sharply to the side. A kill with added certainty. A double blow. An attack meant to bring her to her knees, one that ensured she never got back up.

Reyna Darragh did not trust easily. And yet she had trusted him.

Lorcan, the son of High King Bolg Rothach. Lorcan, the prince of shadows.

A hammer of harsh bitterness pummelled her heart, threatening to knock her down.

Instead, she found her voice. "I suppose you want me to don some sort of ridiculous silken gown for his visit. Hours of preparation for a moment's conversation. Well then, did you bring it along? Where is it?"

Nollaig stood quietly. Her face was obscured by the thick hood, but Reyna could feel the shadow fae's eyes on her, regarding her with an intensity that would have made almost anyone's skin crawl. Reyna, impatient, just wanted her to get on with it.

Reyna let out a huff of irritation. "You know I didn't pack any courtly gowns seeing as I didn't have a chance to pack before Lorcan dragged me here. If you want me to meet with your king, then either give me a gown or let me meet with him as I am."

She gestured down at her silver tunic, her soft, loose hoarfrost silk trousers, and the simple slippers hugging her feet—the only item of clothing that the Shadow Court had provided since her arrival. It was not the attire of a princess.

"That will do," Nollaig merely said.

Surprise flickered through Reyna, but she did her best to hide it. Was Nollaig playing some sort of game? Was the Shadow Court trying to unsteady her? She'd spent so long cooped up inside this bedchamber, with no one to keep her company other than her familiar and her own damn self, that she no longer even knew what month it was. But kings expected certain things, particularly from princesses. Gowns and brushed hair, at the very least.

And then Reyna understood. "I see. As your prisoner, courtly manners do not apply to me."

"Do not play coy," Nollaig said. "You may be a princess, but there is far more to you than that. You're a Shieldmaiden. So, there's no need for you to dress yourself up like a simpering lady in search of a lord husband."

"An unsworn Shieldmaiden," Reyna said quietly. "And that status was removed when my father returned my courtly title to me."

Nollaig waved a gloved hand dismissively. "You're a warrior. The technicalities of your titles don't matter. Besides, you will find we are not so formal as most courts. Now, enough of this. The king is waiting for you. Come with me."

Nollaig moved toward the door and pounded her fist against the wood. Reyna watched, narrowing her eyes. This *was* some sort of trick, after all. She had not been allowed to leave her room since she'd awoken that first day, her head throbbing, her heart raw. Why in the name of the Dagda would they allow her to wander through their castle corridors now?

With a sigh, Nollaig paused and cast a a glance over her shoulder, face still hidden beneath the folds of her cloak's dark hood. "You will be surrounded by armed guards as soon as we step out into the corridor. I do not advise attempting an escape. Remember what the king said. So long as you behave accordingly, you will continue to enjoy your privileges. And if you do not...then he will not hesitate to throw you into the dungeons."

The dungeons did not frighten Reyna. She had seen and experienced far worse than a grungy cell deep in the ground. In the Battle for the Shard, the fields of blood and ice and snow were images burned into her head. Bodies piled on top of each other, faces mottled and black with rot. It had lasted hours. During the battle, she had even forgotten what peace felt like.

No, she did not fear the dungeons. But even though her chances of an escape were next to nothing, there *was* a chance, so long as they housed her inside that room. Inside the dungeons...she would never again see daylight, even the strange, misty red glow of the shadow lands. She was certain of it.

So, when she followed Nollaig into the corridor, Reyna did not attempt to bolt through the half a dozen guards that quickly surrounded her. She could not help but eye them though, and imagine various scenarios where she fought—and won. If she suddenly threw her weight into the smaller guard to her right, she could knock the sword from his grip and take it for herself. She would still have to fight six, not including Nollaig, but she had faced worse odds than this.

"I know what you're thinking," Nollaig said, falling into step beside Reyna. "I don't blame you. I would be thinking it myself."

She rolled her eyes. "You know nothing about me."

"You're thinking about how you might kill every single one of us in order to hatch your escape, including me."

Reyna could hear the smile on Nollaig's face, even if she couldn't see it.

"You're right," Reyna said, seeing no reason to mince her words. Even within the exiled shadow kingdom, lies died on her tongue like bitter ash. The deep dark magic of the fae realms knew what she was. She'd been born in ice, she'd bled on fields of ice, and she hoped that when her death day finally came that she would be buried in ice.

"But you won't make the attempt," Nollaig added. "Especially once you hear what our king means to propose to you."

Reyna cut her eyes toward Nollaig's cloaked form. "It better not be an actual proposal. I am already betrothed to another prince, and I would not marry Lorcan if he was the last male alive on this godforsaken continent."

Nollaig actually chuckled. The sound was odd coming from the hooded form that seemed to eke shadows and darkness with every move she made. But she seemed legitimately...amused, almost. Reyna did not quite know what to make of it.

"The High King has a far more important proposal than that. Arranged marriages and sneaky intrigues are for petty kings."

Reyna frowned. "And your king isn't a petty one?"

"Certainly not." Her voice held a snap, the level tone now replaced by a dangerous edge.

"What is he then, if not petty?" Reyna asked despite Nollaig's reaction. She saw no reason to mince her words here. She was already a prisoner, one they clearly did not wish to kill. "Most kings are." *If not them all,* she thought.

"Clever and purposeful."

Reyna lifted a brow but said nothing more, storing away that small bit of insight into the king. It might prove useful down the line. Clever and purposeful, which meant he was no doubt in possession of ambitious plans. That did not mean he wasn't also petty.

Nothing more passed between Nollaig and Reyna other than their whispered footsteps down the long and mist-enshrouded corridors. As they approached the great, looming doors of the throne room, tendrils of darkness seemed to curl from the depths of the walls.

Reyna could not help but shudder. She had yet to become accustomed to the strange darkness that seemed to lurk in every corner of this strange realm.

The throne room was not far from what Reyna had imagined. Large and lofty, thick black pillars were scattered throughout, bracing the high ceiling. The shadows were deep and dark where every wall—and the very floor itself—had been built from that black stone so present in Findius. Bolg sat idly on his throne, a crown of twisting antlers perched on his tiny head. He was flanked by guards, all donning grey scale armor and helmets made from shadowsteel.

Bolg's black stone throne was a strange little thing, particularly compared to the other Seats of Power that Reyna had set her eyes upon. In the Ice Court, the majestic throne of her father grew from the very ground itself, so much so that the ancient castle had been built *around* the throne, rather than the other way around. It rose high, a hulking, glistening seat of ice that never melted. When she had been little more than a girl, Reyna had watched one of her cousins try to burn it with a torch. The old ice throne had done nothing more than continue to sit there, and Reyna swore she had felt it frown.

"Your Majesty," Nollaig said, bowing slightly. "I have brought the Princess Reyna Darragh of the Ice Court, as requested."

Reyna stared up at the king. He still looked small and strange, just as she remembered, but there was a glint in his eye. That cleverness Nollaig spoke of.

"High King Rothach," Reyna said. "The throne suits you, it seems. I'm sure you feel it's a shame your having it does not mean your kingdom is no longer exiled. I should offer my condolences."

Inwardly, Reyna smiled. She *should* offer her condolences, but she wouldn't. And she would certainly take every opportunity to remind the bastard that try as he might, he was still an exiled king. Nothing had changed.

"Blah, blah, blah," the High King said, waving his hand dismissively. "I care little for these faux niceties. Your words are layered with the truth, and I have more important things to do than dance around pretending that we like each other. I had you brought here for a reason. Let's get on with it."

"You won't get very far with the kings and lords of Tir Na Nog if you refuse to play their games," Reyna said frankly.

He grinned. "Swords are sharper than words."

"Then, you have never parried with my father."

"Yes, yes," he said, leaning back into his onyx throne. "Your family is why I have brought you here. I have your sister."

A heavy slab of iron dropped into Reyna's stomach, burning up her gut. The world seemed to tip sideways as she stared at the king, certain that she could not have heard the truth of his words. Her legs slightly trembled as she took a step toward him, and a dozen swords sang in the air around her.

"Best not step any closer, Shieldmaiden," Nollaig muttered.

Reyna froze, glaring at the king. "You're lying. You can lie."

"You are right, of course. I can. But lying rarely does me any favors. It is a weapon best used scarcely." He shrugged. "I have your sister."

Reyna's heartbeat pulsed in her ears, and a horrible dizziness swept through her. This couldn't be real. It just couldn't. Eislyn was back in the Air Court, close enough to their father to be safe.

"Then, let me see her," Reyna said in a rush of words. "If you have her, then show me her face."

"Absolutely not," he said. "I will not risk putting two ice princesses in the same room so they might speak in riddles to plot some sort of scheme."

Reyna stared at the king, and then let out a harsh laugh. "You have just proven you don't have her. That's a terrible excuse."

"Are you not the one who just told me how dangerous words are compared to swords?" he asked, lifting a brow. "I'd prefer not to test that little theory of yours."

The smile on Reyna's lips died, though she still did not

believe his blatant lies. "What is all this? Has your fortune teller given you another ridiculous vision?"

"Indeed she has." His smile grew wider. "And I need you to become my Shieldmaiden. It seems you never did swear your warrior oaths to the Ice Court. So, you are free to swear them to me."

Reyna choked out a strangled laugh. "You are far more delusional than I thought."

He lifted a knowing brow. "Am I truly? Because I believe that you deeply care for your sisters, particularly the youngest. You will swear your oaths to me so that she will not die here in this castle, never to see your northern lands again. Do not tempt me Reyna Darragh. I will happily kill an ice princess."

His words were tinny and distant as a strange darkness began to creep into the corners of her eyes. Fear thudded through her veins like thick globs of molten iron. Every single part of her was on fire. She had never before felt fear quite like this.

"You may refuse, of course," the king continued, his voice garbled and distant through the haze in her mind. "*You* will not be executed if you do. Eislyn, on the other hand, will perish here."

She shook her head and opened her mouth to scream at him, but no sound came out. Her words were swallowed by her fear.

He leaned forward and draped an arm across his leg. "You will fight for me, or your sister will die."

## 2

## LORCAN

"He did *what?*" Lorcan's voice was low and quiet, but every word was as violent as a punch. The past few hours he'd been cooped up inside his chambers while his father met with Reyna Darragh, the Ice Court princess who he'd not seen once since her arrival in the shadow realm.

He'd discovered only last night that his father planned to request her presence in the throne room. At first, he'd been hopeful of finally setting his eyes on her. He was desperate to see her face. To confirm she was safe and unharmed. Alive.

But then his father had prohibited his presence. Normally, Lorcan wouldn't care a damn about his father's bloody commands, but he had decided to take a different tactic these days. He would play the part of a dutiful son. And then he would end Bolg Rothach's miserable reign.

It was becoming increasingly difficult to stick to that plan. His father made him angrier than everyone else in the world combined.

Teutas, one of his father's most trusted warriors, stood tall by the door. When Lorcan had briefly lived in the shadow realm, the two had been thick as thieves. They'd trained together. They'd fought together. Teutas had been one of his only true friends at court. As such, he told Lorcan far more than any of the other guards inside the castle, though he was still fiercely loyal to his king. He, like all the others, thought High King Bolg Rothach was answering the call of their god. He was doing the Unseelie's bidding by restarting this war and driving the Air Court out of Findius.

And he spoke of the fortune teller, Tarrah, in awed, hushed tones. Out of all the shadow fae, Lorcan trusted her the least.

"Tarrah has seen a vision of Reyna fighting for our side. Somehow, the future of our realm rests on her shoulders. If she joins us, then we will find victory against the Wood Court, who is now mobilizing forces against us. But if she doesn't...we will fall once again, and this time, it will be for certain."

"Did you ever consider that these visions might be fragments of an overactive imagination? Unseelie has not spoken to a single fae in nearly a hundred years. Why now? Why Tarrah? There is nothing particularly special about her that I can see. And look at her now. It has given her an esteemed place by the High King's side."

"You mistrust her."

"I mistrust everyone," Lorcan said. "Even you, Teutas. We once were close, but you are my father's sword now, through and through."

Teutas gave him a thin-lipped smile. "Careful. You have become far too accustomed to speaking your mind. The air fae have rubbed off on you."

"And that's where you're wrong, old friend. They hide the truth as much as anyone else. They're merely far more careful about it. In all my years spent at that court, I very rarely heard anyone truly speaking their mind. Except..."

Reyna Darragh.

He ground his teeth together, fighting back the urge to charge down the castle corridors, seek her out in the throne room, and shout at her to run. Run as far as she could, and never stop until her feet bruised and bled and tumbled out from under her.

But he couldn't. His father held Thane Selkirk in his dungeons. If Lorcan helped Reyna escape, he had no doubt Bolg Rothach would murder Thane on the spot.

Taking a steadying breath, he returned to his father's newest plot. "And what did Reyna say to my father's proposal? Surely she did not agree to such folly."

Lorcan couldn't imagine his father could say anything that would convince Reyna to make those vows. Full of ferocity and edged with skin as tough as shadowsteel, the former Shieldmaiden had little time for games. She would sooner swing a sword than bind herself to a cruel king's every command.

Unlike Lorcan himself.

Memories of the past filled his mind like ghostly spectres. The mark being cut deep into his skin, forever binding him to his father's orders. His father smiling, cruelly, as he ordered Lorcan to spy on his mother's people in the air fae lands. The sight of Comharra, Lorcan's childhood village, a ghost town, every fae who lived there murdered by his own father. Out of spite. Every memory burned in his mind, as fresh as the day it had happened.

"She did not take the news very well. It seems our king is now the proud owner of two Darragh sisters. He has Eislyn, too." Teutas had the decency to grimace at that. "The High King of the Ice Court will be none too pleased when he learns both his daughters are now our prisoners. I fear they will no longer ignore our existence. On the bright side, there are several realms between us and them, and they would sooner hack their way on land through the Air Court, and then the Wood Court, than chop down their precious trees for ships."

Lorcan barely heard Teutas's final words. His mind had locked on the first. "The king has Princess Eislyn?"

Teutas frowned. "It seems so. He had the warriors collect her when they took your Thane."

Lorcan ground his teeth together. He should have seen this coming. It was his father's classic style of manipulation. Find someone, or something, that his enemy cared about, and then threaten it. His father had used this tactic on so many occasions now that Lorcan had lost count. The trouble was, it always worked.

And he knew Reyna. Oh yes, he knew her well. She had only been in his life for months, but he'd spent hours upon hours by her side, guarding her for Thane. Lorcan knew what made her tick, what angered her, the way her eyes flashed with ice when she felt wronged.

If there was one thing in the entire bloody continent that could convince her to make vows to High King Bolg Rothach, it was her sister.

"Damn him, Teutas. He's gone too far," Lorcan said, pounding his fist on the table. "I need to speak with Reyna before she does something she'll regret for the rest of her life."

"She's made it clear she doesn't wish to see you," Teutas said quietly. "And it sounds as though you plan to stop her from making the vows. You know I can't allow you to do that."

"I swear to the Dagda, Teutas, if you don't let me see—"

"We don't worship the Dagda here, Lorcan." Teutas shook his head and backed up, his eyes shuttering over the warmth and friendliness they'd held only moments before. "I serve the king now. And Unseelie. You should, too."

With a growl, Lorcan whirled on his feet and stormed down the corridor and away from his old friend. He should have known he would find no help inside this castle, not even from someone who had once hated Lorcan's father as much as he did. That was the trouble. The king looked frail and weak and too incompetent to hold his seat, but it was all an illusion, just like everything else inside this bloody realm.

The king was strong, and he held a kind of power that most fae could only dream of. Too long spent in his presence, and one started to believe he was in the right. About everything.

Lorcan knew better than anyone. He had not always been the Prince of the Shadow Court. Once, he had been but a bastard, starving in the grasslands. His father's warriors had found him one dark Beltane night and had dragged him back to the shadow lands. There, he'd been forced to make his own vows. Vows that had come with a mark. At first, he'd hated every word his father said. The war against the air fae was not his own. But over time, the mark began to poison his mind until he almost believed that he was right. An unexpected need for vengeance had poured through his veins like molten lava. It had almost dragged him under. Almost.

But his love for Thane had washed it all away.

When he reached the throne room, he found his father whispering quietly with two of his closest advisors, including that bloody trickster, Tarrah Glas. Lorcan did not understand how she had wormed her way to his side, nor why the High King of the Shadow Court believed the nonsense pouring from her mouth. So much talk of visions and dreams. She was playing him. Lorcan knew it. To what end, he could not say, but he had no doubt that it would end with far too many dead.

"Father, we need to speak."

At that, Tarrah stiffened and hurried out of the throne room, leaving Lorcan and his father to argue, like they always did. He did not blame her for wanting to get out of the way of the storm.

The High King of the Shadow Court did not even raise his eyes toward his son. He lounged against the black stone, eyes shut to the world around him. "My dear bastard son. I'm beginning to think I made a mistake with you."

Lorcan merely ignored him, as well as the dismissive title. His father had legitimized him over a decade ago. He was no longer a bastard, but he would not have cared if he was. Lorcan did not value titles the way most fae did. "It's about the Darragh sisters."

His father snorted. "I daresay it is. You have been moping around the castle day and night, pining over the middle one for weeks."

Lorcan's back went taut. "At least have the decency to call her by her name."

"I am the High King of the Shadow Court." Eyes still shut, Bolg smiled. "I may call the middle one whatever I damn well please."

His mark burned as a wild thought flew through his mind. The king was drunk, and only Heremon, the financial advisor, stood by his side. It would not take much to kill him.

But then what? Bolg would be dead, and every shadow fae inside the castle would want to execute Lorcan for treason. There would be no one left to protect Reyna. Another king would rise up to take his father's place. The next one might not be as interested in visions and prophecies. And an ice princess would be a very satisfying murder indeed.

One day, he would destroy his father, but that day at yet to come. He needed to bide his time.

So, he held his anger in check, though he spoke through gritted teeth. "I have heard what you demanded of Princess Reyna."

"Yes. And what of it? I suppose you're here to talk me out

of it." Bolg sighed dramatically. "My mind cannot be changed. My champion has visioned Reyna fighting for our side. Unseelie was clear. If Reyna makes the vow, the war is won. And if she doesn't, then we all die, every one of us. Surely you do not wish all shadows to die, do you?"

His father had always been a superstitious male, one enamored with prophecies, visions, and gods. He did not doubt that Tarrah took advantage of that. She could get the king to do whatever she pleased, just so long as she said it was the command of their god.

"And what makes you think this Tarrah of yours is telling you the truth?" Lorcan tried. "Have you seen the visions yourself?"

"She has proven herself to me, son. Time and time again. Unlike you."

As much as Lorcan hated the king, his dismissive words stung harsher than the mark. He had done everything his father had commanded. He'd even betrayed the one he loved. The one and only thing he had never done, the one command he had disobeyed, was killing Thane.

And it still had not saved him. Lorcan knew that when his father was done with him, Thane's life would become forfeit. The High King of the Air Court was more valuable to Bolg alive, for now, but only so long as he could be used as ammunition. Once that was gone...

Lorcan steadied his breath and his anger. "Apologies, Father. I know I have disappointed you at times, but I worry about this stranger's control over you. Her visions make little sense. Why would you be successful with an ice princess by your side? They are as different to us as fae can get."

At that, Bolg Rothach finally opened his eyes but only just. They were two black slits on his pockmarked face. "And what would you have me do instead? Not listen to the girl and risk failing? Think about this, my bastard son. Say that I let your pretty princess run free because Tarrah could be lying to me. Very well then. Everyone is happy. But say that Tarrah is right. What then? The wood fae attack, and we all die. This entire realm? Gone forever. That is the price of being wrong. I'm not as dumb as I look. I know you have little love for me. But what of the rest of them? All those poor helpless souls trapped in their exiled realm, starving?" He sat up straight, leaned forward, and braced his arm on his leather-clad knee. "Who would you rather see win? Me or the wood king?"

Lorcan's hands clenched. It was a terrible choice. His father had a twisted mind and was hell-bent on destroying every realm who had wronged the shadows. But that was nothing compared to what the wood king was. Bolg Rothach's ire fell onto his enemies. Ulaid Molt's wrath was felt by innocents. His mind was so far gone that he could no longer tell friend from foe. While Lorcan's father suffered the consequences of worshipping a dark and vengeful god, the wood king embraced the darkness in a way that Bolg never had.

If Lorcan had to choose, he would be forced to side with his father.

But there were not a mere two realms, or two kings, in the upcoming game of war. Ice, and Air, and Sea would have something to say about it as well.

"I would never side with the Wood Court," Lorcan said.

Bolg gave him a thin-lipped smile. "Your time at court truly has changed you, my bastard son. Such an expert at mincing words you've become."

"Better mincing than outright lies. Something you'll soon have to become accustomed to if you wish to return the shadow lands to their rightful place as part of the great continent of Tir Na Nog. If you are no longer exiled, you will be forced to tell the truth just like the rest of them."

"Be that as it may," Bolg said, sighing and shutting his eyes once more. "You now know why I cannot allow the Darragh sisters to leave this place. Reyna must make her vows to me. There is no other way."

With a frustrated growl, Lorcan spun on his heels and left his father to his lonely perch on his beloved Seat of Power. There would be no convincing him now, not so long as Tarrah believed that Reyna was their savior.

But they did not know Reyna as he did. The ice princess would never be the savior of the shadow fae. If anything, she would be the end of them.

## 3

## EISLYN

A fist pounded the door so hard that the wood rattled on its hinges. Eislyn's heart shattered. The book slipped from her trembling fingers and fell with a loud *thunk* on the stone floor of her chambers. Bunching her silver gown into her hands, she scurried backward, trying to think around the terror spilling through her veins like venom.

The time had finally come, far sooner than she'd thought.

The door swung wide. In the corridor, a hooded figure shook with belabored breaths before rushing inside and kicking the door behind him. He dropped back his hood, his entire face lined in pain. Vreis Floinn was one of Thane's closest guards and had taken it upon himself to look after Eislyn in the High King's absence. With short-cropped light brown hair and mismatched eyes, he stood out among the gleaming golden air fae nobility. Still, they rarely paid him any mind.

His voice was rough when he spoke. "The Grand Alderman has had Imogen hanged. It's time for you to leave this city, Eislyn. It is no longer safe for you here. Aengus will clearly do whatever it takes to hold onto his power. He will set his sights on you next. While I don't believe he would kill you outright, he will use you in some way to prevent Thane from retaking his throne."

Eislyn swallowed hard and nodded. Word had spread through the city. Everyone now knew Thane intended to marry Eislyn when he returned, making her the future High Queen of the realm. Which meant Aengus knew. And he would see her as a threat.

Vreis had first come to her soon after her sister's disappearance from the castle. He had warned her this day would come. At the time, he had tried to convince her to leave straight away, but Reyna was not the only stubborn member of the Darragh family. Eislyn had stayed for as long as possible, to continue her research into the Ruin.

They had managed to hide Reyna's disappearance from the Grand Alderman for a few weeks, but he had somehow found out the truth. If he learned that Eislyn had helped hide it from him...

"Come," Vreis said. "Grab your things. We must go quickly while he is still in the square. All eyes are on the former High Queen. It is our best chance at an escape."

Eislyn nodded and rushed into her bedchamber, trying not to think about what that meant. All eyes on the High Queen. All eyes on her death. A terrible fate even for a cruel fae. Eislyn had never liked the High Queen, but that did not mean she wished to see her dead. When Thane discovered this...

It would break his heart. And Aengus would face certain death.

She grabbed the leather satchel hidden beneath her bed and tossed it over her shoulder, hurrying back into the drawing room to join Vreis. Even with danger looming inside the castle, Eislyn ached to remain. She had wanted to be here when Thane returned, waiting for him. Now that she knew the truth about his feelings for her, she could not stop thinking about his face, his smile, his hands.

And someone needed to warn him. If he strode back inside this castle, unaware...

Vreis must have seen the doubt on her face, because he gently took her hands in his. "I understand this is difficult for you, Princess. It is difficult for me as well. I have served the Selkirks for so long that I scarcely remember a time in my life before them. Thane, in particular. He is out there somewhere. Missing. A pretender has stolen his throne and murdered his mother."

Eislyn nodded, her heart aching.

Vreis continued. "There is little I can do. Aengus is surrounded by guards who appear loyal to him. So, if I cannot remove him from the throne, I will do the one thing I know Thane would request. He would want me to ensure that you are safe."

"I know," she whispered, tears burning her eyes. "But what will happen to him when he returns? Will Aengus try to—?" Her voice cut off. She could not bear to speak it.

Vreis's mismatched eyes hardened, one a deep brown, one golden. "Aengus should try if he likes. He will not get very far. Thane is the High King of this realm. As much as Aengus wishes otherwise, that is something he cannot change. If he attempts to kill our Thane, this entire city will rip him to shreds. And then he truly will be cursed for eternity."

Eislyn shivered, both exhilarated and terrified by Vreis's words. She did not want to see a male ripped to shreds, even one as terrible as Aengus. And yet...she yearned for justice in a way she never had before. It was not right what Aengus had done. He'd stolen the throne, he'd had the queen killed. And now, there was nothing standing in his way. True power was in his grasp.

If Thane died, the Seat of Power would transfer straight to his greedy little hands.

"Come," Vreis said. "We cannot waste any more time. The boat is waiting."

Nodding, Eislyn followed Vreis into the dimly-lit corridor outside of her chambers. Two stone walls rose high on either side of the narrow tunnel that twisted through the castle's many towers. There were six of them in total—connected by looming white-stone walls. When Eislyn had first arrived in Tairngire, the expansive, maze-like corridors had put the fear of the Dagda into her soul. She had rarely left her rooms, so long as she could weave together an acceptable excuse. Without lying, of course.

But Eislyn had grown accustomed to these strange and twisting halls. She had sneaked through them with the prince, that fateful night when they had escaped into the city for a night of mead, bards, and dance. Until that night, Thane had always worn his cloak as if it weighed five hundred pounds, the weight of an entire realm pulling him deep into the dirt. Away from court, he had come alive in a way she had never expected.

And now he was gone.

She followed Vreis through the corridors, her feet moving quickly along the white stone floors. Down they went, rushing through stairwells that led them into the very guts of the castle. Soon, they reached the hidden tunnel and then rushed out into twilight.

To their right, the Witchlight Woods rose high into the scarlet sky, the thick limbs of the yew trees whispering in the soft wind. Even though the sun had only begun to set, the woods were dark and ominous. Thankfully, Eislyn knew that their journey would lead to their left, where the Bay of Wind rippled, boats and ships bobbing in the water, the blue turned scarlet beneath the sky.

"Which boat is ours?" Eislyn asked, frowning. There were none anchored by the shore this night.

"Apologies, Princess, but that way would only lead to death," Vreis said quietly before motioning toward the dirt-packed path that cut through the tall grass and into the forest of shadows. "We must cut through the woods and head to the eastern shore. There, our ship will be waiting for us."

Fear staked Eislyn's heart. She swallowed hard. "Surely there must be some other way."

"I'm afraid not. There are many eyes and ears in the Bay of Wind. We could not leave that way without being seen. Perhaps those eyes would belong to someone who would be sympathetic. Or..."

"Or they might belong to someone loyal to the Grand Alderman," she finished for him, her lips trembling as she pressed them tightly together. "Are there really that many fae in Tairngire who are loyal to that vicious male? He stole the throne."

"Some might say that he stole the throne, but others might also say that he is defending the throne for when their true High King returns. And others might even hope that Thane is gone for good. The realm has always been torn in their opinion of the Selkirks. You know the story of how they came into power, yes?"

Eislyn nodded. It was a story full of betrayal and death. Thane had not been alive then. He'd had nothing to do with his father's lust for power. But there were many out there who would blame him all the same.

She swallowed hard and took in the path before her. Eislyn had never been courageous, not like her sister. Her *sisters*, really. Glencora was just as brave as Reyna, only in different ways. She had not once complained about her fate. She would have walked into the Air Court and taken her seat beside Thane graciously. But the Ruin had gotten to her first.

The very thought of the horrible magic filled her head with noise. It was loud, loud, loud. Screaming filled her ears, and visions swarmed across her vision, blocking out the dreadful Witchlight Woods. Bodies fell to the ground, and then spasmed. Black fingers of dust singed their skin. Their eyes turned black; their lips went white. Her mother reached out…

"Princess?" Vreis's calm, strong voice cut through her dark thoughts. She sucked in a sharp breath, and shook the madness away. Eislyn did not remember much from that fateful day, nor the days after. But those horrible images flashed before her every now and again, reminding her that it was her fault that her mother was dead.

Eislyn was the reason her mother had even been in the village that day. And as her sisters had dragged her to safety…

"Very well then. Let's go," she whispered, brushing aside the hot tears that splashed onto her cheeks.

As they rushed quickly through the thick forest, Eislyn's fear began to thaw. Up close, the trees were nothing but trees rather than the looming sentries that she had seen from a distance. The canopy's cover felt like a blanket, hiding them from the ever watchful gaze of courtiers, spies, and gossipers. In fact, Eislyn could not help but think this was the safest she had been in weeks.

The path wound through thickets of yew trees, past lazy brooks burbling down gently sloping hills, and over fallen logs cast down across the path. Victims of the realm's insistent wind. Wind that grew in strength with every step they made closer to the shore.

They reached the eastern edge of Tir Na Nog long after twilight had deepened into full dark. The twin moons, Brigantu and Danu, were high in the sky, their full glow splashing silver onto the sea that stretched out before them. Under their brilliant light, Eislyn spotted a ship waiting in the distance.

It was a merchant ship formed from great timber beams, its mast bearing the sigil of the Sea Court: twin teal waves bursting forth from an unseen sea, the frothy crests pushing away from each other. A small wooden boat had been pulled onto the shore, cutting a line through the waterlogged sand. Beside it stood a sea fae.

Eislyn took a step back toward the safety of the tree line.

"No need to fear, Princess," Vreis said quietly. "This is a friend, not a foe."

"That is a ship of the Sea Court," she whispered, her eyes darting back to the sea fae's face. Unlike Imogen, this fae looked as though he had been born in the sea itself. His skin shimmered beneath the glow of the moon, creating the impression that he wore translucent scales. His deep blue hair was long, almost to his waist, and parted by his viciously sharp ears.

"That ship once belonged to the Sea Court, but you'll find that it does not belong to them now. There are sea fae on board, but there are air and ice as well. None of them pay allegiance to any court."

She twisted toward him then, searching his eyes for confirmation that she could trust him. He had never mentioned the sea fae before now. Had she been wrong to believe Vreis's words? Her heart thumped as worry twisted her gut. For awhile it had seemed that there was a shadow fae inside Dalais Castle. *Someone* had lied, several times, in the lead up to Thane's gruesome coronation where Eislyn had been stolen away. And that someone had used Vreis.

Or had Vreis been the liar all this time?

*Never trust an air fae.* Eislyn could hear her sister's voice whispering in her ear, reminding her that no one inside of Tairngire meant them anything but harm. But Vreis might not even be an air fae. If he'd lied to get her here, he was nothing but the worst of them all: a fae of shadows.

She shook her head and stumbled back, her feet knocking against the root of an ancient tree. "I've changed my mind. I'm going to stay in Tairngire."

Vreis frowned. "The city isn't safe for you anymore."

"Maybe I'll take my chances. Reyna wouldn't run."

Hurt flickered in his mismatched eyes. "Princess, I have put my own life at risk to ensure you escaped this city safely. I…" He shook his head, ground his teeth together, and glanced at the horizon. The sea fae still stood on the shores, silently watching them from a distance, the frothy waves lashing his bare feet.

"You what?" she asked.

"I am no lord, nor a baron or a druid or a landowner of any kind. But I have dedicated my life to the crown, and I have been rewarded well with airgead. I have spent very little of it. Until now, to hatch this escape. It has required all of my coin to buy not only this ship and the crew on board, but to purchase their silence."

Eislyn stayed rooted to the spot, her mind reeling.

"Eislyn." Vreis had never spoken her name until now. It was always Your Highness or Princess, a warrior's respect for titles never faltering. So, it made her listen. "If I wanted to do you harm, if I worked for the Grand Alderman, do you truly believe that I would have done what I have? Would it not have been much simpler to merely march you to the foot of his dais, to throw you at his feet and to his mercy?"

He had a point.

But more than that, she knew she had little choice. She still stood on the path that led from the castle to the sea. There were only two directions she could go. She could choose to return to the castle where Aengus would no doubt have her punished, used, or executed. Or she could go with Vreis.

So, Eislyn swallowed her fear, stepped off the path, and strode to the waiting ship.

# 4

## REYNA

"This is the first time I've been outside." Reyna strode beside Tarrah in a courtyard just outside the tower where she'd been held prisoner these past weeks. Tarrah wore full plate shadowsteel armor, the Shadow Court's twisting antler sigil etched deeply into the dark breastplate. Her ebony hair swished at her waist, vibrant and healthy, a direct contrast to her sunken cheeks and haunted eyes.

Out of all of the High King's closest confidantes, Tarrah was the most like an enigma. At first, Reyna had believed her to be nothing more than a con artist. A shadow fae skilled at weaving convincing lies. Pretty smiles could go a long way toward convincing lonely males to listen, and the High King was nothing if not lonely.

But now, Reyna was not so certain. Perhaps Tarrah truly did believe her own words. Perhaps the visions were true. Other magic had begun to spark throughout Tir Na Nog in recent months. As strange as it may be, and as difficult as it might be to believe, it was not impossible that the gods had passed visions on to Tarrah.

Of course, Reyna *might* have been able to believe the girl if it weren't for Tarrah's *latest* vision. Reyna Darragh, fighting for the shadow king. It was an impossibility.

"What do you think of the gardens?" Tarrah asked as her lips twisted into something resembling a smile, almost as though she were not accustomed to the expression.

With an impatient sigh, Reyna took in the surprising number of flowers blooming along the path that cut through the center of the castle courtyard. Most were varying shades of lilac with a few bunches of silver and gold mixed in with the rest. The vines were twisting and full of sharp edges, choking the path tight. It looked as though they had only been cut away recently, remnants of the wild brambles flaking the path.

"I've never seen anything quite like it," Reyna said honestly. She would have said they were beautiful, but she was not certain she could find pleasure in anything inside these black stone walls. Even the most delicate and vibrant flower would look like a token of death.

Tarrah's odd smile crested her lips again as she continued down the path with her hands twisted tightly behind her back. Reyna cast a quick glance behind them. They were heavily guarded. There must be fifty or more warriors watching them, and Tarrah carried her own sword by her side as well as a bow upon her back.

Reyna's eyes flicked to the castle wall they approached. It would be the perfect opportunity to hatch an escape, regardless of how many guards stood behind them.

But somewhere inside that castle, her sister was trapped.

"I don't blame you for your feelings, nor your reaction," Tarrah said quietly. "In fact, I imagine I would have had a very similar response if I were you. I am sorry for what we have done to you. Truly."

Reyna frowned and narrowed her eyes suspiciously. "A

few kind words won't trick me into making a vow to your king."

"I would hope not," Tarrah said, snapping off a snake lily as they passed by, before lifting the flower to her nose and taking a long inhale of the sweet yet bitter scent.

Reyna's frown deepened. What was this strange shadow fae up to? She seemed calm and pleasant enough, but Reyna knew that there could only be one reason why the High King would allow Tarrah to take Reyna out into the courtyard for a relaxing stroll. Tarrah had been tasked to convince Reyna to yield. And yet, she was doing nothing of the sort.

"You think I am a liar," Tarrah said lightly as they reached the wall looking out upon the undulating, misty city. "You believe that I proclaim falsehoods."

"You are a shadow fae. You are not bound to your words."

Tarrah smiled her strange smile. "If you could lie, would you?"

Reyna turned her gaze to the city before them. From the tower, all she could see were lights and vague figures scurrying through the mist. But down here, those figures transformed into faces with smiles. There were dozens pouring in through distant castle gates, carrying packs as their bloodied feet carried them into the safety of Findius. Cheeks were painted with dirt, and eyes were sunken, hollowed out by years of starvation. Despite herself, Reyna felt her heart soften. The low fae of the shadow lands had struggled to survive for so long. And now they had a home again.

"I'm certain I would lie if given the chance," Reyna finally answered.

"Yes, no doubt you would, as would anyone. But how often? And why? Would your every word be a falsehood? Would your entire existence sit on a bedrock of lies?" Tarrah turned to face Reyna, her dark eyes sparking with intensity.

Curious, Reyna cocked her head and considered the shadow fae's words. If Reyna could lie, would she? Yes, she would. She could not pretend she wouldn't. Any fae would lie if given the chance. But all the time? No. Just as with word mincing, and answering questions, one needed to be careful. Answer too many questions, and one could easily give the true secrets away. Lie too often, and one would never be believed.

Tarrah gave a nod and motioned for them to continue down the path, apparently satisfied by what she saw in Reyna's eyes. As they walked, Reyna plucked a stray silver flower and took a small sniff. Strangely, it smelled of ozone, as if it came from the sun itself.

"I came a very long way to get here," Tarrah said quietly. "My mother died during a raid on our village when I was only ten, even though I was certain she would live forever. She had so much power, but she could not survive a cut to the throat. My father died a long while before that. I don't even remember his face. He died during a raid, too, or at least that is what my mother said. She was what you expect from all shadow fae. A liar to her very core. I am not certain she ever spoke the truth. She lived before the exile, so she understood what it meant to be bound to your words. And she relished in the absence of it."

Reyna nodded, wondering why exactly Tarrah was sharing these personal details with her. What did she hope to gain from it? Reyna knew it was not a simple conversation.

Tarrah continued. "After her death, that's when I began to see the visions. There were only a few of us left in the village after the raid—I had a hiding spot in a cellar hidden beneath the floor with our stores of food. That year, the crops had yielded very little, as is often the case. You have seen the sun and our mists. Only a few plants thrive under the orange glow. Back before we were exiled, the shadow fae relied on trade with the other kingdoms. Now, we have to rely on ourselves. Raids are common…as is murder for goods."

Reyna opened her mouth to speak, but Tarrah waved her hand dismissively. "No, do not offer me your pity. That isn't what I want, and despite what I am certain you believe, that is not the reason I am telling you my story."

Reyna dropped the silver flower to the ground. It was crushed beneath her boot as they continued ever forward. "Then, why are you sharing your past with me? I know this isn't a simple conversation. There is a purpose to your words. To convince me to make vows to your king."

"At the very heart of it, yes, but not in the way you imagine." Tarrah rustled her fingers through the brambles, not even flinching when a thorn pricked her thumb. She licked away the blood that bloomed on her skin and smiled. "This isn't some sort of trick or trap or strategy. I simply want to tell you what I know, to make you understand what is happening here. And then, I want you to consider what we've asked you. If you refuse, then…you are free to leave this kingdom."

A strange dread slithered past Reyna's heart like a snake, twisting and whorling inside of her, desperate to strike. "That's a lie."

Tarrah shook her head. "It isn't. If you refuse, then I was wrong. You are not the warrior we seek."

"And my sister?" Reyna asked, not even daring to allow herself even a sliver of hope. "What of Eislyn?"

"Come. We will get to Eislyn." Tarrah continued to walk. For a moment, Reyna stayed rooted to the spot, staring after the warrior, watching the orange glint off her scaly armor. Reyna felt unmoored. Surely, after all these weeks held captive, they would not allow her and Eislyn to simply walk out the castle gates and return home to the ice and the snow and the soothing cold. It would be a long, difficult journey, with the Wood Court standing in their way…but they would finally get to go home.

No, she could not dare to hope.

Tarrah would not dangle freedom before her unless she was certain that Reyna would never take it.

Frowning, she followed after the shadow fae. When she reached her side, Tarrah continued on as if the conversation had not paused at all.

"The food stores beneath our cottage diminished quickly. I was only a child. I did not understand the concept of rationing, nor did I keep my food to myself as I should have. I shared them with the other survivors. Weeks passed, and then we were hungry again." Tarrah sucked in a sharp breath. "When the starvation flickered like pain in my belly, that is when the visions began.

"At first, they were small and quiet and few. The faces in my mind were always blurred. I thought they were waking dreams at first. But then my mother's old words came back to me. Words of visions, prophecies of the futures, images flashing before her until she drowned in them. I had once thought them lies, but now I was experiencing them myself. I thought I was going mad."

For some reason, Reyna found herself believing the shadow fae. Tarrah's voice sounded so raw, so earnest. Whether these visions were from the gods or not, Reyna was certain of one important truth: the visions were real to Tarrah.

"Soon, the visions grew and grew, and I was having wild thoughts of a king sitting on a throne. A king and a throne I had never before seen, not with my own two eyes. Only in my mind." Tarrah smiled. "This time, I could see faces very clearly. It was our High King, Bolg Rothach, sitting on the shadow fae's Seat of Power. Only we didn't have the Seat of Power then. And our king was only a king. The images spurred me on, telling me to seek out Bolg Rothach and convince him to press forward against our enemies, to take back our own lands. So, I did. And then *we did*. The image I saw in my mind became real."

Reyna's heart thumped. It was eerie and unsettling. There was no doubt about that. It also wasn't enough. *Nothing* would ever be enough. "And now you've had visions of me fighting for your king."

"No." Tarrah stopped suddenly, twisting to face Reyna.

"No?" Reyna stared at the shadow fae, confusion rippling through her. "Then, why…but that is why your king wants me to fight for him, isn't it?"

"My visions as of late have become like those I had before. Those with blurred faces." Tarrah shook her head, furrowing her raven brows. "It makes it more difficult to understand what Unseelie is trying to tell me. I don't understand what I have done for him to dim my power, but alas. In my visions, I see *someone* fighting for the king."

Reyna's heart thumped faster. Fear clutched her veins.

"That someone is without a doubt a princess of the Ice Court. She has long, flowing silver hair. She wears a circlet on her head with the Ice Court's sigil carved from ice glass. She is strong and powerful, and a snow owl perches on her shoulder." Tarrah's eyes glittered. "It sounds like you, does it not? But I cannot see your face. And if it is not you because you refuse to fight for us, then it must be your sister, Eislyn."

All the blood drained from Reyna's face. At last, she had found Tarrah's true purpose. Another threat against her sister's life. Rage simmered in Reyna's gut. "Eislyn does not have a familiar."

"No, that is true. Not yet, at least." That strange smile slithered across Tarrah's lips again. "But perhaps when she becomes our warrior, she will acquire one then."

Her rage boiled, poisonous and churning with hate. "If

your visions are even real, you know as well as I do that you saw me and not my sister. Eislyn is a great many a thing, but she is no warrior. She wouldn't last more than a moment on the battlefield. She's never even held a sword."

"Be that as it may, one of you *will* fight for us. I would rather it be you."

With a roar, Reyna launched herself at Tarrah, fists curled. She fell on top of the shadow fae easily, knocking her onto the hard-packed ground. Tarrah's eyes went wide, but she did not scream in fear, even when Reyna's hand closed tight around her neck.

Reyna glared down at her, chest heaving as she dug her fingernails into Tarrah's skin. Her entire body was alive with a pulsing hatred so deep that her body trembled from the force of it. "You have made a terrible mistake. Swear you will release my sister or I will kill you before the guards can reach us. You know I am not lying. I can't. I mean every word I say, shadow fae. I will not let you harm my sister!"

Tarrah merely stared up at Reyna, her face impassive. "I had a vision that you would do this."

"You're lying," Reyna spat.

"I wish I were," Tarrah replied, smiling faintly. "You are hurting my throat."

"Then why didn't you have the guards stay closer?" Reyna demanded, leaning down to hiss into her face. "If you're so all-knowing, why did you let it happen?"

"Because you won't kill me. You know what will happen if you do. The High King loves me. Kill me, and your sister is dead, regardless of whether or not you agree to become his Shieldmaiden."

Reyna felt like she'd been punched. She released her hand from Tarrah's throat and stumbled to her feet just as the guards closed in around them. One of them caught Reyna in an instant. She did nothing to fight back, heart hammering a drumbeat in her ears.

She still wasn't convinced the Shadow Court even had her sister, but it didn't matter. They *could* have her. Which meant they could kill her, too. And as long as that was a possibility, there was nothing Reyna could do but go along with whatever they demanded. If Eislyn was executed…if she was forced to fight a battle she could never win...

Reyna could not bear the thought. She would tear apart the very fabric of the world to stop it from happening.

"Dungeon time for this one, eh, Champion?" the guard asked in a dangerous growl.

"No, no," Tarrah said, frowning at the guard. "There will be no need for that."

"She attacked you. Our Majesty will not—"

"The High King has placed every decision about the princess with me. She will not be going into the dungeons. In fact, I daresay she has business in the throne room."

Reyna ground her teeth together, hating Tarrah with every fiber of her being. The vengeance was welcome. For so much of her life, her entire focus had been the Air Court. Battling against them, destroying them. Somewhere along the way, her hatred had dimmed. She'd begun to see them as friends and as allies. But now her lust for blood had come alive again.

Tarrah had forced her hand. Reyna Darragh could kneel to her bloody king, but she would never see him as anything but her greatest enemy. And, one day, when they least suspected it, she would slaughter every single fae who had threatened her sister.

And she would relish in it.

# 5

## TARRAH

Her triumph had come at a cost. It always did. Nothing in life was free, least of all victory. Tarrah Glas had convinced Reyna to swear fealty to the High King of the Shadow Court, but she had been forced to tear the ice princess's soul apart. And she had been forced to lie.

It was the first time in her life she had lied.

Her mother had loved falsehoods. It made Tarrah hate them.

She glanced toward the princess, who stood beside her in the throne room. They were just below the dais where High King Bolg perched on his black stone throne. His expression was one of smugness, and he swirled a goblet of thick, sickly-sweet wine that he'd smuggled in from the southern regions of the human lands. It seemed his own victory to reclaim Findius Stronghold had come at a price as well. He had gained a second layer of dough around his middle, and he rarely left his chambers. It was said that he kept air fae prisoners in the dungeons, leftover survivors from the reclaiming of the city. Females, only. Every night, he commanded the guards bring him another. Sometimes, Tarrah swore she heard muffled screams echoing through the castle, whorling to mix with the thick, impenetrable mist.

And yet, Tarrah continued to serve him. His champion still. Regardless of how she might view his dishonorable actions, she would stand by his side until Unseelie told her otherwise. Her god had chosen Bolg Rothach for a reason. What that reason was, Tarrah could not comprehend, nor did she even expect to understand. Unseelie was all-seeing, all-knowing. Tarrah was nothing more than an ant in the dirt.

"Princess Reyna. I must say, I did not expect to find you inside my throne room so soon."

Beside Tarrah, Reyna scowled. "The only reason I'm here is because your damn champion threatened to involve my sister in this. It's me or her, so here I am. What would you have me do?"

He took a long sip of his wine, forcing Reyna to wait. She had come to him with her head hanged low to give herself to his mercy, and he revelled in it. It was a cruel move. Finally, he set down his empty goblet and wiped the red from his lips. When he smiled, crimson stained his yellow teeth. "I would have you make your vow to me."

"Show me Eislyn," the princess said, her voice as frozen as the icy north. "And then I will fight whatever battle you deem necessary."

"I think not," the king said smoothly, without a moment's hesitation, as if he had expected the demand. "As I said before, I cannot risk putting the two of you into a room together."

Reyna's hands clenched. A guard shifted closer to the king's side. "You are a shadow fae. You are not bound to truth. How can I be certain you have my sister if you will not allow me to see her?"

"Well, here's how it is, princess. You *cannot* be certain I have her, but are you willing to take that risk?"

Tarrah was an expert in controlling her expression. She learned long ago not to show her mother the truth of her emotions, and Tarrah had carried that with her even here. So, outwardly, she knew she was the picture of calm serenity. Inwardly, however, she was troubled. The High King seemed to take delight in this game of lies. It revealed a level of corruption in his soul that she had not realized he had.

Tarrah had seen the very same corruption in her own mother. She might worry that they suffered from the same affliction, but she knew it to be impossible. When her mother had been pregnant with Tarrah, she had travelled to a land far from the shores of Tir Na Nog, and she had stared into the face of deep, dark magic. That magic had transformed her, changed her. It had turned her into something full of rot and dread.

But the king had never been to Inishfall. He didn't even know the truth of the two powers hidden there. If he did, she knew what he would do. He would want to go and take one for himself. And, just like her mother, he would choose wrong.

Reyna let out a long exhale. "Fine. You win. I'm not willing to take that risk. Tell me the vows, and I will speak them, but you must promise me you will not harm my sister. I know your words are meaningless, but on your honor as a king, I ask you to promise."

The High King smiled, victory dancing in his beady eyes. "Very well then. I promise you, I will not harm Princess Eislyn." His gaze slid to Tarrah. "Now the vows, Tarrah."

Tarrah swallowed hard and nodded before turning to face Reyna. "Princess Reyna Darragh, you have come before the High King of the Shadow Court, and our Seat of Power, to make vows to serve this realm. To bond your vows to your life, repeat these words after me."

Reyna's eyes were two thin slits of hate, but she nodded all the same.

"I promise to serve the High King of the Shadow Court. I promise to protect his life and fight for him when he commands. I promise to never attempt an escape, nor shall I ever attempt to kill him. I am his to command, now and always." Tarrah stopped and sucked in a sharp breath of hope. Regardless of how they had come to this moment, they finally had. The Shadow Court needed Reyna to make these vows, but as the moments ticked ever forward, Tarrah began to doubt.

The High King had chosen force as a way to procure the princess's vow. But Reyna Darragh did not seem the kind of fae to respond very favorably to force.

But finally, Reyna spoke, repeating the words that Tarrah had said. And then finished with, "But these promises are hereby revoked if you harm my sister."

Tarrah swallowed hard and glanced sharply at the king, who swirled his wine, lips pursed. But then he smiled. "Such a fiery little thing you are for being born in the ice. I should make you repeat your promises, only this time, as you were instructed. But as I have no intention of harming your sister, I'll leave it be. Thank you for your service, princess. You're excused now. I have some other matters to attend to this evening, and they do not require your presence. Unless, of course, you would like to join me and my companions in my bedchamber."

Eyes flashing, Reyna twisted on her heels without another word and headed straight toward the door, her long hair a whirlwind around her shoulders.

"I need to speak with you, Your Majesty," Tarrah said quietly as Reyna stormed out of the room.

He jerked his attention away from the retreating princess and waved dismissively in Tarrah's direction. Now that he had what he needed—his throne—he seemed far less interested in what Tarrah had to say. "Go on then. New vision, eh? I hope it involves a head on a spike, preferably the wood king's ugly green head."

Tarrah frowned. "Now that Reyna has made her vows, we should tell her the truth about her sister. The lies will only turn to dust in your mouth if you don't."

Bolg coughed out a laugh. "What and tell her that she's not here? That she's gone missing? That might be the worst counsel you have given me yet, Tarrah."

"She would do better knowing the truth."

"Do better at what?" He laughed again and waved at a nearby serving girl to refill his goblet. "At plotting ways to escape so that she can run to her sister? No, I think not. As long as she believes we have the girl, then she will do whatever we say."

"She made vows that cannot be broken. The magic would kill her before she stepped foot outside this castle. If we told her the truth—that we are not in fact threatening her sister's life—she might not view us as her ardent enemy." That was the real truth of it. Tarrah had seen the hate churning in Reyna's eyes. She'd made her vows, but she would forever hold a deep-seated grudge against the Shadow Court, and Tarrah could scarcely blame her.

When Tarrah had first been blessed with a vision of the ice princess, wielding her sword on a bloody battlefield, she had been full of hope. She'd imagined Prince Lorcan delivering her to the feet of the king, who spoke with ardent, poetic words, convincing her of their need to end the exile.

She had not imagined such trickery.

"Harrumph," he said, smiling at the serving girl refilling his wine. She was a pretty thing with flowing brown locks and big blue eyes. He likely had plans to take her to bed. In fact, Tarrah doubted that he was paying much attention to her counsel at all. Not with a future conquest in his presence. "Reyna Darragh is more clever than you think. She will spend her nights dreaming up ways to kill me, ways to circumvent her vows. But if she believes her sister's life will be forfeit if she makes a move against me, she is much less likely to follow through on those plans."

Tarrah opened her mouth to argue, but then snapped it shut. She could see now that his mind would not be changed. He wished to keep up the charade, and his mind had already grown bored with the conversation. She should have known. He would never release a lie once he had committed to it. Because Eislyn Darragh was not the only false prisoner he had.

# 6

## THANE

Three weeks past, the High King of the Air Court had rushed through the grasslands to escape an ambush from the shadow fae. His mind had run as fast as his legs, trying—and failing—to come to grips with the fact that his oldest friend had betrayed him.

Although, that was not entirely the case, he admitted to himself as he charged past the crumbling fortress to his left. Feurach Fortress, his family's castle—what was left of it. Only moments before, the Ruin had poured from bulbous, sleet-grey clouds, along with blasts of icy snow. Thane had never seen anything quite like it before. It had looked like a swarm of black-and-white locusts had descended from the Court of Dead where their forsaken dead looked down on them and laughed.

It had been long believed that there was nothing more tragic than the death of a fae. Cursed, they were called. Cursed by mortality. Once, the lives of fae had seemed endless. A king could live three hundred years, or more, unless another took up arms against him. To then watch the light die in eyes that had witnessed hundreds of years…

But Thane was beginning to believe the dead were the lucky ones. The fallen, the ones left behind in these dying realms, they were the ones who were truly cursed. They would have to watch the world burn down, and it was a fire that none would survive.

Not even a High King. *Especially* not a High King.

Thane reached the docks that lined the shores of the Mag Mell Sea. Feurach Fortress had long been the home and training grounds of many of the realm's warriors. As such, his uncle had kept the bulk of the warships in the cove just beyond the castle. Thane had visited often when he had been younger, and he had always gaped at the glistening golden ships and their billowing sails. The way the sunlight gleamed on the freshly-polished wooden decks. At the time, he had dreamt up glorious adventures where he was a ship's captain, off on some grand adventure. Perhaps he would visit the human lands or even beyond. Perhaps he would even sail around the bottom tip of Tir Na Nog and press on to the Empire of Fomor.

As a boy, it had not mattered that no fae ever returned alive from Fomor. He would do it all the same. And survive.

The first fae to see Fomor and live to tell about it.

Now, he could think of nothing worse than sailing to a certain death.

He had slowed to a stop when he reached the docks. The warships were there, same as they always were, but their decks were eerily empty. Even from a distance, Thane should be able to see activity on board. There was always work to do. Cleaning the decks and repairing broken wood. Then, there were the drills. Warriors would clamber on board, and push off with speed, sailing to a position in the sea only provided moments before.

He'd heard footsteps behind him. With hope in his heart, he had whirled toward the sound, imagining that Lorcan had escaped the shadow fae and followed him to the sea. In that moment of hope, Thane had thought he might turn back toward the Air Court after all. If Lorcan had found him, he would not flee.

But it had not been Lorcan.

It had only been one of his uncle's warriors, one he recognized from his time spent in Feurach Fortress as a boy.

"Oh, it's you." Thane had shook his head and sighed. "Apologies, Marlon. I thought you might be someone else. Are you all right?"

Marlon had swayed on his feet, and a thick layer of ash covered the top of his head. The Ruin, Thane had thought grimly. The warrior had clearly been inside the castle during the attack, and he'd likely hoped he could escaped. But none escaped the Ruin.

No one but Reyna Darragh.

"Here, let me help you." Thane had reached out to clasp the warrior's elbow, but Marlon's knees buckled beneath him before he had a chance. The poor fae fell forward, landing heavily on his face. A bone crunched. Thane shut his eyes. The fae shuddered his last breath, and went still.

"Eislyn, I do hope you find your cure," Thane had whispered into the wind. The Ruin was a terrible thing that must be destroyed. But he would not be the one to stop it.

He had left the warrior behind. There was nothing Thane could do for him now. The Dagda's hidden servants would collect his soul, carrying it away to the Court of Death.

The Court of Death. Thane had clenched his hands. Had his father been taken to that place? Or had he been banished to Ifrinn? It was likely the second. Sloane Selkirk had broken so much; he had destroyed the lives of many. The Dagda would not look kindly upon the former High King of the Air Court.

Still, Thane could not help but feel doubt in his heart. He

no longer knew if he believed in the laws of the Dagda at all. What kind of god would allow such terrible things to occur in his own lands?

But there had been no time for those thoughts.

Thane's feet had thudded on the wooden beams of the docks as he searched for a boat that he could man himself. He had no crew. He had nothing but his own two hands.

Movement at the end of the dock had snagged his eye. He had turned, spotting a small merchant ship bobbing in the water, the crew scurrying about like ants to food. Thane had picked up his pace, hope in his heart. This ship might be his only chance.

"Oy!" He had called out when he reached the plank that led to the ship's deck. A moment later, a head popped over the side. The man gave him a dismissive flick of his fingers, showing off half a dozen glistening silver rings. He wore a scarf-like hat made of the finest felt, two feathers poking out. A favorite style among the wealthier merchants.

"Sorry lad. No time to chat. We're busy."

"I only need one moment of your time," Thane had shouted up with a frown.

"We're getting out of here, son." The merchant had pointed a trembling finger toward the smoldering castle. "Whatever that is, I don't want it coming for me."

"I'm the High King of the Air Court," Thane had said roughly, his voice carrying on the light breeze.

The merchant had blinked at him, glimmering green eyes drawn to the elaborate tattoo that stretched across Thane's tanned forehead. "Yes, I suppose you are. What's it to me?"

"I have business with the Sea Court," he'd said. "Take me there, and you will be rewarded for your bravery."

The merchant had snorted. "Bravery? It ain't bravery if it's for coin." And then he'd added, "Your Majesty."

"You know who Imogen Selkirk is, yes?" Thane had asked, ignoring the jab. "Daughter of—"

"Yes, yes," the merchant had said, flapping his hand in dismissal. "She's a sea fae, and your family are royals. I probably know more about you than you do about yourself, son." The man had squinted, white bushy caterpillars dancing on his forehead. "Alright then. Come on board. I'll get you there, and you'll get me that coin. If you don't, then I'll have to tell the Grand Alderman where you've gone. And I doubt anyone wants me to do that. Me included, but I will."

Thane had nodded, climbed on board, and that was how he found himself on a merchant ship, docking on the island of Gorias, home to the Sea Court's capital city, Gorias City. The salt in the air thickened as he strode down the wooden dock, head tipped back to gaze up at a clear, turquoise sky. Colors in Gorias were unlike anywhere else. The blues were far more vivid; the greens deepened into teal. A soft wind blew his golden strands away from his curving-tipped ears and rustled the silken tunic around his waist.

Thane drew a deep breath into his lungs and sighed. It had been years since he'd visited the Sea Court. His father had forbidden it, too focused on the wrongs between the two realms. The Air Court and the Sea Court had been at war for a century, just like the rest of the realms, but Thane's mother had always kept the lines of communication open with her sister. She'd brought Thane here, only a few times, and always when he'd been no more than a boy. He had always loved it here. It felt more like home than Tairngire.

"Thank you, Doughlas," Thane said to the merchant. The fae had been shockingly kind during their journey. Something Thane realized he was not accustomed to, at least not without a deceptive reasoning hidden behind the smile.

"No need for thanks," Doughlas replied, straightening his

ever-present hat. "Just don't forget us merchants when you wage your wars. The past century has not been kind to us."

Thane nodded. He'd always known the merchants had suffered. With the borders between kingdoms as closed as they were, trade was not what it had once been. Many merchants had taken to smuggling, risking their lives for a chance at enough coin to survive. Those who had chosen to trade within the laws of the realms had lost a great deal, having to rely on enough business within a single kingdom to get by. The only other options were to trade with the humans across the Mag Mell Sea, or with the Fomorians. Neither were particularly attractive options.

After bidding his farewell to the merchant and his crew, Thane made his way through the city of Gorias. Much like Tairngire, Gorias had been built on a foundation of kingdom colors. A dirt-packed road led through a bustling city center with buildings built from teal stone that glimmered beneath the strong, steady sun. The markets were bustling, and music drifted through the streets. It was a happy place. Calm, serene.

It made Thane take the long way around to reach the castle gates.

"I'm Thane Selkirk, here to see my aunt." He did not use his title here now, and he never had before. It would be seen as a slight to the sea fae. His father had never understood that nor had he cared to try. To him, the sea fae were nothing more than fish to fry and feast upon.

No doubt the sea fae would celebrate once they learned of his demise, if they hadn't already. The journey had taken several weeks, long enough for a message to reach Leaghan Castle.

The castle itself sat upon a cliff that rose high above the churning Mag Mell Sea, a glistening tower of rocks flecked with turquoise stones only found in the waters surrounding the Thousand Islands. Gorias was the largest and most prosperous island of them all, boasting ten thousand residents.

The guards led him through the castle and into the Great Hall where he had dined many times as a young boy. His aunt's family sat around a long wooden table, halfway through breaking their fast, though the king and queen were absent. The scent of delicious breads and soft cheese rose up to greet him.

"Thane Selkirk here to see you, Your Grace," the guard said, bowing slightly and then stepping back into the shadows of the nearest corner.

His aunt turned and stood. Iona Leaghan was a twin to her sister, even though they had been born two years apart. She was tall and lithe with an angular face, sapphire eyes, and blue hair that hung down to her waist. A sea fae circlet sat on her head, glittering from the sunlight that poured through the wall-to-wall window that looked out on the sea on the western edge of the Great Hall.

"Thane." His aunt's voice wobbled when she saw him, fear and pain churning through her eyes. He hesitated, fearing that he had made a terrible mistake. Their realms were at war. He might be family, but that did not mean that he would be welcome here.

But then she jumped up from the table, rushed forward, her long blue hair trailing down her back. She clasped his hands between hers and squeezed so tight that his fingers ached. "Oh, Thane. I had hoped you would come here. We will kill him, we will. This, I promise you."

Thane shook his head in confusion. "What do you mean? Kill who?"

She furrowed her brows. "Aengus, of course. That horrible fae who has stolen your throne and killed our beloved Imogen. He—" She stopped when she saw the look of devastation that must have passed across his face. He staggered back, and his heart ached as though someone had punched a sword through his chest.

"What?" His voice came out a croak as the world spun before him.

His aunt's face swam in his blurred vision. "Oh, Thane. I am so sorry. I thought you knew."

"Thought I knew," he mumbled dumbly, grasping at the wall. Surely it could not be. His aunt must be wrong, or he'd misunderstood her words.

His aunt's grip tightened on his arm, her sharp fingernails digging into his skin, talons into flesh. "When you disappeared, that lover of hers took the throne in the name of the Grand Alderman. He showed everyone some letters she tried to send to me, letters discussing how we planned to get Sloane off the Seat of Power and…" She trailed off, but Thane knew what she would say next. His mother had worked against his father, and against Thane, in order to sit on the throne herself. In the end, she had given it up, but it had been a source of strife between them.

"He declared her a traitor to the realm," she said in a soft whisper. "She was a sea fae. So, of course, no one tried to stop him…"

"Aengus killed my mother." Thane's own words sounded foreign in his ears, as if they were coming from someone else, and were about someone else. This couldn't be happening. His mother could not be dead. Despite the strife between them, he had loved her dearly. And he knew that regardless of what she had done, she had loved him, too.

It was Aengus. He had done this.

Thane's tears turned to dust, and finally, his aunt's face became clear before him. Her eyes reflected all of the hate he felt inside. "We will make him pay for this."

# 7

## REYNA

"Your new chambers, milady," the small, timid serving girl tiptoed away from Reyna as she took in the spacious rooms that stretched out before her. Now that she had made her vows to the bloody shadow king, her words bound her to her fate. There was no longer any reason for barred windows. Reyna should have felt some relief in that, she knew, but it resulted in the opposite effect.

She felt even more trapped than she had before.

Rather than the one room, she now had three. The first room was a lush, well-furnished bedchamber with silk sheets draped over a feather mattress. The black stone floor twinkled beneath the candles lit in the chandelier hanging overhead. Through one door, Reyna found a sitting room with two lush sofas, a fireplace—not that it was needed in this dreadful heat—and a soft bearskin rug covering the smooth floor. Another door led to her bathing chamber. A small, simple room with a wooden tub and nothing else.

"Thank you," she said to the serving girl. "You may go."

The serving girl gave a nod and then vanished into the

corridor. Reyna sighed and glanced around. The quarters were nice. Almost too nice, as if the shadow fae expected her to *appreciate* them. Did they truly think she could be so easily bought or that she could feel at ease just from a comfortable bed and a sitting room?

*They had her sister.*

Not even a room fit for a king would make her forget that.

Wingallock settled comfortingly on her shoulder as she moved to the window and pushed open the thin glass. He hooted, though his was not the sound of joy. Her familiar always reflected her own mood. When she was sad, he would curl up mournfully in the corner. And when she felt strong, ready to tackle the world, he would soar through the sky with his magnificent wings outstretched, talons arching toward the enemy like swords.

Now, Reyna did not know quite how to feel. She'd just given herself to the shadow king. Had it been the right thing to do? Did he even *have* Eislyn? They'd put her in an impossible situation, unable to do anything but speak vows that tasted like ash in her mouth.

She would have to follow his every command, do his every bidding, and comply with his every folly. In the wrong king's hand, that kind of vow could turn cruel very quickly indeed.

But the right king would have never made her take that vow.

She would likely die in this place. But as long as Eislyn did not, that was all that mattered.

*Eislyn.* Her heart clenched tight. Her little sister would be terrified, captured once again by the enemy.

"How did they get their hands on her, Wingallock?" she whispered to the bird. He was merely silent. Reyna knew the answer, though she did not want to think it.

*Lorcan.*

A knife sliced through her gut, reopening a wound she'd failed to heal, over and over and over again.

It was one thing for him to capture Reyna. It was quite another for him to take her younger sister. He *knew* Eislyn. How fragile and troubled she was. He knew how afraid she'd be and how much she'd been through in her life. It pained her to think he would stoop to such a deed. Eislyn. Out of everyone in the entire world, how could he hurt *Eislyn*?

How else would the shadow fae have gotten their hands on Reyna's sister? He must have taken her just after he'd poisoned Reyna. She even bet they'd been on the very same boat, heading toward the same terrible fate. If only Reyna had known, if only she could have battled against the poison in her veins, pulling her into that strange dream where the line between reality and horror bled together like the opposing lines on a crushing battlefield.

She began to pace, a frown etched deeply into her face. Where would they be keeping Eislyn? Would they have given her chambers similar to hers? She would likely be trapped behind iron bars, unless they'd forced her to make her own vow. Reyna's frown deepened. She needed to find Eislyn. If they had harmed her…

She would kill every single last one of them. Except she couldn't, she thought with a growl, pounding her fist against the black stone wall. They'd made certain of that. Her hand smarted, stinging from where she'd hit stone.

Wingallock let out an agitated hoot, and then flew out the window to join the reddened skies. Reyna gave a grim nod as he disappeared out of sight. She didn't blame him. She wanted to fly out of this hellhole, too.

After watching him soar across the city, she turned toward the door and pushed out into the corridor, bracing herself for impact. But no guards stood in her way. Instead, she found the twisting black tunnel eerily empty and silent. Surely they did not trust her this much already?

Of course, why wouldn't they? She had vowed to serve the High King, in whatever capacity he demanded. There was nothing she could do against him. Escape was an impossibility. Her only relief would be his death, but she could not kill him herself, nor could she conspire with anyone else to do the deed.

She was as helpless and as harmless as a mouse in a snake pit.

It made Reyna's skin itch. It made her head pound with rage.

Still, she had made no vow to remain in her chambers. Nothing could stop her for going in search of her sister unless the High King suddenly appeared before her and commanded it. So, search she would. All she needed was to see her sister's sweet face, to confirm her safety, to make sure she was alive. It was the only thing she wanted, the only thing she desperately needed.

It would make it all worth it.

Moments blurred by as she searched the castle. There was little to be found. The corridors were winding tunnels, twisting and turning like a dozen angry snakes. She passed no one. According to the few whispered conversations she'd heard, few courtiers had arrived in Findius since Bolg had retaken the city. Were they too afraid to step foot inside their ancient home? Or were they plotting against the king? They'd accepted him when he'd been nothing more than a title in an old forgotten fortress. Now that he sat on the true Seat of Power, he might find enemies behind the smiling faces of his friends.

After finding nothing but empty rooms, Reyna gave up search in the eastern tower. She had backtracked to the throne room, intent on searching the west wing of the castle, when she heard voices drifting along the shadowy breeze. Both were familiar. One so much so that it made her gut quake.

"I have done everything you commanded. Now, please. I need to see Thane." Lorcan's booming words echoed through the throne room.

"No wonder you fell for the ice princess. You two are so alike it's giving me a headache. Begone with you, son. I have no wish to argue with anyone about prisoners any more this day. There is somewhere I need to be. And some*one* I need to see. Heh."

Reyna had noticed his leering eyes on the serving girl earlier. She had no doubt who he meant to see this night. But what had Lorcan said about Thane? Reyna inched a bit further down the corridor.

"Father," Lorcan's voice was low and dangerous. He almost sounded as though he wanted to rip the king to shreds…a thought that brought a slight smile to Reyna's lips. "I have done nothing but follow your every command since we arrived in Findius. Please. Just give me this one thing. I committed the worst betrayal of my life to ensure Thane's safety. Let me see him now."

Reyna gripped the wall, her heart thundering.

"It is a grave thing when a father cannot trust his own son as far as he can spit," the king answered in just as dangerous a voice. "If I allow you to see your air king, I know what you will do. You will break him out of his cage, and then you'll free the Darragh girl, too. It seems my power over you has faded with time. My mark no longer holds the bite it once did. You found a way to force your way around it once, when I commanded Thane's death. I have no doubt you'll try it again. Your loyalty to this court is gone. If it was ever there to begin with.

"Heh. I should have known when my people found you in

those bloody grasslands. A bastard will never replace a true-born son. I should have never given you a title. You should have stayed in that hellhole and starved. I'd send you right back there now, but...that village is full of nothing but the dead."

Lorcan let out a roar so loud it echoed far and loud. The heavy thudding of footsteps soon followed. Reyna twisted on her heels and raced down the corridor. She ducked out of sight just in time. The throne room door flew open, slamming into the wall, only seconds after she'd slid around the corner.

Heart hammering, Reyna waited with her back against the slick stone wall, listening to the footsteps receding in the opposite direction. She couldn't believe what she'd just heard. Eislyn was not the only prisoner in these halls. Somewhere in the darkness, Thane was here, too. And Lorcan...

Suddenly, everything made sense. Horrible, twisted sense. Thane had never gone missing. When the shadow fae had attacked Lorcan and Thane in the grasslands, they had taken Thane captive.

And Lorcan's reaction...he was loyal to Thane. Reyna could scarcely believe it. Ever since awakening in the shadow kingdom, she'd assumed Lorcan had been working against Thane all this time. But no...it was the opposite, in fact.

Lorcan had betrayed her to save Thane.

For a moment, her hardened heart softened. Regardless of who and what Lorcan was, he had always cared for Thane. They'd been brothers, even if not by blood. It was no wonder that he had done everything he could in order to spare his life.

But then her heart hardened once more. There had to have been another way. There was *always* another way. In order to save Thane, he'd sacrificed Reyna and her sister. Eislyn was an innocent, far more than the High King of the Air Court. As much as Reyna had come to respect Thane, she would never choose him over her sister.

Reyna could not forgive Lorcan that easily. In fact, she was certain she never would.

She might have promised herself to Bolg, but she had done no such thing to his son. If Lorcan truly had brought her sister to the shadow king, to save Thane's life or not, she would find a way to repay him for the favor. By stabbing her blade right into his heart. And he would never see it coming.

## 8

### REYNA

There was a shadow fae in her chambers when she returned. Reyna slowed to a stop as she held her door half open, her fingers still clutching the wood.

"What are you doing here?" she snapped at Tarrah. After hearing Lorcan's voice and his words, she needed time alone to deal with her grief. And come up with a plan to kill him and all the rest of the shadow fae without breaking her vow.

That damn vow.

"Enjoy your stroll through the castle?" Tarrah asked. Pretty chirpily, Reyna thought, for someone whose eyes looked perpetually hollow.

Reyna narrowed her eyes. "And what of it? There were no guards at my door. If you didn't want me to leave my chambers, your bloody king should have ordered it."

"You may leave your chambers whenever you like. This castle is your home now."

"It will never be my home," she snapped.

"I understand your anger," Tarrah said, brushing her raven hair over her shoulder. "We certainly haven't handled this as well as we could have. That's why I thought you might like to join us for dinner in the Great Hall. It will give you a chance to meet everyone."

Reyna coughed out a bitter laugh. "You must be joking."

"I'm not. You've been kept to your chambers for far too long."

"I was kept there because of *you*."

Tarrah pursed her lips. "Well, the offer stands. Join us in the Great Hall and meet the rest of the court. Or stay here. It's up to you."

Just to spite her, Reyna wanted to stay in her chambers. Going to dinner almost felt like giving in and accepting this ridiculous situation that she had been forced into against her will. Tarrah acted as though Reyna was suddenly a shadow fae, as if a few words would take the ice from her heart and burn it down to ash.

But Reyna was not dumb. She realized she had been given an opportunity to learn more about the court. At the moment, she knew very little about the shadow fae. She did not know the players in the game, the lords and the ladies, who was loyal to the king. And who wasn't. There would always be at least one who wasn't, who had ambitions, who craved power. If she befriended them, they might be willing to help. There might be a way for her to get out of here yet, but she would have to rely on her brains instead of her sword.

And that meant infiltrating the court.

"Fine. I will join you on one condition," Reyna said.

Tarrah gave her a knowing smile. "I have a feeling I know what that condition is. He won't be there tonight. I'll make certain of it."

"Then, it's a deal."

The Great Hall needed a dusting. It was just as gloomy as the rest of the castle, even with fifty fae crammed inside, filling the space with heat and noise. Sconces lined the walls, all lit by flame. They cast ominous, flickering shadows across the black stone floors, dancing and whorling in the light breeze that poured in from the open windows.

Reyna was led to what she assumed to be the head table, though she would hardly call it that herself. It was an ordinary table crafted from old, spotted wood and had been packed to the brim with courtiers in various states of dress. Some were prim and proper and pristine, wearing courtly attire in varying shades of grey. They wore silken tunics embroidered with deep crimson and glistening jewellery around their necks. The females were expertly dressed in billowing gowns that cut sharply between their breasts.

But then there were the others. They looked as though they'd barely managed to scrape together a clean outfit, some with ragged holes in the knees. Their faces were scrubbed clean, but their hair and nails were long and wild.

At the opposite table, warriors packed in tight. Their laughter boomed; their drinks splashed onto the table.

This was not a standard night at court, that much was certain.

"I thought you might like to sit near me and Nollaig." Tarrah, still donned in her armor, motioned to a chair by her side. Across the table, Nollaig sat waiting. Her hooded cloak hid every single inch of her from view except the gloved fingers of her right hand.

"Of course," Reyna said sarcastically. "Why would I want to sit anywhere else?"

She felt Nollaig smile. "Careful, Princess. One might think you were trying to lie."

"A question is never a lie," Reyna said, dropping into the chair. "A lesson you should learn since you're so hell bent on undoing the exile. If you succeed, you'll lose your ability to lie."

"You can be frank here," Tarrah said, settling in beside her. "We know you're not thrilled to be here. No need to pretend otherwise."

"Some kings like to execute courtiers who have nothing to speak but insults."

"Our king won't hang you," Tarrah replied, motioning to the food. "I hope you like potatoes. Unfortunately, it's mostly what we have. Few crops grow beneath the mist. And you know all about our trade issues, so I won't bore you with that."

Tarrah had not been exaggerating. Several platters were spread across the packed table. Four of them held different variations of potatoes while only one had meat. There was no fruit or bread or green vegetable in sight. She'd noticed her meals were bland when she'd been kept in her barred chambers. At the time, she thought they were trying to make a point. Now, she knew why. They literally had no other food to eat.

"Don't you get sick of eating the same thing every night?" Reyna asked, scooping some fried ones, seasoned with rosemary, onto her plate.

"I like potatoes," Nollaig said.

Tarrah made a face. "When I was a child, I had mashed potatoes for breakfast, boiled potatoes for lunch, and then meat for dinner if we were lucky. Often, we weren't. I would like nothing more than to eat something else for a change."

"Enough to make someone your slave apparently," Reyna said in a faux-chirpy tone, before scowling. She would not feel sorry for these fae. No matter what sad tales they spouted, they were her enemy.

"You are not our slave," Tarrah insisted.

"You brought me here against my will. You captured my innocent sister. And you threatened to kill her if I didn't make a binding vow to your bloody king. If that is not a slave, then what is?"

Tarrah frowned and poked at her potatoes with a twisted fork that had seen better days. "It wasn't supposed to happen like that."

"Then, how exactly *was* it supposed to happen?"

"I was hoping you would agree to help our majesty willingly."

"Ha! That's rich." Reyna glanced around the table, noting a glaring absence amongst the various warriors and courtiers present. "Speaking of, where is your king?"

"High King," Tarrah corrected, but then frowned. "He is otherwise engaged this evening. He won't be joining us."

Reyna noted a hint of disappointment—and disapproval—in the Champion's voice. *Interesting*. So, his right hand did not approve of his dalliances. Was it jealousy? Did she wish she was the king's chosen bedmate? *No*, Reyna thought, examining Tarrah carefully. The shadow fae's hollow eyes were drawn to someone else, a warrior at the far end of the second table. A rugged male with piercing silver eyes, chiseled features, and an impressive physique, who wore grey scale armor imprinted with the Shadow Court's sigil.

That could only mean one thing. Tarrah was not wholly pleased with her king. Very interesting indeed.

Reyna took a stab at the fried potatoes, chewing them carefully. They weren't bad at all. "Yes, he did seem quite interested in the serving girl. I realize things are different in this realm, but I'm surprised he isn't attempting to make a much more politically beneficial match. A marriage with one of the ladies would make his reign more stable."

She had no intention of helping the shadow fae at all, but

she wanted to gauge their reaction to her words. She knew next to nothing about his plans, other than an impending attack on the Wood Court. After that, he might very well aim to join his court with another. Not the Air Court. He'd made it clear he wanted to snuff out every last air fae royal, including the ladies he might choose to wed.

That left Sea and Ice. And he had Eislyn, or so he said.

Of course, Reyna's father would never agree to such a thing. But High King Bolg Rothach did not know Cos Darragh as she did.

Tarrah sighed. "The High King's dalliances are just that. Dalliances. But let us talk about something more entertaining. Princess Reyna, is the north truly as cold as they say?"

*The north*. Something inside Reyna's chest twisted. Her beloved kingdom. Her people. It felt so long ago that she had set her eyes upon fields of ice and trees cloaked in snow. When she had been a Shieldmaiden in training, her father had asked her to never make the vow that would have bound her to be a warrior for the Ice Court for as long as she lived. Princesses could not become true sworn Shieldmaidens. Her heritage must always come first.

And so she had agreed. She'd done that one thing for him, to keep the peace with her family. He never would have forgiven her if she had turned her back on the court for good, even if it had been to fight for her people.

But now she saw she should have done it anyway. If she had, she would not be here now, trapped in a vow that could never be broken, stuck serving an enemy court, and forced to bow to a cruel king who cared little about the innocents who would die in his impending war.

"Princess Reyna?" Tarrah asked, her voice breaking through Reyna's troubled thoughts.

Reyna sighed and poked at another potato. "The air is so cold that your breath frosts as it leaves your lungs.

Icicles cling to your eyelids, and baths must be taken indoors, lest the water freeze while you are in the middle of it." She gave Tarrah a sad smile. "It is as cold as they say."

Nollaig popped an entire boiled potato into the folds of her cloak—and presumably her mouth. "That sounds intriguing. I would like to go there someday."

Irritation ripped through Reyna's gut. "Why? So that you might destroy every village there in your quest to conquer the entire continent?"

"We are not going to destroy every village," Tarrah said with a frown.

"No?" Reyna arched a brow, dropping the fork onto her plate. "Then, how do you plan on doing it? None of the courts are going to want you back, especially not when we're all already at war. You'll just be one more enemy added into the mix, with a load of innocent low fae stuck in the middle, desperately trying to stay alive."

"There are some fae we do need to destroy. I will not lie to your face about that, but they are not the innocents you speak of," Tarrah argued, fist tightening around her fork. "Once we kill the wood king, we will turn our sights on the Air Court. But it's the royals we want. And that throne. Once we have that, we can end the war."

*That* throne?

"Why do you need that throne?" Reyna asked. "You have a Seat of Power here."

Tarrah pressed her lips together, and then glanced at Nollaig, who merely shrugged. "Might as well tell her."

"Tell me what?" Reyna demanded.

Tarrah tapped her finger against the table, as if considering, but then she began to explain. "The Air Court's throne is the strongest. It holds the most power. That was how the Selkirks found the magic to exile us despite the Fall. If we get that throne, we can undo the exile, and we can be part of Tir Na Nog once again."

The most powerful throne? Reyna had never before heard that. But it made sense. Terrible, perfect sense. The Air Court had always been the strongest realm. They'd always held the most power, had the biggest army, and had not suffered as deeply as the other courts had. All this time, it had been because of that throne.

Reyna took another bite of food. "Why do you want to undo that magic so much?" she asked, honestly curious to know. In her eyes, she could not see much of a benefit for the shadow fae, other than access to trade. But that could easily be accomplished in other ways. Winning a few battles here and there, forcing the borders to reopen. Taking down the Wood Court would be enough for that. Then, they would have a direct line to the Empire of Fomor. It would be enough for their realm to not only survive but to thrive. And they would still have the ability to lie.

Why push further? Why fight harder? There was only one reason a realm would do that. Power. Tyranny. Control. They not only wanted to restore their kingdom to its previous glory. They wanted to dominate everyone else.

Tarrah blinked at Reyna in confusion. "For Unseelie, of course. Our god is the rightful ruler of this great continent, but he's been pushed out by a pretender."

"You mean the Dagda..." Reyna arched a brow. This was a first. She'd certainly never heard anything like it before.

"Yes, of course," Tarrah said, her hollow eyes unblinking. "Only a follower of Unseelie should sit on the throne with the greatest power. Then, and only then, will our god have the power he needs to bless us all with his wisdom, goodness, and strength."

"Well, that doesn't sound at all terrifying," Reyna muttered to herself. She didn't know if she believed Unseelie even existed. But if he did, it would be a terrible day when he gained power over them all.

"Are you a follower of the Dagda then, Princess Reyna?" Nollaig asked from where she had fully polished off her plate. She leaned forward, gathering a second helping of the various potatoes. "You don't seem like the type."

"And what is that supposed to mean?" she asked hotly, suddenly remembering that this was no ordinary dinner with ordinary courtiers. She was dining with the enemy. They needed to be treated as such.

Nollaig put down her fork, her cloak's long arm rustling against the palm of her hand. "It takes a certain kind of mind to get caught up in religion and prophecies and myths. You seem far too level-headed for that. Swords wield far more damage than the empty words of an invisible god, am I right?"

"Hey!" Tarrah scowled and whacked Nollaig's arm. "Don't speak blasphemy at the dinner table. And stop insulting my mind. We got our castle back because of me, remember?"

Nollaig chuckled. "It's so easy to get a rise out of you, Tarrah."

Reyna merely gaped at them. When she had imagined the Shadow Court, she had never once envisioned a relaxed dinner table full of joking jabs and laughter. It had been all darkness and gloom and despair. Backstabbing liars, murderous kings.

Well, the king part might have been right, but the rest seemed anything but what she'd expected. Of course, maybe they were putting on a show, trying to put her at ease so that...so that, what? They already had her word, her vow. She was already forced to do the king's every bidding, even if they kept her locked up in a cage for the rest of her life.

They laughed and joked around for a few more minutes, before finally turning their attention back on Reyna.

"So, what *do* you believe, Princess Reyna?" Tarrah asked. "Are you a follower of the Dagda?"

Her heart ached. Once, she had believed in him more than anything else in the world. She thought he would protect them, always. But then reality had smacked her in the face. Repeatedly.

"If the Dagda exists, he will never allow you to take the Air Court's Seat of Power for Unseelie. He'll fly in from the Court of Death and burn every last one of you to a crisp."

Tarrah cocked her head and smiled. "Word mincing."

Reyna scowled. "What?"

"You just minced your words. I've always been curious about it." She shrugged and popped a potato into her mouth. "Where I'm from, everyone just lies."

What a strange way to put things. "Where you're from? You mean here, right? In the Shadow Court."

"No, I mean in the Southern Plains beyond the Dorcha Mountains. They lied so much there that it was almost as though they were allergic to the truth." She shrugged and glanced around. "Here, you'll mostly find the truth."

"Mostly," Nollaig said. "There is the occasional fib."

Reyna continued to stare. "You mean to tell me that you lot don't lie your arses off all day long?" She snorted. "Wait. You got me with that one. You just lied about lying. It's going to take awhile to get used to this."

Tarrah reached across the table and patted her hand. Reyna flinched.

"No, Princess. We're telling the truth. I can understand your doubt though. In time, you'll see."

Reyna scowled and dug back into her food, done with the conversation. It was too much. She'd almost felt more comfortable locked away in a room with iron bars. Then, it had been easy to draw a line in the sand. Black and white was always easier to see than the murkiness of grey. They had been liars, the lot of them. Cruel, evil, wrong. None of that had truly changed, of course, but now they seemed almost *normal*. Like this was any old dinner at court. Reyna did not want to think of them as normal. They'd abducted her. They'd forced her to make vows to their king. She was here against her will, and so was Eislyn. They had threatened her sister's life.

The shadow fae were monsters. Every last one of them.

Suddenly, Reyna felt the air in the room *shift*. Shadows seemed to reach out from behind her and pulse along her skin. The scent of leather and smoke and steel drifted into her nose, pushing aside the salty aroma of the food spread out before her.

It was *him*. Her gut twisted, and her heart began to pound. He'd entered through the door at her back. She could have kicked herself for not choosing a seat facing it. Then, she wouldn't have ended up stuck, glued to her seat, with Lorcan striding toward her. She could feel him moving through the room.

Frantically, she pushed up from the table so fast that her chair toppled to the floor, and a wooden chunk cracked off the side. "I have to go."

Tarrah scrunched her eyebrows together, and then glanced behind Reyna. Immediately, the friendliness in her eyes vanished. "Your Highness, I thought we told you it was best if you stayed in your chambers this night."

Reyna gripped the edge of the table, carving her fingernails into the wood.

"Reyna," he said softly.

She came undone. Her name on his lips was the worst and best thing she'd ever heard. Ice splintered around her heart, threatening to shatter completely. A pain so raw scraped against her soul and made her stumble to the side. Gritting her teeth, she hissed to Tarrah, "I can't do this. I have to go."

The sadness in Tarrah's eyes—her enemy's eyes—sent a new wave of turmoil through her heart. "Of course, Princess. I understand."

*I understand.* Ha! How could she possibly understand? Reyna had never opened her heart to a male. Ever. She'd spent her life training for battle, refusing to even entertain the idea of getting distracted by something as pesky as lust. Or even more. She'd made herself hard and strong and fierce. It was what she'd had to do to survive.

And somehow, Lorcan had broken through it all. She had trusted him. She had cared for him.

He'd betrayed her so utterly and completely that she did not think either one of them could survive it if they ever again came face-to-face.

In fact, she hoped he *wouldn't* survive it.

Her anger toward him did not mean the pain was no longer there. The wound was still fresh and festering.

"Reyna," he repeated. His own voice sounded wounded, but he did not know the true meaning of pain. Not like she did. "Please. It's been weeks. Let me speak to you." A pause. "Let me apologize for what I have done."

"Never," she growled through gritted teeth, punching away from the table. She kept her eyes averted from where she knew he stood, glaring hard at the timber beams she quickly rushed across. The door was only a few meters away. Soon, she would reach it and be away from him. Back in her chambers where she knew he wouldn't come. At least she had a sanctuary there.

A shadow loomed before her. Strong hands grabbed her arms and rooted her in place. Heat and pain roiled through her at his touch.

"Reyna, I am sorry." His breath whispered across her face, infused with berry wine.

She kept her eyes squeezed shut. She couldn't look at him. *She wouldn't.*

Instead, she smacked at his hands, desperate to get away from him. Her heart roared in her ears. She knew he wouldn't let go. He would hold her here, force her to stay when her entire body itched to run.

"Don't touch me," she hissed, pushing past him. She stumbled toward the door, glad the tears had waited until she got away. The last thing she wanted was for him to see her cry. He didn't deserve her tears. Not after what he had done to her, and to Eislyn.

Still, she cried for him anyway as she rushed through the mist-enshrouded corridors. They left hot streaks down her cheeks, reminding her just how far from home she truly was. Tears were meant to freeze.

# 9

## MARIEL

Mariel stood in the midst of three hundred screaming fae. The crowd had stuffed itself into the square just outside of the Adhradh, the warm spring sun beating down on the tops of their golden heads. The stone statue of the Dagda loomed over them all, his flared wings casting dark shadows on the sight at the top of the steps.

Aengus had called for yet another execution. This was his fourth in mere weeks. Today, he'd brought forth Lady Epona, one of Imogen's old friends. She'd been hiding out in the castle the day Princess Eislyn had escaped. Rumors had been swirling through Drunkard's Pit for weeks. Some said Lady Epona had even seen the princess leave and had done nothing to stop her.

And so Aengus had turned his wrath on her next.

Mariel frowned as he motioned to the executioner, a druid Aengus had conned into his schemes. He knelt beside Lady Epona, his brown robes bunched up around his feet. With furrowed brows, the druid gently wrapped the noose around her neck and whispered something into her ear.

Lady Epona gave Aengus a wan smile. "I curse you just as Imogen did. My loyalty is to our former queen."

Mariel had seen enough. Turning on her heels, she pushed through the teeming crowd to escape the square. She had been witness to three executions thus far, including Imogen's, and she need not witness another. It would not change a thing. She knew what kind of king—temporary or not—Aengus had become. Sloane Selkirk may have wronged her family, but Imogen and her lady friends had not.

Aengus's actions were doing nothing but creating turmoil for the realm. For *her* people. And she knew what lay south. The shadow fae had retaken their Seat of Power. They were intent on vengeance. They wanted to make the Air Court pay for what they had done to them—for their years spent in exile.

War was coming for them, and meanwhile, Aengus continued to strike down anyone who might doubt him, even if the throne was not his to take. He was sowing uncertainty, fear, and division. If he did not stop, the realm would tear itself to shreds far before the shadow fae even stepped foot on air fae soil.

Something must be done.

She heard the crowd let out a collective gasp just as she stepped through the gates. Setting her jaw, she only gave herself a moment's pause before she started off again, pushing through the wealthy streets that surrounded the castle. Mariel had once known these streets better than she knew the lines in her own palm. They'd been her home. She'd ran through them, barefoot, despite her mother's protestations. She'd made friends with every merchant, had bought their wares even when they insisted the princess have them free.

When she reached Drunkard's Pit, she breathed in the familiar stench of dirt and rot. To many, the slums were a dangerous, disgusting place full of thieves, murderers, and fools. They were not wrong, but Drunkard's Pit was far more than that, too. It was full of kind faces, laughter, and sparks of hope. The fae who called the slums home had nowhere else to go. They'd been beaten down, and yet, they found the will to survive.

These were the fae who would suffer because of Aengus. Not the courtiers safe up in the castle, hidden behind thick stone walls. If the shadow fae descended upon the city, the slums would die first.

"You have that look in your eye again," her brother said as she pushed into their empty tavern. He glanced up from where he mopped a wet rag across the wooden bar top and shot her a grimace. "I thought you were done with all the Bloody Dagger business. Thought you didn't want to risk getting caught."

Indeed, it had been weeks since Mariel had agreed to take on another job. She hadn't wanted to catch the attention of Aengus, knowing full well that he would like to see her dead. And Mariel would be no help to the fae of Tairngire if she hung from a rope.

"I need the birds," she said quickly, pushing through the empty tavern and past a burlap flap whose deep color had faded over their years spent in hiding. She entered the storeroom and glanced around the familiar shelves packed full of spirits, wine, tankards, and salted meats. Jumping on top of the stool, she reached over the bottles of wine on the top shelf and extracted a yellowed journal she hadn't touched in years.

Her brother had followed her into the storeroom. He stood just beyond the burlap flap, staring up at her with pinched brows and a furrow that was all too familiar. He had used it on her many a time before now.

"The birds?" he asked. "Why do you need the birds?"

"It's time we end this, Mavis," she said gravely. "It's time we stopped cowering in the slums. We need to help our people."

"Mar," he said hoarsely, his eyes flicking from her face to

the journal she clutched tightly against her chest. "You're scaring me."

"Aengus killed another royal today," she said. "That's the fourth in only a matter of weeks."

He stared at her for a long moment before throwing up his hands. "That's none of our concern. It stopped being our concern when the Selkirks killed our entire family and drove us out of the castle! Why do you think we're still alive, Mar? It's not because they spared us. It's because they think we're *already dead*."

"The truth is they don't think of us at all," she said quietly but forcefully. "But they will."

He shook his head, and then threw his arms toward the packed shelves. "We've built a good life here. I know it's a pit of filth out there, but we have a good thing going on in here. You want to help the people? We do. We give them somewhere warm, safe, and happy to go anytime they need it. We don't need to stalk the streets and dispense justice to help our people. And we certainly don't need to go charging into the castle, reminding everyone that the Dalais family built this city and that they're still alive. Aengus is killing traitors, yes? What do you think he'll do when he finds out we exist?"

Mariel smiled. "He will welcome me with open arms."

Mavis blinked. "You've truly lost your damn mind, Mariel. He will have you killed on the spot, unless he decides to make a spectacle of you like all the rest."

"He won't." She continued to smile. "I have a plan. All I need from you is the location of the birds."

"You're actually serious about this." Shaking his head, Mavis crossed his arms over his chest. "I will not help you with this. I will not be a party to my sister's death."

"If you don't help me, Mavis, then I will merely find the birds from somewhere else," she said with a dangerous edge to her voice. "And that is less likely to be as safe."

He ground his teeth together. "Damn you, Mariel. Damn you to the Court of Death. You will be the death of the both of us. You know that, right?"

"No," she said, smiling. "I will be our rebirth. Prepare yourself, big brother. Once I'm finished with Aengus, no one will ever utter the name Selkirk again. We're going home."

❧

Her brother had been very fond of birds when he'd been a boy. Their mother had never approved, but that had not stopped her from supporting Mavis's strange obsession. She had bought him a flock of birds from the Empire of Fomor, said to live as long as the fae. He'd spent hours nurturing them, training them, loving them. When the Selkirks had sacked the castle, Mavis had cried all the way through their escape, terrified the birds would meet the same bloody fate as the rest.

But the birds had escaped, and they'd found him, despite it all. They were the best trained birds on the continent, or so her brother said. Mariel believed it was far more than that. He'd bonded with the birds. They loved him.

But he could not keep them, not if they wanted to survive in the slums unnoticed. Gutter rats did not have flocks of fully-trained birds.

Instead, he'd hidden them away somewhere safe. He'd never even told Mariel where he'd taken them. Until now.

"I should have known," she murmured, glancing up at the looming yew trees of the Witchlight Woods. Above, a dozen golden birds perched on the thick branches, the sun glittering off their luminous feathers. "You never would have left them in the hands of someone else, not in the city."

"Of course not," he grunted. "The poor get hungry. They'd sooner eat them than feed them precious grain."

"And you've been coming out here all this time?" she asked, arching her brow. "Every single day?"

"Not every day. Once a week, unless things are busy at the tavern."

"You've been giving me so much stick about getting caught, and yet, you've been coming out here all this time. If anyone had spotted you…"

"It's not the same, Mar, and you know it. No one ever comes out here. The Selkirks don't like these woods, not like we did. They don't understand it. They think it's full of darkness and dread."

But still, if someone had seen him, they would have realized he was more than a mere low fae, though she could not find it within her heart to argue with him. Her brother's birds were alive and well and thriving from the looks of it. No doubt they preferred the canopy of green to the stone walls of the castle tower. They were free now, like Mariel and Mavis. But Mariel would not be free for long.

"You've been eating the sap?" she asked him. No one but Mariel's family had ever known about the sap. It had left Mariel feeling young when every fae around her had begun to wither and die after the Fall.

"Of course. And you have, too. I can see the glimmer in your eyes."

"You might have told me," she scolded but only gently. "I've tried time and time again to bring some to you."

He let out a heavy sigh. "You never asked, Mar. You've been so focused on vengeance and death that you didn't think to ask me what I've been doing to stay sane all these years. Well, here you are. This is how." He gestured up at the woods. There was yearning in his voice, in his gold-flecked eyes. He missed this place just as much as she did, and she'd never even realized.

"You said you liked the tavern life. That we had a good thing going on in the slums."

"I cannot lie. Those words were truth. But it did not mean I don't miss home."

Squaring her shoulders, Mariel nodded. In his attempts to convince her to stop, he'd only added more fuel to the fire in her gut. She knew her brother wanted nothing more than for her to give up this plot and settle in at the tavern, where they would live out their lives without intrigue, and murder, and war. But the war would come for them, whether Mariel did a damn thing about it or not. So, she would make certain they were on the winning side.

"Call them down," she said. "I'm ready."

Mavis sighed and let out a low whistle. Two short bursts of high-pitched sound followed by a single low blow. Instantly, the birds pushed off their branches, wings flapping against the strong wind. A million golden feathers filled the air as the birds swooped toward the ground.

Several landed on her brother's shoulders and outstretched arms. Some settled by his feet. Not a single one had anything to do with Mariel. They did not even deem her interesting enough to blink in her direction.

She dug the scrolls from her pocket, tied together with golden string. "I need four of these delivered."

Mavis sighed. "Where are they going?"

She flipped open her journal and pointed at a list. Four names, all underlined in red. Mavis sucked in a sharp breath, his eyes widening. When he glanced up at her in shock, she nodded. "Yes, those."

"Alright," he nodded, surprising her with the intensity of his tone. "I'll agree to that."

Mavis took the scrolls and pressed them into the curved talons of four of his golden birds. He murmured to them as he did, whispering instructions into their eager ears. It had been a very long time since they had followed their master's orders.

One by one, the birds took flight, rushing up into the cloudless sky. Mariel watched and clutched the journal tight to her chest. Wings speared the sky, gleaming beneath the golden sunlight. Her hopes were carried away on the wind, hopes of a future that was finally theirs after so many years spent hiding in the shadows.

# 10

## REYNA

"It's time for you to make yourself useful," Nollaig said as they stood clustered around a small table in a room just beyond the throne room. It was a small strategy room, lit by flickering candlelight. Bookshelves lined the walls where leather-bound tomes were packed tight. An oversized globe sat in one corner, the continent of Tir Na Nog stretched wide across the side that faced them. It reminded Reyna too much of her father's study, where he spent hours pouring over battle plans.

Nollaig pointed at the map, where the grey border melted into green. "I'm taking a scouting team through one of our hidden gates. The goal is to establish what the Wood Court is planning, and to determine their numbers. You'll be coming with us."

Reyna frowned. "I thought my purpose was to fight, not to spy."

"We're not spying," Nollaig said. "We just have no intention of being seen. We get in, we see what they're doing, and then we get out."

"Again, I thought the visions had something to do with me fighting."

Reyna did not wish to leave the castle. Her sister was here, and she still hadn't found her. This quest could take days, if not more. How far into the wood fae lands would they have to venture? If they intended to trek all the way to the capital of Murias…she could not abandon her sister with the shadow fae that long.

"As careful as we intend to be, there is always the chance we might be seen. If we are, we need strong and capable fighters."

Reyna crossed her arms and lifted a brow. "And if I choose to stay here in case some Air Court ships appear in the Midnight Bay?"

"You don't have that choice," Lorcan said quietly from the corner. "My father has decided we're going on this mission, and you must follow his command or die."

Reyna's head jerked up as her entire body locked tight. Horror churned through her, and she had to fight against her every urge to run. At some point, he had sneaked into the room, or he'd been hiding unseen in the shadows all this time. Heart roaring, she could do nothing more than stare at him for a good, long while. The rest of the room was quiet.

Her skin was hot, and a hammer sounded in her ears. If anyone would have spoken, she would not have been able to hear their words. It had been weeks since she had laid eyes on him. He looked the same as he always did. Tall and strong and corded with muscle. His dark hair framed a face full of strong angles and a lightly-stubbled jaw. The tips of his ears barely broke through his thick locks. Even here, in the shadow lands, he wore the same armor he had back in the Air Court. Boiled leather hugged his frame. Only here, nothing covered his muscular arms. Lorcan had never been fond of the cold, but it was warm here.

His expression was the only thing about him that had changed. Instead of the self-assured, stoic set of his jaw, he wore an uncertain frown that looked as though it had been permanently etched into his face. His eyes flashed with fury, though it did not seem directed at her at all. She wet her lips and stared, her heart trembling. A rush of memories and emotions flooded her mind, feelings she had tried so hard to burn away. But they were still there. They had always been there.

That did not mean she would let him see it on her face.

Regardless of what she had learned, Reyna found that she could not forgive him. The betrayal still stung as sharply as it had the day she'd awoken trapped inside an enemy court.

Reyna swallowed hard and turned back to Nollaig. "Surely, you cannot expect me to go on a quest with *him*."

"Prince Lorcan has been assigned to this quest, as have you. I discussed it thoroughly with the High King, and he is adamant in his decision."

Reyna scowled. "He's trying to torture me. I made my bloody vows, and he still has every intention of making me miserable." She whirled toward Tarrah, whose face at least Reyna could read. Her eyebrows were pinched, her lips set in a straight line. Clearly, she did not think this was a good idea either. "Did you see this in a vision?"

"I have seen you fighting for the king. You know that."

"No, but this," Reyna said, waving her hands at Lorcan, Nollaig, and herself. "This quest. This team. Did you see it in a vision?"

"Not all of the king's decisions are based on my visions."

"So, then wouldn't it—"

"Reyna." His growl was so familiar that it made her belly twitch with need. Her name on his lips, his face in her thoughts. It had taken every ounce of willpower to pull her focus away from him, but she could not stop it any longer.

She braced herself and turned to face her former lover once again.

Desperately, stubbornly, she had avoided him until now. The High King had been oddly agreeable when she'd demanded he keep Lorcan away from her. Of course, Lorcan had been less so. He'd appeared outside her chambers on more than one occasion, shouting to be heard, but the guards had turned him away.

Her heart ached as she stared into his dark eyes. She wanted to fight him and kiss him and hate him and love him and throw anything in the world right at his face. Instead, she gave him the iciest stare she could conjure. "Yes?"

He flinched, almost as though she had hit him. Perhaps aloofness was the best defence after all. If he truly wanted fire, then she would give him ice. "I know my father well, unfortunately. It seems he's intent on your presence on this quest. He has Eislyn. And you made vows."

Reyna ground her teeth together. "All right. So, then *you* stay here."

"Alas, I am in no better position than you are, I'm afraid." He crossed his arms over his muscular chest and leaned against the wall, his eyes momentarily flashing with a hint of rage. "I am certain this is some sort of test. If we fail..."

Reyna's heart jumped. She understood instantly. Before putting her in a real fight, the king wanted to test her, to ensure that she hadn't found some way around the vows. She scowled. He was far more clever than he looked.

"I just need to know one thing," she said in a harsh whisper, hating the tears that pricked the corners of her eyes. "Did you take Eislyn? When you delivered me to your father's feet, did you do the same to my sister? *Did you take her?*"

Lorcan's jaw twitched, but his face remained impassive. A blank slate. An empty canvas. The only emotion was in his eyes, but it was so chaotic that she could not tell if it was hate, pain, or fear. "No." A beat passed. "But what is my word to you? Right, Reyna? I am a shadow fae and a liar, and I cannot be trusted. I poisoned you, stole you away on a ship, and delivered you to the enemy. An enemy who has forced you into submission. So, what does it matter if I didn't take your sister? I've done enough for you to hate me for the rest of our miserable lives."

Reyna could do no more than stare, her heart in her throat, a roar in her ears, even in the silence of the room. She had not expected him to be so brutally honest, almost casual in the way he had admitted what he'd done. What did he expect? For her to suddenly forgive it all, based on what? His ability to own up to his mistakes?

"You did do those things," she said, her voice hoarse with raw emotion.

Lorcan's hands clenched. "I did."

She stared at him through blurring eyes, eyes that burned. "Is that all you have to say about it? No explanation? No apology? Nothing more than a confession is all I'll get from you?"

"Would any explanation be good enough for what I have cursed you with?" he said in a harsh whisper. "You're forever bound to my father. No, I agree with you for once, Reyna. Hate me. Hate me for eternity."

His words burned. Why would he not tell her about Thane? Why wasn't he even trying to make amends with her? Instead, it was as if he had given up. It was if he didn't care. Not about her, not about anything.

"Ahem." Nollaig cleared her throat, and Reyna suddenly remembered that she and Lorcan were not alone in the room. There had been an audience to their fight, and several pairs of eyes were looking anywhere but at them. Her neck flushed, and Nollaig continued as if there hadn't been an interruption. "There are two hidden gates that the Air Court never found during their occupation of the city. The wood fae shouldn't know their location either, so it is unlikely we will be spotted. We will leave at nightfall to be certain."

Nollaig paused and appeared to glance around the table, waiting for questions or objections. When no one spoke, she continued. "The wood fae prefer to stick to the trees, and they know their forests well. Some are most likely camping out here." She pointed to a spot inside the forest the began several hundred meters from the border between the realms.

Teutas frowned and peered down at the map. "If they're that close, then we are at a great disadvantage. We're not yet ready for a siege."

Reyna glanced up, eyebrows lifting. That was interesting. She hadn't known that. If the shadow fae were not yet ready for a siege, she almost *wanted* the Wood Court to attack. If she could somehow find her sister and extract her from her cell while the shadow fae were distracted by an army at their gates...

Of course, her vows would never allow her to do that either. She'd promised not to flee...but she had never promised a thing in regards to her sister. She could get Eislyn out of these godforsaken lands. She just couldn't leave herself.

"Indeed," Nollaig mumbled. "We have already sent a few scouts. None of them have returned. Odds are, the wood fae are already nearby. But we need to confirm it."

Reyna frowned. "They never returned? So, the king is sending us out on a death quest."

"The previous scouts were not protected by a trained Shieldmaiden, a king's own guard, and *me*." Nollaig smiled, or at least, Reyna thought it sounded like she smiled. It was impossible to tell, the strange shadow fae's face always hidden beneath her black hood.

"And I am going," Tarrah said quietly from where she bent over the map, studying it with a deep crease between her eyes. "I'm protected by Unseelie."

Reyna fought the urge to roll her eyes. "If you're protected by Unseelie, then why do the rest of us need to go?"

Tarrah blinked up at her. "Because I have seen every one of you in my visions. Unseelie wishes for you to be with me always. I do what my god commands."

Any doubt Reyna once had about the girl's beliefs, she no longer had now. There was an earnestness to her words that could not be faked. Reyna did not believe for one second that Unseelie protected her, but she knew that Tarrah believed it wholly.

But Unseelie protected no one. He was the god of darkness and cruel hate. His magic poisoned the minds of any who used it, and then twisted them into believing they were right. Unseelie made those who followed him see the world upside down, sideways, through mirrors. Good was wrong, and wrong was good. Murder was the greatest display of honor.

*Once,* Reyna reminded herself. That had *once* been the message of Unseelie, if he even existed at all. But just like all magic, his had vanished after the Fall. He held no power anymore.

Unless...

Nollaig tapped the map again. "Of course, the scouts were instructed to carry on up to here." She now pointed to a spot near Murias. It was just as Reyna had feared. "It is possible they were caught much further north than we fear. It would still mean that the Wood Court is on the march, but we would have far more time to prepare."

"Why don't we just send our familiars?" Reyna asked. "My owl and your crow can see where they are."

Nollaig's voice went razor sharp. "Absolutely not. It is impossible to spot the wood fae through the canopy of trees, and I will not send Holas down below it. The wood fae are skilled in archery, and there are no snow owls or crows in their woods. As soon as they spotted a foreign bird, that bird would be dead."

A chill swept down Reyna's spine. "All right. Scratch that idea then."

Nollaig continued with her plan, pointing at various spots on the map and explaining the obstacles they might encounter along the way. Reyna found her mind wandering. It was impossible to stay focused when she could feel a pair of eyes on her skin. Swallowing hard, she twisted her head toward the back corner where Lorcan still stood. His gaze was unflinching, but his expression was utterly unreadable.

Her heart pounded. Over the weeks of her captivity, she had imagined, time and time again, what she would do once she saw him. She'd known she could not avoid him forever. Eventually, the past would catch up to her, the ghosts transforming into fully-formed beings.

She had recited words. She had closed her eyes and imagined their steel clashing together. She had wondered how it would feel to face him on the battlefield. In her mind's eye, there had always been a standoff. Lorcan against her and everything she loved. A blade pointed at his heart. Instead, she had gotten *this*.

It was not enough.

Nollaig cleared her throat, drawing Reyna's attention from Lorcan's face. She could not see the strange shadow fae's face and yet Reyna could swear she saw Nollaig frowning. "Your vows prevent you from killing shadow fae, Shieldmaiden. *Any* shadow fae."

Reyna scowled. "As long as you understand that I would kill every last one of you if I could, that's enough. For now." She turned her glittering eyes back on Lorcan, hoping he caught the meaning of her words. "You wouldn't be the first enemy I've plotted against. Did you truly think I agreed to marry Thane so that I could become his sweet, silent wife? My other sisters might have, but me?"

Shock flickered in his dark eyes. Good. She'd surprised him, shown him that he wasn't the only one willing to commit terrible deeds in the name of the ones he loved. She might not be able to shove a dagger into his flesh, but she could do one better.

His shock vanished as he shuttered his eyes. "You aren't that stupid, Reyna. You would have been hanged for treason. You would have shattered the alliance and restarted the war between ice and air."

"Or I would have done it in a way that *no one* would have known it was me. And then I would have become reigning High Queen."

He shook his head, jaw rippling. "You're just saying this to get a rise out of me."

"I cannot lie."

He stared at Reyna. She stared right back, her heart thumping. A small part of her hidden deep inside her bones wanted to take it back. She'd never wanted Lorcan to know the reason she'd first gone to the Air Court. But she'd blurted it out now, knowing that it would hurt him. Wanting to make him feel the way she did. Betrayed.

His jaw flickered as he ground his teeth, whirling toward Nollaig. "Make your plans. You don't need input from me. When you're ready to leave, come find me."

He kicked open the door and stormed into the corridor, his black cloak trailing behind him. Reyna stared after him, hands fisted. She wanted to call after him, dare him to come back. She'd expected something else. Shouting, screaming, rage. Instead, all he'd done was leave.

It wasn't enough. She needed more. Her skin itched for a fight.

Nollaig cleared her throat. "Not a fan of the Air Court then? I'm surprised you're so resistant to fighting for us."

Reyna whirled toward Nollaig, ready to take her fight out on the cloaked fae. But her rage died in her throat. "It wasn't the Air Court itself that I hated. It was the prince. I thought he'd make a terrible king, one who would ruin my kingdom. And if I thought it about Thane, then you'll have a pretty good idea how I feel about your ruler."

"Thought?" Tarrah asked. "Or think?"

"It doesn't matter," Reyna said. "Because my feelings for your court will never, ever change. And I will never forgive your prince for what he's done to me."

## II

### LORCAN

Lorcan charged through the castle, hunting for something to break. How could he have been so stupid? Reyna had hated Thane. They'd fought on the same battlefield, and she'd seen him kill her fellow fae. She was far too stubborn to forget something like that, not even when Thane had come charging in on his gleaming white stead, proud and strong, announcing alliances and peace. Not when she had known all along about the slaughter at the Sapphire Axe.

Lorcan had always wondered why she'd agreed to the betrothal, and now he knew why. She'd always planned to kill Thane once he'd become the High King. It would have kept her sister safe and provided vengeance for her kingdom. That was Reyna Darragh, through and through.

But even though it made horrible, twisted sense, Lorcan needed to smash something. His father's nose sounded like a fantastic option, but his bloody mark would no doubt put a stop to that as soon as he tried.

His father was wrong. Lorcan had pushed down the mark's command when Thane's life was at stake, but he hadn't been able to replicate it since. Every time Lorcan tried to *resist,* the dark magic in his skin sent shockwaves of pain throughout every inch of his body. Often, it brought him to his knees. And if he resisted too hard, the mark would blind him with such intense, unimaginable pain that it would knock him out like a sword against his skull. It had done it once before.

So, if he was going to get out of this damn quest, he would have to ask his father. He couldn't think of a worse punishment.

Swallowing down the tornado of emotions in his throat, Lorcan stalked through the castle to the king's chambers at the top of the central tower. As ruler supreme, Lorcan's father had staked his claim on the grandest rooms. His chambers covered two floors connected by majestic curving stairs. Lorcan had never been inside. He didn't understand why his father needed all that room, and he had no desire to find out.

Lorcan thought back to Reyna's face as he passed torch after torch. For weeks, he had ached to see her once again. To look into her eyes. To touch her. To hold her. Well, he had finally gotten what he wanted. Part of it, anyway. And now he would do almost anything to undo it.

She was so angry she could scarcely look at him, and when she finally did, all he saw was ice. The fire he knew so well, that he loved, was gone. In the Air Court, he'd thought she'd hated him at first, but he'd been wrong. Because *this* was hate.

Lorcan strode up the curving stairwell and found Segonax stationed outside of the king's chambers. The old commander was one of the few tolerable fae inside of Bolg Rothach's court of chaos, a steadying presence most of the time. His black hair was peppered with a grey that matched his eyes, and his nose reminded Lorcan of the flat end of a shovel.

He stood outside a commanding wooden door that had been reinforced with iron bands. The better for protecting the king in case of an invading army. One of the reasons he had no doubt chosen these rooms. If the battle came to Bolg Rothach, he would hide in his bed.

"Segonax, I need to speak with my father."

The commander pursed his lips and shifted on his feet. As he did, the grey scales of his armor jingled like pockets full of coin. "I'm not sure that's wise, Your Highness."

"I don't care if it's wise." Lorcan took a step closer to the door, and Segonax shifted to block his way. Narrowing his eyes, Lorcan dropped his hand to the golden hilt of his Tamaris steel sword. He did not want to fight Segonax—in fact, he wouldn't—but if he had to threaten him to get inside, then so be it.

Segonax sighed. "Lorcan, son. You don't want to go in there. The king is…ah…well, he will be in a state of undress."

"Of course he is," Lorcan said, his voice rising. "He won't rest until he's impregnated every fae from here to the northern tip of Tir Na Nog."

The door suddenly swung wide. Bolg stood in the doorframe, tunic off, trousers rumpled and bunched at the waist. His crown sat crooked on his head where sweat clung to his thick hair. Behind him, several females lounged on the bed, all naked. They appeared happy enough. One of them pressed a hand to her lips and giggled.

Lorcan just scowled.

"What's all this yammering out here?" Bolg demanded, scratching his pink, hairy chest. "I was in the middle of regaling the serving girls here with stories from before the exile."

Lorcan scowled at his father. "No prisoners for you tonight then, Father? Didn't feel the need to drag a poor air fae in from her cell?"

Bolg's eyes narrowed into two thin slits. "Get out of here. I didn't call for you."

"I need to speak with you, and it can't wait." Lorcan hated that he had to stand before his father and practically beg for his time. It made him feel small, like the young boy in the grasslands who had cowered before the charge of the Fomorians.

"I'm busy." Bolg grasped the door and pushed it shut, but Lorcan thumped his palm against the wood. The door stayed in place, half open. Bolg might be able to make Lorcan feel small, but he was not the stronger of the two and he knew it.

If they ever fought, Bolg Rothach would not stand a chance. The mark suddenly screamed with pain, and Lorcan flinched.

"It can't wait. You've put Nollaig in charge of a quest to scout in the wood fae lands, one that you've commanded both me and Princess Reyna to be a part of." Lorcan curved his fingers against the wood. "I need to stay here. It would be a mistake to force me to go along. Reyna and I are like bottled lightning. Your precious quest will fail if we both go."

Bolg stared at him for a long moment, and then dropped back his head. His booming laughter echoed through the corridor, and the serving girls even joined in. "Well, isn't this rich! Son, you have been hailing abuse at me for weeks, demanding I let you see that princess of yours. Stomping around, throwing fits. And now you have a chance to spend some time in her 'esteemed' presence, and you want me to let you out of it?" Bolg laughed again.

Lorcan's gut churned with irritation. He hated to say what he was about to say, but it would be the only way to get Bolg to agree to his request. "Well, it seems you were right all along. It is a terrible idea to put us together."

"Ha! Look at you, grovelling! I should have brought the two of you here together ages ago. I've never seen you so compliant before." Bolg's grin widened. "I like it. I want it to stay. So, I'll tell you what. You go on this quest with the ice princess. Clearly, it will be good for you."

Anger boiled in Lorcan's veins. "I came here to ask something from you, Father. I've never asked anything from you before."

Bolg just smiled smugly.

"I cannot go on this quest. Say I can stay here."

"No. I don't believe I will."

"Dammit!" Lorcan shouted, hands clenching. "Can't you just do one thing for me? Once? That's all I'm asking!"

Bolg arched a brow, and his tone lost its laugh. "Once? *Just* once? I wonder, son, did I not do something for you when I brought you here from your starving grasslands and made you my prince? I gave you power. I gave you everything." He leaned forward, eyes flashing. "I made you what you are."

"You gave me nothing," Lorcan spat into his face. "And then you *took* everything. I'm not going on that quest, Father. I refuse it."

The mark pulsed with pain. Blinding, excruciating shards of it streaked through his gut. It dragged through every inch of his skin, tearing all his flesh from his bones. Shuddering, Lorcan stumbled back. He couldn't think. He couldn't breathe. Every single part of him burned with the heat of a thousand blazing suns.

"You will go," Bolg said with a sneer. "Or I will let that mark kill you."

At that, Bolg leaned back and kicked the door hard. It slammed right into Lorcan's face. Seething, Lorcan stared at the wood and contemplated how many ways he could destroy it completely. He could take out his sword and chop the thing down, but fire would do a better job. There'd be nothing left but a blackened husk where the door had once been.

More pain burned through him. He was so destroyed by it

all that he had to lean against the wall to keep from toppling to the ground.

"Lorcan," Segonax said quietly, snapping Lorcan out of his thoughts. He'd forgotten the commander was even standing there, bearing witness to the terrible cruelty of the king.

"He's impossible," Lorcan spat. "Regardless of what I do, he just wants to torture me. Look at what his mark has done to me."

Lorcan still trembled, though the worst of it was over now. Now that the king had vanished behind his iron-banded door, the piercing pain of the mark had dulled to an ache.

"Only because you allow him to. You let him get under your skin." Segonax gave him a thin smile. "You aren't very good at hiding your emotions from him."

"I can't go on this quest, Segonax."

"Unfortunately, son, you have to."

"We'll end up killing each other."

He arched a brow. "Do you truly believe that?"

"She just told me that she agreed to the Air Court's alliance so that she could get close enough to Thane to kill him."

"Ah, I see." Understanding dawned in Segonax's eyes. "Your loyalty to Thane, while not ideal for the Shadow Court, is commendable. Loyalty is *always* commendable. But, and please don't take this the wrong way Lorcan...*you* originally plotted your way to Thane's side so you could spy on him for your father. And you always knew that he would eventually command you to kill him."

"But," Lorcan said, but Segonax held up a hand to signal that he wasn't done.

"Yes, you became close to Thane, but that came later." Segonax shook his head, laughed. "In truth, Lorcan, you and Reyna Darragh are far more alike than either of you realize."

Lorcan's tension in his hands relaxed, just a bit. "What are you saying?"

"You both went to the Air Court to avenge your kingdom. And then you realized that the world isn't as black and white as you thought. Enemies can end up not being enemies at all. Enemies can turn out to be good people." Segonax's smile died. "And allies can be terrible ones."

"Even if I agree with you, Reyna will never see it that way. This quest is madness."

He still did not know if he could forgive her fully for what she'd planned for Thane. Lorcan had gone to the Air Court with the very same plot, but he'd done so under the curse of his mark. He'd had no choice. Reyna'd had every choice in the world.

And it wasn't as though she had apologized. She'd thrown it right into his face when she knew it would hurt the most.

"Most of the king's plots these days are madness," Segonax muttered beneath his breath, and Lorcan wasn't entirely certain he'd heard him right. The commander never questioned his king.

"What was that, Seg?"

"Nothing," the commander said quickly. "You best get ready for your adventure. The hour is growing late. Try not to get yourself killed, eh? We need you."

Lorcan frowned at that. The last thing the shadow fae needed was a prince who had no control over his own damn actions. Whirling on his feet, he strode back down the corridor, heading to his chambers to prepare for the days ahead.

And brace himself for the inevitable battle that was looming. His battle with Reyna Darragh. He hoped it would not be a bloody one.

# 12

## EISLYN

"We're fully north of the mouth of the Bay of Wind now, princess." Vreis stood tall on the deck beside her, the salty air rustling his brunette locks. An amber jewel hung from his neck and swayed with the rock of the boat. "No ships have been spotted in pursuit. We truly may have escaped."

Eislyn exhaled, a rush of relief. She had been tense from the moment they'd stepped foot on the Stingray, her eyes ever wandering to the western horizon, fearing a sail would be seen fluttering in the distance, bearing the Air Court's golden crown sigil. It had taken them a full week to sneak north. At first, they had headed east, deep into the Mag Mell Sea and away from Tir Na Nog's shores.

"I wish we could head to shore now," she said, yearning for the icy forests of her homeland. She had forgotten how much she missed them.

That first night, Vreis had sat her down at a rickety wooden table below deck with an ancient map stretched out between them. He had explained their strategy for getting her home. Sail east, then north, and then even further north. They would not stop at the villages along the eastern edge of the Hoarfrost Forest. Too close to the Bay of Wind, Vreis had said. Eislyn was inclined to agree with him, as desperate as she was to reach Falias.

The next closest stop would have been the town of Deigh. But the cursed place had been destroyed by the Ruin five years past. No one lived there any longer, and they needed food and supplies when they landed. That left Margaidh far up north. Lord Killian lived there, old friends with her father. From there, it would be a long trek to Falias, but they could get an owl off to Father when they arrived and fill him in on what was happening at the Air Court.

And it would give her a chance to peruse the eastern markets again. Perhaps she could find another book to help her with her quest to end the Ruin.

"The Grand Alderman likely has ships waiting on the coast," Vreis said. "We would be ambushed."

She sighed. "I know. It doesn't stop me from wishing."

Vreis smiled. "You seem more at ease now, Your Highness. I'm glad to see."

"You know you don't need to call me that. You may call me Eislyn." Ever the honorable warrior and guard, Vreis had not once uttered her name since they had stepped on board.

He arched a brow. "I don't know any such thing. Most courtiers insist upon their titles, particularly princesses, kings, and queens."

"You spent all of your money to get me out of that city so that I wouldn't end up like the Imogen Selkirk." She sucked in a lungful of brine-clogged air. "You don't need to use my title, Vreis. In fact, I'd prefer it if you didn't."

"Very well then," he said with a smile. "If you insist, *Eislyn*. But only when we aren't in the presence of royals. We wouldn't want them to believe you'd become too friendly with a mere warrior."

She felt herself flush as she caught the implication. Only husbands, wives, sons, and daughters were permitted to drop titles at court. Family. Those bound by blood and vows and flesh. If Vreis were to drop her title in front of a lord or lady, some would think them lovers, ruining any chance she had at truly marrying Thane.

A High Queen could not be blemished. That included sex.

Eislyn cleared her throat, suddenly unable to find any words at all. As she turned her gaze to the horizon, a heavy darkness rolled across the crystal sea, blotting out the blazing sun.

"Storm's a coming," Aisten, the captain of the ship, shouted as he scurried toward them, flapping his shimmering arms. "You two best get below decks. I don't fancy fishing a princess out of that there sea."

Eislyn's stomach flipped with fear. Their journey thus far had been nothing but pleasant. The waters were calm; the skies were clear and blue. It had lulled her into a false sense of security, it seemed. Eislyn hadn't imagined what could happen if there was a storm.

They could all die.

"No need to be frightened, Your Highness. Er, sorry. Eislyn." Vreis wrapped a strong hand around her elbow and ushered her toward the stairwell that led deep into the belly of the ship. "This crew has sailed through many a storm, and we'll be safe down below."

"All right," Eislyn said, doing her best to appear steadied and calm, like her sisters would. They would not show fear, not when faced with something as simple as a storm. But storms made Eislyn think of something she wished she could forget. The ash in the sky. The falling flecks of black. Her mother's scream as she died.

Eislyn shuddered and followed Vreis down the creaking steps. He led her to the cabins where a small, dark room held about half a dozen tables. Large barrels were stacked in the corner, and shadows bounced through the room from teal orbs that hung from the curving walls. It stank in here, Eislyn could not help but notice. Like stale mead, sweat, and grime.

They settled into a pair of wooden chairs just as distant thunder crackled through the skies. It was so loud, Eislyn clamped her hands over her ears. If it was that loud below decks, she could not begin to imagine what it had sounded like up there.

"Here, let's play a game to pass the time." A glass bottle landed heavily on the circular table between them. It was quickly followed by two mugs. "You guess something about me. If you're right, I drink. If you're wrong, then you drink."

Eislyn couldn't help but laugh. "Is that truly wise? We're on a bouncing ship in the middle of a storm. We'll both end up nauseated."

"Those are rumors and nothing more." He shot her a devilish grin. "Fae do not get nauseated on ships. Only humans do."

She arched a brow, trying on a slight smile. "All right then. So, all I have to do is guess something about you, and you have to drink."

He gave a nod, crossing his arms over his chest and leaning back into his chair.

Eislyn regarded him carefully. She knew his face well, but she had never really *looked* at him before now. Not like this, considering every detail, noting every piece that made Vreis who he was. He was tall, even for a fae. In fact, there was nothing slight about him. His arms were corded with muscle, and Eislyn could tell he had a full chest beneath his leather armor. His hair was a light brown not often seen in the Air Court. He had the coloring of something else with his bronze skin, and an eye that was deeper than golden. And it crinkled in the corners when he smiled.

"You can trace some of your ancestors back to the fire lands," Eislyn said, feeling confident in her choice. He did not have flaming red hair, but he did have *something* about him that felt like fire.

Vreis's smile widened. "An obvious attempt, and a correct one. My great-grandmother was a fire fae." He lifted his mug to his lips and drank deeply. "Now, it's my turn. I'll guess something about you, Eislyn."

A little flutter went through her belly as his eyes roamed across her skin. It felt as if his gaze dug deep, revealing the darkest truths about her. She could feel his eyes flick to her wrists, back up to her face, and then...lower. Was this how he'd felt beneath her own gaze? There was a strange intimacy to it, one that made her flush. What would he say? What kind of truth would he reveal? She was almost scared to find out.

"You miss your sister," he said simply.

She snorted a laugh. "And you said *mine* was obvious." Shaking her head, she took the drink. It burned all the way down, and then her belly turned as hot as coals.

"Alright then," he said smiling. "Let's make it harder this time. Nothing obvious. Nothing that we know is true. Real guesses now."

Eislyn shifted on her seat, and the wood creaked beneath her. What could she guess about Vreis? Something that might be true. Something that wasn't obvious. She glanced at his hands. They looked strong. Some of the skin on his palm looked rough. He clearly used them to great effect in his role as a guard.

But that was obvious.

Her eyes drifted to his leather armor. He'd donned a well-fitting tunic that stretched tight across his strong chest. There was no sigil on it. No splash of gold. She flicked up her gaze to meet his eyes. He was watching her just as intently as she watched him.

"You have no intention of returning to the Air Court." Her voice was a hush when she spoke.

Vreis sighed, swirling the spirits in his wooden mug. "Is that one not obvious, princess?"

"But…of course you would return. Once Thane returns to Tairngire and throws Aengus off the throne, then…" She shook her head, eyes widening. "You don't believe Thane will go home. You think he's gone for good."

"I'll take my drink now." Vreis tipped back the liquid and slammed the mug on the table.

"But you mustn't give up. He wouldn't abandon his throne." *He wouldn't abandon me.* "You don't think…you think he's dead."

"No," he finally said. "He isn't dead. I believe he fled. Why, I cannot begin to imagine. I suppose he had good reason for it. If I were to guess, he felt his reign cursed. And he likely did not take his father's betrayal well. Where to…? I have my theories."

"Where?" Eislyn whispered, swallowing down the pain. Thane could not have left. If he had, it meant that he had turned his back on her. On everything they had shared. She was to become his wife, his queen.

"His mother's family would likely welcome him gladly, particularly now. It won't take long for them to learn what Aengus did to Imogen."

"The sea fae." Eislyn sat back into her chair, frowning. "If that's true, then we should sail there first. We need to talk some sense into Thane, and—"

"Eislyn," Vreis said quietly.

"What?" she snapped, though she immediately regretted her tone. Vreis had done nothing but help her, at so much expense to his own life, his own future, his own soul. He was only trying to help her now. Help her understand something she did not want to accept. Because it would mean that Thane was not the male she thought he was.

"You know I cannot take you to the Sea Court." He spoke in low, measured tones, though his eyes were full of the fire of his ancestry. "They might not see you as a friend but as a foe. You could end up a prisoner in their wave-crashed castles, held as a ransom against your father."

"You just said they would welcome Thane gladly. I am his betrothed."

"You are an ice fae. And a princess at that." He left the rest of his words unspoken, but she could hear them clearly enough. Eislyn was not Thane's betrothed, not truly. They'd never had the chance to make that designation. Oh yes, he had meant to take her hand. Before he had vanished.

Before he'd fled.

"My turn."

At first, Eislyn was confused. What did Vreis mean? *His turn?* And then it dawned on her. The game. The drinks. The horrible rush of their conversation had made her forget about any of that. After the revelations, she wasn't certain she wished to continue.

"Go on then," she said with a sigh. "Make your guess."

"You love Thane," he said easily, without a moment's hesitation. As if he had been ready to say it for a good, long while.

"I thought we agreed to avoid obvious guesses," Eislyn answered with a frown.

"And is it obvious?" he asked quietly.

His gaze was heavy on her face. Eislyn opened her mouth. No sound came out. Was it obvious? To the casual witness, perhaps. She and Thane had grown friendly over her weeks spent at court. He had helped her with her studies. He'd shown interest in her quest. And there had been some fluttering in her belly, the hope of something more.

But that more had never come. They hadn't been given that chance.

"No, I suppose I don't," she whispered, unexpected tears burning her eyes. "I mean, not yet. We only spent a brief time together, now and again." She shook her head and spoke more quickly. "They were good times. I was happy to hear he'd changed his mind about the betrothal to Reyna, happy he'd decided to choose me. Love would have come. It *will come.* I refuse to believe he fled."

Vreis nodded. "Well, I guessed wrong. That means I have to drink."

Eislyn watched him slowly lift his mug to his lips and sip the fiery liquid. As strange as it seemed, she was almost certain he'd guessed incorrectly on purpose. He had expected her to say she didn't love Thane. But why?

Eislyn lifted her chin. "You know, as someone who vowed to protect his king's future queen, you seem awfully convinced she'll never be said queen."

"And as someone who has vowed to destroy the dark magic plaguing your realm, you seem awfully distracted by a king who willingly left you in a castle with his enemy." He stood suddenly, dropping his mug on the table. "The boat is steady. It seems we've passed through the storm. I'm going to get some sleep, Your Highness. I'll see you in the morning."

Eislyn frowned and glanced down at the floor. She hadn't even noticed it had stopped swaying.

# 13

## REYNA

They left at full dark when the twin moons had risen fully into the sky, their glorious light obscured behind dark rolling clouds and the ever-present mists of the shadow lands. There were five in their company. In addition to Nollaig and Tarrah, the shadow fae had sent a warrior named Teutas to join them. It seemed the king was taking every precaution imaginable.

Lorcan appeared just as they gathered in the castle courtyard. He said nothing to Reyna. She had nothing to say to him either. His glowering eyes were cast on the distant horizon. Now that he finally knew her darkest truth, he would likely never look at her the same again.

*Good,* she thought. She did not want anything from him but his blood on her hands.

Nollaig took the lead, winding through the castle courtyard and down a long flight of stairs where a rusted metal gate clung to the ground by their feet. Teutas and Lorcan knelt down and pried the gate open. Loud creaks screamed through the quiet night.

Reyna peered into the tunnel, her stomach tumbling.

Wingallock hooted from where he sat on her shoulder. He was coming with her, even if he wouldn't be scouting ahead. "When you said that we would be going through a gate, this was not what I had imagined."

Once again, Reyna swore she felt Nollaig smile. "It would not be a secret gate if it merely opened on one end of the wall and again on the other. We must go underground to reach the other side."

Reyna had never been particularly fond of underground. There were caves in the north where ice glass formed. Miners spent hours of their day deep in the pits, cutting shards from the rocks. But Reyna had never laid eyes on them herself. She liked the fresh air and the forests and the skies.

"I would rather spend a week knee-deep in mud on the battlefield than go down in that cave," Reyna said.

"Perhaps you will get to do both." Nollaig let out a laugh before motioning her gloved hand toward the entrance. "Why don't you go first since you are so eager?"

Reyna glared.

Nollaig chuckled again. "I'm only joking. You don't know the way, and I doubt your eyes are as accustomed to darkness as mine."

"Nollaig, enough," Lorcan said.

"Oh, relax. You once enjoyed jokes, Lorcan, but it seems the air fae have destroyed that as well as our kingdom."

Reyna couldn't help but smile, and she swore she could hear the tinkle of laughter coming from beneath Nollaig's cloak.

Once again, Nollaig took the lead, throwing her legs over the side of the hole and shuffling down a hidden ladder. Reyna waited for her turn, her stomach twisted together like a dozen angry snakes. After the top of Tarrah's raven head disappeared, she couldn't stall any longer. Taking a deep breath, she plunged inside.

The rickety ladder led deep into the ground. Moments stretched by in terrible silence as they descended into the dark. At long last, they reached the bottom. Reyna jumped off the last rung and glanced around. The tunnel had opened up into an enormous cavern. The walls were covered in jewels lit up with yellow and teal, shimmering with light.

"What is this place?" Reyna's whispered voice echoed off the glittering walls.

"The Caves of Lysa," Nollaig replied from the front of the group. "You won't find it on a map. The shadow fae who discovered it hundreds of years past did not wish to share their discovery with the rest of Tir Na Nog. It seemed even then they sensed future strife, knowing that one day they would need somewhere to hide."

Reyna glanced around, wondering. "Why didn't you use these caves during the Exile War?"

"Some did. Mothers and children, those unable to fight. The rest stayed in the city to battle the onslaught of the Air Court. It did not save them." Nollaig sighed. "In the end, they refused to flee and abandon the warriors fighting in the city. They stayed in these tunnels, waiting for their loved ones to come down and tell them it was safe. But they never came."

Reyna's heart thumped.

"Eventually, they ran out of food and water. Too afraid to leave this place, they starved."

The caves did not look so glittering and bright anymore. A heavy darkness settled upon it. The ghosts of lives long lost. She could not imagine how those people had felt, trapped in a cave, desperately waiting for hope to arrive. It had never come. Innocents who had no doubt heard the clang of battle above, and then silence.

Reyna blinked. Innocents? Ha! They had been anything but. It was another sad tale, one no doubt intended to pull upon her heart strings. Perhaps it wasn't even the truth. It could easily be another one of their lies. Reyna needed to remember that she could not believe a single word they said.

Nollaig motioned for the party to follow. They left the glittering cavern behind to enter a much smaller, much darker tunnel. Reyna inched forward, grinding her teeth as the tunnel grew thinner with each passing step. Lorcan was just ahead of her, and she could not help but stare at the taut muscles of his back and remember how silky his hair had felt between her fingers. She still hated him, of course. He was a demon if there ever was one.

Suddenly, as if hearing her thoughts, Lorcan spun toward her and blocked her path. Her heart stopped in her chest. She swallowed hard. There was nothing else but him. He took up the entire width of the tunnel.

"I just have one question for you," he said quietly. "And then we never have to speak to each other again."

She lifted her chin, bracing herself for the impact. She knew what he would want to hear. He'd ask her all about Thane. He'd demand to know how she could have hidden it from him all this time, even after everything they'd shared. That or…he would just want to shout at her.

"Those vows you gave my father," he growled. "Have you found a way around them?"

She blinked, caught off guard, and then glanced around. The others had continued, unaware that Lorcan and Reyna had stopped. They were not near enough to overhear their words. "If I have, I certainly wouldn't tell you."

"You should be careful," he replied. "My father isn't a smug air fae lord. If you poke him with a stick, he will bite. And his fangs are venomous."

"Is this some sort of trick?" she asked, taking a step back. "Only hours ago, you looked at me as though you wanted to rip off my head. Now, you're trying to warn me about someone who thinks I'm going to save his entire realm?" She narrowed her eyes in anger. "I thought you were better than ridiculous games. If you want to hate me, then hate me, but at least be bold enough to say you do."

His expression hardened. "Just as you were bold enough to share your true feelings about Thane to the world, yes? Because surely *you,* Reyna Darragh, would never stoop to pretending you wanted to marry him, when really you wanted to shove your dagger into his back."

"I hate you," she whispered, tears in her eyes.

He smiled. "Feeling is mutual, princess."

She slammed a hand into his chest and pushed him back against the tunnel wall. Her skin felt as if it pulsed, twitching off her bones. Surprise flashed through his eyes. She smiled at his shock just as a strange desperation poured through her. Her body ached to do something, anything at all. The fury, pain, and fear was almost too much to bear, and—

Lorcan wrapped his hand around her wrist, pushed her away from him, and then spun her to the side. Her back hit the rock hard, and her breath whooshed from her lungs. He edged closer, pressing his chest tightly against hers, and leaned down to whisper into her ear. Every cell in her body buzzed.

"Now who's the one playing games?" he murmured. "Fighting me? That's not allowed. Trying to see how far you can push until your vows stop you?"

"I'm not allowed to kill you," she hissed back. "But the vows said nothing about making you bleed."

She pushed up onto her toes and sunk her teeth into his neck, biting his flesh as hard as she could. He tasted sweet, and he smelled of boiled leather, smoke, and steel. The scent of him made her ache, but she would not allow something as dumb as sentiment to stop her from making her point. She dug her teeth in deeper.

He let out a harsh grunt and yanked back. As he pulled

away from her, she managed to nip his skin. A few droplets of blood stained her lips. She licked the blood away and smiled.

"What the fuck is happening here?" Nollaig barked, striding toward them with an angry flap to her cloak's hood. "What are you two doing? Fighting? Or fucking? Nevermind. I don't want to know. Neither is allowed on this quest. Your Highness, go to the front with Teutas and keep your damn hands to yourself."

Grumbling, Lorcan stalked away, taking his spot at the head of the party next to Teutas. Nollaig scowled at Reyna, or at least that was what Reyna thought she was doing.

"Look, I know you don't want to be here with us, but you're going to get us all killed unless you at least try to get your head on straight."

"My head is on very straight, Nollaig," Reyna said evenly. "It's just that our roads do not line up. Your king forced me to bind myself to him. That doesn't mean I suddenly want him to win this war. In fact, I want him to lose more than I did before."

"Hmph," she said. "At least you're blunt about it."

With unshed tears burning her eyes, she glared at Lorcan's retreating back. "He betrayed me. I trusted him, and he twisted that trust into pain." Reyna did not understand why she was telling this to Nollaig, an enemy shadow fae who probably couldn't wait to burn Reyna alive once this war was over and done with. "I can't pretend that he didn't."

"Yeah, well, that's a prince for you." Nollaig huffed. "Unfortunately, Tarrah thinks he's needed here. As long as that's the case, you two are going to have to coexist in peace somehow. Otherwise, the quest fails."

"Maybe I want to sabotage this quest."

"You don't. Because if we fail, the wood king wins. And as much as you hate us, you hate him even more." Nollaig reached out and gave Reyna's shoulder an awkward pat. "We're on the same side, Princess Reyna."

"We are not," she growled in response.

"Okay." With that, Nollaig turned and trailed down the tunnel, her cloak billowing behind her like a wraith.

A red glow loomed large down the path ahead. The party exited the tunnels and strode into a cavern that looked like something straight out of the fire realm. The rock walls around them crumbled from a blasting heat that sank deep into Reyna's skin. The parched ground led to a thin, rocky path over the center of the floor. On either side of that path were pools of churning, molten lava.

Swallowing hard, Reyna stopped.

"What is this?" she asked as evenly as possible.

Nollaig turned toward her, and even the darkness of her cloak looked crimson in the deep reddish light. "We need to go through here to reach the other gate."

Reyna pointed at the lava. "That looks like death."

"Accurate," Nollaig said. "It's molten iron. Fall in, and you're not getting out."

Reyna's eyes bugged out of her head. "It's *iron?*"

"I don't like it either, but Unseelie will keep us safe," Tarrah said in a soft voice, her hollow eyes glued on the roiling lava.

"Come," Nollaig said. "The path is short."

Reyna didn't like it, but she also had no choice. She could feel her vows tugging her forward, away from safety and toward the molten iron that would be poison to her fae skin. Grimacing, she followed after the others, stepping carefully on the jagged, cracked ground. Mist swirled around them.

Suddenly, a heavy blast of wind slammed into Reyna's side. Her balance faltered. She stumbled forward, and her foot caught on crumbling stone. She tipped over the side of the path, a terrified shriek ripping from her throat. Throwing out her arms, she grabbed the edge as she fell, her fingernails digging into the rough stone. Her legs dangled beneath her, and the heat of the lava melted the bottoms of her boots.

Wingallock screamed, darting frantically through the cavern.

Terror burned through her as she clung on with every ounce of strength within her body. She did not dare glance down. She didn't need to. The churning sea of red was alive in her mind's eye. Molten iron. Even if she survived the heat, she would never live through the poison of the iron.

Not even a fae before the Fall could survive that.

Sucking in a deep breath, she closed her eyes. Deep down in her soul she knew, she was going to die.

A warm, strong hand curled around her wrist. Another soon followed, rougher and courser than the first. Gritting her teeth, she stared up to see Lorcan and Nollaig leaning over the ledge. They held onto her as tightly as they could. Determination clung to the harsh set of Lorcan's jaw, his eyes sparking with the red glow of the lava beneath Reyna's dangling feet.

Nollaig wound her hand under Reyna's shoulder. "We've got you. Let go, and we'll pull you over."

Reyna swallowed hard and nodded, releasing her desperate hold on the ledge. Instantly, the world dropped out from beneath her, and she bit back a scream. Nollaig grunted as she took Reyna's weight, toppling slightly forward. But Lorcan pulled her back, and then reached down and wrapped an arm around Reyna's waist.

He pulled hard. They all collapsed into a heap on the ledge. Relief was an avalanche on top of her. Reyna pressed her cheek against the comforting coolness of the stone and sucked in frantic breath after breath. She'd almost died. She *would* have died…if Lorcan had not saved her life.

A soft gasp echoed in the cave. Reyna glanced up to see

Tarrah standing over her, her cheeks white and her eyes as round as moons. "Are you all right, Shieldmaiden?"

A tiny chunk of ice that surrounded Reyna's heart threatened to break away from the wall she'd erected to keep herself safe. But she just stared up at the shadow fae, grumbling, "I'll never be fine as long as I'm a prisoner."

Reyna climbed to her feet, inwardly sighing as Wingallock's comforting form settled onto her shoulder. She always felt better with him there. He brushed his feathers against her face, cooing.

Nollaig pushed up from the ground, brushing the dirt from her midnight cloak. "You're welcome for saving your life."

Reyna glared at her, refusing to turn her eyes toward Lorcan. He had helped save her, too, even after she'd admitted to her plot against Thane. Maybe it was instinctual. Or maybe he was just following orders, same as the rest of them. "You only saved me because your king believes I'm going to save your court from getting slaughtered in your war with the Wood Court. In any other situation, you would have let me fall."

"Yes, because we're bloodthirsty monsters who enjoy watching fae get swallowed up by pools of molten iron," Nollaig said, her voice full of an eye roll.

"Well, I'm glad we're in agreement," Reyna said.

"The day we're in agreement is the day it snows in Findius," Lorcan snapped. He pushed his way past them. "Let's stop stalling and get on with it. Reyna, watch your feet. Next time, I might not be in the mood to help you. These lot have orders to keep you alive." He paused, and Reyna's heart paused right along with him. She knew what he'd say next. She *wanted* him to say it, if only because it would prove that he was exactly everything she feared he was. *Next time, I'll let you die.* But instead, he said, "My father knows I don't need orders to keep you alive. But for the love of the Dadga, Reyna, I wish I did. Fuck, I wish I did."

For once, Tarrah didn't even correct his reference to the 'wrong god' as he strode gruffly down the rest of the path, reaching the lava cave exit and disappearing through the gap.

"You two have a very complicated relationship," Nollaig remarked, clearly over the lack of a 'thank you' far sooner than Lorcan.

"I wouldn't call mutual hatred a relationship," Reyna said, staring into the shadows where Lorcan disappeared. She was pretty certain he had done his shadowy vanishing act, which did not bode well for the success of the mission. Not that she wanted him to be part of the mission. Tarrah had said he was important. That was the only reason she wanted him to stay.

Tarrah gave her a knowing smile. The color in her cheeks had returned. "Mutual hatred?"

"What else would you call it?"

Nollaig and Tarrah exchanged a look.

"L," Tarrah said.

"O."

"V."

"Enough." Reyna rolled her eyes and brushed off her trousers, flinging the dirt into the roiling molten lava below. "I just almost died because of falling into that iron sea, remember? We should get out of this cave before another one of us ends up encased in poison."

Tarrah beamed. "You just said 'another one of us' as if you'd rather see us live than die. We're making progress."

"That's right," Nollaig replied.

Reyna scowled. "You two are reading far too much into my words."

Tarrah cocked her head. "Isn't that what we need to start doing? Soon enough, we'll be surrounded by fae just like you, who mince their words and always hide meaning in every statement they make."

Reyna had warned them of that. She hated that she was unintentionally training them to survive in the world they hoped to claim. So instead, she gave them a vicious smile. "Reading too much into words can be just as dangerous as not reading enough. I may be helping you now—because you've forced me to—but that does not change anything at all. I still want every one of you dead."

# 14

## REYNA

The sun was a glorious thing, all bright and yellow and free of the reddish haze that marred its brilliance in the shadow lands. When they pushed through the gate hidden in the folds of a small hill, Reyna breathed a sigh of relief. The landscape was a tapestry of green with towering, gnarled trees that twisted together, their limbs heavy with lush, oversized leaves. Rolling hills stretched toward the forest, carpeted in a luxuriant grass that looked soft enough for sleep. Unintentionally, Reyna felt herself smile.

"Careful, princess," Nollaig warned, placing a finger against the side of her head, tapping the thick fabric that obscured her face. "This place might look like an oasis to you, but it is nothing of the kind. Here, there is not even a speck of ice."

"There's also no mist, thankfully," she countered dryly. "Or iron lava."

"Ah, but there are plenty of shadows," Nollaig said with a smile in her voice.

It seemed to Reyna that there were shadows all

throughout Tir Na Nog. Every court had them. They were inescapable. As long as there was light, shadows would not be far behind. She wished she could say the same for ice, but this far south, there was none to be seen.

The group clustered together just outside the gate, lurking behind a dense row of hedges. It hid them from the view of any wood fae who might be scouting along the forest's edge. Reyna frowned and surveyed their surroundings. If there were any enemies hiding in wait, the hills would be the shadow fae's undoing. They would need to cross them to reach the forest, and they would be out in plain sight.

"Where exactly are we?" Reyna hated to make them think she was interested in this godforsaken quest, but she could not hold back her curiosity. They'd travelled for hours underground, beneath the towering fortress walls that stood between the Shadow Court and the Wood Court. Through the twisting and tunnelling maze, she had not been able to keep track of their direction.

"Two miles north of the border's wall, almost as far east as one can go before falling into the Sea of Fomor. Except for the village of Oxgrove, of course, which is not far down the coast from here. But we won't be paying them a visit, I'm afraid. Rumor has it they aren't too fond of their wood king. So, if we want to find the army, it won't be there." Nollaig turned to point a gloved finger at the closely-packed trees just ahead. "That there is the Forest of Thorns. We're several days' journey from Craobhan if we head northwest. Two weeks to Murias if we go east."

Reyna sighed. "And we're going east, I imagine? To the capital?"

Nollaig glanced over her shoulder at the rest of their party. Lorcan had not yet returned from the shadows, and no one had even mentioned his disappearance since it happened. Which was more than fine with Reyna. She did not want to dwell on it more than she had to. Of course, that hadn't stopped her from replaying their argument over and over again in her mind. The look on his face, pinched and angry. And then the softness that had soon followed when she'd almost fallen to her death.

She didn't want to think too much about that.

"Tarrah?" Nollaig asked. "Anything new?"

"Not this again," Reyna muttered to herself.

Tarrah, with her eyes shut tight against the world, nodded. "I thought we would need to go east, but it seems Unseelie has other plans for us. West it is."

Reyna let out an audible sigh.

Tarrah's eyes flew open, curiosity flickering in the darkness of her irises. "You do not want to go east. Why?"

"Because Murias is two weeks away, and then two more weeks return. My poor sister is trapped alone inside your castle. I can't bear to imagine her inside a grungy dungeon cell with no hope, scared."

"You wouldn't be able to see her even if you were there, Princess," Nollaig replied, albeit gently.

"I don't care," Reyna snapped. "At least I would be there instead of half a realm away."

Tarrah frowned. "Princess Reyna..."

"I know what you're going to say," she said, cutting Tarrah off before she could prattle on about vows and commands. "I took a vow. I have to follow the king's orders, and there's nothing I can do to change it. Trust me. I'm well aware." She coughed out a bitter laugh. "But that does not change my bone deep desire to keep Eislyn safe. If you had a sister, you'd understand."

But it wasn't just that. Reyna had never felt the same intense protectiveness toward Glencora. True, she loved her, but it was not the same. Eislyn *needed* her in a way that no one else ever had, and she could not bear the thought of letting her down, letting her suffer. And yet suffer she had. Terribly.

"That was not what I was going to say at all," Tarrah said in a quiet whisper.

Nollaig snapped her head in the prophetic fae's direction, tsking loudly. "Tarrah, I think that is enough."

"It isn't right, Noll."

"That may be so, but now is not the time."

Reyna glanced from one shadow fae to the next. "What is this? What aren't you saying? Is there something wrong with my sister that you've kept from me?" Her voice began to rise, higher-pitched with every word. Panic clutched her heart. "If you are, then I—"

"You'll kill us. We know," Nollaig said dryly.

"That didn't answer my question." Reyna balled her hands into fists. "Is there something wrong with Eislyn? Has she been hurt?"

Tarrah reached out and rested her hand on Reyna's arm. When she spoke, her voice was as soft as a whisper on the wind. "There is nothing wrong with your sister. That I can swear to you."

"You're a shadow fae," Reyna whispered back, unshed tears burning her eyes. "You can lie."

"I can. But I don't." Tarrah smiled. "When we return to Findius, I'll show you where she is."

"Tarrah," Nollaig muttered.

"What harm can come of it?"

"Our High King could burn you alive."

"He wouldn't," Tarrah said, lifting her chin. "I'm his Champion."

"Because you've proven yourself to be loyal and useful," Nollaig countered. "The moment he no longer believes you're either of those, he will throw you into the pits to an audience of thousands. Fire will devour your skin and soul, and your life will end in screams. I have seen him do it to others."

"And you would both serve a king like this?" Reyna asked, shaking her head from a strange mixture of horror and awe. Bolg Rothach had once been nothing more than a minor lord, who had only risen to the throne because of the vacuum of power after the exile. What Reyna could not understand was why someone else had not murdered him to take his place. He was terrible and cruel and weak.

"Your father is a High King," Nollaig said. "What would he do to traitors?"

"I..." Reyna fell silent. Her father had been responsible for his share executions. As the High King, he'd had little choice. Traitors must be dealt with swiftly and surely to prove a point more than anything. Anyone who made a move against the crown was deemed an enemy of all. They were marked by death. If rebels ever thought they might live after staging a revolt, others would quickly follow in their footsteps.

But that was different. Her father was *nothing* like the shadow king.

"There is a very long path from mild disobedience to full-on treason. It sounds as though *your* king cannot see the difference. My father is a friend of mercy, as well as justice."

"Your father sold out his daughters to an enemy," Lorcan muttered, suddenly appearing out of the shadows of the cave. "As I recall, he was more than willing to wed Eislyn to the court you despised so much that you planned to murder them all."

Reyna scowled even as her heart throbbed in her chest. She had not been prepared for his sudden return to the group. He'd reappeared just when she'd least expected it. Her guard was down; her heart was lacking steel. His familiar face sent a jolt of pain through her soul.

"I did not plan on murdering them *all*," she snapped. "You

are getting your courts mixed up, Prince Lorcan. It's the shadow fae I plan to destroy. Every last one. Including you."

"Threats begin to lose their shine when you repeat them every hour of every day," he said with a wry smile. "Careful. We might stop taking you seriously. If we ever took you seriously."

A low growl rumbled from her throat.

"Lorcan." Nollaig sighed. "*Must* you constantly agitate her?"

Lorcan didn't answer. He simply vanished into the shadows again, leaving a gulf of cold air where he'd stood. Reyna sucked in a sharp breath, her body itching to feel his presence again. Her soul longed to see his face again, just so that she might spit in it.

She hated everything about it. She did not want to see him, and yet she hated that he wasn't there. The whole situation left her endlessly annoyed.

"Honestly, he is the most frustrating male I have ever met in my life!" She glared at the rolling hills, desperate to just get on with the damn quest. The sooner they tracked down the wood fae's army, the sooner they could return to Findius. And the sooner she could go back to avoiding Lorcan every minute of every day.

"How exactly are we to cross these hills and enter the forest without being seen?" she snapped at Nollaig, though she knew she shouldn't take out her anger on the rest of them. They weren't the ones who deserved her wrath. Lorcan was.

She blinked. Where had *that* thought come from? They were still her enemies, same as Lorcan. Just because he was the one currently riling her up didn't mean she could forget they were just as terrible as he was.

"We'll wait for nightfall," Tarrah said, turning the group's attention back onto the task at hand. "That is when we cross.

The wood fae will not see us. Then, we camp and make for Craobhan in the morning."

Reyna frowned. "What makes you so certain we won't get shot with arrows as soon as we step out into the open?"

"Because Unseelie told me," Tarrah said, blinking those wide, vacant eyes of hers.

"Wonderful. We're relying on an invisible death god to keep us from dying."

---

To Reyna's relief—and slight irritation—they made it into the Forest of Thorns without incident. She didn't want to trust Unseelie nor believe Tarrah's visions were real to anyone but the girl herself. But not a single arrow flew their way when they made their hasty trek across the hills. It seemed the wood fae were nowhere near this section of the border.

They settled in to a small clearing a few hours into the forest. Teutas got a fire going and found a rabbit for them to share for a meal. Lorcan even reappeared, though he stayed far from Reyna, taking a seat on the opposite side of their strange mix of a circle.

Reyna glared across the fire at him, watching the shadows of the flames dance along his sun-kissed skin. He sat with his sword draped across his knees, his body tense, his eyes darting through the trees. He looked so much like the male who had come to her aide in the Air Court. Why had he even bothered to help her then? If he'd only planned to capture her and bring her to his father, what had been the point of it all? She had asked herself those very questions so many times throughout her captivity. Not once had she conjured up a logical answer.

His eyes landed on her face. Instinctively, she stiffened and blood rushed into her cheeks. *It's anger and nothing more,* she thought. She hated him so fiercely that she could have kicked the burning logs of their camp right into his chiseled face.

"Reyna, I want to understand something," Tarrah said quietly from her side, jolting Reyna's attention away from her arch-nemesis and her desire to see him pay for what he had done to her. Tarrah was staring into the flickering flames, her eyes wide and distant. "You wanted to kill Thane Selkirk. Why?"

Reyna frowned and glanced back at Lorcan, absentmindedly petting Wingallock's soft feathers. He'd returned to searching the trees. He must not have heard Tarrah's question. "I'm not sure how much you know about what has been happening in Tir Na Nog these past few decades. The war still rages on, even now. Have you ever heard of the Battle for the Shard?"

Tarrah tore her gaze away from the fire and shook her head. "The Shard is the piece of land that stretches between your two kingdoms, yes? Between yours and the Air Court's?"

"That's right. It's all ice fae land. It belongs to our kingdom, a single strip of ice as wide as a bridge. It protects us from an invasion from the south. The Air Court tried to take it so that they could set up their army just north of it. If they controlled the Shard, it would have been a death sentence for us all." Reyna thought back, remembering. It was all so vivid in her mind, even now. "The Air Court has the superior army. Better steel. More warriors, most far better trained than ours. We are a peaceful kingdom. The ice fae are not good at being fighters."

"You are," Tarrah pointed out. "I've seen you in my visions. You are a force of nature, Reyna Darragh."

Reyna gave her a wry smile. "I thought you couldn't see my face in your visions."

Tarrah stared up at her with those unnerving hollow eyes.

"My god has given me several visions of you, Shieldmaiden. Ones that show your face. In many of them, you fight."

"So, it was a lie then," Reyna said with a sigh, turning back to the fire. She'd suspected as much. "You knew your god wasn't showing you my younger sister."

As she gazed across the fire once more, she noted that Lorcan no longer sat in his place between Nollaig and Teutas. Frowning, Reyna glanced around. Where had he gone? Back into the shadows again? Perhaps he had overheard their conversation after all.

"No, it wasn't a lie," Tarrah said. "The important vision—the one where I see you fighting on the battlefield for our king—I cannot see a face. Silver hair frames a strange darkness, like a smudge left behind by a pile of ash."

A chill swept down her spine. The image was a terrifying one, though she would not admit it to Tarrah.

"But you know it's me," Reyna argued. "Even if you cannot see my face."

"Do I?" Tarrah arched her brow. "It is strange that Unseelie will not show you to me. If it is you, then why is there so much darkness surrounding you? It makes me wonder if there is something wrong."

She bristled. "Maybe it's something about you that's wrong, Tarrah. Not me. I'm not the one who claims to receive visions from a dark god."

Tarrah smiled. "You misunderstand him, as many do. He is not a dark god. He is good, pure, and right."

Reyna rounded on her. "How do you explain all of his twisted servants? Those whose minds have been warped, damaged, gone wrong? That is what he turns fae into."

"False prophets and nothing more," Tarrah said softly. "There are ancient books speaking of these things, prophecies proclaiming that his name would be sullied by his enemies. The magic that twists and burns minds—it comes from somewhere else. It blames Unseelie for the darkness so that none will know the truth."

"How very convenient. Let me guess. These prophecies came from visions."

"I'm not lying to you, Reyna. I am able to, but I don't. It's not something I believe is right."

"I don't think you're lying to me, Tarrah," Reyna said, feeling a sadness creep into her heart. "I think Unseelie has found a loyal servant, and I think you're being used."

A twig snapped in the looming forest that surrounded them. Panic clutched Reyna's heart as she whirled toward the sound. Footsteps crunched fallen leaves in a path that was clearly heading straight toward their camp. Heart in her throat, Reyna stood. Had the wood fae found them after all?

But it was Lorcan who appeared between the trees. His face was pinched, eyebrows knitting tightly together. His sword hung from his white-knuckled hand, the tip skimming the ground.

"Lorcan, what is it?" Reyna asked sharply.

He met her eyes. Understanding passed between them at once. Lorcan had stumbled upon something terrible. "A group of wood fae were here not that long ago. A few days, perhaps. No longer than a week judging from the…state of them."

Reyna's heart leapt into her throat. "What do you mean, the state of them?"

"The wood king has been here."

Those six words were enough to make Reyna's gut quake. She had heard the rumors. They all had. And yet, she had desperately hoped they weren't true.

"How do you know it was him?" she asked quietly.

"He left behind a painting of his sigil on the ground. If it wasn't him, it was someone working for him."

"Come," Nollaig said, striding toward Lorcan. "I need to see this with my own eyes."

Reyna frowned but followed. She knew that what they would find would be terrible indeed, but she found she could not turn her back on the brutality. Avoiding it would be like pretending it didn't exist.

When they reached the wood fae's campsite, bile rose in her throat, choking her. Through blurry eyes, she took in the horror. There had been six of them, as far as she could tell. All of them were in pieces. Arms and legs were missing, along with some of the torsos. The heads had been lined up in a row beside the Wood Court's sigil that had been painted onto the dirt with the dead fae's blood. The blood had baked into the ground, staining it crimson. The scent of rot swirled through the air.

Reyna pressed a hand to her mouth just as Tarrah gagged. The shadow fae whirled away from the sight. Wingallock hooted mournfully.

"They are wearing the armor of the court," Nollaig said in a low, gravelly voice. "These were his own people, his loyal warriors."

It made so little sense. Why had the wood king murdered his own warriors? And why had he left them scattered in pieces? What had happened to the rest of them?

Reyna tore her gaze away from the carnage to find Lorcan watching her with a hooded look in his dark eyes. Pain roiled through her stomach, though she did not know what had caused it this time. Perhaps Lorcan. Perhaps the wood king's brutality. Perhaps everything, all the horror and pain in their world.

She might not be able to stop all of it, but she could do something about *part* of it. For once, Reyna hoped that Unseelie was real and that he was right. The wood king needed to die.

# 15

## MARIEL

"The Grand Alderman would like to see me privately," Mariel said to a guard clad in gold-dyed leather. He stood barring entry to the Great Hall, along with four others. A rookie mistake, Mariel thought with amusement. The strongest number of guards was always six.

"We have not been informed of such a thing," the guard muttered with an eye roll before casting her a curious sideways glance as he attempted to peer beneath her hood. "Who are you? You look familiar."

Indeed, that was the point, though she did not wish to reveal her full appearance to the guards, not before she had her audience with the Grand Alderman. Some eager guards might get the wrong idea.

"A tavern owner from the slums," she said as quietly and demurely as possible. "I have some important information for the Grand Alderman. It is about the Princess Eislyn. I know where she's gone."

Now, that got the guards moving. The one she'd been speaking to disappeared through the door within an instant. As the door opened and shut behind him, Mariel caught a glimpse of the throne. That old, ugly thing rose high from the very stone it had been planted into, gnarled limps and thorns twisting together like snakes. Still, she ached to sit on it, if only to claim the power for herself.

Aengus did not sit on the throne. He must have learned he could not, not so long as the High King lived. Thane would have to abdicate or die for another to claim the power from the seat. He was stuck until he figured out a way to take care of Thane.

A sigh slipped through her parted lips as the door shut against the view from within. The guards continued to stare at her, no doubt wondering who she was and what she had seen. Of course, Mariel had not seen a damn thing, but she *did* know where Princess Eislyn had gone. Even a fool would have known the answer to that mystery.

The door reopened, and the guard motioned her inside. "The Grand Alderman will see you."

Aengus sat on an elaborate golden chair beside the throne, the plush seat of red velvet clashing against the ancient wood beside him. Gaudy and harsh versus purity. How could he not see the contrast? How could he imagine he belonged here?

He was an odd male, unlike any Mariel had ever met before. She'd thought so the first time she had laid eyes on him, and she thought it even now. His hair was a bright ginger that would suggest a heritage in the Fire Court, but the accent did not match. There was a strange slurring of certain words where the fire fae spoke in crisp, sharp tones. Every vowel short and to the point. Mariel had never heard an accent quite like Aengus's even in her long years spent in Tairngire, a city teeming with a multitude of fae.

He wore pristine armor and a cloak spun from the most expensive silk found throughout all of Tir Na Nog. The golden material fell to the floor, rustling around his booted feet. It was a statement, one that was impossible to miss.

Subtlety was not one of Aengus's strongpoints. Mariel made note of that.

"My guard tells me you witnessed the princess's escape." He leaned forward, eyes flashing with greed. "Tell me where she's gone."

Mariel frowned and glanced at the two guards on either side of her and then at the lords clustered around the Grand Alderman. "I am certain that what I wish to say, you would prefer to hear it privately. Without audience."

Aengus gave her a thin-lipped smile. "I did not find myself in this desired position by being thick in the head. I am certain there are many who wish me dead. You could very well be one of them."

"That's very clever of you. However, killing you would result in the opposite of my aim."

He arched a brow. "You mean to say that you have no intention of killing me?"

"That's right."

"Very well." He nodded at the guards, and then at the lords by his side, accepting her spoken truths. "Leave us be."

Several of the guards frowned but they did as they were bid by their "king" in command. They quickly exited the Great Hall, leaving Aengus alone with the former would-be queen. If only she could kill him now, hidden behind closed doors. There was nothing anyone could do to stop her. Aengus wouldn't be able to fight her off if she jumped at him with blades. He wore that rapier, but she had a hunch it was purely ceremonial. Another statement, a symbol of the power he pretended to yield. In the end, he would fall, just like pretenders always did.

But no, she could not kill him. Her god did not look kindly upon kingkillers, even ones who weren't blessed by seats of power.

"Explain yourself then," he said, lounging back in his gaudy chair, crossing one leg over the other. "What couldn't be said in front of the others?"

Mariel smiled and pushed back her hood, revealing her new head of cascading silver hair. Aengus, to Mariel's great satisfaction, sat up straight, his spine as taut as a ship's mast. He leaned forward, squinting. "Am I seeing this right? You're a bloody ice fae."

He didn't recognize her then, even though they'd already met. Interesting.

"Wrong. I am an air fae. I've only made myself look like an ice fae. A princess, in particular."

"You can glamour yourself? Does that mean you are a shadow fae?" Aengus asked curiously, and he did not seem the least bit alarmed. Not when confronted with the most dangerous type of fae in the world.

"I'm far more useful than a shadow fae. I simply dyed my hair."

"To what end?" he asked, squinting some more.

"I asked to see you because I know where Princess Eislyn has gone. Straight back to the Ice Court," she said.

"She hasn't," Aengus said with a frown. "She wasn't seen leaving the Bay of Wind, and I've had my ships watching the coast further north. There's been no sight of her. She's gone somewhere else."

"She's gone *far* north. It's what I would have done," she said with a shrug. "It makes the journey much longer, but it stops you from finding her."

Aengus's frown deepened. "So, she's gone to the Ice Court. That's what you came all the way here to tell me? That's why you've dyed your hair silver? Are you mad?"

Oh, Mariel was mad, just not in the way Aengus imagined.

"Eislyn will likely sail to Margaidh. From there, she will be able to send word to her father about what has happened here. The High King likely does not know the fate of his daughters yet. Once he does, he will march on these lands. And you have no army here to stop him."

Aengus drummed his fingers on the arm of the chair. "That has occurred to me, yes. In part, that is why we've been so intent on finding her. She cannot be allowed to get word to her father."

"She is far out of your reach by now," Mariel said. "Regardless of what we do, she *will* get word to her father, but you have some time yet. Time to prepare, time to call the lords of the Air Court to your side. And their armies."

"I've already tried," he said with a wave of his hand. "Half of them were already here, and half of those got slaughtered at the coronation feast. The other half, they see me as their enemy. They've refused to come."

"And that is where I come in."

Aengus arched his bushy red brows.

"Hardly any of those lords will have met Princess Eislyn. The silver hair will be enough for them. The ones who are already here at the castle, the ones you've ensnared in your web…when they realize the plot, they won't dare say a word of it."

He barked out a laugh. "This is ludicrous. You want to pretend to be Princess Eislyn? What good will that do any of us? She's an ice fae, not a beloved folk of the air."

"She might be an ice fae, but she is far better than whatever you are," she said bluntly. "I say with the utmost respect, of course, but surely you see that for yourself. None of the lords know you or care about you. You're a foreign stranger with no titles, no family, and you've stolen the throne." She took a deep breath and played her hand. "Eislyn is a princess and the daughter of a well-respected fae who has just become their ally. Thane, the High King, who they *do* love, was going to marry Eislyn before he vanished, and now she will be 'speaking for him' in support of you. She can gain their trust in a way that nothing else can, at least right now."

Aengus continued to drum his fingers on his makeshift throne's arm. "It is a very convoluted plot."

"And it's the only plot you have." She smiled. "Sloane Selkirk sent most of your army into the wood fae lands. You don't have much protection against an invading army. You need my help."

He drummed his fingers ever onward, and then stopped, leaning forward. "I just have one important question."

"Yes?" Mariel asked, trying her level best not to sound as eager as she felt.

"You are not Princess Eislyn. You cannot say you are because that would be a lie. How will your scheme ever work?"

Mariel smiled. "We mince our words. We're fae. It's an easy enough thing to do, especially when we've both had years of practice. You, of all people, should know that."

Aengus pursed his lips. "Perhaps. I also know that fae do not offer favors. You'll want something in return. What do you hope to gain from this?"

Should Mariel tell him the full truth of it? She had toyed with the idea the entire walk from Drunkard's Pit. If he knew who she was, he would take her much more seriously. He would understand at once why she had come here to hatch this strange plot. But he would also see her as a threat.

Because Mariel was *very* much a threat.

"I want power," she said instead of revealing her true name. "A seat on your council. A seat by your side."

"I should have known." Aengus nodded slowly. "All right then. You'll have your seat. Let's summon the lords."

# 16

## EISLYN

The crew was wild. Eislyn had never seen anything quite like it before. They were up on the tables, stomping their feet, shouting out the words to a song she'd never heard, drinks sloshing from their mugs as they danced. Half of them were fully naked. Now, *this*, this was a revel.

Neck flushed, Eislyn backed toward the door. They looked like they were having fun, of course. The kind of fun that Eislyn had never experienced for herself. She just did not feel prepared to face it now. Not when her thoughts were so thick with shadows. The visions had gotten worse as the days went on. Memories of death and screams were always so close by.

It was the first time that Eislyn had joined the crew since they'd set off from the shores of the Air Court. Most of the time, a servant brought her meals to her cabin or to a small table on the main deck when the waters were calm enough to allow it. Even though the crew of the Stingray had wholeheartedly agreed to spirit her away from Tairngire, she knew they still viewed her as an outsider. A stranger in the mists.

Vreis had joined them a few times, he'd mentioned. So, she

had decided to seek them out this night. By the time she'd arrived, plates had been already cleared, and the naked dancing was well underway.

One of the females was dancing right near Vreis.

She twisted on her heels and pushed out of the cabin, racing up the stairs to the cool safety of the main deck. Leaning against the thin wooden railing, she pulled pocketfuls of air deep into her lungs, relishing how the spray of the water on her face made her feel alive. After several moments passed, she heard footsteps approach from behind.

Vreis's familiar presence curled around her like a cloak. "Are you all right, Princess Eislyn? Did the revel frighten you?"

"I'm fine," she said as the salty air rustled her silver strands. "I envy them more than anything. They don't have a care in the world. They seem so free of darkness."

Why had she said that aloud? Vreis did not need to know about the twisted visions in her mind, the darkness and fear that plagued her always.

"No one is free of darkness," he said, taking a place by her side and leaning against the railing. "Some are just better at ignoring it, or finding a way to smile through it."

"Hmm," she said.

They fell into companionable silence. Even though Eislyn had yearned for solitude, she found she didn't mind Vreis's company. There was nothing dark about his presence, nothing overwhelming. Where most fae left her feeling unsteady on her feet—even Thane—Vreis felt more like a steadying rock. A rock she knew very little about. She didn't know where he'd come from, what he'd dreamed of as a boy. She didn't even know what he believed in or if he even believed in anything at all.

Suddenly, she was desperate to know what he thought of it all.

"Vreis, do you ever wonder..." she trailed off, not even sure what she wanted to ask. "What are the gods doing? Why have they taken our magic? Is there a way to get it back?"

"At times, I've wondered." He stared out at the sea, black beneath the dark clouds above. "I assume we'll never learn the answers to those questions."

"That's not very satisfying."

"Do you ever wonder if the gods even exist?" he asked, turning to face her.

Surprised, she laughed. "Now *that's* something coming from an air fae. You lot take the Dagda's laws very seriously. And it's very much against the rules to question his existence."

"Oh, I believe the Dagda existed—or exists. What I am uncertain of...was he a god? The tales say he was, but why?" He shook his head. "No, if there is a god, I doubt he's walked these lands."

"Of course he's walked these lands. Our magic had to come from somewhere. He couldn't very well imbue the lands without touching it, without running his fingers through the grass and brushing his feet against the dirt."

Vreis gave her a long, thoughtful stare before responding, which made her flush. "If that is how we got our magic, then how did he take it away? Did he return to Tir Na Nog? If so, why did no one see him?"

"I..." Eislyn frowned. "His hidden servants must have taken it, just as they carry away the souls of the dead. He didn't need to return to Tir Na Nog himself." She thought for a moment, and then added, "*Or* he was hidden himself."

"Or something else took away the magic," Vreis said quietly as he absentmindedly fingered the amber jewel that hung around his neck.

A shock of alarm zapped Eislyn's heart. Vreis's suggestion went against everything she had ever believed about the Fall. Once, the Dagda had roamed Tir Na Nog, far before the fae ever did. He knew that one day a people would rise up in need of help. His magic was his gift to the fae. It was their armor, their strength in the world. And then, centuries later, he decided to take it away.

There was no other explanation. The gift of a god could not just *vanish*. Not without a reason.

"You don't truly believe that," Eislyn whispered. "You're only tossing about theories to pass the time while we're stuck waiting for the dawn."

Vreis gave her a strange smile. "I don't believe any particular thing, Eislyn. That was my point. We don't know if he took it or if someone else did. It's only a possibility, one that is no less plausible than the rest."

Eislyn leaned back against the railing. Vreis was wrong. He had to be. If the Dagda had not taken away their gift, then something else had. Or some*one* else had. And that was a terrifying thought.

It also meant…

"But," she said breathlessly, "if there is some other reason we lost our magic, then could that mean…" It couldn't. She dare not speak it aloud. She shouldn't even be entertaining these thoughts in the first place. It would lead to nothing good. Despite Vreis's uncertainty, Eislyn believed in the Dagda. She always had, even in her darkest times.

"That we might be able to get it back?" Vreis finished for her. And then he shrugged. "Perhaps we could…if the kingdoms were not intent on their theory about what caused the Fall. They are all content believing in the Dagda. Only Fire and Shadow might have questioned it. But Fire is gone, and Shadow is exiled. We'll find no help from either of them."

She could not help but laugh. "We? You speak as though the two of us are about to embark on a grand adventure to find the thief of our magic."

"Well, we're certainly not far off, now are we? Or have your priorities changed since boarding this ship?"

The smile fell from her lips. "You speak of the Ruin."

"Of course. It is your life's purpose is it not?"

Eislyn had never quite thought of it like that, but Vreis was not wrong. If there was only one thing she could ever accomplish, one thing in all her years spent walking these lands, it would be that. To end the Ruin.

She nodded.

"Then, you see." He smiled a smile that shot tingles into her toes. "Your aim is not far off at all."

Her forehead crinkled as she frowned. "You don't mean to say that the Ruin and the Fall are connected, do you?"

"I would be more surprised if they weren't," he replied. "A dark magic begins sweeping across our lands not long after we lose all of our own? It would be too much of a coincidence otherwise."

"But…the Dagda would never send the Ruin to destroy us."

"No, I don't believe he would," Vreis said evenly. "God or not."

Heart thumping, Eislyn turned her attention to the icy sea. Had she been approaching this the wrong way all this time? The Ruin had appeared in the Ice Court only twenty-odd years before. The Fall had happened nearly a century ago. But that was not entirely correct, of course. Eislyn had found what appeared to be mention of the Ruin in some books, and Thane's research had turned up several mentions of a dark magic in ancient tomes. So, the Ruin had been around far before the Fall.

A strange thought sprang forth in her mind. "You don't think…the *Ruin* is what took our magic…?"

It made little sense, but now that the idea had occurred to her, she did not think she would ever be able to get it out of her head. The Ruin was a terrible, horrible thing. It destroyed villages. It murdered innocents, leaving behind nothing but smoke and ash. And Eislyn had always wondered if there was even more to it than that. It felt wrong. Like a malevolent force.

"The Ruin took our magic, twisted it into something wrong, and then decided to use it against us?" Vreis asked with a nod. "That could very well be what happened."

"I don't like it," she said so softly that her voice drifted away on the cool sea wind. Eislyn shivered.

"You're cold." Vreis shrugged off his jacket and quickly draped it around her shoulders. She smiled up at him, touched by his kindness. So much so that she couldn't bear to tell him that she wasn't cold at all. At times, she had felt a chill in the air fae realm, only when the brittle wind attacked from the east. But that sensation was gone now. The icy wind soothed her now that they were in the waters so far north. She had not realized how much she'd missed it.

"Thank you, Vreis," she said, blushing as she glanced up into his kind eyes. "In fact, thank you for everything. I don't believe I've told you that enough."

"You don't need to thank me," he said gruffly. "I'm merely doing my duty for Thane. I swore an oath, after all."

Her heart sunk a little, though she did not know why. It must have been the reminder of Thane. She hoped he was safe, wherever he was. She hoped he was alive.

"You and Lorcan," she said, clearing her throat, "you always seemed closer to Thane than the other warriors. Did you meet him when you were quite young?"

"I was a low fae, a street urchin in Tairngire. One day Thane found me and took a liking to me for some odd reason. Thane seems fond of broken things, I suppose. Lorcan joined us not long after. He found him withering away in a tiny village when Lorcan saved his life. From then on, those two were as thick as thieves. If I were to trust anyone with finding Thane, it would be Lorcan."

"And Reyna," Eislyn added. "She never gives up when she dedicates herself to something."

"She gave up on her dedication to the Shieldmaidens," Vreis said, though not unkindly.

"Did she?" A slight smile ghosted her lips. "I'm not so certain. She'll always be a warrior, even if she made those vows, and whether she sits on a throne or not."

She thought Vreis might argue against that. Most would. Her father, most particularly. A true sworn Shieldmaiden could not become a High Queen, nor the other way around. It was a rule that had never been broken.

But he surprised her, and not for the first time. "Perhaps that is how it should be. A queen who cannot fight for her people is not much of a queen at all."

"Well, I won't make much of a queen, then will I?" she said, trying her best to laugh, but finding it far harder than she liked. "I cannot fight."

Vreis frowned, tucking a finger beneath her chin. A thrill went down her spine. "Princess, you fight harder for your people than you think."

She swallowed hard. There was something so calming about his touch, even though her pulse had begun to race. Something in his words, no doubt. The suggestion that she was far stronger than she was. She wished he was right, but of course he wasn't.

Taking a step back, she ignored the heat in her cheeks. "I could take lessons, I suppose. The least I could do is learn how to protect my own self."

"That is not what I meant, Eislyn, and you know it." He smiled. "But that is not a terrible idea at all. I could teach you if you'd like. We have plenty of time on the ship to practice. By the time we reach the shores of your great kingdom, you could be skilled enough to take on your Shieldmaiden of a sister herself."

She couldn't help but choke out a laugh. "I believe you were a jester before you became Thane's guard."

"I mean it, Eislyn," he said insistently. "Reyna does not have to be the only Darragh sister who can fight well."

"I would settle for being able to fight decently." She grinned up at him. "And I daresay you won't find a student worse than me. I don't even know how to hold a dagger properly."

"You could never be the worst at anything, Eislyn," he said.

Her heart twitched.

Vreis cleared his throat. "So, what do you say? Meet me here at first light tomorrow, and I'll make a fighter out of you yet."

"It's a deal," she whispered into the wind. Her cheeks felt flush, and her hair was wild around her shoulders. In that moment, she imagined she did not look much different than Reyna at all. Perhaps she could even learn to be a little more like her.

Of course, Eislyn thought sadly, Reyna would never have fled Tairngire or the Grand Alderman. She wouldn't have let the enemy get the better of her. Instead, the enemy would be dead.

## 17

### REYNA

Sleep was a wily creature. It crept closer and closer in the darkest part of the night, but then scurried away just as it was in reach. Reyna stretched out on the leaf-strewn ground, staring up at the towering canopy of the trees where Wingallock sat watching over the camp with glowing, bulbous eyes. The limbs swayed in a gentle wind, rustling and whispering amongst themselves. The sound reminded Reyna of the hoarfrost worms back home, the tiny translucent silk-spinners whose voices only she could hear.

Nollaig sat on watch, perched in a tree nearby, fire extinguished. The rest of the party slept soundly while the nightmare of her life kept Reyna's eyes from shutting.

Lorcan lay on the ground only a few meters away. At first, she had kept her back aimed firmly in his direction. But that had not helped. She could feel him nearby. His body seemed to thrum like the steady sounding of drums. He was there. It was inescapable. And she could do nothing but glower in the night.

After hours like that, Reyna had dropped onto her back, her neck aching from jutting sideways for so long. Now, she could see him clearly out of the corner of her eye. His body looked relaxed, one arm draped across his eyes, the other stretched out on top of his sword. A warrior, through and through. Always ready for a fight, even when asleep.

She would respect that, from anyone other than Lorcan. From him, it was probably all for show. Another illusion. A lie.

In fact, she bet she could toss a pebble in his direction, and he'd never know.

Heart tripping in excited trepidation, she dug around in the dirt until her fingers found stone. She tossed it in his direction. It fell only a millimetre away from his ear.

His eyes snapped open. Biting back a grin, Reyna's lids slammed shut as she desperately tried to steady her breathing to mimic sleep.

"I know that was you, Reyna," he said in a low growl. "No one else would throw a rock at my face in the middle of the damn night."

"It was only a pebble," she whispered back. "If it hit you, it would barely even sting."

She probably should have found a larger rock.

He sighed. "Go to sleep, Reyna."

"I can't. I've been wide awake all night."

He cracked open an eye again. "So, you thought you would throw rocks at me to pass the time?"

"I just wanted to see what your reflexes were like." She pushed up to her elbows and pointed at the sword. "You barely even flinched. You failed."

"I heard you shuffling around over there. I knew something was coming."

She cocked her head. "Can't sleep either?"

"No."

"Maybe it's your conscious keeping you awake, reminding you that you betrayed someone who trusted you with her life."

He let out a low growl, pushed up from the ground, and glared down at her. "You cannot talk to me about *trust*."

Whirling on his feet, he stomped away from camp. Reyna scowled and jumped to her feet. She followed after him, shooting daggers into his back with her eyes. He'd removed his armor, leaving most of his skin free of clothes. She tried not to notice that way his muscles tensed, the way his skin glistened beneath the dappled light of the moon.

She realized that she had never seen him like this in the northern kingdoms. There, he had always been cloaked in leather armor and furs. She understood why now. His body yearned for the south, for the crushing heat of it. Shadow fae, through and through.

"Where are you going?" she shouted after him.

He stopped and jerked toward her. "I'm going to find a place to sleep where I won't be pelted with rocks."

Huffing, she stalked through the trees, erasing the distance between them. She jabbed a finger into his bare chest, ignoring the warmth that spread into her hand. "You're just running away because you're too cowardly to face the consequences of your betrayal."

He let out a bitter chuckle, wrapped his hand around hers, and yanked her hard against his chest. Eyes sparking, he leaned down and growled into her face. "At least I recognize myself for who I am and what I've done. You can't bring yourself to say that what you did was wrong."

"I didn't actually do anything," she hissed back. "I planned to kill him. But I didn't. Meanwhile, you *more* than followed through with your little plan. Because here I am, forever bound to your arsehole of a father."

"You never followed through because you never got your chance. You never became the High Queen. The realm wasn't yours to steal," he sneered. "Thane chose Eislyn in the end.

And you know why, don't you? Because you're wild and impulsive and a bloodthirsty, stubborn-as-hell fool."

Reyna gritted her teeth and tried to yank her hand away, but his nails dug into her skin. His words cut deep, slicing through the carefully-constructed ice she'd frozen around her heart. Every single word of it was the truth. She was everything he said. For once, she knew he was not lying.

"Let go of me," she hissed, hating the tears that burned her eyes. She did not dare let them fall. Lorcan could not see the pain he'd caused. "Stop forcing me to look at your stupid face."

"You're the one who followed me, Reyna. You're so desperate for a fight? Well, here it is."

She glared up at him, the heat of anger flooding her cheeks. As they'd argued, they'd shifted together, and now they were only millimetres apart. Reyna swallowed hard at the feel of his bare chest beneath her hand, where he still trapped her fingers against his skin. She could feel his heart pounding, racing. It matched the frantic beating of her own heart.

"If this is a fight, then you're doing it wrong," she whispered up at him. "Draw your sword."

His eyes flashed. "You would have us exchange blows?"

"Too scared?" She grinned.

"Your vows mean you would die within an instant." He leaned down and brushed his lips against her ear. Anticipation shivered through her. "I take no pleasure in hollow victory. When I win, I want to know there's *nothing* you could have done to best me."

She glared at him, her heartbeat tripping in her veins. "You had the chance to get rid of me in the caves. Why didn't you?"

He edged even closer, his chest brushing against hers. "And why didn't you pull me down with you?"

His breath was warm against her neck, shooting a rush of

electricity along her skin. She didn't dare breathe, and she felt as if the words had been sucked out of her mind. They were so close. Too close. She could feel the thump of his heart and hear the whisper of his breath. Memories flooded her mind. His mouth on hers, his strong arms wrapped tightly around her.

She blinked, chasing the images away. "Let me go. I want to go back to sleep."

At long last, he dropped her hand. He gave her one last look, one that seemed to pierce her very soul, and then he vanished once more into the shadows. With a shaky sigh, she shook her head and returned to the camp. Nollaig was standing by the glowing embers of the fire, warming her hands against the dying heat.

She didn't glance up when Reyna returned, at least not that Reyna could tell with the massive hood hiding her face from view. "Did you two finally get it out of your systems?"

Reyna frowned. "Get what out of our systems?"

"He really isn't so bad, you know. A little broody at times, but he's far more good than bad. You can't say the same thing about most fae royalty."

Reyna scowled. "He betrayed me."

"He didn't have much of a choice, but I think you know that."

"There is always a choice."

Nollaig glanced up then, though the folds of her cloak still settled carefully around her face. "What would you have done in his place? Say the High King threatened you with your sister's life. The only way to save her would be to deliver Lorcan to him. I think the answer is clear." She crossed her arms. "You made a vow to your enemy in order to save your sister's life. Something tells me you would do far more than that."

"That's different."

"Is it?"

"Yes, that's choosing between two lives, two fae I care—I mean, *cared* about. Past tense. My vow to your king only hurts me."

"And whose life would you choose, if you were forced to make that decision?" Nollaig asked. "Lorcan's? Or Eislyn's?"

Reyna balled her hands. "That doesn't really matter now, does it? He isn't the fae I thought he was, so it wouldn't even be a question. Of course I would save Eislyn."

"You would have chosen her before, too," Nollaig said gently. "The gods know why, but Lorcan loves Thane like a brother. But you already knew that. Besides, Bolg Rothach has a way of forcing one to do exactly what he wants, regardless of their honor, regardless of the goodness in their soul."

Nollaig strode to the edge of the camp. Even now, she was fully decked out in black. Reyna wondered if the strange shadow fae ever let down her mask. What was it that she was so desperate to hide?

And why had her words unnerved her so? Reyna couldn't let it get to her. She couldn't let herself see Lorcan as anything but her enemy. Or her heart would shatter all over again.

❧

They started off at sunrise. Reyna had found only scraps of fitful sleep. Even though Lorcan had no longer lain beside her, she still felt the remnants of his presence. The scent of him hung there like a thick, unmoving fog.

"Enjoy your rest?" she asked in a snap when he rejoined them in their trek through the forest.

"Very much," he replied with a faux-pleasant smile. "It turns out that it's far easier to sleep when someone isn't throwing rocks at you."

"How unfortunate." Reyna leaned down and scooped up a rock. She bounced it in her hand. "Perhaps I should make up for what you missed."

"Go on then." He crossed his arms over his chest. "Throw it."

She glared at him, desperately wanting to do just that. His smug smile and stupid muscled chest needed to be knocked down a peg. She hated that he'd managed to sleep while she'd flailed in the dirt and leaves, eyes puffy, mind whirring.

He certainly wouldn't feel so smug anymore if she actually did it.

But no, this wasn't how she wanted to battle him. Rocks were boring. Swords were much more her style. And she would not dare risk Lorcan's father harming Eislyn because she couldn't keep her rocks to herself for more than one measly quest.

She dropped the rock. "That would be giving you what you want, and that is the last thing I want to do."

A flicker of a genuine smile ghosted his lips. "If that is what you say, Princess Reyna."

She decided to ignore him. That would be the better option. For now. Later, she would figure out how to stab him in the heart.

The party fell silent as they crunched through the trees. Tarrah took the lead, Teutas by her side with his sword held high. She motioned the group forward, often stopping to cock her head and gaze through the trees. At first, tension radiated throughout Reyna's body, reflected in the uneasy hoots of Wingallock. At any moment, wood fae could come swarming from the trees. Arrows could punch the ground at their feet. They had managed to slither into the forest unnoticed, but that would not last long. Eventually, they would be spotted.

Boredom quickly set in the longer nothing happened, and exhaustion began to take its toll. Reyna was weary. She'd had very little sleep for several nights in a row, followed by one without any at all. Tiredness tugged at her eyelids. She tried to fight it, but it proved impossible. Her eyes shut once, and then twice. It took all of her concentration to pry them open again. She stumbled onto a thin, fallen limb that snapped beneath her heavy boots.

"Reyna, stop!" Lorcan roared, grabbed her shoulders, and threw her to the ground behind him. Wingallock screeched and took to the skies. Half a heartbeat later, a string unravelled from around the branch she'd just snapped. Half a dozen arrows landed where she'd just stood.

Reyna gaped, her heart in her throat. It had been a trap, one meant to obliterate an enemy. If she had been standing there when those arrows hit, she would be dead.

And she *had* been standing there. Until Lorcan had shoved her out of the way.

Slowly, she dragged her gaze away from the arrows. Lorcan had already turned his back on her, leaping lightly over the arrows and continuing down the path as if nothing had happened.

Nollaig loomed over her and held out a gloved hand. "Like I told you, Shieldmaiden. These woods have teeth."

But Reyna didn't care about the teeth. All she could think about was Lorcan. He'd saved her. Again. Once could be an accident. A mistake. Twice was something more.

She took Nollaig's hand and climbed to her feet, smiling as Wingallock settled back onto her shoulder and gave her an annoyed hoot.

"I know, I know. Sorry, Wingallock."

He nuzzled her neck, forgiving her for her misstep instantly.

"Lorcan," she called out, a strange hope solidifying in her chest.

He slowed to a stop beside Tarrah, stiffening. Twisting on

his heels, he shot her a withering glare. "Be more careful. Watch where you're going. I don't want to have to explain to my father how the savior of his realm died on our watch."

"All right." She brushed the dirt off her trousers, but the thin hoarfrost silk was already stained brown.

He arched a brow. "*All right?* You're not going to argue?"

"You just saved my life."

He eyed her suspiciously. "Yes, and I'd do it again in a heartbeat. We need you."

Her heart fluttered. "We? So, you *are* on the side of the shadow fae. You're one of them."

"Of course I am. I have no other choice." His eyes flashed. "And neither do you."

## 18

### REYNA

"There's smoke just ahead," Nollaig whispered as she dropped onto the ground from the trees. Tarrah's 'compass' had failed several hours back, so Nollaig had taken over. According to her calculations, they were still a full day away from Craobhan, but they would soon pass small villages and hamlets. Most would be far up in the trees rather than on the forest floor, so they had little choice but to climb every now and again to ensure they were not walking straight beneath the enemy.

"How far?" Tarrah asked. "If we stick to the forest's edge, can we avoid them?"

Nollaig shook her head. "It was impossible to see where the village began and where it ended. The canopy is thick in the Forest of Thorns. The wood fae are very clever about not being seen unless they want to be seen."

"Fantastic," Reyna said bitterly.

"Draw your sword, Shieldmaiden," Nollaig replied. "It might be time for you to use it."

"Can I use it on you?"

"You can certainly try."

Reyna sighed and drew her sword. If only she truly did have the freedom to attack these shadow fae, she knew that she would win. The cloaked one might be tricky, and Lorcan was a force to be reckoned with at times, but it would only take a single shove to knock Tarrah down. The other warrior, Teutas, could fight. But he could not fight as well as Reyna Darragh.

"Teutas, you and Lorcan take the front. Tarrah stay in the middle. Reyna and I will round out the back. Everyone stay alert." Nollaig motioned the party into position, and they began a slow crouch-walk through the dense trees beneath the dappled light of the sun.

Nollaig fell back beside Reyna, holding a longsword tightly in her right hand. "I am going to give you one piece of advice. It is the same advice I gave Prince Lorcan many years back."

Reyna pushed her brows to the top of her head. Nollaig had given Lorcan advice? She shook her head in awe and kept her gaze focused on the limbs that stretched over their heads, her eyes darting through the trees in search of hidden wood fae, poised to attack.

"All of this will go much better for you if you—"

"What? Give in? Accept my fate? Just be happy that I'm stuck inside an enemy court forever?" A new flash of irritation went through Reyna's gut. They'd already taken her free will from her. She would not let them take her spirit as well. She would fight back the only way she knew how. With her words.

"You don't have to accept any of it, Princess Reyna," Nollaig said, her soft voice almost lost beneath the rustle of the leaves beneath their feet. "You just need to pretend."

She jerked her eyes away from the trees. "Pretend?"

Nollaig nodded, which caused her hood to rustle around her hidden face. "Play the part. Convince the king that you do not hate the shadow fae. Make him trust you. Make him lower his guard."

"I don't see what good that will do," Reyna muttered, turning her attention back on the canopy above. So far, there had not been any sign of the wood fae. That did not mean they weren't there.

"He'll no longer see you as a threat. You can get far more out of him then." Nollaig nodded at where Lorcan strode at the head of the party. "How do you think Lorcan got to leave for so many years? It wasn't from him shouting all the time about how he wanted to murder us all."

Reyna frowned. "That's different. Lorcan was—"

"Brought to our court against his will," Nollaig cut in. "That's right." She nodded when Reyna shot her a shocked glance. "Lorcan was as angry as you are. Perhaps even more so. In the end, he decided to play the part of a dutiful prince, even if his hatred toward his father never died."

"But this *is* his court. I don't understand why he would feel the way I do about any of this."

"This is not Lorcan Rothach's court." Nollaig sighed, stepping over a bramble of thorns. "He was a bastard, born in the air fae lands. He lived most of his life there until his father forced him to join the Shadow Court. I'm afraid his story is a sad one, and it is not mine to tell."

Reyna's eyes went wide. So, he had been telling her the truth about his life in the grasslands. When she had awoken inside an enemy court, stolen away by a male she'd grown to trust, she'd merely assumed he'd been lying about everything. But he had told her this part of it true, at least. His mother, the air fae lands, the father he had never met. Reyna shifted her gaze to Lorcan. He strode tall in front of them all, taking the lead as if he'd done it a hundred times before. His raven hair curled around his neck, just above the edges of his tightly-fitting leather armor. Silver bands cinched his biceps, highlighting the strength in his arms. Everything about him was sure and strong and steady, and yet she could sense some darkness there. She always had.

What had happened to him? How had he gotten to this place?

Why should she even care?

Suddenly, Lorcan stopped and motioned for them to fall behind him. Breath catching, Reyna lifted her sword and scanned the trees. Had he seen something?

An arrow suddenly whistled over the top of her head. She swallowed hard and ducked down behind a tree, her heart hammering out a drumbeat in her chest. Glancing up, she saw Nollaig just standing there like a golden ship gleaming in the middle of the sea. Frowning, she tugged on the shadow fae's cloak. Nollaig sighed and squatted down beside her.

"I do not like crouching," she muttered. "It feels like letting the enemy win."

"Well, the enemy is going to win if you don't duck," Reyna whispered fiercely. "They're shooting arrows at us. Stay low."

As if to punctuate her point, another arrow stormed toward them and thunked into the tree only a millimetre to the left of where they'd just stood. Reyna pointed and gave Nollaig a frank look, as if to say, *See? You're not the only one who can dispense useful advice.*

Just in front of them, Tarrah was trembling and fumbling around with her own arrows. She finally got one nocked, stood shakily on her feet, and loosed it in the direction of their attackers. She immediately dropped back behind the line of trees, chest heaving.

"Are you all right?" Reyna hissed.

Tarrah shook her head. Her entire face was a brutal white. "Unseelie did not warn me of this. I don't like battle and bloodshed."

"And that doesn't make you question this whole vision thing of yours?" Reyna asked incredulously.

"Of course not. There must be a reason why he didn't want me to know." Trembling, Tarrah curled her fingers around another arrow, but she dropped it into the brush before she could nock it.

"Here, give me the bow," Nollaig demanded, holding out her gloved right hand.

Tarrah hesitated, but then passed the bow and arrows to Nollaig. The cloaked fae nocked it easily, lifting the feathered end to what must have been her eyes, as if she had done this very thing a thousand times or more.

Reyna frowned. "Shouldn't you remove your hood? You won't be able to see a damn thing."

Nollaig stood, aimed, loosed the arrow, and then ducked down in one fluid motion. A strangled scream echoed throughout the forest. Reyna raised her brows.

"All right, that was impressive," she admitted.

Nollaig sent a few more arrows flying in the direction of the wood fae. Some hit the mark. Others failed, at least that they could hear. But soon, there were no more arrows to sail.

"Lorcan!" Nollaig hissed as a storm of enemy arrows punched the ground all around the trees where they hid. "We need to move."

"Aye," he said gravely, twisting to face them. "They're growing closer, and their arrows will soon find their marks, even if we stay behind these trees. There's nothing to protect our heads. We need to rush forward and force them into close combat. It's our only choice."

Reyna's stomach tumbled. Close combat was all well and good—preferable in her eyes—but *getting there* would pose a problem. The wood fae seemed to have an endless supply of arrows, and they'd launch another dozen of them as soon as their party stood from the brush.

Of course, Reyna had experience with this. She'd dodged her fair share of arrows at the Battle for the Shard.

"Lorcan," she hissed. "Let me up front."

He glanced over his shoulder at her and scowled. "Absolutely not."

"Just trust me. Let me up front."

Lorcan narrowed his eyes but motioned for Reyna to scuttle forward. She left Wingallock with Nollaig and a terrified Tarrah, and then edged to the prince's side in a crouch.

"What is it?" he demanded in a tone of voice that suggested he had zero patience for nonsense. Despite the many tight spots they'd gotten into together, she'd never actually seen him transform into pure warrior mode. She kind of liked this side of him.

"All right. I'm going to rush them. The rest of you hold back until my sword draws blood," Reyna said. "I'll get right in their faces. Trust me, they won't be able to ignore me. That will give the rest of you a chance to charge."

Lorcan gaped at her incredulously. "Hold back? Are you out of your fucking mind?"

"Maybe, but I've trained to do this. I'll be fine."

"She's right," Nollaig cut in from where she patted her gloved hand on top of Wingallock's head. "Shieldmaidens train to dodge arrows."

"And Unseelie has shown her standing on the battlefield in our shadow lands. That means she doesn't die here now," Tarrah whispered.

"You're all in agreement with this, are you?" Lorcan growled as another arrow slammed into the ground not far from where they hid. He whipped his head toward Teutas. "Do you have anything to say about this?"

Teutas shrugged. "I'm not sure we have much of a choice."

Lorcan growled. "You're all mad, the lot of you."

But there was no time left to argue. An arrow rushed

through the air, the sharp point aimed right at Reyna's head. She ducked just in time, and the arrow sailed past, vanishing into the forest.

Teutas let out a low whistle. "She's got my vote."

"Stay back," Reyna whispered, determination curling in her gut. She leapt to her feet and released her Shieldmaiden's roar. It was a sound as powerful as the thunder in the sky, and just as loud and deafening. Her cry spilled from her throat in a tumultuous rage, and every single part of her sparked with life. It had been far too long since she had truly roared. She grinned and charged.

Instantly, the air was full of arrows, and every last one of them hurtled straight toward Reyna's chest. With hands curled into fists, she steadied her raging heart and focused on the sharp points. Her breath stilled in her lungs, and the world seemed to transform around her. Everything slowed down. The wind in the trees drifted away.

Reyna narrowed her eyes. There was one arrow to her left and three to her right. With a deep breath, she ducked down, avoiding the three, and then shot to the side to miss the last. The arrows carried on past her, thunking hard into the trees.

The world came back in a rush, and sharp cries filled the air. The wood fae were just ahead. She could see them now. There were six in total, all decked out in light leather armor dyed a deep green to match their surroundings. Their ears were longer and sharper than the fae in the north. Some had lightly-tinted green skin while others appeared almost translucent.

One in the front, a female with ginger hair hanging across her shoulder in a thick braid, lifted her bow and aimed.

Footsteps thundered behind Reyna. She frowned, keeping one eye on the fae while glancing over her shoulder. Lorcan was stumbling through the brush with his sword raised high and a scowl as deep as the night plastered across his face.

"Damn it, Lorcan!" she shouted. "I said stay back!"

Irritation roared through her. Couldn't that godforsaken male just listen to her? Just once!

A *snick* echoed through the forest as the fae loosed her arrow. Reyna spun toward her, watching the weapon slice through the thick, humid air. She gasped, and her heart almost stopped. In the flicker of a moment, she glanced over her shoulder to envision the path of the arrow.

Lorcan. It would hit Lorcan.

If Reyna dodged the arrow, the sharp, steel point would bury itself in his neck. He wore no armor there. Nothing could save him. He would die within an instant.

"No!" a furious scream ripped from her throat, and Reyna leapt high into the air. Not *away* from the arrow but toward it. She threw herself into its path, holding her breath to brace herself against the inevitable blast of pain.

The arrow slammed into her gut, punching her back several feet. Agony stormed through her stomach with white hot fire, blinding her from feeling anything else but the utter torment of it all.

She fell to her knees, gasping, pressing her hand to the wound that was already slick with blood. Grimacing, she reached around to feel her back. The arrow had punched clean through, and the end stuck out the other side of her.

"Reyna! Reyna, no!" Lorcan dropped to her side, his words a roar of utter anguish. "No, no, no!"

She collapsed into his arms, and her head lolled against his chest. The scent of him filled her mind. Leather and smoke and steel. Reyna peered up at him, at his impossibly handsome face.

"Lorcan," she croaked out. "I think I'm going to die."

# 19
## LORCAN

The pain was unyielding.

"Reyna. Reyna no." He cradled her head in his arms and blasted fury at the sky with a roar. Blood poured from her wound, painting his armor crimson. This couldn't be happening. Reyna was one of the strongest fae he'd ever met. A tiny little arrow couldn't kill her like this. She couldn't die.

*Reyna can't die.*

"I won't let you die!" he roared, gently curling around her fallen body. Her beautiful, sparkling, full-of-life eyes had slipped shut, and all the color had drained from her face. Panic and fear punched into him like dozens of blunt knives.

His utter anguish must have frightened the wood fae because they were now darting through the forest, vanishing into the thick tangle of trees, thorns, and death. The dappled sunlight glanced off their green-dyed armor just as they slid out of sight.

"Nollaig!" he roared. His hands shook as he pressed them against Reyna's slick wound to staunch the bleeding as best he could. He couldn't go after the enemy himself. He wouldn't leave Reyna sprawled out on the forest floor alone, dying.

"I'm already here, Your Highness," Nollaig said quietly from behind him. "What would you have me do?"

"Stop those wood fae. They're no doubt rushing ahead to warn the king. I caught a glimpse of them. They look like scouts, not villagers." He ground his teeth together as he pressed firmly against the wound. His hands were now wet with her blood, his fingers stained the color of death. "They're fleeing, which means they're likely low on arrows. The three of you should be enough to stop them. Kill every last one of them. Make them pay for what they've done."

"And what are you going to do, Your Highness?" Nollaig asked, already taking off at a run, her billowing cloak flaring behind her like dark wings.

"It's too far back to Findius. I'm taking her to Oxgrove," he said hoarsely. "I have to save her. And they're the only hope I've got."

Lorcan raced through the forest with Reyna's limp body in his arms. He'd left the arrow where it was, but it burned him up to see the cruel piece of wood sticking out of her, as if the enemy had left its mark on her. He would make them pay for this. He would. His feral scream ripped through the forest, threatening to tear a hole in the entire sky. As he ran, Reyna's familiar flew by his side, darting through the trees. He gave the owl a grim nod. As long as the bird was alive, that meant Reyna would be, too.

He ran half the day, not once stopping to rest his feet or drink from a stream. He didn't want to lose even a single moment, for that moment could be the very last one that Reyna ever saw. She would not die because of his mortal weaknesses. It did not matter that he could scarcely breathe, that his heart pounded so hard that it threatened to stop at any moment. It didn't matter that his mouth was parched or that stars had begun to dance in his eyes. And it didn't matter that his feet throbbed with blinding pain. Lorcan knew blinding pain, and he could block it out better than anyone else.

He laughed bitterly to himself as he ducked beneath limb after limb of the dense forest. Perhaps his bloody mark had done some good, after all.

At long last, Lorcan reached the tree line. He came to a sudden stop and gazed out at the green, rolling hills that led to the sea. Reyna's blood drenched him completely, and the crimson had seeped through his tunic. It was as hot as fire on his skin.

"Don't die on me, Reyna," he said softly, cupping her pale cheek before pushing off into a run once again. "One more hour, and we'll be there. Don't let your bloody stubbornness fail you now."

Lorcan could no longer feel his feet in his boots. He knew they would be bloody and raw when he finally stopped, but he didn't care. They were so close. He could even see smoke curling from distant chimneys, and small specks on the horizon where the land met the sea. He could not fail her now.

The moments passed in a blur. Lorcan could no longer think about anything but the simple movement of putting one foot in front of the other.

The village was before him now, a small cluster of mud-encased buildings squatting on top of a lush green hill overlooking the sea. The thatched roofs rustled in the soft breeze, reminding Lorcan at once of his childhood. The familiar din of village life rose up around him. Laughter drifting from the open tavern doors. The sound of wood splintering from the heavy blow of an axe. The clang of metal from the local blacksmith. And the soft hum of a mother hanging linen out to dry.

Lorcan's heart ached for home. The village from his childhood. The people who he had known and loved and lost.

The ones his own father had killed.

Gritting his teeth, he shook the memories away and raced into the village, shouting for help.

There were several cottages clustered together at the edge of the village, squatting beside a tavern that buzzed with the steady hum of conversation and laughter. A few fae were wandering along the road that wound through the village, chatting together in groups or lugging barrels of water from a nearby stream.

Several of the fae slowed to a stop, eyeing Lorcan warily.

There were three of them. One was an older male with white strands peppering his mossy green hair, and deep lines around his eyes carved into his face like an ancient tattoo of wisdom. He had a flat nose and large verdant eyes, and the two younger females with him had matching features. All wore the simple garb of villagers: linen tunics and trousers, worn and faded.

"What's this?" the wood fae asked, glancing at Reyna, at all the blood. "We don't want any trouble."

"We were attacked. She's been hurt." Lorcan inched forward, showing the fae the blood that had soaked through Reyna's tunic. "Please. She's dying. Is one of you a healer? Can you help her? Please." His voice cracked on the last word.

He would have given them anything in that moment to save her. He would let his mark finally burn him up and tear his limbs apart. The world had taken so much from him already. This was all he had left, and he would die if it meant she could live.

One of the females stepped forward. Her eyes were kind and her voice soft. "Who attacked you?"

Lorcan did not know how to answer that. Nollaig believed this village to be safe and free from the wood king's influence, but what if she was wrong? What if these wood fae were loyal to their court? His mind spun with lies, but he knew they would not believe a one of them. It was clear why he was here, a shadow fae with a dying ice princess in his arms. All he could offer them was the truth. "Some archers in the woods. Scouts for the king."

"All right then," she said, waving Lorcan forward. "You're not the first bloodied fae to come rushing in here with an arrow poking out of a belly. She's lucky she has you. She looks half dead."

Lorcan's heart twisted.

"Don't worry," she said with a kind smile. "I'll stitch her right back up again. I'm Meredith, by the way. The local alchemist."

Lorcan hadn't known the Wood Court had alchemists. He didn't think they believed in such things. From what he'd heard, they'd turned their backs on the ways of the Dagda, welcoming darker things, just like their king.

He followed the female past the cluster of cottages. She led him toward the tavern, up the rickety stairs, and into a room where a dozen wood fae fell silent in a hush of tense air.

His entire body tensed. His eyes flicked from fae to fae, spotting swords on backs, bows leaned against walls, and daggers on mead-stained tables. These were warriors. Every last one of them.

"Avalon," she called out to the tavern wench with cascading ginger hair, who stood behind the curving oak bar at the back. "I need the following herbs: rowan, knit-bone, and willow bark. Some nettle tonic, too, please. And Duff, give the lad a drink or two and get him cleaned up. Don't forget to burn that tunic. It's drenched in her blood."

Every single fae inside the tavern sprang into action. Avalon, the tavern wench, disappeared through a burlap flap behind the bar. Duff jumped to his feet, rushing to the bottles that lined the wall. And several other males joined in as well. They gently wrenched Reyna from Lorcan's arms. At first, he resisted. He didn't dare let her go. But then Meredith had given him an impatient slap on the arm, and he had relinquished his vice-like grip around Reyna's broken body.

Meredith motioned for the warriors to follow Avalon into the back. Lorcan trailed behind them, his eyes locked on Reyna's frail form, but Duff clamped a strong hand on his shoulder and pulled him back. The fae shoved a small metal mug into Lorcan's hands. Amber liquid sloshed inside. "Drink."

Lorcan shoved the mug aside. "I'm going with them."

"You're staying here," Duff said steadily. "Have a drink."

Lorcan shoved his shoulder against the wood fae's, knocking him out of his damn way. The mug clattered onto the timber floor, the spirits splashing onto his boots. But three others stood from the table and blocked the path to the back of the tavern where they'd taken Reyna.

"Get out of my damn way," Lorcan growled.

"We get why you're angry, but there's nothing you can do to help her now. The room's not big enough, mate. You'd just get in the way." Duff knelt down, grabbed the mug, and tipped a new splash of spirits inside. He held it out for Lorcan. "Besides, we need to get rid of all that blood. You're covered in it."

Lorcan glowered at Duff, and then turned his attention on the other three. They all wore well-worn boiled leather with no sigil stamp anywhere to be seen. They were broad and muscular, but much shorter than most of the air and shadow warriors Lorcan had met over the years.

The closest gave him a nod. "I know you're worried about your lass, but Meredith can't do her thing if you're in there growling and knocking people over."

"You came to us for help." Duff's voice softened. "Let us help you, mate."

Lorcan's shoulders slumped as he relented, even though it was the last thing he wanted to do. He couldn't bear the thought of Reyna trapped in the back room of a tavern, being tortured by wicked wood fae who just wanted to watch her bleed.

But if they'd wanted to kill her, they wouldn't have bothered trying to hide it from Lorcan. And Meredith had said she would help. As a wood fae, she couldn't lie. With a shake of his head, he grabbed the mug and downed the amber liquid in one gulp. He winced as the burning liquid hit his throat. Wood Whiskey. The strongest spirit in all of Tir Na Nog, and the most fiery.

"What's all this about the blood?" Lorcan asked after he'd downed another shot. His nerves were spent, he realized. His entire body hummed as if it had been shot too close to the sun.

"You don't want to leave too much of your blood lying around in these parts. Unseelie's magic is blood magic." Duff peered at Lorcan. "Though I suppose you know that, don't you, mate?"

Lorcan stiffened. "I'm not a follower of Unseelie. I know nothing of the sort."

"That's good then," Duff said. "We aren't big fans of him here either, at least not in Oxgrove. The rest of the realm though?" Duff shook his head. "Well, that's why we've got to get rid of this blood."

Frowning, Lorcan pulled the crimson tunic over his head and tossed it onto the round wooden table they indicated. "What exactly would they do with it?"

"A great many a thing, I'm afraid. They could use her face as an illusion or find her no matter where she might go. But worst of all, they could use her blood to control her and make her do whatever they damn wanted." Duff grabbed the tunic, strode over to the hearth, and tossed it inside. The flames engulfed the fabric, burning away the blood. Fear squeezed Lorcan's heart. He'd never heard of such a thing, but admittedly, he'd purposefully avoided anything that involved the Unseelie god. He'd never wanted to know, and this was why. Unseelie was the god of monstrous things.

A small quiet voice whispered in his mind. A voice he had not heard in a great many years. It was the voice of his mark. *You are right, Prince Lorcan Rothach. I am.*

# 20

## REYNA

The sweet scent of fresh grass, the salt of the sea, and spring flowers drifted into Reyna's nose. She drew a deep breath into her lungs, sighing in contentment. She was warm but not too hot. There was no wind to speak of, and she could feel the soft, calming touch of her mother's ice glass ring on a necklace at her throat.

And then suddenly, memories of the attack assaulted her mind. The wood fae in the forest. The arrows. The pain that had exploded in her gut. The sound of Lorcan's fury when he'd seen how badly she'd been hurt.

Her eyes flew open, panic and fear churning through her like the wind during a brutal storm. Lorcan leaned over her, his dark eyes flashing with charged emotion. His raven hair was down, falling into his face and brushing his shoulders corded with muscle. Her gaze dropped south, drinking in his smooth, tanned skin. He wasn't wearing a tunic. Was this a dream?

"You're awake." His voice was full of relief. He reached out to grasp her hand, his grip strong but gentle.

"Where am I?" She pressed a hand to her throat. It felt as raw as an onion fresh from the ground.

"We're in Oxgrove," Lorcan said quietly. "A village on the coast of the wood lands. The one Nollaig told us about."

She jerked at his words, sudden terror charging through her. "Why in the name of the Dagda are we in a wood fae village? Have we been captured? Are we prisoners?"

"Relax," Lorcan said with a soft smile. "The fae here are not fond of their king."

"And Wingallock? Where is he?"

"Off hunting in the fields for mice."

Reyna sighed and relaxed back onto the pillows. "Well then. That's a relief. You gave me quite the fright though."

"I could say the same to you." A pause. "You were supposed to dodge the arrows. Not jump into their path."

She scowled. "And you were supposed to hold back."

"I wasn't going to let you rush into a barrage of arrows all alone." His voice went sharp. "I know you're reckless and stubborn as hell, but that doesn't mean you're invincible, Reyna."

"Have you had Shieldmaiden training?" she snapped. "No? Then you should have let me take the lead."

"I may not be a Shieldmaiden, but I've spent most of my life training for combat, in one manner or another. And one of the most important things I've learned is never let ally to rush into danger alone."

"Oh, I'm an ally now, am I?" She scowled and shifted away from him, her cheek plastered against the pillow. "You know what else you don't do to allies? Betray them. Threaten them. Hold their loved ones captive for your own aims."

He sighed heavily and sank into the chair beside the bed, the wood creaking beneath his weight. "I see we're back to this now."

"We never left it, Lorcan."

"And here I thought you leaping in front of an arrow to save my life meant you might not hate me as much as you insist."

"That's just your delusional mind getting the better of you." She glanced over her shoulder and shot him an icy smile. "It's a classic symptom of being an Unseelie worshipper, or didn't you know?"

Lorcan growled. "I swear to the Dagda, one day you are going to be the death of me."

"No, I'm not," she said sweetly. "I just took an arrow in the gut for you. I saved your life."

"And I saved yours. Twice."

"It's a competition now, is it? Because if it is, I'll win. Every damn time."

Suddenly, Reyna's throat tightened. She coughed, hard, and pain exploded in her gut. Grimacing, she pressed her hands against the dressing on her wound, stars dotting her eyes.

"Ow."

"All right. Enough of that. Let me check your wound," Lorcan said gently, shifting onto the bed. With gentle fingers, he lifted the edge of the dressing. She gazed down at the wound, heart hammering. There was a mottled and bruised hole in the very center of her stomach where her skin should be. The bleeding had slowed, but it hadn't stopped. It still bubbled ominously in the candlelight.

Lorcan gently pressed the bandage back onto the wound. "Let's put a pause on the arguing for now. At least until you heal."

Reyna grumbled.

"You can shout at me as much as you want when you can stand again." He gave her a strange smile. "Or you can keep trying to do it now. You'll probably end up passing out and never get to say all the terrible things you have in mind."

She huffed. "You might have a point with that."

"Or you can admit that you don't hate me after all."

"Don't push it." She shifted on the pillows, trying to regain the comfort she'd felt before opening her eyes to the reality of her life. For a moment, she just wanted to return to the sweet scent of grass, the softness of the pillows, the safety of it all. Just for a moment. And then she would get straight back to the business of slaying her enemies.

"Are you uncomfortable?" Lorcan asked as he watched her flop around on the pillows.

"I'm..." She wanted to say *fine,* but that was a lie. Nothing was fine at all, and she doubted it ever would be again.

Lorcan shifted a little further onto the bed, and then gently pulled her into his arms. She opened her mouth to protest, but the moment her head rested against his chest, she forgot every word she meant to say.

He was solid and steady and familiar in the midst of so much chaos and pain. Lorcan had been the cause of a lot of that, of course, but that didn't matter right now. She breathed him in, leather and smoke and steel, and emotions she thought she'd lost washed over her.

*I still hate him though,* she reminded herself. *I still hate him, and I'll remind him when I don't feel like I've been through another round of the Battle for the Shard.*

But she wasn't entirely certain she would be able to get the words out. Not because they were lies. Of *course* they weren't lies. She didn't feel anything toward Lorcan Rothach, the Prince of Shadows, but hatred. Hate, hate, hate, and nothing else.

His heart thudded against her ear. Despite how muscular he was, his chest was surprisingly comfortable. Not soft like a pillow, but smooth and warm and safe. With a contented sigh, she snuggled in and gave in to the exhaustion that tugged insistently on her eyelids.

Her eyes drifted shut as she basked in the steady warmth of him. Reyna had never liked the heat. In fact, she hated it. The burning cold of the northern ice was far better than anything created by fire. But this was different. A good kind of heat. The best kind, really.

Distantly, she was aware of Lorcan stroking her hair and pressing soft lips against her forehead. The stubborn part of her wanted to wake up and slap him right in his stupid handsome face, but the other part of her—the part that was enjoying this far more than she should—begged her to yield. Just this once.

*You're healing. You need the rest. There's no reason to be so stubborn all of the time.*

Time passed as slumber pulled her into the darkness of a dreamless sleep. Eventually, she heard the clattering of footsteps on a wooden floor, but she did not have the strength to rouse. Her face was still plastered against Lorcan's chest, her limbs heavy, her stomach still throbbing with pain. She stayed right where she was, eyes still shut against the world.

A familiar voice cut through the silence, a grating voice she would recognize anywhere. "Your Highness. Thank the gods. We were worried you hadn't made it to safety."

More thudding of footsteps followed.

"How's the princess?" Tarrah asked in a soft voice.

"She's in a lot of pain, but she'll live." A pause. "These wood fae saved her, Nollaig. If they'd turned us away, she'd be dead."

"Yes, quite right. We're lucky they aren't loyal to the wood king."

"This village is awfully close to the border," Lorcan said, so quietly that his words were almost garbled in Reyna's tired brain.

"What are you saying?" Teutas asked.

"I'm not sure. All I know is that I will not let another

village full of innocents burn down." He cleared his throat, his voice sounding strangled. "Did you stop the scouts?"

"Some," Nollaig replied tensely. "But not all. The wood king will soon know we're here, if he doesn't already. And he will come for us."

# 21

## LORCAN

Lorcan paced a line from the window to the door and back again. He did not know what to do or even if he should do anything at all. At least one of the wood king's scouts had made it back to Craobhan. Now, the Wood Court would know that shadow fae had been poking around the forest just north of Findius. And they would likely know why. As cruel as the wood king was, he was not dim-witted. In fact, he was very clever indeed, if the tales were true.

Only a male of great cunning could have gotten as far as he had.

Duff suddenly strode inside Reyna's healing room, flanked by two of his fellow warriors. They eyed Lorcan's frantic pacing, and then exchanged knowing looks.

"Sure you don't want to join us at the tavern tonight for a round of ales?" Duff asked, still donned in boiled leather armor even now. "Our local bard is a sea fae, and he's got some tall tales he loves to sing about. You ever hear of the Ghaisgeach, the one who's supposed to save the world?"

"I'll pass. Meredith said Reyna is getting better, and I don't want her to wake up alone."

"If she does wake up soon, it likely won't be for long," Duff said. "It'll be several more days before she's back to normal."

"I don't care. I'm staying here."

"Suit yourself." Duff shrugged. "In the meantime, I thought you might like something to wear. I've brought you a tunic."

The wood fae tossed a small bundle of green his way. Lorcan caught it, held it up, and frowned. "I appreciate it, but this looks a bit small."

Duff chuckled. "That's because you shadow fae are so damn big."

Lorcan bristled, but he didn't bother to correct him. He might have inherited his father's court, but he'd never considered himself a true shadow fae. He belonged to his mother's court. The Air Court. Even though he'd betrayed them, he would have the heart of an air fae until the day he died.

A knock sounded on the door, and then Meredith bustled inside without waiting for an answer. Duff and his friends gave Lorcan a quick goodbye, and then backed out of the room while Meredith fussed at Reyna's wound, wrapping a new bandage and wiping away the fresh blood. Before covering it back up, she spread an ointment across the wound. A healing salve meant to speed up the process, though it would never replace the powers the fae had once had.

If only the Fall had never happened, Reyna would already be fully healed by now.

And the kingdoms would not be at war.

"How is she doing?" Lorcan asked as Meredith finished up with the bandage.

"Much better. She is a strong one, this Reyna."

Lorcan audibly sighed. "Good. We will leave first thing on the morrow."

Meredith frowned. "I said she's better, but she is not fully healed. The poor thing needs to rest, to gather her strength back."

His heart pulsed. The wood fae knew they were somewhere in the area. It would not take them long to realize where they'd gone. If the shadow fae knew Oxgrove was a welcome place for strangers, the wood king would know it, too.

"How much longer?"

"A few more days." With a gentle smile, she patted his shoulder. "And then she will be good to go."

"A few more days," he echoed.

A few more days, and the wood fae would be here. That or they would cut off their return path to Findius. If they did, Lorcan and his party would never be able to cross beneath the wall. The wood fae would spot the hidden tunnels if they used them. And they couldn't risk the enemy discovering the only path across the border.

"And there is no way to speed up her healing?"

She swatted at his arm. "No. You're lucky she's even alive. Now why don't you go join the lads and leave her be? The more she rests, the faster she'll heal."

Lorcan merely crossed his arms over his chest and kept his feet firmly rooted to the timber floor. With a roll of her eyes, she gave Reyna one last glance and left. As she departed, another visitor announced her arrival with a rustle of her cloak against the floor.

"Your Highness," Nollaig said, bowing slightly. "I didn't mean to eavesdrop, but I heard what the wood fae said. It appears our fate has finally caught up with us."

Lorcan twisted to face her with a frown.

Nollaig continued. "We will fight our best, of course, but the wood king will send far more warriors than we have here, even including the many villagers of Oxgrove who know how to wield a weapon. I suppose it is a matter of how soon we will fall, not if."

"You would stay here with me and fight?"

"Well, yes, of course," she said with confusion in her voice. "What ever else would I do?"

"Return to the court," he said. "Abandon this fool-hardy quest. Save yourselves."

Nollaig stiffened. "I am not leaving your side. You are my prince, my liege. Whatever you might think of me, you must know I would not leave you behind to fight the wood fae alone."

He noted that she didn't ask whether he would leave Reyna in Oxgrove so that they might return safely to Findius. She already knew the answer to that. He would stay and protect her healing body with his dying breath if he must.

"I appreciate your loyalty, Nollaig," he said quietly. "More than you'll ever know. But here is not where I need you. There's something else I need you to do."

"And what is that?" she asked crisply, clearly unhappy that Lorcan did not wish for her to stay and throw herself into a fight against an army too large to even contemplate.

"I need you to go ahead and return to Findius. Warn the court of what's happening."

"I just told you I'm not leaving your side," she growled. "And even if I wanted to, the king would have my head."

"Somehow, I doubt that."

Nollaig answered with a moment's pause, and then, "I'll do this, but only on one condition. We need to make the Wood Court believe that all of us have gone. Otherwise, they might come here looking for you."

Lorcan exhaled in relief. For a moment, he did not believe that she would go. He might be the prince, but she was his father's creature, not his. She would always defer to the king. He need not forget that.

"What did you have in mind?" Lorcan asked.

"We'll make plenty of noise and leave behind a lot of mess. When we camp, we'll make it look like there was five of us instead of three. When Reyna has healed, take a small boat instead of the tunnels. It will take longer, but the wood fae won't expect it. And if they show up unexpectedly, run, use the boat. They won't swim after you. The salt burns their skin."

Lorcan nodded. "I hate separating our party like this, but Reyna is not ready to go. She needs to heal."

"Yes, she does," Nollaig said quietly, and Lorcan knew that if he could see her eyes, there would be a glint in them. "I've never seen you like this, you know."

"Like what?" Lorcan narrowed his eyes.

"So focused. So determined." A pause. "You were going to save that lass no matter who and what stood in your way. You would have ripped apart the very fabric of the world. I daresay she knows it, too."

A snake squeezed tight around his heart. "I betrayed her, Nollaig."

"Hmm." Nollaig turned to go, but then paused in the open doorway. "One last thing I thought you should know before we all return home to Findius. I wasn't going to tell you yet, but your actions have proven you to me. Your father does not hold Eislyn Darragh captive. And he doesn't have your Thane either."

Nollaig vanished out the door. Lorcan's hands clenched and then unclenched as he ran Nollaig's words over and over again in his mind, just to be sure he had not misheard her.

"Father," he growled to himself, rage rising up within him even as relief loosed the hold of fear around his heart. Thane was not only alive, but he was safe. The king of the shadows did not have him in his grasp, and he would not be able to kill him at any moment with a single-worded command. Lorcan staggered to the side, placing a palm against the rough wall to hold himself steady.

Thane was fine. He was safe. He would not die by Bolg Rothach's cruel hand.

His father had lied to him.

For once, he *had* lied. Bolg Rothach had been able to make this bluff because he had followed through on his cruelty so many times in the past. Painful memories flashed through Lorcan's mind. The faces of old friends. Cadman of Comharra, the only father Lorcan had ever truly known, even if they hadn't been related by blood. Aoiffe, the old snarky widow who had made sure he'd had a sword as soon as he could hold it in his hands without falling over from the sheer weight of it. And little Elen. Lorcan's heart ached. The new babe of Comharra. He'd never even had a chance to meet her. Because Lorcan's father had murdered them all.

"Lorcan?" A soft voice dragged him back to the present. Lorcan pushed away from the wall and turned toward Reyna. She peered up at him, her hair spread like ice across the pillow, concern flickering in her clear eyes. "What's the matter?"

"Nothing is the matter," he said in a rough voice, striding to her side at once. "Nollaig just informed me that my father has been lying about his prisoners. He doesn't have your sister, Reyna. Eislyn is safe. He can't harm her. And he doesn't have Thane either."

Reyna jolted, and a strangled choke ripped from her throat. Her entire face crumpled as she pressed a shaking hand to her heart. And then she started to cry. Heaving, painful sobs that shook her entire body. Lorcan did not quite know what to do. He'd never once seen Reyna Darragh break. He didn't think she could. Her fear for her sister must have been twisting around her entire body like a venomous snake all this time.

His hands fisted. Bolg Rothach had done this to her.

"Reyna," he said softly, dropping to her side and wrapping his arms around her. Her sobs were almost violent now, shaking her entire body. They sounded like a deep rumble that came from the deepest part of her soul. "It's okay. He doesn't have her."

"I will kill him," she said in a hiss.

"Only if you let me help you do it."

She pulled back and gazed up at him, her tear-streaked eyes searching his face. "He has been playing both of us. He used what we love and twisted it against us so that we had no choice but to do what he said."

"That's what he does," Lorcan said quietly. "If you love something, you can depend on my father to rip it apart or use it to hurt you. Often both."

Realization dawned in her eyes. "He's done this to you before."

He clenched his jaw and glanced away, staring hard at the door where Nollaig had disappeared. A part of him wanted to call after his old shadow fae friend and make her explain why his father had done this to them. But Nollaig knew as well as he did that there was no point in explaining. Because Lorcan already understood. The King of Shadows had a plan. He wanted to reign over the entire continent and crush the other courts beneath his boot. And he would do *anything* to make sure it happened.

"The village I told you about," Lorcan said in a haunted voice. "The one from my childhood. You remember it?"

Reyna nodded. "The one from Beltane when the Fomorians chased you through the grasslands. Yes, Lorcan. I remember. To be honest, I've been thinking about that village a lot lately. When I first realized you'd captured me for the Shadow Court, I thought you'd been lying about the village, too. But I don't think you were, were you?"

"I was not," he said through gritted teeth.

"Tell me about it," she said softly as she slipped her small hand into his. Her touch was warm and strong, even though she had been on the brink of death only a couple of days before. He took comfort in it.

"The Fomorians attacked my village that night, killing almost every fae inside of it, including my mother." He stopped short, catching his breath, and Reyna squeezed his hand. He collected himself and continued. "There were few of us left, but we lived peacefully—if not poorly—in Comharra for ten good years. Until my father sent his warriors to collect me."

"Let me guess. He did not give you much of a choice."

"It was no choice at all. He threatened to kill every living fae of Comharra if I did not go to the Shadow Court and become his legitimized son." He laughed bitterly. "It worked. I did it. And for years after that, he held their lives over my head, always knowing that I would do whatever he bid as long as he had that."

Reyna pushed up from the bed and leaned forward, pressing her forehead against his as emotion shook his voice. Lorcan had never spoken to anyone about this, not fully. He'd never wanted to, nor had he ever known someone who would understand. The wounds were fresh and raw, even though it had been years since that day he'd stumbled into Comharra and fallen to his knees in anguish.

The day he'd found the village empty, barren, and full of blood. The day he'd found out his father had killed almost everyone he loved. Cadman, Aoiffe, and all the rest.

"Eventually, my father realized I was not the loyal servant he hoped I was. He discovered I'd come to care for Thane, the prince I was meant to kill one day."

Reyna blinked in shock. "You were meant to kill Thane?"

Lorcan nodded. "After he became the king and before he

sired an heir. It would have created a vacuum of power, throwing the Air Court into chaos. Chaos is exactly what my father wants from his enemies.

"After spending several years by Thane's side, I decided that I wouldn't do it. That I would find a way out of it. I don't know how my father found out, but he did. Likely through the mark he gave me to make me his." He closed his eyes. "So, he murdered every fae inside of Comharra."

"Oh, Lorcan," she said softly.

He brought her hand to his chest and pressed it firmly against his skin. "I am so sorry for what I have done to you, Reyna. I should have known he never had Thane. Now, you're stuck with him, same as me. And that is not a fate I would wish on anyone. Especially not you."

A low growl rumbled in her throat, and she tightened her grip around his fingers. "He needs to be stopped. We cannot let him get away with this."

Lorcan could not help but smile, even if her rage was nothing more than folly. There was no way to stop the High King of the Shadow Court. He had them both wrapped around his pinky finger, Lorcan with the mark and Reyna with her vow. "You must be feeling better. It's been hours since you had that murderous glint in your eye."

"Better enough that I could rip off his smushed little head."

He chuckled. "He does have a particularly smushed head, doesn't he?"

"*So* smushed," she replied. "Lucky for you, you only inherited his hair and his eyes."

His brows winged upward. "Was that a compliment?"

"Hmph," she said. "Maybe I like smushed faces."

He slid his hand up her arm to her neck, and then to her cheek. She stiffened beneath his touch, but she didn't pull away.

"Tell me you hate me then. If that's your truth, then speak it aloud."

"I want to hate you," she whispered back. "You betrayed me. Terribly."

"I did. And I deserve your wrath."

"Stop that," she hissed.

"Stop what?" His voice dipped low as her lips drew agonizingly close to his. He could smell the alchemist's medicine on her breath, the tangy scent of herbs and rowan berries.

"Apologizing." She swallowed hard, the skin at her neck trembling. "It makes me want to forget everything you did."

"Then, I'm sorry," he whispered, brushing his thumb across her bottom lip. "I'm sorry. I'm sorry." He slid his nose across the soft skin of her cheek, and then murmured into her ear. "I am sorry, Reyna Darragh."

With a gasp, she slid her fingers into his hair and pulled his mouth toward hers. Her soft lips collided into his, warm and sweet, but as ferocious as every single thing that made her who she was. Distantly, he was aware that his mark had begun to ache. But for once, it was nothing more than a dull, pesky fly.

Now that she was in his arms once again, he would never again let anyone—or anything—take her away from him.

## 22

REYNA

Reyna wound her fingers through Lorcan's hair and relished in the feel of him. She opened her mouth to his, kissing him with the ferocity of a thousand roaring lions. Everything within her squeezed tight. Her core ached. Her heart felt close to bursting.

She felt whole again, as if her world had finally right itself after so much time spent askew. Murmuring, she slid her hands over his smooth, rippling shoulders and down the front of his bare chest. She had no idea what had happened to his tunic, but she was glad for whatever it was. He was the most gorgeous male she had ever laid eyes on, particularly when he wasn't clothed.

"Reyna," he murmured against her mouth. She gasped at the sound of her name on his breath. There was always something in the way he said it that made her insides quiver in anticipation.

Suddenly, he pulled back and gazed into her eyes. "Tell me you don't hate me. Tell me this is what you want."

She curled her lips into a demure smile. "*What* is what I want?"

A low growl rumbled in his throat. "Shall I show you?"

"Please do," she whispered, cheeks flaming.

With a devilish smile, Lorcan leaned down and dragged his tongue across her ear. White hot desire exploded inside her core. Moaning, she sagged against the pillows, digging her fingers into his skin.

He pulled back and braced his hands on either side of her head. "I need to hear it."

"Lorcan..." He pressed a finger to her lips, his eyes flashing.

"I need to hear it from you, Reyna," he said softly. "I need to know you aren't bored or confused or maybe just angry at my father. Do you hate me, Reyna Darragh?"

Her breath caught as she stared up at him. Those churning eyes, that hair that looked like the darkest part of the night. The way he gazed at her at times, as if he could see the truth of her, the best and worst parts all at once. He was as steady as a rock on a wave-tossed sea, and the strength of him could put most fae to shame.

Yes, he had betrayed her. It had been a terrible thing for him to do. But Reyna had done many terrible things, too, and Lorcan had forgiven every one. When she looked into his eyes, she did not see only darkness. She saw both shadow and light.

"I don't hate you, Lorcan Rothach," she whispered, pressing her lips to his.

He let out a victorious growl. Bracing himself on top of her body, he kissed her with an animalistic need, only for a sharp pain to rip through her gut. She whimpered, squeezing her eyes tight against the torment roiling through her.

His weight vanished in an instant, his voice full of concern. "What's wrong, Reyna? Did I hurt you?"

"It's my wound," she hissed through the pain in her stomach. "It hurts like hell."

"I'll go fetch the alchemist."

She heard him bustle out of the room and wished she could stop him. She felt as if she had torn her heart open wide, and now that she was lying bare before him, she never wanted to see him go. A moment later, he returned with Meredith, who was making a lot of agitated tsking noises.

She fussed with the bandage, poking and prodding. At one point, she spread another dose of the herbal ointment across the wound, and a million tiny stars danced in Reyna's eyes from the sting of it. After applying a clean bandage and making Reyna drink another dose of nettle and rowan draught, Meredith took a step back and looked at the both of them very sternly.

"Might I ask what caused this?" she asked, her eyes aimed very pointedly in Lorcan's direction.

Lorcan pressed his lips together. Reyna coughed. She knew she was blushing furiously.

"I see." Meredith tsked again, crossing her arms over her chest. "Reyna, would you say you're well enough to stand up and walk a circle around the room?"

Reyna pulled the covers up to her chin. This was mortifying. "Unlikely."

"Until you are, you'll be doing *nothing else*," Meredith said firmly. "Particularly *vigorous activities*."

With a heavy sigh, the alchemist twisted on her heels and stormed out of the room. Reyna stayed hidden beneath the covers. Partly because she was pretty exhausted after all that. Meredith had given her another dose of her infamous draught, and it had the tendency of making the world slow down almost instantly.

Lorcan grabbed a chair and dropped it on the opposite side of the room, as far away from Reyna as he could get. He crossed his arms, smiled, and tipped back.

She narrowed her eyes. "Why do you look so smug?"

"I'm too much for you to handle."

"Oh, give me a break," she muttered.

"It's true." His smile widened into a full-on grin. "You got so hot and bothered that your wound popped open."

Her jaw dropped as a new wave of heat rushed into her cheeks. "You're delusional."

"Is that so? Then, prove it." He tapped a finger against his chin. "Oh wait. That's right. You can't. Alchemist's orders."

"You're having way too much fun with this," Reyna said, rolling her eyes. "You get one little kiss, and you suddenly think you're the Dagda's gift to females."

"Not females," he said. "*Female*. This gift is purely singular."

Her heart began to thump again, pulsing in time with the ache in her core. She wanted him fiercely, even while her wound throbbed with pain. He'd tried to lighten the mood after the embarrassment with Meredith. It had worked, but it hadn't made her forget how they had been moments away from screaming each other's names.

Her eyes began to drift shut as the healing potion took hold. She fought against it. There was still so much unsaid, so much more she needed to know. About *everything*. His life. His feelings. The world he'd been forced to inhabit all these years.

"Rest, Reyna," he said softly. "We'll have our chance again. That I can promise you."

# 23

## LORCAN

Duff burst into the room, knocking the door clean off its hinges. It fell with a heavy thunk, but the wood fae scarcely even noticed. Lorcan was on his feet at once. He'd nodded off in the chair, having drifted off while watching Reyna sleep. She'd grown stronger over the past three days, so much so that Meredith had said Reyna would be ready to leave on the morrow.

"We've just had a scout rush in, wounded from an arrow in the knee." Duff growled. "Damn wood king. He's on his way. He'll be here within the hour."

"Within the hour?" Lorcan's heart thundered in his ears. "Are you certain?"

So much for the wood king following the trail left behind by Nollaig. The diversion hadn't worked.

"Aye. Meredith's getting a boat ready for you. If you leave now, the army won't catch sight of you."

"And if I stay and fight?"

Duff's lips went white. "Then all of us will die."

"Allies never leave each other behind." Reyna's clear voice cut through the room. The two warriors turned to find her standing tall at the edge of her bed, shoulders thrown back in stubborn ferocity. Lorcan's heart swelled. It was the strongest he'd seen her in days.

"You can't stay," Duff argued. "The king doesn't know you're here. When he arrives, he'll take a look around, find nothing, and leave. Same as every other time he's tried to catch us housing the enemy."

"Nollaig tried to draw him away," Reyna said, putting voice to Lorcan's thoughts. "If the king is coming here, it's because he knows where we are."

Duff let out a curse, one that Lorcan felt deep within his bones. And yet, he felt strangely ready for whatever might be coming for them. Reyna had brought him alive again, in a way that he had not been in a very long time. He could not remember the last time he'd had hope in his heart.

"But his army is marching this way," Duff said, face draining. "We're just a village. A strong one, but just a village all the same. We cannot fight against the numbers of the wood king."

"*All* of his army?" Reyna asked.

Duff shook his head. "The scout doesn't believe so." At the look of confusion on Reyna's face, he explained. "We don't know the full extent of the wood king's army. He's been very secretive about it for years. We know he has some air fae companies now as well, but our scout did not see any banners with the golden crown sigil waving in the wind."

"Those would be Lord Bowen's warriors," Lorcan said grimly. "The ones Sloane Selkirk sent, and the Grand Alderman never called back."

"The Grand Alderman?" Duff asked. "You mean, the foreigner?"

Lorcan nodded.

"He would never get those troops back now, even if he called them. The wood king will not be concerned with a pesky nobody playing at thrones."

"That's a good description of him, really," Reyna said with a strained smile. "That said, I think right now I'd rather Aengus be in control of—"

"Wait," Lorcan suddenly said. "Does that mean Aengus is *still* in control of the throne?"

Duff nodded. "As far as we know."

Lorcan let out an irritated huff. All this time, Lorcan had thought his father had Thane, so he'd thought little of the prince's disappearance. But now that he knew the truth, there was one question that begged for an answer. Where the hell was the High King of the Air Court?

*Where is Thane?*

Reyna's soft touch, a gentle hand on his arm, pulled him away from his dark thoughts. "We'll find him, Lorcan. I don't know how, but we will."

"If you're going to be finding anyone, we're going to have to survive this attack first. Any bright ideas?" Duff asked.

The three of them stood quietly in the room. The sound of their silence was a death knell to come. There would be no answer to this, Lorcan knew. A tiny village could never win against the brute force of an entire army. One well trained, one that no doubt had a plan. They might be able to hold their own, for a short time, but in the end, Oxgrove would fall. Brutally so.

Lorcan had tried to cut off an army once. He'd tried to stop the Battle for the Shard from ever happening by making it impossible for the air fae to cross the border. He'd failed then, too, but that…that had been because his mark had stopped him.

"Wait. I have an idea," he said, hope sparking in his gut. He turned to Duff and grinned. "How does the wood king feel about fire?"

The conflagration rose high into the tormented sky. Big puffs of smoke met the clouds, filling the air with ash. As Lorcan stared up at it, he could not help but be reminded of the Ruin. The black specks that rained down around them all were a chilling reminder of that terrible magic that spread throughout the lands like a plague.

The villagers stood clustered on the hill around him. Each wore a similar expression. Horror swirled with regret. Several sobbed as the trees cracked and tumbled. They were burning down their own lands, all in the hope that they might survive.

Lorcan hoped it was enough.

"That's it then," Meredith said with a sniffle, where she stood by Reyna's side. "The fire is unstoppable now. He has no hope of getting past that."

Duff grunted in agreement. "And it will spread even further over the course of the night. He'll get pushed back. That gives us time enough to leave this place and make certain no one gets left behind."

Lorcan's heart ached. "I am sorry, Duff. I've brought destruction to your village."

"We brought it on our own damn selves, shadow fae," Meredith replied crisply. "We've been rebelling against the crown for years. It was only a matter of time before they finally came for us."

"Where will you go?" Reyna asked as she absentmindedly ran her fingers along her familiar's feathers. "Do you have somewhere? I'm certain we can find a place for you in the shadow lands—"

Meredith cut her off with a chuckle. "I appreciate the offer, princess, but we'd be no better off there than here." She cut her eyes toward Lorcan. "Nothing to do with either of you, you understand. It's that king of yours."

"Ah." Reyna's voice filled with ice. "We certainly do understand."

Meredith rose her brows. "He might be mighty, but so are you." The wood fae leaned forward and hissed, "Resist."

Reyna blinked at the wood fae for a moment, but then she laughed. "You don't have to tell me twice. Besides, I wouldn't call him mighty. Unless your idea of mighty is a toad."

Lorcan chuckled, but Meredith gave them both an odd look. "I heard he was a great monstrous thing, as tall as a bear with horns growing out of his head. Isn't that why everyone followed him, even though he had no true claim to the throne?"

Reyna laughed. "Bolg? Monstrous? Well, he is monstrous, but not in the way you think. He's smaller than you and he has nothing resembling horns. That's a rumor based on nothing more than lies. A rumor he most likely started himself."

The wood fae began moving away from the fire, rushing to their cottages to collect their belongings for the journey ahead. They would likely have to flee to the Air Court. With all of Aengus's warriors wrapped up in the Wood Court, the villagers might be lucky enough to cross the Mistmoor Mountains without being spotted. There were many villages and hamlets that far south, many with friendly faces. Would they welcome wood fae? Lorcan could only hope so.

"Meredith, wait," he said, just as she turned to go. "If you struggle to find a home, there is an abandoned village not too far north of the border, on the western coast of the realm. There's enough room there for two hundred fae. There are fields to grow crops. Wheat is popular there. It's called Comharra, and it could use some honorable fae to bring it alive again."

Meredith smiled. "Well, then to Comharra we'll go."

An arrow slammed into Meredith's forehead. Her clear green eyes widened into shock, and her lips parted as a strange, gurgling hiss rose from her throat. And then she crumpled to the ground.

Reyna screamed.

Lorcan could only stare at Meredith's unseeing eyes as shock nailed his feet into place. A moment before, Meredith had been laughing. She'd spoken of the journey, of choosing Comharra.

And now she was dead.

"Lorcan!" Reyna shouted. "Lorcan, please, come on!"

The world snapped back before him. The entire village was screaming and racing across the hills. A loud *smack* sounded in the air, and a sharp sting exploded in his cheek. He looked down to spy Reyna's outstretched hand and a furious determination set in her furrowed brows.

"The wood fae are attacking, and I swear to the Dagda, if I have to jump in front of another arrow to save you…"

"You slapped me."

She threw up her hands. "Of course I did."

"You know, there are better ways to snap someone out of shock."

"You two." Duff launched toward them as he shoved a long, willow arrow into his bow. "Take the boat and get the hell out of here."

Lorcan pressed his lips together. "I thought we made it clear that we don't leave allies behind."

"Bah," Duff growled. "Only a dozen of these arseholes made it through the wall of fire. If you want to help, make sure some of them see you. That'll split 'em up. You take on some. We take on some. And then we win."

Reyna frowned. "What if they don't follow us?"

"Oh, they will," Duff said grimly. "The wood king will want to get his bloody hands on you. In fact, he's likely salivating about it."

Lorcan saw Reyna visibly shudder.

With a nod, Lorcan said a goodbye to Duff and raced across the field. Reyna stayed in sync with him every step of the way with Wingallock soaring by her side. Every now and then, Reyna would wince when her foot hit the ground a bit too hard. It was a reminder that she'd been close to death only a few short days ago by making an unfortunate acquaintance with an arrow. He would have to make certain it didn't happen again. He didn't think she could survive a second wound like that.

Their feet hit the sand just as anguished cries filled the smoky air. Lorcan risked a glance over his shoulder. Three of the archers had followed them, striking down a villager who had placed himself between Lorcan and the attackers. He roiled on the ground, an arrow sticking out of his thigh.

Lorcan cursed and threw himself forward, hating that there was nothing he could do to help.

The archers galloped after them on glistening white steeds. They were growing closer. Within moments, they would be within striking distance of the arrows, and the boat was still too far away.

Reyna came to a sudden stop, skidding against the sand. She grasped his arm and glared up at him fiercely. "Do you trust me, Lorcan Rothach?"

His heart tripped over itself. Whatever she was about to say next, he knew he would hate it with every fiber of his being. "Of course I do, but—"

"You go that way, and don't let them see you." She pointed further down the shore. "I'll go this way. While I distract them, you sneak up from behind."

Lorcan's heart thundered. "*Are you out of your bloody mind?* You just got hit with a fucking arrow!"

"Because you didn't trust me! Because you didn't stay back!" She gripped the front of his tunic and yanked his forehead down to hers. "If I say I can do something, then trust me to do it. And if I need your help, I'll call for you. It's our only hope of getting out of here alive."

Lorcan ground his teeth. The last thing he wanted to do was let Reyna throw herself into the path of danger again. But as much as he hated to admit it, she was right. He hadn't trusted her before. He'd wanted to sweep in and be her hero. He'd ignored her, thinking she was too stubborn to know how to keep herself safe.

All he'd done was get her hurt. She had almost died because he hadn't listened to her.

With a tormented sigh, he took a step away from her, feeling his soul come apart at the seams. "Don't make me regret this, Reyna."

The smile she gave him was blinding.

With dread in his heart, he ducked low and raced down the shore with his shadows pulsing around him. They hid him from view of anyone who might turn his way. When he'd gone several meters, he paused and craned his head over the hill, spotting the wood fae instantly. But Reyna was what drew his eyes the most.

She stood with her feet planted in the sand, her familiar fluttering in the wind by her side. One hand held a rock, and the other was curled into talons like her bird. The three wood fae charged toward her. One eyed her warily while the others aimed their arrows. Her back faced him, but he did not need to see her face to imagine her devilish smile.

His stomach twisted uneasily. He hated this. Every single moment of this. But he had made a promise to trust her. He had to believe that she could do this.

Keeping low to the grass, he inched his way behind the wood fae, flinching when he heard the unmistakable *snick* of arrows being loosed.

He twisted toward Reyna. She dodged them easily, knocking one aside with her rock as if it were nothing more than a pesky fly. Wingallock grabbed another and dropped it into her waiting palm. With a smile, she bounced it in her hand. And then she caught it mid-air, flipped the end in the direction of the wood fae, and let it fly like a spear.

It *thunked* into the center of one of the wood fae's heads, landing right between his eyes. He tumbled from the horse, his eyes vacant, his body still.

Lorcan shook his head and resumed his crouch-walk to the rear of the trio that was now merely two. While he lurked, shadows pulsing along his skin, Reyna and Wingallock managed to take out another, using the same trick they'd used on the first.

But she had played her hand—twice—and the third had clearly caught onto her plan. Instead of lobbing more arrows —and potential weapons—in her direction, he leapt off his horse and charged.

Reyna's body tensed. She jogged back, eyes wide. With a frustrated grunt, she pulled her arm back and launched the rock at the wood fae's head. She missed. His heart dropped into his gut. She didn't have her sword. She'd lost it in the forest when she'd been hit.

"Lorcan!" she shouted.

That was all he needed to hear to run. He pushed up from the grass and shook off his shadows, throwing himself forward at an impossible speed. His eyes zeroed in on Reyna. Determination and fear swirled like snakes in his gut.

The wood fae stopped and twisted his head over his shoulder, hearing Lorcan coming. Reyna darted out of the way and leapt into the sea. The still waters rushed over her head, hiding her from view, but Wingallock darted back and forth over the sea where she'd jumped in.

Lorcan stalked toward the wood fae, sizing him up, just as his opponent did the same. He was muscular like the rest, though several inches shorter than Lorcan. He wore boiled leather stamped with the sigil of the Wood Court—two crossed arrows with vines binding them in the center. His green-grey hair squatted in a bun on the top of his head, highlighting the dagger-like points of his ears.

His weaponry was impressive. In addition to the yew arrows tipped in iron, and a bow carved from an alder tree, he had a bastard sword crafted from Tamaris steel. The steel of the forgotten fire fae. Tamaris steel blades were stronger than any other weapons found within Tir Na Nog. Except for swords spun from iron.

Unfortunately for the wood fae, Lorcan wielded Tamaris, too. And he was a much better swordsman.

Lorcan threw himself toward the wood fae with a roar, his blade outstretched. Eyes wide, the wood fae reached behind his back for a poisonous arrow to slam into Lorcan's gut. But while he was fast, Lorcan was faster. He slashed his blade at the wood fae's hand, cutting the fingers clean off. The wood fae screamed in agony, grasping the bloody stump to his chest.

Lorcan thrust his blade into his enemy's chest, and the wood fae died with terror in his eyes.

Reyna pushed out of the water, her skin soaked with the salt of the sea. He drank in the sight of her, entranced by the tunic clinging to her shapely breasts and by the bloodlust singing in his veins.

"We should go," she said, snapping him out of his trance. "More are coming."

He noticed she pressed a hand lightly against her wound. "Have you been hurt? Did that reopen your wound?"

"I'm fine," she said, wincing slightly. "It just aches a little. Dodging arrows is more difficult than you'd think."

"I think it's impossible. *You're* impossible, and yet here you are." He strode toward her and scooped her up into his arms.

"Wait, what are you doing?" She glared up at him. "I said my wound aches, not that my legs have suddenly stopped working. I can walk to the boat on my own, thank you very much."

"I let you dodge arrows, and now you're bloody well going to let me carry you to the boat," he said, stomping forward. "And if you argue with me about it, I'll bend you over my knee and spank your bloody stubbornness right out of you."

Pink dotted her cheeks. A moment later, she cleared her throat. "Promise?"

Every single part of him went rock hard. "Don't tempt me, Reyna."

"Maybe I want to tempt you."

He jumped into the boat and deposited her onto one of the wooden benches, grabbing an oar just as several more wood fae thundered onto the beach. He shoved the oar into the sand, pushing them into the waters.

The wood fae tried to launch a few arrows their way, but it was too late. The boat had already made it out of their striking distance, and they would never dare step a toe into the sea. Lorcan continued to row, watching the shoreline disappear from view, and with it, the ones they'd left behind to fight the enemy alone.

It felt wrong to leave them like this, and yet, Duff had seemed as though he had everything under control. One day, Lorcan hoped he could journey once again to his old home in the grasslands and pay Comharra a visit. Perhaps the fae of Oxgrove would have settled in, living happily off the grain in the fields, bringing the old bustling market back to life.

It felt like a dream of a different life, one for a different Lorcan. A Lorcan who had not stumbled into the path of the Fomorians that night so long ago. One who had not ended up a prince of shadows.

"They'll be okay, you know," Reyna said from behind him. "There were only a handful of archers, and we drew a lot of them away from the village. Duff's a good fighter. So are the others. They'll win quickly and escape to the border. I'm certain of it."

"Then, why do I feel as though we've lost something?"

Reyna wrapped her arms around his waist and took one hand in hers. "Because for a few days Oxgrove felt safe, like somewhere we could stay forever. It felt like home, like your village back in the grasslands. The kind of home one could settle into and spend many long and happy years. And I don't think you've been somewhere that feels like home for a very long time."

Shuddering, he squeezed her hand. "Well, there you're wrong, Reyna Darragh. Because you feel more like home than any place I've ever known."

# 24

## MARIEL

The lords and ladies were arriving to court. It had not taken as much convincing as Aengus had thought. A few carefully worded letters had done the trick. All they'd had to do was convince just one, and then the others quickly fell in line. Over the past week, four royal families had come to Tairngire, bringing with them thousands of fighters. If the Ice Court attacked, it might just be enough.

A mere day after the arrival of Lord Finnbar and his family, the final courtiers who had made the trek to Tairngire, Aengus decided to celebrate his impending victory against his enemies. Lord Finnbar had come the furthest, all the way from Tawold, located on the southeastern coast beyond the Blade's Pass. Their banners rippled in the Tairngire wind, embroidered with a scythe on a field of golden wheat. It was a familiar sight to Mariel's sore eyes.

She remembered those banners well from when she'd been nothing but a child. Lord Finnbar had been lord even then, and he'd always been kind to her.

That night, they called a feast to welcome the lords and ladies to the castle. Aengus ordered the servants to transform the Great Hall into a celebration fit for a king's coronation. The banners were freshly washed and then rehung along the walls, highlighting the glittering golden crown that was the sigil of the Air Court.

New tables had been built especially for this feast, the timber taken from the Witchlight Woods. Mariel had many a thought about that, but she kept them to herself. Now was not the time to argue, and it had already been done. Whoever had chopped them down would be dead soon enough. The trees of the Witchlight Woods did not take kindly to an axe.

Mariel sat at the head table, to the right of the Grand Alderman. Wearing the sizeable golden crown that had once sat on Sloane Selkirk's head, Aengus had clearly taken up the mantle of what he thought was his. He sat where the king should have sat, smiling broadly as he motioned for the servants to lay out the roasted pig before him.

Luckily for Aengus, it was not boar.

The rest of the tables seemed to have been divided into two camps. On the left side of the room sat the lords and ladies who Aengus already considered loyal to his cause. They had already been in Tairngire when he'd stolen the throne, and they had yet to scurry back to their manors and castles. Mariel thought they were not loyal so much as scared. He'd already executed some of their peers. If they spoke too broadly, he might just turn his murderous glint on them, too.

The right side of the room held the new arrivals. In addition to Lord Finnbar and his wife, Lord Malcolm from The Plains, and his daughters, had answered the summons. Next to them sat Lord Neil and Lady Regan from the great city of Faladrast and old friends of poor Lady Epona. Finally, at the very end was Lady Keely from further south, down where the villages were poor and scarce and had been ravaged by war. Mariel wondered if Aengus saw these courtiers as enemies or as friends.

She knew how she saw them.

When she'd asked Aengus why he'd decided to separate them so thoroughly, he had mumbled something about wanting to be able to tell who was who. Mariel thought it odd. Did he not know the names of his own lords? Likely not.

With a deep breath, she pushed back her chair and stood. "Welcome, everyone. Thank you to the lords and ladies who have journeyed from all around the realm to be with us this day. Many of you have not been seen in court for years. Aengus and I feel very grateful you have come now. Don't we, Grand Alderman?"

She smiled as Aengus shifted uncomfortably on his seat, clearly taken off guard. Aengus was the kind of cunning male who was always searching for a way to best his opponent, whether or not they knew he was his opponent at all. He had never sparred with Mariel though.

Once, she had breathed and bled courtly life.

Smiling, she spread her hands wide, and her fingers glistened from the remnants of her silver dye. Lord Neil and Lady Regan latched their eyes on her hands, their faces impassive. But when Mariel turned away, she could see them whispering fiercely out of the corner of her eye.

"As is often customary, we have some bards here to regale you with some wonderful lore, but I thought I'd start the night off with a story myself." She held back a smile when Lord Neil and Lady Regan looked keenly interested. She'd caught their attention. Now she merely needed to hold their throats and force their eyeballs to see.

"This is quite out of the ordinary," Aengus murmured, but he did nothing more than that to stop her. He couldn't, or he would make himself look bad. Poor Princess Eislyn, stuck inside a court without her sister or her betrothed. A sweet little thing she was, or so the tales suggested. Mariel knew she did not perform that part of Eislyn well.

Mariel cleared her throat. "Once, there was a golden crown. It was small and dingy. Faded and dull. It had been cast away into a corner of the castle, and no one had thought of it for years." She kept her voice steady, her eyes roaming the hall. Her gaze landed firmly on Lady Keely, a slight yet strong noble with gold-and-silver hair who had seen far more death than most. The villages and hamlets down south had not fared well in the war.

Mariel continued. "The crown belonged to the previous king, so it needed to be tossed away. Meanwhile, the new king and queen fashioned glorious new crowns that sparkled in the light. These crowns were a sight to behold, and the realm spoke of them in awe, so much so that the banners were remade and embroidered with this new vision of the crown.

"Until, one day, a child stumbled upon that old crown. She liked it very much, but she thought it needed some sprucing up, so as to save it from being tossed away again." Mariel smiled as Lord Malcom, an old male from The Plains, leaned forward, his golden eyebrows pinched together.

" So, the child dipped the crown in silver dye and proudly wore it atop her golden head. Unfortunately, the king and queen were not fond of that silver crown, so they took it from the child and threw it out of their window, straight into the middle of a terrible storm. The child cried, of course. She'd loved that crown and vowed to find it the next morning. Only when she did find it, it was no longer silver but golden once again. The rain had washed the dye away and had polished it clean. Now, it gleamed brighter than every other crown in the kingdom. And so it sat on the queen's head forevermore."

Mariel sat, heart hammering.

Aengus awkwardly cleared his throat. "That was, uh, quite the tale, though I've never heard anyone get quite so emotional about a bloody crown!"

A few of the lords laughed. The ones who sat on the left.

But all the rest were staring right at Mariel. They'd heard her story true. She'd done her part. Now, she just needed to wait for the rest.

It came only an hour into the feast. The bard had been playing a jolly old song, but scarcely anyone had been dancing. When the song ended, Lord Neil from Faladrast stood and motioned for the lad. The lord murmured something into his ear, and the bard rushed back to the center of the hall.

"Our good lord here has requested I play The Heart of Tairngire. A bloody good song." The bard dove toward his harp, and the music began in earnest. Smiling, Mariel stood and joined the bard in the middle of the hall. She picked up her silver skirts and danced, letting the music fill the empty parts of her heart. She whirled this way and that, feet stomping, arms flailing like windmills.

The music filled the hall, and soon, more fae had joined her in the dance. It had been years since she had heard the song, and yet she danced it as if she had only danced it yesterday. Bodies whirled through the hall. Laughter filled the air. And Mariel's hardened heart felt full enough to burst.

Lord Neil suddenly appeared before her, grabbed her hand, and spun her round and round. As their bodies pressed together, he leaned forward with rowan berry wine on his breath and whispered the one word she longed to hear. "Dalais."

She gasped as the blood filled her face. And then he was gone again, a new lord dancing before her. Lord Malcom leaned in and whispered the same. Lady Regan was next, followed soon by Lord Finnbar and then Lady Keely. Every single one who Aengus had called to court whispered her that word.

Her name.

Her legacy.

*Her* court.

When the song ended, Mariel was left breathless. She tiptoed back over to the head table and perched on her chair, her heart a drumbeat in her ears. Aengus leaned over and grinned. "I daresay you are making yourself very useful indeed. You got them all dancing, and they look thrilled to be here. I'll get this entire court on my side even if it kills me."

He hadn't seen them whispering amongst themselves. She'd gotten away with it all.

Mariel smiled.

# 25

## EISLYN

She stared up at the turquoise sky, her head spinning as the boat tipped beneath her bruised and aching body. Vreis stood over her, a hand outstretched, a grin on his devilish face. With a growl, she swatted his hand aside.

"I am capable of standing up by myself, thank you very much," she snapped.

The truth was, she *could* stand up, but she wished she could lie on the wooden deck for the rest of her days. A week into training with Vreis, and Eislyn had never been more tired in her life. Was this what Reyna had felt like during her Shieldmaiden training? It was a wonder she had never given it up.

Eislyn was not improving in the least, of course. At times, she had a flicker of hope. It would seem that she might actually get the better of Vreis, and then he would quickly prove that she had learned nothing. And she would end up in yet another heap on the deck to her extreme embarrassment.

Vreis just grinned as she rose unsteadily to her feet, brushing off her dirty hoarfrost trousers. If only her father could see her now, he would be mortified. Another daughter, lost to the wild ways of swordplay. Not that she had even touched a sword since they began. They'd only been battling with wooden mop handles.

"That was better," Vreis said.

"Better?" She glared. "Honestly Vreis, sometimes I truly do think you must be a shadow fae for how many lies spill from that mouth of yours."

"Not a lie," he replied easily, draping his arm across the ship's railing. The breeze ruffled the hair that framed his chiseled face. "It's true. You were on your feet a full minute longer than the last time."

She narrowed her eyes. "You're mocking me."

"I'm not mocking you."

"You are."

"It's merely good-natured ribbing, Eislyn." He still smiled at her, his mismatched eyes twinkling.

"See." She lifted the mop handle and pointed the end at his chest. "That's mocking."

"No. Mocking is something I only do to fae I don't like. This is..." He cleared his throat and glanced away. "Shall we try again?"

Eislyn reached up and felt her cheeks. They were impossibly warm. The sun had climbed high in the sky while they'd been training on the deck, and even this far north, Eislyn could feel the heat of it on her skin. The hours had flown by. They always did when she trained with Vreis. It must have been the physical exertion. It made her forget the rest of the world. Her troubles. The darkness. Her fear.

She felt alive.

But now that they had stopped, reality came creeping in like the mists. She'd once felt alive like this before. When Thane had taken her into Tairngire. They had drank and they had danced. It had been a whirlwind of innocent pleasure. At the time, she had been scared of everything. She had not known how easy she'd had it then.

Before she'd been abducted by Sloane. Before Aengus had taken the throne. And before Thane had vanished into nowhere.

She sighed. "I think that will be all for today, Vreis."

His smile vanished. "You're thinking of him again. Our king."

"I'm so worried about him." With a frustrated sigh, she dropped the mop to the floor and pressed herself up against the railing to stare out at the churning waves. The sea was a bright, clear blue today, a match to the crystalline sky. The color of home.

"Thane is strong."

Eislyn pushed off the railing, her hands fisted. "But where is he, Vreis? Despite what you think, he wouldn't have just left. Something must have happened to him. He got attacked, taken, or even…" *Killed.* She closed her eyes.

"If he didn't leave, then Lorcan and Reyna will find him," Vreis insisted. "He might be trapped somewhere. He isn't dead. He can't be."

Eislyn glanced up at her warrior, searching his eyes. She saw now what he refused to say aloud. He was just as scared as she was. He refused to consider the idea that Thane might be dead because it was too painful for him to think. So, he had to believe that Thane was out there somewhere, hidden in the grasslands, waiting to be found. Or even with the sea fae.

"Oy! Princess!" A small, bright-eyed fae named Maeli rushed across the deck, the wood creaking beneath his thick leather boots. His golden hair was tied up into a tight bun on the top of his head, bouncing as he bustled toward her. "You must get below decks immediately."

"What?" Alarmed, she glanced at Vreis. "Why? What's wrong?"

"There's another ship approaching, passing close enough to see you on board," he said quickly. "It looks like a merchant ship, but merchants can be known for being cut-throat. Anything for a bit of money. We're taking down our Sea Court sigil just in case."

Vreis narrowed his eyes. "This is a merchant ship. *You* are merchants."

Maeli flicked up his eyes, smiling devilishly. "Yes, so you see, we understand how merchants think. They will size us up, hoping to find something amiss."

Eislyn wrung her hands. "Can we not adjust course? Sail far out of their line of sight?"

"We could," Maeli admitted. "But they would find that suspect. No doubt word is out now. Aengus will be looking for you. If the passing ship thinks we're hiding you..."

"But if I'm nowhere to be seen, might they not realize I am just below decks? How has this not been a problem until now?" She was almost shouting her words, but she realized she was not truly angry at Maeli. Nor should she be. Her anger should be directed at someone far more deserving. The Grand Alderman of the Air Court.

"We have passed no other ships thus far, Princess," Maeli said with a small bow. "Now, please. They will be upon us soon."

"Yes, alright. I'm sorry." Heart hammering, she twisted on her heels and rushed toward the stairwell. Vreis followed quickly behind, after murmuring a few words to the fae. Down and down they went, hurrying into the hold beneath the cabins. It was a dark and dreary place and crammed with barrels, wooden boxes, and dust. A rat scurried by her feet, and she bit back a scream.

The boat creaked as it slowed to a stop. Eislyn could feel the shudder, even if she could not see it for herself.

"What are they doing?" she whispered to Vreis.

"The other ship likely asked them to stop," he murmured. "They'll have agreed to avoid arising suspicion."

"But why would a merchant ship ask another to stop?" she hissed.

He frowned. "They wouldn't."

"What are you saying? It's one of Aengus's ships?"

"Unlikely. The ship was seen approaching from the north. It could be one of your father's few ships."

"Well, if it's one of my father's ships, then why in the name of the Dagda am I hiding in the dust?" She turned toward the ladder, but Vreis caught her hand. His palm was warm and rough and strong.

"I said it was unlikely one of Aengus's. Not that it was impossible. The Air Court could have been keeping a few ships in the northern waters all this time, waiting for the precise moment they would be needed." His smile was grim. "I could see Imogen using this tactic. She might have believed the alliance with the Ice Court would turn sour. Or, more likely, the former High King himself. He never wanted an alliance. He yearned for an empire instead."

Eislyn's heart pounded. "And Aengus might have known of these hidden ships. He could have sent a bird ahead, alerting them of my escape."

"Perhaps."

"So, then they will search this ship for me," she hissed, her heart pounding so hard she could scarcely stand the overwhelming beat of it. "We're not safe, not down here."

Vreis nodded, glancing around. "We'll need to hide you in the hatch."

The warrior stepped aside and tugged open a compartment hidden in the floor. Eislyn had not even known it was there. The door had been carefully obscured by the floorboards, so that a seam could not even be seen.

"This ship is a smuggler's ship," she announced. It was

clear as day now. She should have seen it before. The ragtag crew. Their wild and reckless nights. Their knowledge of how best to avoid being spotted by other ships. They had done this before. She could not help but wonder who else they had stolen across the Mag Mell Sea.

Vreis nodded. "They carry as much as they can across kingdom lines. Some lords are willing to pay a pretty airgead for certain things that cannot be obtained inside their own court."

"And they were in Tairngire because they were dropping off smuggled goods. Weren't they, Vreis?"

He shrugged. "Unless the ice fae alliance doesn't fall through, the Air Court doesn't have a trade route with the Empire of Fomor or with any other kingdom within Tir Na Nog. Smugglers are inevitable."

"They're criminals," she hissed, heart hammering. "They could sell me to the highest bidder."

"They won't." He motioned toward the open hatch. "Now climb inside before you get found out. They're willing to smuggle you. I doubt they're willing to fight for you."

With a frustrated harrumph, Eislyn climbed into the hatch and settled onto the rough wooden floor. There was nothing inside but darkness and empty shelves. They had likely cleared out their coffers at the Air Court. Eislyn did not know how to feel about being stolen across the seas by smugglers. She'd heard the tales of them. They often killed for their bounties. Coin was far more important to them than life.

But she supposed she didn't have much of a choice now. She was on the ship, and the only way off would be jumping the plank.

Vreis shut the lid of the hatch, and the tiny room plunged into a darkness so pure that Eislyn could not even see her own hand as she wiggled it in front of her face. A familiar fear clawed up her throat and tightened sharp fingernails on her heart. Eislyn did not like the darkness. It was like an unseen rope wrapped too tightly around her neck. Dark things lurked in the shadows. They always had.

Her breathing became shallow as she struggled to retain control of her panic. It would be fine. There was nothing to worry about. She was only down in a hatch on a smuggler's ship. Vreis was on the other side of that door...the door she couldn't see.

What if he left her down here? What if she never got out?

A low scream of panic built in her throat, desperate to shoot out for all the ship to hear. The darkness pushed closer. It plucked at her skin. It shivered down her spine. She swore she could feel rough fingers slither up her arms and then rest dangerously in the center of her chest, at her hammering heart.

Suddenly, Vreis let out a muffled curse, lifted the lid, and dropped down into the hatch beside her. Light momentarily speared the small space, and Eislyn gasped at the illuminated emptiness. There had been nothing there. It had all been in her mind. The darkness had not been ready to kill her. She'd only imagined it.

Again.

"What are you doing?" Eislyn gasped.

"I recognized their voices. Air Court warriors. They'll know who I am and that I disappeared along with you."

Her heartbeat thrummed in her neck. "They're from the *Air Court?*"

He nodded. Or at least she thought he nodded. She couldn't see his face. "When they realize the ship is full of smugglers, they'll likely let them go. Rumor has it that Aengus was once part of a smuggler's ring."

"That would explain where he came from," she said quietly, hoping her voice did not give away the panic that had almost made her scream bloody murder a second ago.

"Are you all right, princess?" Vreis asked.

She sighed. She should have known he wouldn't miss a thing. He never did. "I..."

How did she explain it to him? Regardless of how kind he had been to her, he wouldn't understand. No one did. No one except for Reyna. Even her own father had looked at her as though she were a strange animal he couldn't quite tame. It was why he'd allowed her to spend so many hours holed up in the library out of his way.

She'd never even told Thane about the depths of her torment.

"Eislyn, I hope you know you can trust me with anything," he said gently. "If you're afraid, I won't judge you."

"It's more than being afraid," she said in a rush of words, plowing forward before she lost the nerve. "I have...terrors, I guess you could call them. Nightmarish thoughts creep into my mind. Sometimes I see things or even hear things. Horrible things. None of it is ever real. I'm just...not quite right. I never have been. Not since I saw..." She ground her teeth together and blinked back the tears.

"Not since you saw your mother die?" His voice was so soft and so gentle that it soothed some of the raw pain away.

She nodded, and then realized he couldn't see her any better than she could see him. "It traumatized me. I didn't speak for years, and I barely remember my childhood. Reyna and Glencora were there when it happened, but the Ruin...it didn't get into their minds the way it did mine. Even when Reyna left court to become a Shieldmaiden, she wasn't the odd one of the family. It's always been me."

"I've always liked the odd ones," Vreis announced with a smile in his voice.

The corners of Eislyn's lips tipped up. "You don't want to run away from me then?"

"Never."

Her heart grew thrice as large.

Suddenly, heavy footsteps thudded down the ladder and continued across the wooden floor just above where Eislyn and Vreis hid inside the hatch. Fear clenched her heart, and she sucked in a breath, holding it inside of her so that she would not make a sound.

"We know this is a smuggler's ship," a deep voice growled. "Show us your hatch."

Eislyn clenched her fists, and tears burned her eyes. This was it. They would be found now, and she'd be taken straight back to Tairngire where she would face her death. It had been hopeless, trying to escape. Aengus was always going to find her.

But then a creak echoed through the quiet of the ship. Another door swinging open, hinges groaning. "See? There's the hatch. We don't have anything in it, I'm afraid, or I'd offer you some of the Sea Court's best wine."

"Hmph," the growly voice replied. "You see any other ships around here lately?"

"Not a one."

Eislyn clenched her hands, hopeful for once.

"And the Princess Eislyn. You hear anything about her whereabouts?"

A pause. "This is just a rumor, I'm sure, but perhaps there's a chance she sailed to the Sea Court. Thane Selkirk has family there. She might have hoped to take refuge with them."

"The Sea Court you say? Thanks for the tip."

The smuggler cleared his throat. "I would be careful about sailing there yourselves, of course. The Sea Court often looks harmless, but they have sharp teeth."

"So does the Air Court."

# 26

## REYNA

The energy at the castle was like lightning. When Lorcan and Reyna arrived well over a day after setting off by boat, every corner of the once-vacant city seemed alive with activity. Nollaig and the others had returned several days past, and they'd informed the king that the Wood Court was on the march.

Bolg Rothach declared war. He decided they must make their move at once. He was gathering the entire army, every last shadow fae who could fight, and he was sending them through the caves and into the wood fae lands.

Lorcan braced his hands on the strategy table, frowning down at the map while Segonax and Nollaig looked on.

"Well?" Segonax asked from where he stood beside Lorcan, decked out in full commander armor.

"You're right," Lorcan said. "This is a terrible idea. Findius is a stronghold. I'd say it's impenetrable, but it's clearly not. Regardless, it's far better to stay in here than to storm out into enemy territory."

Segonax sighed in visible relief. "That's what we've told

him, Your Highness, but he refuses to listen. We were hoping that if you brought our thoughts to him, that he might…"

Lorcan glanced up, his eyebrows winging upward. "Listen to his bastard son that he doesn't give a single damn about?"

"You're no longer a bastard, son," Segonax said evenly, pinching the bridge of his flat nose.

"Legitimized or not, I'm still an unwanted bastard in my father's eyes." Lorcan turned toward Nollaig, who had been strangely silent thus far. "He listens to you."

"Not on this, I'm afraid," the hooded fae said quietly, her voice hushed beneath the thick folds of her cloak.

Reyna watched, torn. On the one hand, she didn't want to see the wood king win this battle. On the other hand, she didn't want to see Bolg Rothach win either. He was a disease.

Her relief had known no bounds when Lorcan had told her Eislyn was free. Her sister would not die in these dark lands. She would not perish beneath a red sun. Eislyn was safe. Her father would call her home from the Air Court if he hadn't already. Most likely, she was sitting in her favorite chair in the Ice Court library, chatting about books with Albin.

She had yet to decide how she would handle Bolg Rothach and his lies. The more she thought about it, the more she felt inclined to say nothing about it, to let him continue to believe she was scared for her sister's life.

Let the trickster become the tricked.

Nollaig hadn't mentioned it either, so Reyna thought it best not to bring it up. The castle walls likely had ears. They usually did in fae courts.

"What about Tarrah?" Lorcan asked with increasing frustration. "He has no issue basing his every action on *her* words."

Segonax rolled his eyes. "Tarrah has told the king that she hasn't heard from her god about this blasted battle, so he's taken that to mean he should go ahead with it. It seems Unseelie has suddenly gone mute."

"If he ever spoke at all," Reyna muttered.

Every eye in the room turned her way.

"I'm just saying that he doesn't seem to be very *consistent* with his visions," she answered. "Sometimes, he's happy enough to pop in with some advice, but other times, like when people are getting shot with poisonous arrows, he's off doing another death god thing."

"Hmm," Segonax said.

Reyna noticed he did not argue.

"So, it seems that regardless of what we think, we must go through with this foolhardy plan. The gods have mercy on us all." Segonax looked up at the ceiling and sighed before vanishing out the door to round up more warriors.

Nollaig hesitated, shook her head, and then followed the commander. At long last, Reyna was finally alone in a room with Lorcan again, but the circumstances were not forgiving.

"I'm not thrilled by the idea of heading back into the wood fae lands just as we escaped it." Reyna glanced down at her clean trousers. It wouldn't be long before they were bloody again. "I'm even less thrilled about fighting against them for your father."

Lorcan let out a heavy sigh and dragged a hand down his face. "If I knew how to free us from our bonds, I would."

But the both of them were stuck. They were forced to go along with whatever plan Lorcan's father concocted. The shadow king might not have Thane and Eislyn held captive, but he didn't need them now. Reyna's vow bound her to his will, and Lorcan still had his mark. He'd been able to defy it a handful of times but not always. And she knew in her heart that he would never step into the light as long as she was stuck in the shadows. He would stay there until she found a way out.

Reyna sighed and glanced down at the map. "So, who do we want to win?"

Lorcan tucked a finger beneath her chin. "Us."

❧

It took two days for the entirety of the shadow fae army to march its way through the hidden tunnels beneath the border wall and out onto the fields that stretched beneath the shadow of Findius. This night, the city seemed to glow like a thousand fires burning. In expectation of a brutal and glorious victory, High King Bolg Rothach had left behind a handful of trusted servants to light the infamous fire pits where he would torture his captured enemies.

Reyna thought it odd a shadow king would be so fond of the flames. But it was merely a fleeting thought. There were far more important things on her mind.

Namely, survival.

The camp sprawled across the rolling hills at the base of the looming Findius wall built from pure black stone. The great fae sky glimmered with the light of a million stars scattered across the inky splendor. Ten thousand burlap tents had been erected almost seemingly at once, servants and warriors bustling around the camp like ants beneath the boot of the king. Every tent had been dyed grey, the better for blending in with the darkness. No torches were lit this night. The camp was bathed in shadows.

Reyna sat in the commander's tent without her familiar, having left Wingallock in the safety of the castle, tensely watching Segonax attempt to make sense of the king's plans. A single candle sat on a table holding the map of the realms.

"Have you seen anything in those damn visions of yours?" the commander grumbled at Tarrah, who merely stared hollow-eyed at the map of Tir Na Nog. She pointed at Findius, *inside* the very city itself rather than outside of the walls on either side.

"Unseelie has only shown me a battle there," she said softly, as if in awe of her god's powers.

*His very limited powers,* Reyna thought.

"You've said that!" Segonax wiped the map of the table. It tumbled to the floor of the tent, painted kingdoms stained with the dirt. "But that's not the battle that's happening now. What we need to know about is *this one*."

"Seg," said Nollaig quietly. "This isn't the poor girl's fault."

"She's the one who has bolstered our idiot king," he said, seething. "It is, in fact, partly her fault."

Reyna jerked up her head, and the entire tent fell silent. Her heart flickered, hope and curiosity battling for dominance.

*Did he just insult his king?*

"I didn't mean that," he said, running his fingers through his short-cropped dark hair. "I'm just on edge because of the impending battle. We all are."

"Bolg Rothach is our High King," Tarrah said before clearing her throat. "And he is the one who will lead us to victory. It doesn't matter what we think of him. All that matters is seeing this battle through, so that we can get to the *real* battle."

"Child." Segonax said, sighing. "This is a real battle, whether you have visions about it or not. There will be real blood. Real death. And all the shadows in the world cannot change the fact that we are currently camping in the realm of the enemy. I fear…" His jaw rippled, and he glanced away.

"You fear what, Seg?" Nollaig asked.

The silence was as heavy as a guillotine.

Segonax lifted his gaze, but it was not toward Nollaig, or Tarrah, or even Reyna. He stared right at Lorcan. "I fear

Unseelie has twisted our king's mind past repair. I fear he's finally gone mad."

A trail of terrible fire burned down Reyna's back. Ominous words. A mad fae in control of an entire kingdom, one who'd claimed a Seat of Power as his own.

Tarrah let out a tense laugh. Her face had gone deathly pale. "I told you. Unseelie does not twist minds. It's all a lie. Another god does that, one with even more power than you could ever comprehend."

"What god is that, child?" Segonax asked wearily.

She frowned. "I don't know his name, but I know where he lives. Inishfall, the island in the middle of the impassable sea."

"Did Unseelie show you this, too?" he asked.

"He did, but—"

"That island is a terrible place, even for a god. What's more, there is no route to get there anymore. Many have tried. Even if you manage to sail past the Fomorians, the sea swallows you whole."

Tarrah lifted her chin, and a spark flickered in her eyes for perhaps the first time Reyna had ever seen. "There is a route there. My mother took it."

Segonax chuckled, glancing at Nollaig with incredulous eyes. Lorcan hadn't said a word, but Reyna could read his face as easily as she could read the map that had been tossed onto the floor. Not a single one believed a word Tarrah said. But in truth, Reyna did.

*Parts of it must be true,* she thought. Tarrah surely believed every word she said, but like the king, her mind had become twisted by the god she thought she knew. If he was real, he'd been using her, much like the king had used Reyna and Lorcan.

A scream ripped through the camp. Reyna stiffened, suddenly alert. Footsteps thundered outside the tent, and then a handful of breathless warriors rushed through the linen flap.

The whites of their eyes were almost as large as their faces. Terror was spoken with every hitched breath.

Segonax took charge immediately. "Tell me the situation. Where is the army? And how many warriors has the wood king brought with him?"

"Not the wood king." The warrior's eyes slid toward Reyna, and fear clenched her gut. "It's something else. Ash. Ash that's turning fae into more ash. It's falling from the sky like snow."

Reyna's gasp ripped from her throat with so much force that she stumbled back. She pressed a hand to the table to hold herself upright, scarcely believing the warrior's words.

"No," she whispered. This couldn't be happening. Not again. She thought she'd outrun the Ruin. It had left her alone for months. Now, it was here. *Again*. At the most southern edge of the kingdom of the wood fae. In the very spot where she stood.

It was not a coincidence. It had followed her here, just as it had followed her to Tairngire, and then further south to Feurach Fortress. All this time, her sister had haunted the libraries, searching for a way to end the Ruin. She'd read page after page, desperate to understand what was happening and why.

Well, Reyna might not know the rest, but she did know one thing. The Ruin did have a purpose. And it was to end Reyna Darragh's life.

Lorcan's face suddenly appeared before her. His brows were pinched with worry. "Reyna, what do we do?"

She gazed into Lorcan's eyes, and then twisted to see Segonax looking to her with hope. "I don't know," she told him, turning back to Lorcan. "I don't know how to fight the Ruin. I never have. It's why my father wanted to make an alliance with another court. It's why Eislyn came with me to the Air Court, so she could do research in the libraries. Our family has searched for a way to fight it all these years. We never found a way, Lorcan. Now that it's here, it will kill us all."

Hope vanished, punching through the ground to join the molten iron in the caves below their feet.

"I won't accept that," Lorcan said firmly, shaking her arms. "You fought it once. At Lord Bowen's castle. You can fight it again."

"I didn't fight it. I fought Sloane Selkirk and a handful of his warriors."

It was true. She *hadn't* fought the Ruin then. Instead she'd just…let it crash down upon her and seep into her skin. Unlike every other fae she'd ever met, she hadn't died when the Ruin touched her. At the time, she'd been so concerned about Sloane Selkirk, and her sister, and finding a way to escape the castle alive.

She hadn't stopped to truly think about what had happened.

It was as though the Ruin had *tried* to kill her, just like it killed everyone else. But it had failed. Instead of killing her, it had given her a strength and a power she'd never felt before and hadn't since.

Reyna pulled a deep breath into her lungs, an idea sparking in her mind. "I might not be able to stop it, but there's something I can try."

Lorcan raised a wary eyebrow. "Why do I have the feeling I'm not going to like this?"

"I could stall the Ruin," she said quickly. "Distract it. Just long enough for everyone to get inside the tunnels. I don't think it could follow us underground. It's never attacked the ice glass caves in the north."

Reyna watched Lorcan's jaw ripple where he ground his teeth in distinct disagreement with everything she had just said. "You're doing it again. Being reckless."

"You're right. I am. And I'm going to *keep* doing it."

Reyna turned to Segonax. "Get all your captains together, and tell them to get all their warriors underground as quickly as possible. Tell them that if they see the Ruin, run. Now is not the time for heroics. The Ruin doesn't care about bravery. Understood?"

She thought the commander might argue with her. She was an ice fae, after all, and practically a prisoner. Just because she wasn't rotting in a cell didn't mean that she was a member of their court. But Segonax nodded and vanished through the tent's flap.

She glanced to her left. "Lorcan, you—"

"I'm not leaving your damn side, and don't even think about telling me to do something else."

Heat filled her cheeks. "All right." She turned to Tarrah. "I think it would be best if you went with Nollaig. She'll keep you safe."

Tarrah stared ahead, unseeing. "Why did I not see this?"

"Because Unseelie is the god of armpits," Nollaig growled. "Come on, Tarrah. Let's get you underground where it's safe."

Tarrah whirled away from Nollaig and disappeared through the tent's flap. Reyna frowned after her. She understood why she was so upset. She was quickly learning that the god she had dedicated her life to was not exactly what she thought he was. Reyna wished she could help her, but the Ruin would not wait.

"Nollaig," Reyna said as she strode toward the flap.

"Don't worry. I'll look after her."

They all pressed out into the night where the camp was descending into total chaos. Strong and steady warriors with brave hearts and honorable souls were screaming in fear as they rushed from an unseen monster. Some had already been hit by the Ruin. Their arms were smoking from the black specks that had touched them, their skin melting off and dusting onto the ground.

Overhead, the once-still sky now crackled and churned with bulbous clouds thick with grey. Lightning ripped through the camp, and Reyna fisted her hands.

"The Ruin," she whispered toward it.

When she had fought the Ruin amidst the snowstorm in Feurach Fortress, she had not known or understood what she was doing. She had been running on adrenaline and pure desperation, her heart crying out in fear for her sister. She had none of that desperation now. While she did not want thousands of fae to suffer and die needlessly, there was no love lost between Reyna and the Shadow Court.

In fact, it was a shame High King Bolg himself wasn't out here in the chaos.

"Reyna, what are you doing?" Lorcan asked as they passed another group of whimpering fae rushing toward the tunnels. His eyes kept flicking up to the churning sky. So far, no flecks of ash had rained down on them yet, but it was only a matter of time before the Ruin turned its wrath on her.

*She* was why it had come here, after all.

"You should go into the caves with everyone else," Reyna said, turning to where she heard the loudest screams. Wind whipped around her, tossing her long hair into a tornado around her throat.

"I would rather sacrifice myself to the Unseelie god himself than to leave you out here to face the Ruin alone," he said, his voice rough.

Reyna stopped suddenly, whirling to face him. Her heart clenched at the look of sheer desperation on his face. It matched the thudding of her own heart. "And I'd rather die than see you turned into a pile of ash!"

He just continued to glower at her as the harsh wind snatched at his hair.

"Look." She pointed toward the left, pleading at him with her eyes. "I've brought you to the other entrance to the caves." She tipped back her head to gaze up at the electric sky. "I don't know where the Ruin's gone, but it's coming back. I think it's searching for me. You shouldn't be here when it finds me."

"Too damn bad!" he shouted into the wind that now whipped around their bodies in a fury.

Her heart cracked in two as she stared into his anguished eyes. If he stayed out here, he would die, same as everyone else. Same as her mother. Same as hundreds and hundreds of ice fae. Same as all those warriors trapped inside of Feurach Fortress when it had come tumbling down beneath the weight of the burning ash.

"Lorcan." She reached out and cupped his face. "It will *destroy* you. Please. Go inside the tunnels."

Lightning crackled overhead, and the bulbous clouds split open. Darkness swirled down in a blizzard of death, large black flakes that sizzled and popped. The clouds stretched out for miles. There was no escaping it.

The Ruin had found her.

# 27

## TARRAH

It looked like the end of the world. Ash rained down from a scarlet sky, and the screams of dying fae seemed endless. Warriors with charred arms stumbled past, their eyes wild with fear and their mouths limp from the utter torment storming through their broken bodies.

Tarrah fell to her knees. She couldn't bear to run any longer. This was it. The end of everything. Even if some survived, the shadow fae army was decimated. Thousands had died. Her quest had been burned up with them all. It was over, and it had barely even begun.

"Unseelie," she whispered at the sky. "Why have you changed your mind? Why have you turned your back on me?"

"All right. Enough of this." Nollaig tightened her grip on Tarrah's arm and hauled her to her feet. She stood directly in front of her, and then slapped her hard right on the cheek. It stung, but it did little to push the pain away.

"He abandoned me," Tarrah whispered, her eyes burning from her unshed tears. She could not remember how it felt to cry.

"He sure did. And you want to know why? Because he's

not a kind and worthy god. He doesn't deserve your unwavering loyalty." Nollaig leaned in, her whisper full of ferocity. "And do you know what *you* don't deserve? You don't deserve to die because you trusted the wrong god."

Tarrah squeezed her eyes shut. Nollaig was trying to help her, and for that, Tarrah was grateful. But her words were like a dagger in the gut, pushed in and then twisted sharply. Tarrah had dedicated her entire existence to Unseelie. She did not know who she was if she was not his loyal servant, the special fae entrusted with his most important visions. She had led the shadow fae army in their return to Findius. She had gotten the king his Seat of Power. How had all that been a lie? How could she have been wrong?

The only thing in the world she had left was Teutas.

"I have to find Teutas," she whispered, grasping Nollaig's hands. "Please. We need to find him and get him to the safety of the caverns."

"If that's what's going to get you moving again, then that's fine with me." Nollaig nodded. "Teutas was assigned to the front line of the eastern side. We'll find him there."

They took off through the camp together. They passed so many ashen bones of former warriors, of former friends. It was impossible to tell how many had died. Most were nothing more than a pile of charred remains. Tarrah didn't even try to count the piles. She didn't need to. The barren, ashen landscape was enough to tell her that most of the army had been lost.

And some were still dying.

A new bolt of lightning ripped across the sky. Thick black clouds spit large flaking mists onto the tents spread out on the northeastern corner of the camp. Tarrah ran. That was where Teutas was. His tent was one of those shivering in the wind beneath the churning clouds spitting out snow-like ash.

But this was no snow, Tarrah knew, even if she had never seen a single fleck in her life. It was death.

"Tarrah, no!" Nollaig shouted from behind her. "We cannot go that way!"

"Teutas!" she screamed back, but her voice got snatched up in the wind and tossed away.

Nollaig charged after her and grasped at the loose sleeve beneath Tarrah's grey scales. The material got caught between her fingers, but then it ripped away. Tarrah kept rushing forward. She would not be stopped. A newfound strength solidified her bones. For the first time in a long while, her mind was clear.

She had to find Teutas.

"Tarrah, we will die if we go into the storm," Nollaig shouted again.

Tarrah didn't care. She raced ahead of Nollaig, reaching the cluster of northeastern tents just as another crack of angry lightning snapped through the sky. It lit up the night, drenching everything in white. She spotted Lorcan and Reyna in the center of it all. The Shieldmaiden gestured wildly as the Ruin drifted down on top of them.

She opened her mouth to shout their names, but her eyes were caught by movement at the edge of her vision. Several figures were stumbling through the camp. She twisted toward them, gasping at once. Teutas, eyes wide, cheeks blanched, was hobbling straight toward her. He was surrounded by several more warriors. Not a single one of them moved with the strength and dexterity she knew they had.

"Teutas?" she called out, taking a step toward him. But Nollaig grasped her shoulder and pulled her back. A black flake fell onto the ground just before her feet, and it sizzled, scorching the dirt.

"We need to go, child. We are far too close to the storm."

"But Teutas," Tarrah cried out, tears bursting from her

eyes. "He needs help. He's—"

"He's gone, Tarrah," Nollaig said softly. "He cannot be saved. Look at him. He's already been hit by it."

"NO!" Tarrah screamed, and then threw herself forward. Nollaig clamped down harder on her arms, dragging her back. Tarrah thrashed against the hooded fae, desperately trying to reach her lover's side. Her future lover's. The male Unseelie had shown to her. The one he'd promised would cherish her, fight for her, and give her his seed. Unseelie had given her visions of the two of them in love, forever entwined. They'd never even had a single kiss.

*The Ruin cannot take him from me!*

Suddenly, Teutas stumbled to a stop, catching sight of Tarrah. He gave her an odd smile, and then spread his hands wide. At once, his arms began to disintegrate. His grey scale armor turned to ash, drifting away on the harsh and bitter wind. Darkness spread across his body, reaching up to his chest like fingers of death. Slowly, every single part of him transformed. His eyes were last. The terror in them was the last thing Tarrah saw of Teutas Rains.

She fell to her knees, sobbing. Pain shook her body. Her heart felt cleaved in two. Nothing would ever be the same after this. They'd lost the army. They'd lost Teutas. They'd lost the war with the Wood Court before it had even begun. The shadow fae would never be a part of Tir Na Nog ever again. Tarrah knew this truth deep within her gut. It had all been a lie.

"Come, child," Nollaig said, gently wrapping her arms around Tarrah and lifting her from the ground. Tarrah's arms and legs dangled limply, her head lolling against Nollaig's chest. The hooded fae carried her away from the Ruin. Tarrah let her. She no longer had the strength to fight.

"It's all right," Nollaig murmured. "I've got you."

Unseelie had lied to her.

# 28

## REYNA

The Ruin whipped through the night with the ferocity of a dragon's fiery breath. The ash had already begun to rain down, big black flakes that sizzled when they hit the dirt. Across the camp, Teutas stumbled forward and shattered into the wind. Tarrah watched on, screaming and falling to her knees.

Reyna pressed her lips together as she glared at Lorcan. "Go with Tarrah and Nollaig. Or go into the caverns. I don't care which, just stay out of the path of the Ruin."

She knew he wouldn't listen. He was being just as stubborn as she was. All she could do was try to draw the Ruin to herself, away from Lorcan and the rest of the camp.

With one last deep breath, she wrapped her hand around her mother's ice glass ring, where it hung around her neck on a chain, and whispered to the sky, "Please help me, Dagda. Please don't let him die."

She rushed into the storm. Wind bashed her face, twisting her long, loose strands into knots. Gritting her teeth against the force of it, she continued to press on, putting distance between her and Lorcan. Ash tumbled down upon her. It fell onto her skin, dozens of black flakes at once. For a moment, she paused and stared down at her arms, fearful that she had been wrong. Perhaps it had been a fluke when she'd stepped inside the storm at Feurach Fortress. Perhaps she wasn't immune to the Ruin at all, and she would die in these strange, dark lands, along with thousands more.

She gripped her mother's ring tighter, the cold ice blazing against her palm. She'd always wanted to be buried in ice. If she died here now, her ashes would scatter into the wind. Even in death, she would never return to her kingdom.

"Reyna," Lorcan growled at her side. "What in the name of the Dagda are you doing?"

She whipped her head toward him, her heart in her throat. Fear twisted in her gut like a venomous snake, and it had already sunk its teeth into her blood. Tears filled her eyes at once. "I told you to run, to get out of here!"

"And I told you I'm not leaving your side!" He held up his bare arm where several flecks of Ruin had dropped onto his skin.

Reyna gasped and stumbled back as more ash hit his face. She watched in horror, bracing herself for the inevitable. She knew what would happen next. She had seen it a hundred times by now. It would start small. A sizzle where it hit him. And then the darkness would start to spread throughout every part of him. In the end, there would be nothing left.

Lorcan would burn away, leaving nothing behind but a pile of ash.

She cried out in rage, ripping her hand away from the necklace and launching herself on top of him. She threw him to the ground with a strength she didn't know he had. She spread herself on top of him, shielding his body from the Ruin. Even though it was no use. Even though he'd already been hit. Great sobs shook her body, but still she remained.

"Reyna," he said in a muffled voice. "I'm fine. It hasn't

hurt me."

"What?" Reyna leapt off of him. He pushed up from the ground, brushing the flakes off his armor. What was left of it. The Ruin hadn't harmed an inch of his skin, but it had burned through the leather. "How is this possible?"

"I don't know, but we need to do your thing and draw this storm away." His voice cracked. "So many have already died, Reyna. Regardless of how I feel about my father, I don't want to see all these warriors gone forever."

Reyna nodded at once. She understood how he felt, and she did not wish to see them die either. Having known Nollaig, and Segonax, and even Tarrah, she had realized that not every shadow fae was the terrible monster she'd thought they were.

That the entire continent thought they were.

There was good and there was bad, but she had seen quite a lot of good. Most of the fae in the camp would be ordinary warriors, just doing the bidding of their king. A king they had to serve, regardless of what they might think. It wasn't as though they had a choice.

High King Bolg Rothach did not allow *choice* in his great court.

Reyna and Lorcan raced through the storm. The swirling darkness pecked at their skin, but it could do nothing more than melt when it hit them. When they reached the edge of the camp, they kept their feet moving forward. They would draw the Ruin down the hillside and toward the Forest of Thorns, giving the warriors in the camp a chance to escape.

They reached the tree line just as a powerful blast of wind knocked Reyna off her feet. The ground rose up to meet her, and she slammed onto her shoulder, wincing at the flash of pain and the crack of a bone breaking. Shaking her head, she climbed to her feet, only to feel Lorcan's strong hand press firmly against her back.

"You all right?" Lorcan whispered as they watched the storm inch across the horizon. Their plan had worked. The Ruin had left the camp behind, and now it was coming straight for them.

"It threw me off my feet," she said, wincing. "It wants me dead. And I think it's realized the ash isn't doing much."

"So, it's going to try another way." Lorcan swore.

"By throwing something else at me instead. Wind, lightning, and whatever else it might have…and I don't know what all it can do. I've only ever seen it kill with ash."

Lorcan's jaw clenched. "What should we do? We can't just stand out here and wait for it to kill you. You're immune to the ash, but you're not immune to wind. And no amount of dodging arrows can win against a storm."

Reyna risked a glance over her shoulder. The Ruin was close now. Too close. "We could go into the forest. That would give us some cover since it looks like the fires of Oxgrove didn't spread this far east."

"Until it destroys all those trees with its ash."

Reyna frowned. "Do you have a better idea?"

"Yes, I can dig a hole in the ground, throw you inside of it, and keep you out of harm's way for the rest of your life."

She gave him a bemused smile. "Only if you'd join me down there. We could start our own little underground village. And we'd never have to leave."

The wind battered her face and hair. There was no more time. The clouds were seconds away from reaching them, and once they did, Reyna was certain the Ruin would have far more in store for her than just ash.

Together, they raced into the forest. The colossal trees loomed all around them, the dense canopy hiding the churning sky from view. They crunched through the thicket at the edge of the trees, and then ducked inside the woods.

Instantly, the rushing sound of the Ruin vanished, replaced by chirping birds and the gurgle of a nearby stream.

"That's eerie," Lorcan murmured. "It's like it's not even there."

"Oh, it's there," Reyna insisted. "It won't go away that easily."

Lorcan tipped back his head to stare up at the peaceful canopy. "What should we do? Go further into the forest?"

Fear burned through her veins like poison. "We aren't wood fae. We'll be too slow through these trees. We won't be able to outrun it."

Lorcan growled. "We can't just let it—"

The entire forest began to shudder. Trees were ripped from the ground by their roots and tossed into the building wind. Lorcan wrapped his arms around Reyna and pulled her to the forest floor. Without even considering what she was doing, Reyna punched her ice dagger deep into the dirt, holding on for all she was worth. The ground crackled beneath them. Ice shot down from the blade, burying itself into the earth itself. It stretched outward, freezing the ground where they huddled beneath the storm.

Reyna buried her face in Lorcan's chest, shivering against the strength of the cruel wind. The Ruin continued to pound at the forest around them. Every branch snapped beneath the strength of it. Every leaf was ripped to shreds. Ash piled high all around them.

They stayed that way for what felt like hours, clinging together as the storm whipped up a fury over their heads. Every moment that passed, Reyna was certain it would be their last.

But after ages had come and gone, the Ruin vanished as suddenly as it had appeared, leaving behind nothing but pure and utter destruction.

And a strange patch of ice.

# 29

## THANE

"We must go to war." Princess Iona Leaghan of the Sea Court stood over the ancient map and pounded a fist against the table, rattling the wooden mugs that held some of the finest wine found in all of Tir Na Nog. Her eyes flashed. The sapphire in them matched the color of the waves that crashed against the jagged rocks below the open window.

Thane merely sat and listened to his mother's family bicker over their next steps. Some frothed like the sea, desperate to sink their swords into air fae necks. Others wanted to continue what they had done the past several decades: hole up and wait things out.

"They killed Imogen. We cannot allow them to get away with this. We need to go to war." Princess Iona turned his way. "Thane agrees with me."

That wasn't *exactly* what Thane had said.

His grandfather, High King Emrys, sat back in his chair, fingering a bushy white beard that matched his shoulder-length hair. "Is that right, Thane? It is your court after all. Is going to war on your own city truly the right step?"

"Of course it isn't," Uncle Calder, the heir to the throne, snapped. Just like his sisters, his hair and eyes were a brilliant blue. "If Thane's goal is to sit on that damn throne, he merely needs to stride through the city gates. This Aengus is nothing more than a Grand Alderman. He doesn't hold the power of the seat."

Princess Iona chuckled. "It won't be as easy as that, brother. Aengus will have prepared for Thane's return."

"It is not our court to reclaim," Uncle Calder said through gritted teeth. "We're the Sea Court. This is not our war."

"But *she* was ours," Iona hissed, her eyes flashing. "We ought to rip him to shreds for what he's done to her." She tossed a letter onto the table that had arrived the day before, stamped with a very familiar yet surprising seal. "This letter could be our hope. A strong alliance could come of it. If we're going to war, then we need this, Father. We need to answer this call."

Thane cleared his throat. "Were we not already at war?"

Princess Iona sighed, twisting back toward him. "In name only, Thane. We ah…" She trailed off and glanced at her father, who nodded. "We knew Imogen planned to redistribute the power inside the Air Court."

She meant that his mother had planned to steal the throne from his father. A polite way of putting it, but that did not change the truth of it. A coup it had always been. Treason and truth. If she had gotten away with it, an alliance with the Sea Court would have no doubt soon followed. She would have never gone to war against her own family.

Thane raised a brow. "So, that was why you went silent. You were biding your time."

"Well…that's the truth of it, Thane. I am sorry for how it was handled. He was your father, but—"

"He was a terrible male and an even worse king," Thane admitted. "I do not blame my mother for what she did. Unfortunately, she trusted the wrong fae with her plans, and he has made her pay dearly for her mistake. And we must make Aengus repay much more dearly in return."

Princess Iona stood. "Does that mean…?"

Thane nodded. "Aengus will never allow me to return to that castle without blood being spilled. He means to become the High King of the Air Court. But the only king he'll ever be is the king of his own grave."

# 30

## REYNA

"How's your shoulder?" Lorcan leaned against the doorframe of Reyna's bedchambers, his hair tousled as if he'd just been roused from sleep. But his eyes, ringed by shadows, said otherwise, and his dark gaze was steeped in concern.

"I'm fine, Lorcan. It's just a small break."

"Is it painful?"

"Not really." She shrugged with one shoulder, the one that *hadn't* been broken. "In fact, I think I might be fully healed."

He considered her for a moment. "It should take weeks for that kind of wound to heal. You broke a bone. That doesn't mend overnight."

She smiled. "One might think you'd rather I be hogtied to this bed."

But he didn't banter right back, as he usually would. Instead, his eyebrows pulled together as he frowned.

"What happened out there, Reyna?" he asked, taking a step into the room.

"The shadow fae army was decimated." She pressed her lips together. "That's what happened."

"You know that isn't what I mean." Another step. And then another. Soon, he stood at the side of her bed, his body pulsing with tension. "In the forest with the dagger and the ice. How did we survive that? Why didn't we get ripped into the wind along with everything else?"

The forest had been left as decimated as the army. The trees had been yanked from the ground for miles, along with every shrub and every flower that had filled the twisted, thorny maze. The destruction had not gone as far as Oxgrove or Craobhan, but the storm must have wiped out every part of the forest between here and there that hadn't been ravaged in the fires. Still, that would do little to stop the wood king from advancing on Findius. His enemy was all but vanquished. There would be no war now, at least not one that would end in anything but the destruction of the entire shadow kingdom.

The camp was nothing more than ash and the remnants of tents that had been reduced to ribbons. Some fae had escaped to the safety of the caverns, including Nollaig and Tarrah. Segonax had survived as well, having taken several companies of warriors through the tunnels. In total, around two thousand had lived. Which meant many more thousands had died.

"It was magic. It was ice," she said frankly.

Despite the Fall, it seemed magic was not dead. It had come to her when she'd needed it the most, in the form of ice. What that meant she did not know.

"It was shadows, too," he said quietly.

"What do you mean?"

He gazed down at her and traced a finger along her jaw. She shuddered beneath his touch, heat coiling in her core. "You've seen my shadows before. They came to me when your ice came to you. I think they hid us from the Ruin. It's why it finally went away."

Her heart pounded as she reached up to wrap her hand

around his waist. "We have magic. Both of us. Is that why the ash couldn't harm us?"

"It might be," he said. "Which means the rest of the realm needs their magic, too. This just might be it, Reyna. The answer your sister has been searching for."

She nodded, though she couldn't help but frown. Something about it still didn't feel right. Magic had protected them but only because they'd done the right thing at the right time in order to ride out the storm. The ice had held them in place as the winds had battered them, and Lorcan's shadows had hid them from view. They could have just as easily died. When Reyna's shoulder had hit the ground, it could have been her head.

They were immune to the ash. But they weren't immune to the storms.

"What are you thinking?" His thumb slid down her neck, tracing a sparking line to her throat.

She shuddered. "I don't remember. You're distracting me."

He shot her a devilish grin. "You said your shoulder has healed. What about that wound in your stomach?"

"I'm all patched up now," she said, voice hoarse. She watched him stalk across the room and quietly shut the door to her bedchamber.

"How fortunate for us both," he murmured.

Her heart pounded so hard that her chest shook. She had not been alone inside of a bedchamber with Lorcan like this since…well, there was one time back at the Air Court when she'd still thought of him as an enemy. He'd only come in to stand guard, thinking she planned to sneak out her window to catch assassins in the night.

He had not been wrong.

The time in Oxgrove didn't count either. That had been an alchemist's healing room, not a bedchamber, and she'd been half out of her mind from pain while the other half was high in the sky from the rowan berry brew. This time, it felt very different. She could scarcely breathe.

With hooded eyes, he prowled across the room. Reyna's pulse trembled in her neck as she curled her fingers around the silken bedsheets. He looked like a lion stalking its prey, and if she wasn't careful, he might take a bite.

"What are you doing?" she managed to whisper, her voice warbling along with the rest of her.

"You know what I'm doing." Eyes sparking with heat, he came to a sudden stop beside the bed and ripped back the sheets. Her eyes went wide, breath catching. "Stand."

She lifted a brow. "Do you seriously think you can command me to—"

"Stand," he growled.

"Hmph!" She threw her legs over the side of the bed, stood, and then poked a finger at the center of his armored chest. "I didn't make a vow to *you*. You can't order me around."

His lips twitched with the hint of a smile. "And yet you're standing."

Before she could come up with a suitable retort, Lorcan grasped her arm and inspected her shoulder. He poked at it, and then pushed firmly with his fingers. Seemingly satisfied, he leaned down and lifted the bottom hem of her nightdress only to find that she wore nothing underneath. She froze, scarcely breathing, as his fingers slid across the faint scar on the lower half of her abdomen. Her skin buzzed from the heat of his touch, and warmth blazed between her thighs.

"Lorcan." She whispered the words since that was all she could manage. "Since when did you become an alchemist?"

"Since you kept recklessly throwing yourself into danger?" He snapped back his hand, and the hem of the nightdress fluttered back down around her hips. "Since I want nothing more in this world than to throw you onto that bed and claim you as mine."

Her breath hitched. Heat stormed through her chest, and any last remnants of the ice wall she'd built around her heart shattered in an instant. She wanted to be his, she knew, regardless of what he'd done, who his father was, and what that might mean when all was said and done. She just wanted *him*.

As if his words were a promise, he wrapped his strong arms around her and tossed her onto the bed. Her back bounced against the soft, feather mattress as Lorcan unbuckled his belt and dropped it to the floor. She drank in his every movement, anticipation thrumming through her veins. His trousers came next, and then his tunic over his head.

Heat spread through her core as she took in his raw masculinity. He was already hard and bigger than she remembered. Wetting her lips, she scuttled back on the bed.

"Where are you going?" he murmured, wrapping his hands around her knees and spreading her thighs wide. He leaned forward between her legs and braced his elbows on either side of her hips.

She could not bear to stay still but she didn't dare move at all. His mouth was agonizingly close to her core, and a sudden wave of need crashed all around her. Softly, slowly, she wound her fingers through his raven locks and tugged him toward her.

With a smile, he glanced up. "Is there something you want?"

"You're teasing me," she whispered.

"No, *this* is teasing you." His mouth dropped onto the skin just above her navel, and his searing tongue drew a line all the way up to the peaked nipple of her right breast. He pushed the nightdress over her head, and then tossed it halfway across the room. Shuddering, she clung to his hair as he dragged his tongue in a circle and then sucked hard.

"Oh god," she moaned, arching her back. Heat sizzled between her thighs. She tucked one leg around the back of his hips and tried to tug him forward, but he growled and clasped her wrists between his hands. His mouth continued its long, excruciating tease, from nipple to nipple and back down to her navel again. By the time he dragged his tongue closer to her core, she was a shivering mess of anticipation beneath him.

"Let me ask again," he murmured, his tongue darting closer and closer to her core, where she could feel she'd begun to soak the bed. "Is there something you want?"

She squirmed beneath him. He was enjoying this, having stubborn-as-hell Reyna Darragh practically begging for his touch. But she didn't care. She did want him. She *needed* him, unlike anything else in the world.

"Yes." She arched toward him again, letting her need consume her. "I need you."

His tongue dove between her thighs, tasting the sensitive spot between the folds of her core. Shockwaves of pleasure poured through her trembling body, and a moan of pure, raw need ripped from her open mouth. A growl emerged from Lorcan's own throat, an animalistic roar that matched her need. Suddenly, his tongue pushed inside of her, and then dragged once again across her heat. Reyna's entire body contracted tight, and then delicious, all-consuming pleasure pulsed through her body, her breath heaving, stars dancing in her eyes.

As her orgasm began to slow, Lorcan inched closer, his aroused length settling between her thighs. He waited, tense with anticipation, his eyes so full of need that it made her own desire rise up within her once more.

"I want you," she whispered again, and that was all he needed to hear. He pushed inside of her at once, and his groan was like music to her ears. He thrusted hard, once and then twice, and then his pace picked up as a feverish need overtook him. Gasping, she dug her nails into his back, her pleasure rushing up to meet his.

Lorcan buried his face between her breasts, kissing her nipples and then her neck, and then trailing kisses up to her lips. As they crashed together, he gazed at her with adoring eyes, dropping his forehead to hers.

She clung onto his sweat-drenched muscles as a new wave of pure pleasure snapped tight within her, and then began to pulse around him. He followed close behind. Every muscle in his perfect body tensed, and then relaxed, his seed pumping deep within her.

They stayed like that for long moments, bound together. Lorcan leaned down to kiss her shoulder and then slowly settled on top of her body with a gentleness Reyna didn't know he had.

"I've been wanting to do that for a very long time," he said with a contented sigh. "Let's not wait so long for the next time, eh?"

She smiled. "Maybe don't capture me for the enemy again, and it won't be quite so long."

He chuckled, and the deep rumble of his voice shot new sparks of heat through her core.

"In fact...why don't we just stay here in my bedchamber forever?"

"That sounds fantastic." He pushed up onto his elbows and gazed down at her, shifting between her thighs so that she could feel his arousal had already returned to him as well. "But I don't want to wait forever for next time."

"I don't either," she whispered.

And so he claimed her as his once again.

# 31

## TARRAH

Tarrah Glas thought her eyes would never dry. She would spend the rest of her dreary life crying herself to sleep, only to awake to another dull, endlessly grey day to sob some more. The loss of Teutas felt like someone had carved a hole in her heart with the sharpest blade in all of Tir Na Nog. She didn't understand how he had been taken from her. He was to be her lover, her husband, the father of her future child.

Together, they were to conquer the Empire of Fomor. They were to rule the world. She pressed a hand against her belly. Now that child would never live. The loss was insurmountable.

Her heart hardened as she imagined the life she would never lead and the child she would never have. The Ruin had taken *everything* from her.

She didn't understand why Unseelie had not warned her of the Ruin. Was this some sort of test? Was he forcing her to stare into the face of her faith and to see which way she would fall? Or was Nollaig right? Could Unseelie simply be the god of nothing? Nothing but pain and strife and death.

With tears in her eyes, she knew what she must do. She stormed straight to the throne room where the High King lounged drunkly on his Seat of Power as he had far too often since retaking Findius. He squinted in her direction when she strode inside, but that was the most he could muster.

"Drinking so you can just forget what has happened to your great army?" she asked in a snap. "Well, that won't change what happened. Two thirds of them are dead."

Bolg Rothach sighed dramatically. "Go. Leave me be. I have better things to do than get berated by a young girl."

"No, you don't." She squared her shoulders. Until now, she had done her best to show Bolg Rothach as much deference as he pleased. But no longer. Her gentle guidance had not been enough. "As your Champion, I demand an audience with you."

He sneered, his head lolling to one side. "You cannot demand anything of me. I am your king."

She ignored him. "I told you that Unseelie hadn't shown me that battle, and yet you sent our warriors to camp on enemy soil regardless. You sentenced them to death."

"Unseelie didn't show you us huddling inside our city in fear either, did he?" Bolg laughed with a crooked smile. "Sometimes, I wonder if his visions have left you. Perhaps he's picked someone else. Someone stronger. Someone better. Someone more kingly, in fact." He grinned at her.

Shock hit Tarrah in the gut. She stumbled back, shaking her head. "Unseelie hasn't given his visions to you."

He wouldn't. He couldn't. Bolg Rothach was…

Suddenly, Tarrah saw the king for what he truly was. All this time, she had followed him because that was what she thought she should do. It didn't matter what he did or who he hurt. He was the king who would save the realm.

*But he isn't.* A fae like Bolg Rothach would never think about saving anyone but himself. He was cruel and wicked and full of hate. He even tormented his own son, his flesh and blood.

"Oh, he has, and they've been very enlightening indeed." His strange, wine-stained smile widened. "Did you know that Unseelie finds power in blood and in death? He is strengthened by sacrifice. And the bigger the sacrifice, the greater the power within his grasp."

Tarrah gasped. She shook her head, trying to shove away a realization that threatened to knock her flat on the ground. But it was impossible. The truth had been laid bare before her. The king thought he'd been given visions from Unseelie. Visions of sacrifice and death.

And so he had sent his own troops to the slaughter, knowing that thousands of them would die on a battlefield of ash.

"You wouldn't," she whispered, a newfound terror and fury roaring through her veins. "Those were your loyal warriors. The fae who serve you."

"Bah. Those fae didn't serve *me*. They only served the title and this seat. For them, it doesn't matter who sits on the goddamn throne. I could be a pile of boiled potatoes, and they still wouldn't care."

The king had truly gone mad. With slow steps back, she began to inch her way toward the throne room doors. If he was willing to sacrifice that many lives, there was no telling what he would do next. Perhaps he would decide Tarrah was an excellent sacrifice as well. She didn't plan on sticking around to find out.

Bolg scarcely noticed. Now that he was talking, it seemed he didn't want to stop. "Unseelie gave me a vision clear as day. He showed me the sacrifices, the blood, and the ash. And he told me, this has to happen. If you give me all this blood, I will give you the power to conquer all of Tir Na Nog."

"I am very glad that he has been speaking to you," Tarrah

said through gritted teeth. She was also very glad she could lie. Unseelie hadn't been speaking to the king at all. Her god, even if he had lied to her about Teutas, would have *never* commanded the king to do something as terrible as this.

"There is something else he has shown me."

Tarrah froze.

"He has shown me a way to defeat this Ruin," he said, flashing his wine-stained teeth. It looked as though he'd been feasting on blood.

"Oh?" Tarrah asked in relief. That was far better than what she had worried. She'd almost thought his latest vision would have something to do with her. And all she wanted now was to get as far away from Findius, and the High King, as she possibly could. Perhaps she would go north to the ice fae lands. Reyna always spoke so fondly of them.

"Yes." Bolg's drunken smile turned razor sharp, as did his sunken eyes. "There is a god-like power in Inishfall that can destroy every last drop of that godforsaken magic called the Ruin. My Shieldmaiden will go collect it, along with my son and Nollaig. And you, my Champion. You will go, too."

# 32

## REYNA

"Inishfall?" Reyna frowned. "Why in the name of the Dagda does the High King of the Shadow Court want us to go there?"

Tarrah winced. "It's in the *name of Unseelie* that he wants you to go. He thinks he's having visions now." The shadow fae's face looked troubled. "He believes the power to destroy the Ruin lies there."

Reyna stood a little straighter. Obviously, a quest for the mad shadow king was not high on her list of things she'd jump to do. But this one...this one was very interesting indeed.

"Lorcan," she whispered, glancing at her lover where he stood glowering by her side. They'd gathered in the strategy room, what was left of them. Segonax was busy looking after the surviving warriors and doing his best to boost morale. Teutas was gone...forever taken by the Ruin. That left Nollaig, Lorcan, and Reyna to listen to Tarrah's pleas.

His lips were a thin, white line. "I don't suppose he gave us a choice in the matter."

"No, but do you need one?" Tarrah replied. "I know how

important defeating the Ruin is to you." She turned to Reyna. "Your kingdom. You've lost many to this magic. I doubt the king is truly having visions, but...he isn't wrong. There are great powers to be found in Inishfall."

Reyna's heart squeezed. "Our great realm is dying because of it. My own sister is sick in her bed, blind. It has been months, and last I heard, she still hasn't recovered."

"It is a terrible magic," Lorcan agreed. "And Tir Na Nog will struggle to survive until we see the end of it. However—and this is extremely important—I do not trust a damn word that comes out of my father's mouth."

Reyna nodded and frowned down at the map of Tir Na Nog and the surrounding lands. Inishfall was in the southern seas, an island that squatted all by itself far away from the rest of civilization. It was impossible to get there.

"Unfortunately, as Tarrah said, you do not have a choice," Nollaig finally spoke up, her voice quiet.

Reyna eyed the hooded fae. "And you do?"

"Yes, but I will go with you anyway."

There was something very odd about Nollaig. She was a puzzle, and Reyna was becoming quite determined to figure her out. "Who *are* you, Nollaig?"

The hooded fae merely continued to stare in her direction. "Who are you?"

Reyna frowned, but Nollaig had already begun to turn the focus of the conversation back to the matter at hand. "I hesitate to ask this, Tarrah. I truly do. But have *you* had any recent Unseelie visions?"

"No, I have not, and I hope I never do again," she replied hotly.

Reyna drew back, shocked. Tarrah had only ever seemed devoted and dedicated to her god's cause. She had been awe-inspired by him. Her tone had always been one of wonder, and she'd insisted time and time again that he was nothing like the tales suggested.

An image flashed in her mind's eye, one of Tarrah and Nollaig, one of Teutas crumbling to the ground. She had seen the way Tarrah had looked at him. There had been love there.

"My father is a delusional liar," Lorcan said. "I don't know why he wants us to go to Inishfall, but it won't be for the reason he says. It's likely a death trap for us all."

"I want to go," Reyna said suddenly.

The room fell into an awkward silence. She knew what they must be thinking, that she was as mad as the king. Maybe she was.

"I don't know if I believe the king. In fact, I mostly don't." She glanced from face to face, seeing concern written in their eyes. Or hood, as it were. "But I think Tarrah has proven that these visions can sometimes be real. That doesn't mean the king is having them or that he even truly understands what he sees. But there's a chance that there is some truth hidden in the middle of all this. Maybe Inishfall is nothing but a trap. Or maybe it does hold the key to stopping the Ruin. I have to go see what's there."

"That's how I feel, too," Tarrah whispered fiercely. "The Ruin destroyed *everything*. We have to find a way to stop it from doing any more harm."

Lorcan expelled a heavy sigh. "I really don't like this, but if it's what you want to do, Reyna, then I'll stand by your side."

They all turned to Nollaig, who merely chuckled. "You lot keep forgetting something. You *have* to go to Inishfall. Two of you don't have any other choice. For now." Nollaig pushed open the door and vanished into the corridor. "See you first thing on the morrow. We should leave at once."

"For now?" Reyna asked, frowning at the door. "What do you mean, 'for now'?"

But Reyna got no answer. Letting out a frustrated growl,

she stormed into the corridor. But the hooded fae was gone. Lorcan stepped up to her side, towering over her like a strong and steady tree amidst a storm.

"What did she mean?" Reyna repeated.

"I don't think we'll get an answer to that," he said quietly. "Not until she wants us to know."

---

They left at first light. Tarrah met them in the strategy room, her hair all a tangle around her face. She'd stayed up half the night, drawing a route from Findius down through the Misty Wastes, and into the Dorcha Mountains. There, she insisted, their company would find a portal that would lead them into Inishfall.

Segonax had joined them to glance over the plan. He looked about as convinced as everyone else. "I have never heard of a portal to Inishfall inside of the shadow fae realms."

"That doesn't mean it doesn't exist," Tarrah argued, propping fisted hands on her waist. "There are a great many a thing in the world that you have never heard of."

"I daresay I know quite a bit more about the world than you." He crossed his arms stubbornly over his armored chest.

"Not about this. Not about magic."

"Hmph," he replied.

Tarrah turned her way. "What do you think, Shieldmaiden Reyna?"

"I think I hope we don't get trapped," she said frankly.

Inishfall was, as most of the realm knew, a strange and terrible place. Few had ever seen it, and even fewer still had lived to tell the tale. It had been a very long time since anyone had journeyed to Inishfall. It could only be accessed through magic, and as magic had vanished from Tir Na Nog, so had the ability to get there.

However, the trickiest thing about Inishfall was not how one got there. It was how one left. For many years before the Fall, the island in the southern seas had been used as a prison. While anyone could travel there by using the right kind of magic, no one could leave, not unless the power protecting the lands deemed one worthy and ready to be freed.

And most prisoners were never deemed worthy. Inishfall had become home to the worst of the fae throughout the history of Tir Na Nog. Luckily, it had been over a century, and most would be dead after so many years spent trapped in that place.

"We aren't being sentenced with anything. We're no one's prisoners," Tarrah said. "There is no reason for the island to decide to trap us there."

Reyna exchanged a weighted glance with Lorcan. "I'm not so certain your king would agree."

"The island has only ever trapped the worst of our kind," Nollaig said. "Monstrous lords and tyrant kings. Murderers. Cannibals. Some kings tried to send their enemies there, but not every enemy is evil. The island always spits the good fae right back out."

Tarrah shivered. "It sounds like a dreadful place."

"You're the one who says her mother went there," Nollaig replied.

"Oh yes." Tarrah nodded. "But that does not mean it isn't dreadful. My mother liked dreadful things very much."

"Tarrah, you always bring such cheer to our quests," Reyna said with a grin. When she had first arrived in Findius, she had felt a terrible hatred toward Tarrah Glas. But she'd begun to feel protective of the girl. Her only crime was trusting in something she shouldn't have.

Nollaig coughed. "Was that a *lie*, Shieldmaiden?"

"What?" Reyna frowned. "That's impossible. It was a joke and nothing more."

"No, that was a lie," Lorcan said insistently. "You've never once spoken a falsehood, not even through a joke."

She laughed, suddenly uncomfortable with the way everyone was staring at her. "I'm certain the Dagda understands the difference between a joke and a true spoken thing. I don't know why you all are making such a big deal of this."

"Because you just lied, Reyna Darragh," Lorcan said.

"I didn't," she insisted. "I can't."

Tarrah gasped and pressed her hands to her mouth, eyes bugged wide. "I know what's happening. Your vow to the king. It's made you one of us. You're a *shadow fae* now."

"That isn't true." Reyna's heart thumped hard. "Only yesterday, I drew power from ice. I wouldn't be able to do that if I'd somehow been transformed into a shadow fae."

"It's true," Lorcan said. "She did."

Reyna sighed in relief, glad that they could move on to the task at hand instead of theorize about a simple joke she'd made. But Lorcan had not moved on at all.

"But I still believe you lied," he said.

"This is ludicrous!" She threw up her hands.

"Prove it then. Try lying now." He grinned. "Try telling me that you hate me."

"Well, I certainly could say that, but I thought you wanted me to try to lie," she shot back.

"So say it then." With a smug expression on his face, he crossed his arms and waited.

"Honestly, I don't know what you hope to accomplish with this," she said, scowling.

"If you're so certain we're wrong, then why are you stalling?" A single raven eyebrow winged upward.

Anger rushed through her like a storm. "You know what? Fine. If you want to play this ridiculous game, then here you are. I hate you, Lorcan Rothach. I hate you with every ounce of blood in my veins. I would rather die than look upon your face ever again."

She gasped and pressed a trembling hand to her mouth. How had she just said that? How had she even managed to form the words? It was an impossibility. The fae of Tir Na Nog *could not lie*. It was one certainty in their world, the one thing that had never changed. The only fae who could were…

"But I'm not a shadow fae," she mouthed, no sound escaping from her parted lips.

She couldn't be. She was born of the ice. She bled in the ice. And she found power in the ice. The ice was her home. It was her strength.

And yet, she could lie.

Nollaig cocked her head. "Well, that is certainly interesting."

"Maybe it's because you're considered part of our court now," Tarrah tried. "You may not be one of us, but your vow binds you to this place in a way. Perhaps that means you've been given the means to lie because of it."

Reyna's head snapped up. "My vow."

Tarrah nodded. "It makes perfect sense. You'll be able to lie until the king releases you, I suppose."

"The king will never release me." Reyna grabbed her ice dagger from the table and threw her hoarfrost cloak over her shoulders. "Wait for me outside the city gates. There's something I must do."

"Reyna," Lorcan said, a warning in his voice. "I don't like that look on your face. What exactly are you planning to do?"

She whirled toward him then, and she knew her eyes flashed with pure, unbridled rage. "I didn't think I could lie, so I haven't been trying. But what if I've been able to for awhile now? Just like I've been able to use the power of the ice in recent months? It would mean that my vow was never binding. It means my promises are nothing but ash. It means there is nothing stopping me from doing the one thing I've wanted to do since I woke up inside this godforsaken castle. I'm going to kill the king."

"Hold on there, Shieldmaiden." Nollaig stepped firmly into Reyna's path. "There will be no king killings this day."

"Why?" Reyna shot back. "You may act like a dutiful servant, but I've seen you. I have heard the things you say. You are not as dedicated to the king as you would like him to think. You believe this realm would be better off without him. You think him cruel and weak."

"You cannot do it. You will be cursed," Tarrah hissed.

"I am already cursed." Reyna pushed past Nollaig, only to find Lorcan standing in her way. She sighed and propped fisted hands on her waist. "Surely you, out of everyone here, don't take issue with this."

"Reyna." He grasped her hand and gently placed it against his chest. Beneath her fingertips, she could feel the steady rhythm of his heartbeat. She swallowed hard, momentarily forgetting her wrath. It was difficult to remain angry when Lorcan gazed at her just like that. As if she meant the world to him.

"Tarrah is right. If you murder a king while he's in control of a Seat of Power, you will be cursed. I watched it happen with my own two eyes. Sloane Selkirk was one of the most powerful males in the world. But you saw what happened to him in the end. He killed a king and his world slowly crumbled down on top of him." His grip tightened on her hand. "If you don't care about the curse, then do it for me. Hold back for me. Bolg Rothach has spent his life destroying everything I love. And I want to be the one who does the same to him."

# 33

## LORCAN

In the depths of the Dorcha Mountains, the Peak of Madness rose up like a great gnarled finger. Behind it stretched half a dozen smaller gnarled fingers, which succeeded in creating a mountain pass that looked eerily like an old man's resting hand. They had spent the past days trekking through the Misty Wastes, past Olc Fortress, and further inward to the south. Lorcan had never before seen this part of the shadow lands, and now he understood why. There was nothing here but the mists.

According to Tarrah's calculations, it would take them another week to reach the portal. It was hidden inside the third gnarled finger, a smaller mountain the previous king had dubbed Cinder Ridge. Here were the caverns the great kingdom had once mined for shadowsteel. Now, they sat empty, save for wicked beasts that were rumored to swallow travellers whole.

Lorcan had been thinking a lot about the words Reyna had spoken as they'd left for Inishfall. She had lied, blatantly so. So much that it could not have been laughed off as though it were nothing more than a joke. He knew what she felt for him, and him her, and it was nothing like hate.

Did that truly mean she wasn't bound to her vow to his father, after all? If she wasn't, there would no longer be anything keeping her inside the kingdom of shadows. Once this quest to Inishfall was done, Reyna Darragh would leave this godforsaken realm. And Lorcan would not try to stop her, even if it killed him to know he would soon lose her again.

"An airgead for your thoughts," Reyna said as she plodded along beside him on the Butcher's Road that wound through the valleys that cut between the mountains. Every now and again, she'd feed Wingallock a worm or absentmindedly stroke his feathers. The reddish light of the sun backlit her silver hair, matching the murderous glint in her eyes. She had still not forgotten about killing Bolg Rothach.

"I'm thinking about my mark. I want to rid myself of it, once and for all."

She cast him a sidelong glance. "I'll cut it out of you."

"You can't. I've tried that before. The mark never lets me make a deep enough cut. It always stops me before I get to that point. Usually, by inflicting so much pain in my head that I can't think straight." He fisted his hands. God, he hated his mark.

"That's because you've been trying to do it to yourself. I'll be in charge of the dagger, and there is absolutely nothing it can do to stop me. I'm fairly stubborn, if you hadn't realized."

He couldn't help but smile. "That sounds thrilling and terrifying all at once. What happens when the mark realizes what you're doing, somehow communicates it with my father, and then my father commands you from across the realm? Your vow will stop you from doing it. We're both stuck."

"Your father can't force me to stop," she said. "The vow isn't binding. It seems I can lie now."

"You're certain of that?"

She shrugged. "Certain enough to try."

Lorcan spent the next several hours thinking over Reyna's offer. Removing the mark had always been a distant dream. He had tried. Time and time again, he had tried. But he had never asked another to do it for him. At the Shadow Court, he assumed anyone he'd ask would refuse. Most were loyal to his father, or so he thought. At the Air Court, no one had known about his mark or who he was. He couldn't have asked Thane without giving up the truth, and he hadn't wanted to lose his closest friend.

It wasn't until now that he'd found someone who was willing to do the deed, who understood who he was, and who wanted to jump into the filth right alongside of him.

That night, they made camp at the southern base of Cinder Ridge in the midst of piles of craggy rocks. The ground was rough and uneven, and not a single patch of grass could be found regardless of how hard they looked. The night was warm with a sticky kind of heat, but they made a fire to roast the potatoes they'd stuffed into their packs.

Lorcan was sick of potatoes, but they had little else.

He settled onto the ground beside Reyna. She'd sat far away from the fire, her arms around her legs, her chin on her knees. She was gazing up at the misty sky, her silver eyes as distant as the hidden stars. In the distance, Wingallock swooped across the barren landscape, searching for mice. He would not find any in these cruel lands.

"An airgead for your thoughts," he said with a slight smile.

"I miss home."

He nodded. "I do, too."

"You should see the night skies there, Lorcan. There are thousands of stars. Every single one is as bright as the sun, or so it feels when they are all out poking holes in the dark." She sighed and pulled a deep breath into her lungs. "And the scent of winter. It is like nothing else I have ever smelled. It is crisp and bright and so, so clear. I want to jump into a pile of snow and bury myself deep within it. I want to feel the cold again."

"You will," he said softly.

"Will I?" She looked to him then with those piercing silver eyes. He felt her pain in the very depths of his soul. "Why can I lie, Lorcan? I am an ice fae, am I not? Tell me how I can feel the way I do and not be one with the ice? It is in my bones."

"I have never met an ice fae who is *more* of an ice fae than you are. You're right. It's in your bones and in your heart. If a fae could breathe ice, then I am certain you would be the one to do it."

She grinned. "Like dragons breathe fire?"

His heart lightened at her sudden smile. "The most ferocious of dragons."

She sighed happily and dropped her head onto his shoulder. "I would like to meet a dragon one day."

"It would bite your head off."

"I'd like to see it try."

"Reyna, I want you to cut out my mark."

She lifted her head from his shoulder, her gaze suddenly sharp. "Did you just say what I think you said?"

"Yes, but only if you're still willing to do it."

"It would be an honor for me to cut that damn magic out of your arm." She reached up and cupped his cheek. "You're certain about this? That magic has been inside of you for a very long time, controlling you. It doesn't want to leave you either. It will try to fight this." She pressed her lips together. "This will hurt you, Lorcan. I imagine quite a lot."

"Nollaig will have brought some spirits with her," he replied. "She always does."

"I'm not certain how much spirits will help in this instance."

"I know what I'm getting myself into, Reyna." He leaned forward and curled his fingers against the rough stone beneath them, the memories pressing in tight around him. Everything he had been forced to do, and everything he had been forced not to do. His father had controlled him for so long. It was time to break free.

Already, the mark had begun to pulse, anticipating the intrusion.

Reyna had already jumped to her feet. She strode toward the fire with a fierce determination in the set of her spine. "Nollaig. I'm going to carve that damn mark out of Lorcan's shoulder. You in?"

"You bet I am." Nollaig pushed up from the ground, leaving her half-eaten potato behind. She went straight to her stash of spirits without being asked, pouring a large shot into a tin mug she'd brought along. She shoved it into Lorcan's hands. "Drink that up, Your Highness. You're going to need it."

Lorcan tipped it into his throat in one fluid motion. It burned as it went down. He slammed the tin mug on the ground and growled, "Another."

Nollaig poured without comment, and then handed him the mug again.

"How much do you think this is going to hurt?" he asked her after he'd taken the second shot.

"I think it's going to feel like your eyeballs are being ripped out of your head." A pause. "So, that would be a lot."

Lorcan scowled. "You know you have the ability to lie, Nollaig."

"Do you want me to lie?"

"Not really."

"Good." Nollaig settled down in front of him with a third and final shot. For now, at least. "Listen. I don't know how this is going to go. No one else with marks has ever tried this before, and there's a reason I never offered to do it myself."

"Because you want him to continue to believe you're his loyal advisor." Lorcan had quickly figured out that Nollaig was anything but, though he hadn't a clue what her true purpose was.

"That's part of it, but I'm more concerned about what kind of magic that is." She pointed at the mark. The black lines writhed through Lorcan's skin, twisting like a snake. "It might try to kill you."

"It *will* try to kill me," he answered in a low growl. "But I'm stronger than my father thinks, and I am done being forced to do whatever he commands. His power over me is over, Nollaig."

She nodded. "There is also the realm to consider. The mark binds you to your father and makes you his legitimized heir. The realm needs you. Right now, there's a mad king sacrificing thousands of warriors because of dark visions from a dark god. They need a ruler they can depend upon. A ruler like you."

"If the realm needs me to remain their prince, then that I can do." He nodded. Staying at the Shadow Court was not on his agenda, but he would do what he could for the people of the realm. He'd spent years living in another kingdom while still remaining their prince. He could do so again, helping them from afar, doing his best to protect them until he could find another shadow fae who would make a good king.

Nollaig gave a nod, and then shifted to the side to make room for Reyna.

"You should remove your tunic," Reyna said at once.

He arched a brow. "Now is not the time for that, Shieldmaiden."

She blushed furiously. "Stop it. I don't mean *that*. At least not right now." She cleared her throat. "You're going to bleed, and we don't want to get it on your tunic. Don't forget what the fae of Oxgrove said about blood magic."

With a nod, he lifted the tunic over his head and sat still while she poked and prodded at the mark. After a few moments, she grabbed her ice dagger from where she'd balanced it on top of her knee.

"Wait a moment," he said quickly. "You need to give me a warning."

"All right. Here is your warning. I am about to stick my dagger into your arm."

"You seem far too eager to do this."

"I like to stab things." She grinned. "Also, you need to relax. Nollaig, I think he needs another drink."

"You can count on me, Shieldmaiden." Nollaig vanished for a moment and came back with another full mug. This time, the contents looked suspiciously pink.

"That isn't what you gave me earlier," he said, pointing out the obvious.

"This is stronger."

"How much stronger?"

"Why don't you drink it and see?"

He sighed and glanced at Reyna. "I'm starting to have second thoughts. Perhaps I'll wait until I can find someone who isn't so gleeful about cutting me open."

"Drink the pink stuff," Reyna ordered.

Lorcan grabbed the drink and swirled the vibrant liquid in the mug. He wrinkled his nose. It looked like something that might be found on the top of a lady's hat at court. Fluffy, pink, and entirely far too scented sweet.

"Drink up, lover boy," Reyna said with a grin that vanished an instant later. "Sorry, I don't know why I said that."

"You heard the lass. Drink up…lover boy." Nollaig snickered beneath her hood.

Lorcan rolled his eyes but drank it all the same. It was as terrible as it looked. All sickly-sweet syrup and something that tasted suspiciously like potato.

"What was that?" he asked after he'd finally downed the whole thing.

"You don't need to worry about that," Nollaig replied.

Tarrah edged closer from where she'd been watching from a distance. "Would you like me to offer a prayer up to the gods?"

"No," all three shouted in unison.

"It would be a prayer to the Dagda," she said, cheeks turning pink. "Not to the god who lies."

"Well then," Reyna whispered beneath her breath before lifting her eyes to meet his. "Lorcan, it's up to you."

"Do you believe it would help?"

"Half the time, I'm not certain I believe the Dagda exists."

"If he's real, do you believe it would help?"

She pressed her lips together, and then gave a relenting nod. "Yes, I do."

He nodded to Tarrah. "Go on then. Perhaps it will distract me from—"

A terrible pain ripped through his arm as Reyna shoved her ice dagger deep into his skin. He let out a vicious roar, curling his hand into a fist and punching the ground. Reyna barely even seemed to register the sound. She leaned in close, her tongue between her teeth, digging her blade into the very soul of him.

The mark thrummed and screamed. It was a vile thing, twisting and curling and shoving its own venom deep into his blood. The torment was blinding. His vision turned black, closing around him until all he could see was his own blood splashing onto the rock by his boots.

"Reyna," he gasped as his body began to buck. The mark shuddered inside of him, throwing out so much pain that Lorcan could no longer remember his own name. Sharp, stabbing bursts spread throughout his every limb. Every single part of him was on fire. On *actual* fire, he believed.

"Hold still," she said, sounding alarmingly calm. "This is a wily little thing. It's trying to get away from me."

"Reyna, I'm on fire," he choked out. Why could he no longer see her? The whole world had gone black. His mark flared large behind the back of his eyelids. The black ink twisted into a living snake, one that bared its fangs at his soul.

"Kill her," it hissed, darting a long, reddened tongue at his heart. "Kill her or she will kill you."

"I think he's passed out," Nollaig said distantly, her voice edged in worry.

"Probably. This thing is putting up a hell of a fight." A familiar voice. A stubborn voice. She wasn't going to give up until this snake was out of his skin.

*What are you?* Lorcan asked inside his own mind, afraid to hear the answer.

"Unseelie," it hissed, lurching forward.

Lorcan roared as it sank its fangs deep into his neck, feasting upon his blood and his death. He was dying. He knew it within his bones. Lorcan was fighting against a god. It would never let him go. Not until the last breath whispered from his lungs.

A fresh stab of torment slashed through his arm. Unseelie screamed. Or perhaps it was Lorcan. He could no longer tell where he ended and Unseelie began. The venomous god was a part of him now. Every drop of his blood had been bathed in the evil of the god.

"It's over. It's won," he whispered, inside his mind or outside of it, he did not know. He would never know again.

"I don't think so," a stubborn voice said. And then the pain became utterly and wholly complete. The fire consumed every part of him.

"I've got it!"

Unseelie dragged him down into the darkness.

## 34

### REYNA

Reyna Darragh would be thrilled if she never had to dig a dark magic snake out of someone's skin again. Then again, she was glad she'd done it, if only so Lorcan could at long last become free.

"That was very dramatic," Nollaig said tiredly, resting what appeared to be her chin on her knee—it was difficult to tell with the hood. "I'm beginning to regret giving Lorcan my secret stash. Do you know how long it takes to brew Buntata?"

"I don't think your pink thing really helped much," Reyna said, grimacing as she replayed the anguish on Lorcan's face. She had never before seen anyone in quite that much pain. At one point, she'd been scared he was dead. The magic had taken ahold of his body and had shaken it until there was nothing left. *Almost* nothing left.

A rustle of movement in the corner of her eye caught her attention. She was by his side in an instant, cradling his head in her lap. Relief poured through her. Even though he'd lived, she'd feared he would never again open those raven eyes. If it had been up to the magic, he wouldn't have. She knew it in the very depths of her bones.

"Am I dead?" he murmured.

"No, you're still stuck with me."

"Reyna." He let out a tired yet happy sigh. "Did you get rid of the snake?"

How had he known it was a snake? He'd been passed out for quite some time by the time she dug the creature out of him. It had grown as large as a full-grown snake, expanding as it became free of his skin. When it had tumbled to the ground, it had hissed and twisted and bared its fangs. And then Nollaig had slammed her sword down on top of its head.

Now, Tarrah was cooking it up in some stew. Reyna would just stick to the potatoes.

"It's all gone," she said, gently brushing her fingers through his hair. "You can rest now. You're free."

"It was Unseelie."

A chill went down her spine. "What do you mean?

"The snake. It was Unseelie."

Reyna twisted toward Tarrah where she was happily chopping the creature into bite-sized pieces. "Um. The snake was Unseelie? Does that mean Tarrah shouldn't eat it?"

Lorcan chuckled, a sound that was music to her ears. "The *snake* wasn't Unseelie. Unseelie was inside the snake, and the snake was inside of me!"

"I think my Buntata is finally kicking in," Nollaig muttered.

"You might be right about that," Reyna said, settling back onto the rock. "I've had my fill of potatoes for the night. I'm going to stay here with him and see if I can get some sleep myself."

Nollaig nodded. "Good luck."

The shadow fae pushed up from the ground and rejoined Tarrah by the fire. A very animated discussion about the snake soon ensued, but Reyna's eyes were far too heavy for her to focus on it for long. Soon, sleep pulled her under, the warmth of Lorcan's body soothing her tired soul.

When she awoke, the darkness of the sky had deepened. She was curled up on the rocks, and a soft blanket had been placed on top of her. Throwing it aside, she stood and padded through the rocky valley, finding Lorcan perched on the edge of a cliff, staring out at the expanse of mist-enshrouded fields they had left behind.

"How are you feeling?" she asked, staying back. She hoped he did not hate her for what she'd done to him. For the pain she'd put him through, even if he'd asked.

"I forgot what it was like to live without that mark inside of me," he said softly. "My mind feels clearer than it has in a very long time."

He stood then and strode toward her. He was still naked from the waist up. The wound on his arm had already begun to heal, but there would always be a scar.

She swallowed hard, flustered by his naked torso, even though they had already shared a bed. "I'm sorry if the pain was too much. I tried to be as gentle as possible, but..."

He tucked his thumb beneath her chin and gazed at her fiercely. "Do not apologize to me for that. You saved me. Again. Before, it was my life. This time, Reyna, I swear it was my soul."

She trembled from the heat of his touch. It was difficult to focus on their conversation when his eyes were raking across her with a feverish need. "Before, when you said it was Unseelie, was that true?"

He nodded, jaw rippling. "What's more, it spoke to me. It tried to make me kill you, Reyna."

"I'm very glad you didn't."

"I would never harm a hair on your head." He pulled her closer, so close that she had to tip back her head to see the fire in his eyes. "Do you know what you have done for me? Do you have any idea how trapped I've been by my father's words? I am finally free, Reyna. I am free because of you. And I would rip apart the very fabric of this godforsaken world to do the same for you."

Reyna could not help but gasp at the intensity of his words. They filled her up with hope and fear, all thrown together in a perfect storm. No one had ever spoken to her this way, with so much conviction and emotion in his words.

"I would do it again a thousand times over," she whispered.

"We should celebrate," he growled into her ear, scattering goosebumps across her bare arms. "Let me claim you under the stars."

Her breath hitched as he lifted her from the ground and carried her to the edge of the cliff. She clung to him, fingers entwined behind his neck, and he slowly lowered her onto her back. As she watched him undress, her eyes caught on a brilliant light behind his head.

Stars.

She pushed up onto her elbows and gazed up at the sky. The mists had cleared, revealing a dazzling display of distant suns, shooting light across the expansive universe. There were hundreds of them. Thousands. The shadows had cleared, revealing a darkness that was as deep as any she had ever seen. But with it came the stars.

"Lorcan, I can see stars," she said, pointing up at the sky.

"I know. I've been staring at them for the past hour, trying to make sense of it all." Smiling, he sank to his knees, fully naked and very much aroused. "Our world is changing, Reyna Darragh. I don't know why and I don't even understand how, but we're a part of it. You and I. And I will gladly face whatever it is with you by my side."

A thrill went through her heart. She did not know what she had done to deserve this male, but here he was laying everything bare before her. She had him, and he most definitely had her. And she would never let him go, no matter how hard the world tried to tear them apart.

He climbed on top of her, gently pressing her back onto the smooth stone. His length pulsed against her core as he gently spread her legs wide on either side of his hips. Hot need dripped from her thighs, her entire body thrumming from anticipation.

"I want you inside of me," she whispered.

A lazy smile stretched across his face. "Patience. We have all night."

Reyna did not think she could wait all night. After everything that had happened, she was desperate for his touch. They had faced down a god together and had won. She'd almost lost him. She needed to feel him, every single part of him.

"I think," he said softly after he dragged his tongue from her neck, down to her naval, and then almost to her very core. She was practically a writhing mess already. "I think I would like nothing more than to see you bathed in the starlight, riding me until you're spent."

Suddenly, she felt very shy, and Reyna Darragh never felt shy. "I'm not sure what I'm doing. You might not like it."

His voice rumbled with a deep growl. "I like everything you do."

"How do I know how to move?" she whispered.

Gently, he wrapped his hands around her hips and flipped her over so that she now straddled him. "Just move in a way that feels good to you."

Her heart pounded in her ears, and she wet her lips. She placed her palms flat on his corded muscles, enjoying the feel of his skin beneath her hands. But before she could move, he grasped her hand.

"Only do this if you want to, Reyna. Because I will gladly take you however you'd like."

"No," she said, suddenly feeling emboldened. "I want to try this."

He smiled and settled back onto the ground, his fingers splayed across her hips. Slowly, she began to rock against him. His length throbbed within her at once. Pressing harder against his chest, she moved faster, gasping when the hardness of his cock hit the very back of her core. A thousand sensations flooded her body at once.

"You're amazing," he murmured. "Everything about you is everything I love."

She moved faster, gasping each time they crashed together. He rose his hips to meet hers, thrusting deep inside of her. Pleasure stormed through her body.

She dug her fingernails into his skin, riding him with increasing wild abandon. With a growl, he grasped her arse and tugged her harder and harder against him, his thrusts growing more eager with each passing beat.

Suddenly, the stars exploded in the night. Her climax hit her like a force of nature, and a million tiny tremors soon followed. When she was spent, she sagged against him, her fingernails still digging deep into his chest.

He flipped her onto her back, his length still deep inside of her. "I am very close, Reyna Darragh, but I will not push you past the edge once more unless you want me to."

"I want you to," she whispered without even a moment's hesitation.

He shuddered hard as his thrusting began again in earnest. Once, twice, and then once more, and Reyna was already a trembling mess all over again. Lorcan grunted and throbbed one last time, emptying his seed deep into her body. They clung together until their trembling faded.

Blissful exhaustion fell down on her. With a sigh, she let it pull her under.

The very last things she saw before she drifted to sleep were the stars reflected in her lover's eyes.

They'd journeyed three more days when trouble came. At the base of the third gnarled finger, the mountain they needed to climb to reach the portal, Nollaig stopped to gaze up at the high mountain pass that zigzagged overhead.

"I see movement in the distance," she said quietly. "I think someone is following us."

"Following us?" Tarrah asked with a frown. "Or tracking us?"

"That's pretty much the same thing where I'm concerned," Nollaig replied. "Whoever it is, they are far more interested in us than I'd like."

"They might just be curious," Tarrah said. "Just because they're following us doesn't mean they wish us harm."

"It does," Lorcan said firmly. "Either they know who we are and they wish to kill us or use us in some way, or they have no idea who we are, and they plan to kill us for a meal. Neither option is one I'd like to face."

Reyna's stomach twisted. "Did you say they'd like to *eat* us?"

"Cannibals are not as uncommon as you'd think in the shadow lands," he replied grimly. "Fae get desperate when there is a shortage of food. Very few crops grow under the misty skies. If they cannot find land to grow potatoes or enough coin to buy them…they turn to flesh."

"Wonderful," Reyna replied, whistling to bring Wingallock

back to her side. She would not risk her owl being shot down for a meal.

Indeed, the mists had swiftly returned with its sticky embrace. The night under the stars had been the only relief. Once again, darkness clogged the skies and rained down mist, forever smudging every rock in their path.

It had made navigation difficult, particularly when it came time to judge east from west. Reyna had learned to read the skies, to understand the constellations. They always guided the way. Here, she felt blind.

"How have they managed to track us when it's impossible to see any further than that rock up there?" Reyna asked, pointing at a large boulder steeped in shadows.

"When you live in the mists all your life, you soon learn how to follow a trail without using your eyes," Nollaig replied cryptically.

"And how did *you* know we have hunters? How did you spot them?" she tried.

"I have my own set of skills, and those I do not plan on divulging to anyone."

"One day, I'm going to figure out who you are, Nollaig."

"You may very well be right." Her voice held the hint of a smile. "But that day is not today, I'm afraid."

"So, what should we do?" Tarrah asked, huddling into a cloak. The temperature had dropped the further they'd trekked up the mountain. Tarrah had grown visibly cold. Reyna had lent her the hoarfrost cloak, but it was a thin and wispy thing and not designed to keep a fae warm.

"They will stick with us until we reach the portal," Nollaig said. "Do we let them follow us through?"

"Absolutely not," Reyna replied tensely. "We will not let brigands interfere with us reaching the power to stop the Ruin."

Lorcan glanced at her, eyebrow raised. "You seem very certain my father wasn't lying to us."

"Oh, I think he was lying to us. But I also think there is something in Inishfall, too."

"A trap," he said dryly.

"A trap!" Tarrah exclaimed. "That's what we should do. Set a trap for the brigands."

Reyna arched a brow. "That's not a terrible idea."

"Why does it always have to be a trap?" Lorcan grunted, but he didn't elaborate.

"Are you certain they mean us harm, Nollaig?" Reyna asked.

The hooded fae was silent for a moment before giving a slight nod. "This realm is full of monstrous things, and these mountains more so than anywhere else. For whatever reason they're following us, it won't be a good one."

The trio turned toward Lorcan, deferring to his command. He was the prince, and it was his call, even if he no longer held that mark inside his skin. With a long, tired sigh, he dragged his hand down his face, and then tensed the muscles that corded deeply through his broad shoulders. He stood tall over them all, strength radiating from his body like a king. "We will set a trap. But I don't want them killed unless we can confirm that they're enemies."

Nollaig gave a slight bow. "We will do as you command."

# 35

## EISLYN

After weeks on board the Stingray, the icy shores of Margaidh drifted into view. Princess Eislyn Darragh stood on the bow of the ship, her wild hair whipping around her shoulders. Vreis stood beside her, stoic and strong. Together, they would find Lord Killian and tell him everything they knew. He would send word at once to her father.

After that, she knew the battles would begin once more. Her father would want to rip Aengus off his throne. Tairngire would fall. Innocent lives would be lost. She wished it didn't have to happen, but she saw no other way. Aengus must be stopped.

Margaidh was the second largest city in all the Ice Court and one of the most impressive. It spread across rolling icy hills that led up to a towering castle that could only be accessed by thin, winding stairs that had been cut from ice. The three towers twisted like skinny tornados, the spires carved from the oldest pieces of ice glass in the realm. Margaidh was a bustling city and still a hub for trade, even though merchants could no longer shift goods between realms.

The eastern market was infamous, full of hundreds of silver tents that dotted the icy fields just to the northeast of the city.

After they disembarked and bid their farewell to the crew, Eislyn excitedly led Vreis into the eastern markets. She'd dreamt of them the past few nights, wondering what riches she would find hidden amongst the stalls. Namely, she wanted to find some more books.

"Here. Wear this hood and cover your hair," Vreis said quietly as he pressed a silken hoarfrost cloak into her fingers. "Put your circlet away, too, while you're at it."

Eislyn cocked her head, smiling at an elaborately-dressed merchant they passed by. "That's silly. Why would I want to hide myself in my own lands? I can be seen walking around the markets, Vreis. This isn't the Air Court. It's safe here."

Vreis shifted uncomfortably in his boots, and Eislyn couldn't help but give him a fond smile. Poor Vreis. He'd only ever lived in the air fae lands, where intrigue and murder were as common as thieves. Prince Thane—*High King* Thane—had often sneaked out of the castle to revel in the nearby taverns, but he'd only ever done so in one specific district where he knew every fae could be trusted. He never ventured out of the castle other than that, and neither did the rest of the nobility. They kept themselves locked up tight behind their looming stone walls, protected against unseen enemies.

"Is it truly that bad in Tairngire?" she asked as they began to stroll through the merchant stalls singing of laughter, conversation, and coin. "I never saw much of it myself."

Vreis sighed. "Yes and no. The city hasn't always been as dangerous as it is now, but recently it's hit a boiling point. It's like the whole city itself is squatting on top of a volcano, ready to burst at any moment. I fear for the low fae when it happens. The royals will be safe. They always are."

"Are they *truly*?" Eislyn asked. "Because I wouldn't say they are. Not even during Thane's coronation." She left the rest unsaid. She herself had not been safe. If it had not been for her sister, Eislyn would be dead.

Vreis winced. "You're right, of course. I wasn't thinking of the coronation, but you're right. Well then it seems that no one in Tairngire is safe now. That city is cursed."

Eislyn was inclined to agree, but her troubled thoughts were momentarily distracted when they came upon a silver tent overflowing with leather-bound books. Excitement tripped through her veins as she gestured eagerly, smiling up at Vreis. "Look. I *knew* there would be a stall."

He did not look as quite as thrilled as Eislyn felt. As she rushed forward, she caught his frown deepening as he stared down every fae that passed by. Despite her attempts to convince him that they were firmly on friendly ground, he could not relax. She supposed that this was what made him such a good guard. He was always ready to protect, even if there was nothing to guard against.

*But no matter,* she thought eagerly. There were books to be examined, pages to flip through, and words to read. These tomes were ancient. Some of them, at least. She could tell by their faded covers and the deep wrinkles etched into the leather. One of these books might have the answers on how to defeat the Ruin.

She grabbed the nearest book and flipped it open.

Immediately, the merchant with his floppy hat and deep crimson robes was by her side, his breath scented with sour wine. "No reading here, I'm afraid. If you want it, you have to buy it."

Eislyn pulled her eyes away from the words and frowned. "How can I possibly know if I want to buy it if I don't know what it's about?"

He narrowed his eyes. "All right then. Take a few moments

to scan the contents, and then put it back or buy it. I'll be watching you."

She shivered, suddenly a bit less certain that she should be walking so freely and boldly through these crowds. The last time she had visited the eastern market, not a single merchant had been rude to her. They'd let her browse the books endlessly, reading whatever she liked. But they had known she was the princess then. Perhaps…

Vreis edged in closer. "Why don't we just grab a few of these and go? I think we ought to go see your father's friend now."

"But there are so many," she said with an exasperated sigh. "I've barely even begun to look through them."

"Let's go see him, Eislyn," he said insistently, prying the book from her fingers. "We can always come back later, after we've spoken to him."

Something in his voice sent a chill down her spine. She let him take the book and watched him pay the merchant his coin. Vreis pressed the book back into her hands, grabbed her elbow, and steered her toward the northern stalls where an exit leading into the city sat waiting.

Her heart was racing as they upped their pace. "What's happening?"

"There were a few curious eyes back there taking an extreme interest in you," he said almost too quietly for her to hear. "A group of them. Maybe a dozen in total. It was difficult to tell."

"Perhaps they recognized me," she said. "I've been here before with my father."

"Oh, they no doubt recognized you. It's what they want to do next that has me worried."

Eislyn frowned. "Ice fae would not harm me."

"No?" He shook his head. "You left your lands to join your sister at the Air Court. The war has been long and harsh and full of death. I wager there are some who might not be pleased by what you two did."

"What, ensure an alliance? Try to end the war? Why in the name of the Dagda would anyone hate us for that?"

"Oh, Eislyn." Vreis shot her a sad smile. "You are far too pure for this world. I wish there were more fae in these wretched lands who see things as you do."

"What's that supposed to mean?" She wrenched her arm out of his grasp and glared at him. "Tell me."

"Grudges are like poison. They get into your blood, and it's impossible to get clean. Once it's in you, it's in there for good. In the end, you either welcome in the poison, take it as part of you, and survive with a festering illness for the rest of your miserable life…or you die."

Tears threatened to burst into her eyes. "You're saying the ice fae have poison in their hearts."

"I'm saying the war has lasted a hundred years, and many of your fae lost their lives to the Air Court. It will take a very long time for those wounds to mend, if they ever do." He pushed a long strand of hair out of her face. "Some will be glad of the alliance. Others will not. I wish it weren't so, and I hate that it feels as if *I'm* wounding *you* now by telling you this, but sometimes harsh truths must be faced."

"You don't seem as if you hate it at all," she whispered fiercely, blinking back the tears. "You've been throwing harsh truths into my face since the moment we left that damn city."

"Only because I am trying my damnedest to help you survive." He leaned in, voice tense with emotion. "You've spent your entire life shielded from the world. By your father, by your sisters, by Thane. That shield is gone, Eislyn. I'm just trying to make you see it's not there and what now lies beyond its shadow."

"And I'm shielded by you," she said, tears now pouring from her eyes, because he was right. He was so right that it hurt. She had long known deep inside her heart that there was something wrong with her, that she could not survive, not on her own. She had been protected, so protected that others had died so she might live. And that wasn't fair. That wasn't fair at all. Her mother should be here now. She would have never needed so many shields.

"See, there you're wrong." He brushed his thumb against her cheek, wiping away the tears. "I am not trying to shield you at all."

"I am not strong enough," she whispered harshly. "I am not Reyna. I'm not even Glencora."

They were both strong in their own way. Even now, Glencora survived something that had killed so many. And Reyna. *Oh, Reyna.* Eislyn did not know what had happened to her sister, but she knew she would be alive. It would take a lot to destroy a Darragh sister.

Every Darragh sister except for Eislyn, of course. She was nothing like her sisters, and she never would be.

"This is what I am trying to tell you." He grasped her shoulders, leaned down, and stared deeply into her eyes. "Look deep down inside of yourself. You are Princess Eislyn Darragh. You do not need anyone to save you. No one but yourself. *Be your own shield.*"

*Be your own shield.*

The thought sparked like a flicker in the darkest dungeon. She gasped at the wave of exhilaration that went through her, but it was quickly pushed away by a tsunami of reality. Eislyn could not be her own shield. Vreis meant well. He truly did. But he didn't understand how useless she was. He didn't understand how terrible the terrors in her mind truly were.

"It's a nice thought," she said with a sad smile. "But not everyone is fit for battle."

Vreis sighed as she pushed away from him. "Eislyn."

She brushed the tears from her face and began to jog. Vreis

was wrong about her. She couldn't take care of herself, evidenced by the fact he himself had been the one to break her out of the castle. *He* had set up the ship. *He* had told her to go to Margaidh. He had done it all, and she'd done nothing!

If she had been left to her own devices, she'd be in a grave next to Imogen Selkirk right now.

He let her go, almost as though he sensed her need for a moment to herself. She hated that she'd let him see her this way, raw and broken, staring her helplessness right in the face. How did he see through her so well and yet manage to get it all wrong anyway?

When her tears were finally frozen on her cheeks, she reached the gates leading out of the market and into the city proper. She slowed to a stop and glanced behind her, ready to face Vreis once again and his all-knowing eyes. But Vreis was not there amidst the crowd, not that she could see. His amber hair should have stood out in a sea of silver and white, but there was not a splash of brown at all.

*He left me,* she thought desperately to herself. *He got sick and tired of being my shield, so he's gone.*

But that could not be right. Vreis had done too much to abandon her now. Something else must have happened. Had he stopped at a stall? Perhaps she'd raced too fast through the crowd, and he'd lost sight of her.

Frowning, Eislyn retraced her steps through the market, heart squeezing tight. With every step, the worry cinched tighter.

"Hello there, princess. How strange it is to find you here in these parts. We thought you were an air fae now." The voice that rang behind her was rough and cruel and terrifyingly deep. Eislyn swallowed hard and turned.

The silver-haired male was a tall warrior, clad in the light armor of the Ice Court. He wore a glistening hoarfrost cloak around broad, muscular shoulders. His grin was wicked. His dagger was sharp. Several more fae fanned out behind him. Murder glinted in eyes that should have been safe, familiar, and kind.

"What do you want?" she whispered, stumbling back.

"I think you know what we want," he growled.

She flew through the market, her feet pounding hard on the dirt-packed street, her hair flying behind her like a dozen silver wings. The males followed close behind. No matter how fast she ran, she could hear them on her heels, their breath ragged, their own feet heavy and loud on the dirt.

"Better give it up and stop now, princess," one of them shouted. "You can't outrun us all."

Eislyn let out a cry of terror, but she did not dare slow her feet. They were right. There were too many of them. She would never outrun them all. Her only hope was to run long enough to catch Vreis's attention, wherever he'd gone. He would help her. He would know what to do.

She raced back through the stalls, searching wildly for any sign of Vreis. There was none. Every head she saw was silver or white, eyes lit like crystal shards. Fear formed a lump in her throat. They'd seen her with Vreis. They knew he was there, protecting her. Had they taken him out first?

Had they killed him?

Tears sprung into her eyes. She wanted to continue her search for Vreis, but the warriors were hot on her trail. Several jumped into the path ahead. With a frustrated cry, Eislyn whirled on her feet and charged through the canopy that surrounded the market.

There was only one place she could go. She ducked beneath the stone arch that led away from the castle. She raced into the forest, praying to the Dagda that the snow-laden trees would hide her escape. Her silver hair and pale clothes melted in with the snow.

Heart aching, she ran.

# 36

## MARIEL

Mariel peered at the lords. It was another day at court after a long line of them. Each one was becoming more uneventful than the last. She had hoped for her plot to move faster than it had, for the realm to finally come together, for the royals to toss Aengus straight into the Bay of Wind.

But court was never that simple.

And now it seemed they had something of a coup on their hands.

She stepped away from Aengus's side and strode down the dais, stopping to stand beside Lady Regan, who had not mentioned Dalais once since that night at the feast. They'd spoken many times, of course, but it had always been minced words and faked niceties.

Mariel leaned in and murmured into Lady Regan's curving ear. "My eyesight must be failing me because Lord Munch and Lord Arlon have a strange look about them this day. In fact, they appear to be entirely different males."

Indeed, it was the oddest thing. Two of Aengus's most loyal lords had arrived just as they did every day. They wore their standard garb. Silken tunics dyed gold and trousers cinched with leather belts. Their hair swooped just to the side, revealing their pointed ears. Same as always.

The only thing was, their faces were wrong.

Lady Regan stared straight ahead. "Oh dear. Could your memory be failing you?"

"Oh, is that what it is? Silly me."

So, Lady Regan wouldn't admit it, which meant either she was involved or she knew who was. Then, it was likely linked to the other new arrivals, Lord Neil, Lord Malcom, and Lady Keely. It also meant that Lady Regan would not explain a word, not here, in court, where Aengus was nearby.

Still, her curiosity was piqued.

"No, I am quite certain they have changed something," Mariel whispered insistently. "Perhaps a new haircut. It looks quite nice. I should suggest Aengus take a closer look so he can replicate it. He doesn't seem to have noticed their new style at all."

"I daresay he hasn't," Lady Regan said, her voice tightening. "The Grand Alderman is as blind as a bat."

Mariel arched a brow and glanced back at Aengus. That would certainly explain why the Grand Alderman hadn't noticed that his loyal lords had been swapped out right beneath his nose. He hadn't recognized Mariel either when she'd first come to him as Princess Eislyn, even though he should have. Was his eyesight truly failing him? How had she not noticed it before? Her heart beat faster, a thrill slinking down her spine.

The loyal lords had been replaced, which meant her plot had worked.

"Tell me, Lady Regan. Do you believe in the curse of that bloody seat over there?"

Lady Regan slid her gaze toward the twisting, thorny

throne. "I imagine you're referring to the High King and what has happened to his family."

"You imagine right."

"Well then. Just between you and me." Lady Regan shifted closer. "Sloane Selkirk murdered the Dalais king, and look where he ended up. He was so frail before he died that he was practically a pile of bones. Imogen Selkirk was executed by her own lover. Their children, save Thane, were murdered by the shadow fae. And our new High King? He's gone. If you ask me, I'd say it won't be long before he's dead, too. So, when Sloane Selkirk killed our king, he cursed his whole damn family. But that's between you and me." Lady Regan dropped her voice so low that Mariel could scarcely hear her. "Your Majesty."

Shivers stormed across Mariel's arms. Her back stiffened, her shoulders straightened, and her chin lifted high. Against all odds her plan had worked. The courtly intrigue war was in full effect, and it would only be a matter of time before the entire house that Aengus built came crumbling down. And he would never truly know what had hit him.

Mariel gave a nod and turned back to the throne. A soft voice followed her, whispering devilish things. "Seeing as Aengus was Imogen's lover, it's likely Sloane Selkirk's actions cursed him, too. And if they didn't, I hear Imogen put her own curse on the little male. I have no doubt his end will come soon."

Mariel smiled.

# 37

## LORCAN

They set up camp halfway up the long and winding path through Cinder Ridge. The journey had grown wearisome for Tarrah, whose feet ached and fingers bled from where she'd fallen after an unexpected encounter with a vine. It had turned out to be a perilous journey. As they'd begun to trek *up* instead of forward, a harsh wind had rushed across the path, threatening to knock every one of them off the side of the mountain. Coiling black vines had appeared not long after. One had twisted around Tarrah's ankle and yanked her off her feet.

It felt as though the very mountain itself was trying to prevent them from reaching the portal. And perhaps it was. Lorcan could feel the hum of a great, ancient power pulsing beneath his feet. Every now and then, he noticed Reyna look down with a frown. She felt it, too. But the others made no mention of it at all.

As they settled in for the night inside a cluster of large rocks, Nollaig curled over a few gathered vines, failing to spark a fire. Reyna sat next to him, the side of her body pressed tight against his. The warmth of her soothed his worry away. Wingallock had taken off to hunt for food, but Lorcan had a feeling Reyna had sent the owl away to keep him from harm.

"How are we going to lure them out of hiding if we can't start a fire?" she asked. "They won't know where we are."

"Oh, they know where we are," Nollaig called out over her shoulder. "I've kept my eyes on them all day. They've grown emboldened as our pace has slowed. They are not far behind us now."

Lorcan frowned. He was not thrilled by the plan to trap their stalkers. There was another trap he'd once set, and he'd regretted it the rest of his life. But that trap had been different, he had to remind himself. The trap for Thane had been a lie, a way for Lorcan to slither his way inside the Air Court. He'd pretended to save him from a crew of brigands, and Thane had been so thankful that he'd invited Lorcan to become his personal guard.

All because Bolg Rothach had forced Lorcan to become a spy. Anger toward his father rose up inside him like a storm, and even now, he braced himself for the inevitable pain. He'd grown so accustomed to it. The torment had become a part of him. But his arm was silent and still now, and his thoughts were merely his own.

He could think what he liked, and there would be no punishment for it.

Nollaig sighed and sat back on her heels. "We will not have a fire this night. The winds are too harsh on this mountain pass. No matter. They know we're here."

The fire had been meant to not only signal their location but to show the hunters that they were sleeping soundly without a single soul on watch for the night. But no matter. They all settled in on the harsh and unyielding rocks, squeezing the ends of the thin blankets beneath them to keep them from getting snatched away by the wind. Lorcan lay quietly on his sheathed sword. It dug into his skin. He was sorely glad they did not plan to sleep.

To his right, he could hear Reyna's steady breathing. He ached to turn and face her, to reach out and pull her close. Since their moments beneath the stars, they'd spent each night wrapped up in each other's arms. Nollaig was always on watch when they stole away for solitude, and while he could not see her face, he could hear the knowing smile behind the hood. Lorcan didn't care. He'd never felt so alive in his life.

Tonight, no one sat on watch, and there would be no stolen moment in the darkness. Tonight, they waited to spill blood.

As the moments stretched into hours, the exhaustion of the day began to creep into his eyes. Try as he might, he could not keep them open, and soon sleep was tugging him into a peaceful darkness.

The rushing of footsteps suddenly woke him. He threw back his blanket and was on his feet within an instant, sword unsheathed. He came face to face with a tall, muscular male with deep-set crimson eyes and hair the color of steel. He wore grey scale armor and carried a shadowsteel blade. His wooden shield was brazened with the sigil of the Shadow Court, the twisting antlers of a beast.

Frowning, Lorcan leapt back as the fae sliced his sword at his throat. Lorcan growled and rushed forward, slamming his shoulder into the attacker's gut. The fae grunted and risked another blow at Lorcan's head, but he blocked the blade with his own before steel met flesh.

Lorcan stepped back, sizing up the shadow fae once again. He had a familiar face. He'd seen him around the barracks. Unease slithered through his gut. This was one of his own damn warriors.

"Stand down," Lorcan barked. "I'm your prince, and this is a command."

"I don't serve the prince," the fae spat back. "I serve the High King of our realm."

So it was as he had feared. This fae was here by the order of the High King, and he was here to kill.

The distant clang of steel caught his attention, and out of the corner of his eye, he could see Reyna in deep combat with another. He fought the urge to run to her, to turn and join her side. But he would only end up with a sword in his back. And Reyna Darragh was strong.

"This is folly," Lorcan said, turning his attention back onto his opponent. "My father has gone mad, and he doesn't understand what he's asked you to do. I am his son. He doesn't wish to see me dead."

Lies, of course. Lorcan knew his father had little love for him, if any at all. He was surprised it had taken him so long to order the assassination. When Bolg had named him heir, he'd hoped for a pawn, an eager servant. Instead, he'd gotten Lorcan, who had fought him at every turn. Lorcan had always done his father's bidding in the end—he'd been forced to—but he had not made life easy for the king.

"Unfortunately for you, it does not matter if he's the sanest fae in the realm or not," the fae replied. "My king gave me a command."

Frustration charged through Lorcan. "I'm giving you a way out of this. Leave now and find a place inside this realm where potatoes grow. I don't want to kill you."

"It is a good thing you won't have to," the fae countered with a sneer, "because I will be the one doing the killing this night."

Lorcan leapt into action, swinging his blade toward the shadow fae's head. But the warrior ducked back, dodging the sword easily. Lorcan rounded on him, testing his skills. A parry to the left got a block, and one to the right got another duck and then a rush forward.

Gritting his teeth, Lorcan made the charge. He threw a quick block to the right, and then followed it with a rushing blow straight down from above, his blade slicing through the shadow fae's head. It cleaved it clean in two, blood and gore splashing onto the black rock that surrounded them.

Lorcan yanked his blade out of the dead warrior's head and whirled toward the fight. Another attacker's body lay at Reyna's feet, handily dealt with by a slash across the throat. He found Nollaig guarding Tarrah in the corner. But that was it.

"Just two?" he asked.

"It seems your father thinks we're easy to kill," Nollaig said dryly.

Lorcan frowned and scanned the mountain pass around them. "And you're certain no more warriors are lurking in wait?"

"I've looked. This is the extent of it. If he has more coming, they are too far behind us to catch up now."

"Well, that's offensive," Reyna muttered, wiping the blood from her sword against her downed opponent's gloved hand.

Nollaig chuckled.

"You sound like you wish he'd sent more of them," Tarrah whispered, her cheeks drained of all color.

"Reyna enjoys stabbing things," Lorcan said, turning back toward the fallen warriors. "This paints a terrible portrait indeed. My father wants us all dead."

"Could they have been lying?" Reyna asked.

"I don't think so. He never intended for us to make it to Inishfall." Lorcan's hands fisted as anger roiled through him. "He sent us to our deaths."

"Either he's so mad he doesn't know his own name…or his trust in me has finally failed," Nollaig said quietly.

"It is a combination of the two," Tarrah replied. "He truly has gone mad. I am certain of it. A darkness has twisted his mind. But...lately, you've done little to hide your scorn for him, Nollaig. He may be mad, but he's clever, too. He will not have missed it."

"It has never mattered before. I—" Nollaig fell silent.

"Nollaig, for fuck's sake, tell us who you are," Reyna insisted.

"Another time, Shieldmaiden."

Reyna's sigh was one of frustration, one Lorcan felt in his very bones. He'd known Nollaig for a very long time, and she had not once let her mask slip. Who she was under that cloak no one knew. No one except perhaps the king. It was odd. Lorcan trusted her with his life but he didn't know one thing about her. Only her name.

"Does this mean we're turning back?" Tarrah asked, the question Lorcan knew was on the mind of every member of this godforsaken party.

"Absolutely not," Reyna said fiercely. "We didn't come all this way to give up when we're only half a day's walk from the portal."

"Reyna," Lorcan said gently. "If there was ever proof my father was lying, this is it. He didn't send us here to find a way to stop the Ruin. He sent us here so we could die. Quietly, without any witnesses, far from the castle walls."

"He's right," Nollaig said. "He may be king, but we have allies inside that castle who would have tried to stop our execution. Segonax, for one, would never stand for it. And there are others. Warriors who witnessed you rushing into the storm to save their lives. The fae of Findius have seen their prince and his beloved fight for them. They will not soon forget that."

Reyna's voice trembled when she spoke. "This is not an invention of his own twisted mind. He might have sent us off to die, but Inishfall, it's real. Isn't it, Tarrah?"

"There is a great power there," Tarrah whispered. "It's true. But it is also a dangerous one."

Lorcan frowned, but Reyna was not quite done yet.

"The High King planned to murder us here on the mountain. Inishfall itself is not the trap, so we don't need to worry about going through to the other side." She stepped up to Lorcan, wrapped her soft hands around his, and peered up at him with so much hope and conviction that he could not help but bend. "We are so close. Can we not just see what's in there? If it turns out to be nothing, then we can leave. It is as simple as that."

Lorcan sighed. "You are going to be the death of me, Reyna Darragh."

Her smile was as bright as the stars.

# 38

## REYNA

The portal to Inishfall was located deep within a cavern that cut through the core of Cinder Ridge. In the deepening darkness, fireflies darted overhead, the cavern walls looming so high that Reyna could not spot the top of them. Moss carpeted the ground beneath their feet, and a strange seductive scent filled the air, one of life.

"Well," Nollaig said sharply, as they came to a stop at the edge of a deep well, one that formed a pool from the gush of water sprouting from the black stone itself. Flickering green light shimmered in the waterfall. Where the waterfall met the pool, there was a sound like a *hush*.

"How in the name of the Dagda is there a waterfall in the middle of the barren shadow lands?" Reyna asked in awe. She had never before seen anything like it. There were no falls in the Ice Court. The waters froze too quickly there.

"Magic," Tarrah said, stating the obvious. "You see now. There *is* a power here. It's just as my vision said."

Lorcan gave Tarrah a sharp look. "I thought you were done with your visions."

"I am." She frowned. "Some of them have been true

though, my prince. That's why I don't understand why some have also been wrong."

"Nevermind all that," Reyna insisted. "We're here, and that's the portal."

"This is your last chance to change your mind," Lorcan said. "We can turn away now and leave this place behind. We don't have to go through with this."

"Yes." She clenched her hands. "We do."

Lorcan sighed. She understood his concerns, and it wasn't as though she didn't have them herself. The king had already proven that he didn't want them to end this quest alive. His 'vision' from Unseelie had been nothing more than a diversion, a way to get them away from the castle where his brutalities could not be witnessed by the low fae of the city.

But she was convinced there was something to Inishfall. She felt the truth of it, the power of it, in her very bones. And seeing the portal before her now, she knew she was right. Power hummed from the rushing waters. She could feel it and hear it. She knew it was there.

This quest might still go wrong. But maybe it wouldn't. It was a chance she couldn't ignore. A chance to save her kingdom. A chance to stop the Ruin from taking the life of even one more fae. And *that* was what stopped her from fearing what was on the other side of that portal.

"Well, I guess we're doing this," Nollaig said. "Who's going through first?"

"I am," Reyna said exuberantly.

"Absolutely not," Lorcan growled.

But she already knew he would say that, and she wasn't waiting around. Without giving Lorcan a chance to stop her, she leapt into the pool. Freezing water swallowed her whole, a welcome relief from the humid heat of the shadow realm. Lorcan shouted as she dove beneath the waters. A splash sounded beside her, but she was already off, pushing through the crashing waters and swimming to the other side of the falls. Wingallock swam by her side, twirling through the soothing waters.

Soon, she parted the waters of the falls and drew in deep lungfuls of air. Her eyes were assaulted by a thousand shades of glistening green. Everywhere she looked, lush and luminous plants wove through the landscape, a dense forest that sagged beneath the weight of the cloying humidity. There were thick vines and trees that sprouted moss. The soft spray from the tumbling falls soothed her cheeks. It looked and felt like paradise, but a deep dark power pulsed beneath it all, reminding Reyna that there was more here than met the eye.

Lorcan pushed up beside her, wiping the water from his face and glaring around. When his gaze landed on Reyna, he growled. "I swear to the Dagda, Reyna, I have never met a more impulsive female in all my goddamned life."

"And you never will," she said sweetly.

Without waiting for an answer, she waded to the edge of the pool and hefted herself onto the thick carpet of grass. She ran her fingers through the long blades, listening as they let out a twinkling kind of song. Lorcan climbed out behind her, followed soon by Nollaig and Tarrah.

Nollaig's cloak was plastered to her skin. Water poured from the thick material, the entire thing forming a puddle of water at her feet. Reyna bit back a laugh.

"Perhaps you should take that thing off," Reyna said as she wrung her hair. Wingallock shook his wings, flinging more water onto Nollaig's cloak. "That looks mighty uncomfortable."

"I am fine," Nollaig grunted.

"If you say so," Reyna said in a singsong voice, turning her attention back onto the new surroundings.

They had arrived in the middle of a luminous forest. Overhead, a large outcropping of rocks formed the mouth of the waterfall on this side of the portal. The water rushed down in a mighty haste, crashing into a large pool. Further down, the water slowed, narrowing into a slow-moving river. It appeared to cut through the deep forest, leading…somewhere.

"This is a rainforest," Tarrah said, gazing around with a haunted look in her eyes. "We don't have them in Tir Na Nog. I never thought I'd see one with my own two eyes."

"A rainforest," Reyna murmured, gazing around once again. The name was fitting, she decided. It was so much denser than a normal forest and thick with wet and mud. They had only just climbed from the pool, and already she could feel beads of perspiration on her brow.

Nollaig had scrunched her cloak between her hands and was doing her damnedest to wring out all the wet. She was not succeeding. The material stubbornly clung to her skin, revealing a very muscular form beneath. Reyna was not surprised. Nollaig was one of the strongest fae she'd ever met.

"Now what?" Nollaig muttered. "I don't see a god lurking in the bushes to bestow world-shattering power on anyone who asks."

"We need to follow the river downstream," Tarrah announced. "You see how it slopes downward? We keep going until we can't go down anymore. That's the lowest point in all the world, and great powers can be found deep within the pool."

Nollaig froze, her hand wrapped around an oozing scrap of cloth. "More swimming?"

"Only for the one who wishes to gain the powers," Tarrah said with vacant eyes, her ominous tone twisting unease through Reyna's gut.

The river stretched on for miles. They crunched through the thick brush, always keeping close to the riverbank, until the skies turned grey with twilight. After they set up camp,

Nollaig sat drying by the fire while Tarrah went on the hunt for some meat.

Reyna took the opportunity to go for another swim to rinse off the grime from the days spent travelling through the shadow lands. She grabbed a bar of soap she'd packed and dove into the cool, crisp river, sighing in contentment. It had been a very long time since she had felt the soothing embrace of the chill. Letting her eyes drift shut, she spread her arms wide and floated happily in the Inishfall river.

A loud splash broke her out of her reverie. She opened her eyes to find a grinning Lorcan swimming toward her, a familiar glint in his dark as night eyes. "You didn't think I would stay at camp when I knew you were out here naked, did you?"

She flushed beneath his gaze, even after all their time spent wrapped up in each other's arms. "I didn't think you'd like how cold this river is."

Furrowing his brows, he waded closer. "It's not cold at all. In fact, this river is one of the warmest I've ever felt."

"To me, it feels as cool as the pools in the southern regions of the Ice Court," she said with a smile. "How odd. It's almost as though the river makes us feel whatever we want to feel."

"This place is steeped in magic," he said, though his face remained troubled.

"Isn't that a good thing, Lorcan?" she asked, swimming toward him. "It's proof that magic still exists in this world. Maybe it means we can find a way to stop the Ruin *and* a way to bring magic back to Tir Na Nog."

"There is power in these lands, but that does not mean we could have it for ourselves."

"But isn't that why we're here?" she asked. "To take the power so that we can fight the Ruin?"

A slight smile crested his lips, rivulets of water trailing down his cheek. "I don't believe it will be that easy, but I love that your determination never wavers, even in the face of a power none of us understand."

"You love it, do you?" she whispered, cheeks growing hot.

"I love your determination, your stubbornness, your ferocity. I even love your impulsiveness. Because it's what makes you *you*."

Her heart thundered. "And I love your protectiveness, your strength, your choice to protect innocents, regardless of their court. I even love that you're so easily annoyed. Because *that* is what makes you Lorcan Rothach."

"Easily annoy me now," he growled, pulling her against his slick chest. Her peaked nipples brushed against his pecs, and a sudden arousal tightened her core. She slid her arms around his neck and hooked her thighs around his waist.

She gasped when his throbbing length pushed inside of her, stretching her wide. His mouth tangled with hers, his desperate need a reflection of the desire within her own soul. They moved in rhythm, the waters raging around them as their bodies crashed together.

"I thought you wanted me to annoy you," she gasped as he thrusted inside her once again with an animalistic growl on his lips.

"I just want *you*, Reyna Darragh." He drew back and stared into her eyes before kissing her fiercely. "Always. I never want to let you go. Never again."

His mouth dropped to her breast, his tongue lashing out. A moan rose up inside of her as he sucked and teased, bringing her body so close to the ultimate release. The waters were a whirlwind around them now as their need became frantic, raw, and more real than anything she had ever known.

With slick hands, he cupped her arse and pulled her against him in a crash. Pleasure ripped through her, lighting up her eyes with a million stars. Her climax throbbed through her as his own growl joined her moans. They came together, their bodies becoming one.

When they had finished, Reyna happily sighed. Her arms wrapped around his neck, her cheek rested on his shoulder. With a murmur, he kissed her forehead, and his heartbeat pounded between them. She could feel every thump in her breasts.

"You might have been right about something," he said with a smile, pulling back to gaze into her face.

She arched a brow. "I don't hear that very often from you."

"This place isn't so bad from this viewpoint."

"No, it's not." She grinned. "So, you're admitting that you were wrong."

"I'm saying you were right."

"Which means you were wrong."

He chuckled. "If I say I was wrong, then you'll never let me hear the end of it."

"Now *that* you aren't wrong about."

"I have an idea," he suddenly said, his voice going soft.

"You have my full attention." Although, with their bodies wrapped so tightly together, and the slick waters still rushing between them, she was beginning to get distracted by a certain ache between her thighs again. It had only been a few moments, and she was already wanting more.

She did not see how she could ever not want more.

"When all of this is over, perhaps we *should* find a place like this. Somewhere calm and free. Somewhere away from all the horrors of war."

She smiled and snuggled back into the crook between his shoulder and neck. "It really is a nice idea."

"I don't mean it as an idea or a nice thing to think about." He squeezed her tighter. "I want this for us. For you and me. Otherwise, I fear the world will try to tear us apart again."

"It won't," she whispered, her heart aching. "And you know

we can't. Our world is too full of turmoil for us to walk away from it."

"Maybe not now, but one day," he insisted. "When the wars are done and Tir Na Nog knows peace. We can find somewhere for us. Our kingdoms won't need us then."

"I fear Tir Na Nog will always be at war," she said sadly. "But I will make a promise to you, Lorcan Rothach. When our kingdoms know peace, I will follow you to the ends of the world."

## 39

### EISLYN

It had been four days since Eislyn had eaten anything but berries. She'd wandered through the forest, using the nighttime constellations to guid her west where she knew she would eventually find the Ice Road. There was little that she remembered from what Reyna had tried to teach her. She'd never been interested in learning how to protect herself in the outside world, far too content holed up behind castle walls. But Eislyn had always liked the stars, especially when viewed through the curving glass roof of the library back home.

She knew she was headed in the right direction, but she had yet to find the tavern where the Ice Road met the Rowan Road. And she did not dare join the road until she did. It would be the first place her enemies would expect to find her, and she'd feel safer once she was firmly outside of Lord Killian's lands.

*Enemies,* Eislyn thought sadly. She had enemies now.

With a sigh, she trudged through the snow, picking a few more berries to power her through the rest of the day. She would keep walking for as long as she could before finding somewhere to sleep for the night, safe and hidden deep beneath the snow-laden trees.

A crunch sounded in the distance. Followed soon by another. Heart in her throat, Eislyn dropped into the snow, thankful that her hair blended in with the ice. She squeezed her eyes shut tight, hoping and praying to her forsaken god that she had not been seen. She'd come so far. To be caught now…and what would they do with her? She didn't dare even think it.

"Eislyn!" A familiar voice called. "Princess!"

"Vreis?" Shock flittered through her as she pushed up from the ground, brushing the snow from her bare shoulders. He stood only a short distance away, the sunlight slanting through the trees and spearing his face. He looked rough, his hair tousled, a thin scar running down his left cheek. When he saw her, he fell to his knees. "Thank the Dagda. You're alive. Dagda help me, you're alive."

Tears filled her eyes as she ran to him. It felt like years since she had seen a friendly face, and even longer since she had heard a voice she did not fear. She flew to him, dropping heavily into the snow by his side, grasping his hand in hers. He was cold to the touch.

"*I* thought *you* were dead." She brushed the tears away before they froze on her cheeks. "I thought Lord Killian had you killed."

"He tried," Vreis said with a sharp shake of his head. "His fae cornered me as soon as you walked away from me. I fought them off, but there were too many to take on my own. I thought they were going to kill me right then and there, but you started racing through the markets. They left me with only two guards. Too few, a mistake on their part." He gave her a grim smile. "I managed to kill them both and get free, but you were gone by then. I've been tracking a pair of footprints for days. I didn't even know if they belonged to you. All

I had was hope. And fear. Fear that you hadn't escaped at all, that you were dead."

The emotion in his voice brought Eislyn to her knees. "You're freezing."

Vreis was not an ice fae. He would not be immune to the cold. And yet, he'd been trekking through the northern forests of the Ice Court without a fur coat and winter leathers. To find *her*. She doubted he even knew how to camp out here in these forests where snow piled waist-high or even higher.

Her heart swelled with an unexpected emotion she did not dare name. Where Thane had run from her, Vreis had charged through foreign lands to find her, risking his life. She wanted to pull him to her chest and never let go.

Vreis shuddered against the cold. "It seems your court's name is very fitting indeed. It is impossible to escape the ice."

"Come," she said quietly, taking his hand. "There are some caves not far from here where we can take shelter for the night. I'll build us a fire, so you can get warm. And then maybe we can figure out what the hell we'll do next."

Vreis's relief was immeasurable. She wrapped her arm around his waist and led him through the snow, wrapping him as close to her as she could get. Her body warmth would do very little for him now. He was so chilled that his skin had gone blue. He needed fire and soon.

And, truth be told, Eislyn wouldn't mind it herself.

She didn't feel the cold, but there was still an ache in her bones. She was exhausted from running for days, and the hunger in her gut felt like sharp claws against her ribs. A rest would be good for both of them.

The caves had once been mined for ice glass, but they were abandoned now. The fae had already carved out every shard they could find, and had then moved on to deeper, darker caves where the glass was seemingly endless. Eislyn led Vreis into the first cave they came across, ducking out of the path of the falling snow.

Even now, the caves glittered from remnants of the ice glass, too small to be deemed useful now. The silver stone walls curved overhead, slick stone that looked as though it had been painted to match the colors of the court. The tunnels stretched on for miles, vanishing into darkness, but Eislyn settled them down near the mouth of the cave where light could still reach them.

"There we go." Eislyn sat back on her heels, smiling, once she had gotten a fire going for Vreis. Glencora had once taught her to make a fire, and Eislyn hadn't been certain she would be able to replicate it without her sister there to lead her through, step-by-step. But she had managed to produce some flames, meager though they were.

Vreis shuddered as he held his hands over the flickering warmth. "I never thought I would be so happy to see fire, but here we are."

"And I never thought I'd *build* a fire myself."

"That's right." He cocked his head, curious. "You're an ice fae. You don't feel the cold, right? Where did you learn how to do this?"

"My sister. Glencora," she said. "Reyna doesn't like fire very much."

"No, I can imagine her very stubbornly resisting it, even if it was needed."

Eislyn laughed. "That is Reyna, through and through."

He answered her laugh with one of his own but then choked, coughing. Eislyn's heart sank. "Have you slept at all?"

"Pitifully," he said with a strange smile. "In five-minute bursts here and there. I couldn't find peace long enough to relax. My thoughts were plagued by your face."

"Oh." She frowned. "I didn't realize my face was so terrifying."

He smiled and took her hand. "Quite the opposite in fact. I was afraid that as I slept, you were somewhere hurt and scared. It seems I didn't need to fear at all."

He fell silent and stretched across the smooth ground. A moment later, his eyes dropped shut. Eislyn sat on her hands, watching the rising and falling of Vreis's chest as his breathing steadied. Now that they were safely tucked away in a cave, the full truth of their situation bore down on her head. They were fine—for now. But what of tomorrow? What then? They could not return to Margaidh, and it was a long, long while until they reached the next town. There would be villages on the way, but would they be full of friendly faces? They were part of Lord Killian's province, and they would be loyal to him. He could have already sent word to each and every one, instructing them to take her by force if she appeared.

"Vreis?" she asked in scarcely above a whisper.

He cracked open one eye. "Yes?"

"I don't know what to do."

"What we do is the same as what we'd always planned. We get you to Falias. It just seems the road is a tad rockier than we first thought."

She frowned. He made it sound so easy, but it would be anything but. "We can't stop in the villages, at least not in this province."

"Hmm." He sighed and closed his eye. "You truly believe so many ice fae would be willing to commit treason by capturing the High King's youngest daughter?"

"You're the one who said the grudge ran deep. I don't doubt the loyalty of the fae in my father's province or even Lord Morcant's from Snowport. He's a distant cousin of ours, and he supported the alliance."

"And how far is Snowport from here?"

"Far," she admitted. "No closer than Falias."

"Well then, Eislyn. I will leave the decision in your hands. You know these lands far better than I do."

As Vreis slept, Eislyn dug out the tome she'd found in the eastern market. That was what had started all this, though she was glad for it. If she had first visited the castle and Lord Killian, she would be stuck there, trapped. The market had actually turned out to be her only chance at an escape.

With a sigh, she pressed open the pages. They crinkled beneath her fingers, old and rough and dry. Whoever had owned this book before the merchant had not taken very good care of it. Albin, her librarian friend back in Falias, had taught her how to care for books to prevent them from turning out like this. At the thought of her dear old friend, her heart ached. He had always known exactly what to say to Eislyn, and when not to say a thing, when her nerves were raw and her mind was filled by terrible, cruel images.

Albin was another one of her shields, she realized. How many did she have?

She flipped another page, but the words blurred before her as the exhaustion of the past few days finally took its toll. Sighing, her eyes slipped shut, and the book tumbled into her lap. Moments or hours later, she awoke sharply, startled. It was dark, save the orange glow on slick silver walls. Owls hooted in the distance, and the soft sound of falling snow was a storm in her ears.

For a moment, Eislyn felt a keen sense of disorientation, forgetting where she was and how she'd ended up there. And then it all came flooding back, an overwhelming tide of memories.

"Oof," she whispered as she recalled Lord Killian's betrayal. She remembered visiting him with her father only a few years past, and how he'd smiled when she told him she wished to visit the markets. He'd even gone with her, showing her the stalls that sold books. That was how he'd known where she'd be once the ship docked, she realized. He'd used her quest for knowledge against her.

The book was still open in her lap. Eislyn lifted it up before her, angling the crisp page toward the still-glowing fire. As soon as she read the first sentence, her heart sank. She'd hoped against all hopes that fate had been kind to her, and that they'd somehow grabbed the only book in the market that provided a detailed cure to the Ruin. But of course fate did not work that way, not in Tir Na Nog.

Still, she read the passage. Her quest for knowledge was far too great to shut the book, even if it would prove to be useless.

*The ancient Fomorians once roamed the lands of all the great kingdoms on wings that flew faster than even the most powerful of ships. They sought the Dionadair, the hero that would save them all from the Unseelie's destruction. A destruction that would transform their world into ash.*

Eislyn sat up a little straighter and turned the page. One word had caught her attention. *The ash*. The fae of Tir Na Nog called it the Ruin, but perhaps it had once been called by a different name. Perhaps it was this ash. If that were the case, then it had been around far longer than anyone thought. That would make it centuries and centuries old. Ancient.

Eislyn's stomach twisted. It was a terrifying thought. The Ruin seemed indestructible as it was, but if it were an ancient thing, heralding to a time before the six kingdoms of Tir Na Nog had even existed...then how in the world would she—little Eislyn Darragh—find a way to stop it?

If the *Fomorians* couldn't even stop it...

*Wait,* she thought. They *must* have stopped it. The Fomorians didn't die out. They were still alive.

Eagerly, Eislyn flipped another page, but there was nothing there. It was blank, the words gone. With angry tears in her eyes, she turned to the beginning of the book and read it through. There was little else about the strange dark magic called the ash. Most of it detailed how the Fomorians once visited the human lands but did not bestow any magic on the peoples there.

"You look as though you've seen a ghost."

Eislyn glanced up. As she'd been reading, morning had dawned, and pinkish light speared the cave. Vreis sat before her with ruffled hair, lounging against the slick stone, watching her carefully.

"I think I may have found something, something that matches Thane's research, as well as something I read in a book that randomly appeared in my chambers one day."

Vreis arched a brow. "Books randomly appear in chambers these days? How very curious."

Eislyn gave him a frustrated huff. "*That* is what you're focusing on?"

He grinned. "You have to admit, it's certainly curious."

"Yes, but—"

"You are terribly easy to wind up, Eislyn." His eyes twinkled. "Tell me what you've found that has excited you so."

"I think the Fomorians have experienced the Ruin. These books seem to suggest they tried to stop it from destroying their lands. The *ash* is what they called it. And whatever they did to stop it must have worked because their empire still exists now. They're thriving, Vreis. Whatever they did, it worked."

Vreis held out a hand. "Show me."

She passed him the book, open to the page she'd read over at least a dozen times. While he read the passages about the strange ash, she knelt beside him, bouncing lightly on her knees. Could she have found the answer? If the Fomorians had conquered the ash, then so could the fae of Tir Na Nog.

After Vreis read the passage, he tapped his finger against

the crinkled parchment. "It does sound extraordinarily similar to what your kingdom is experiencing."

"*Our* kingdoms," she corrected. "The Ruin has made it into the air fae lands now."

"And it will likely stretch further south before it is done," he said with a grave nod. "Of course, I can't say I would be terribly unhappy if it took out the wood king. That bastard needs to be stopped."

"He needs to be stopped, but what about all of the innocent wood fae who just want to live their lives in peace? They'll all die, Vreis. I don't care what their king does. They don't deserve to be turned into piles of ash."

He gave her a sad smile. "You are the best of us, Eislyn. And I truly mean that. You will make an excellent queen."

Her heart ballooned in her chest, threatening to break out of her skin. A gasp slipped between her parted lips, and her darned cheeks filled with heat. She ducked her head, pretending to turn her attention back on the book spread open between them.

"You must be mocking me again," she said, after clearing her throat.

"If I joke with you, it's only because I like you very much." He cleared his throat. "But no, I mean every word I say. Most fae, most future queens, would not care one lick about the innocents trapped inside the Wood Court. They would choose the easy option: kill them all."

"What would you choose, Vreis?" she asked insistently.

"I would follow my liege's commands."

She snorted. "You know that's not what I was asking."

"You want to know what I would do if I were king?" He shook his head. "I cannot say. Even Thane was not certain what he wanted to do about that court. To tear down the wood king would be to sacrifice many lives. Not doing anything would mean allowing a cruel king to reign terror over his realm. And to make an alliance would mean to consort with a fae who would be just as likely to eat his own kin as to give him a kiss on the brow."

Eislyn shivered. She had heard the tales, of course. High King Ulaid Molt, the cannibal of the woods. He chose his victims based on dreams, carving them up and eating them piece by piece. Sometimes, he left parts behind, scattered in strange symbols he claimed would return immortality to his fallen fae body.

His victims were always his own subjects, those who had pledged fealty, who called him their liege. Sometimes, Eislyn could not understand why they did not rise up against him. It would only take one arrow pointed right at his heart, and he could terrorize them no longer. The expert aim of wood fae was legendary.

"And the innocents," she insisted. "Those too afraid to run from their cruel king?"

He sighed. "I suppose we ought to try to save them, too."

She beamed at him. "I see you, Vreis. You're as soft as a cake inside. You just don't want anyone to know it."

"Oh, what I would do for some cake." He grinned.

She couldn't help but laugh. "When we reach Snowport, you can gorge yourself on mountains of cake. I will make certain of it."

He arched a brow. "Snowport it is, then? Not straight home to Falias to see your father?"

"There is something in Snowport that I cannot get in Falias," she admitted, bracing herself for his reply. Vreis would not like what she would say next, and she expected that he would try and stop her. But Eislyn knew what she had to do with a kind of certainty that she had not once felt in all of her life, at least the part of her life that she could remember.

"And what's that, Eislyn?"

"A ship to the Empire of Fomor."

# 40

## REYNA

The river path was one of a great many sights and sounds. As they trekked through the humming rainforest, they spotted a crumbling castle in the distance, set upon a distant hill. It was made from a shimmering stone that reflected the island's many gleaming shades of green, and the twisting towers had once been topped with spires spun from emerald gems. Now, it was nothing more than a ruin with two of its many towers appearing to have been blasted out from within.

Tarrah did not have the answers to any of the questions Reyna lobbed at her. Who had built the tower? Who had lived there? Had there once been kings and queens on Inishfall? Had it been home to hidden kingdoms? But the shadow fae had no more answers than she did, nor did she know why the birds sang songs from Reyna's home, melodies she had heard a hundred times in ice fae taverns or in the hall during feasts.

After two more days spent roaming the riverbank, they came upon the end of the ever-narrowing river. It was now nothing more than the trickle of a stream no wider than the length of a finger, pouring the last remnants of its water into a deep, dark pool.

Their party stood around it in a circle, gazing into the murky depths. They could not see the very bottom, but Reyna did not doubt it went deep into the ground beneath their feet. Power hummed, a strange melodic tone that tugged at her ears, whispering, pushing, tempting. It wanted her to jump inside the pool and swim.

"I don't like it," Nollaig said, clucking her tongue. "It does not feel right."

"It holds two incredible powers," Tarrah said, her hollow eyes wider than Reyna had ever seen them. She looked as though she might fall face-first into the pool, giving herself up to the power that sought to claim them all.

"Yes, I can feel that," Nollaig said. "But who owns these powers, Tarrah? Your gods? Or mine?"

Reyna glanced up. "What gods are yours?"

"*Not* what is down there, I am certain of it."

"Well, there's nothing to it, I suppose." Reyna unbuckled her belt and dropped it onto the forest floor. "I came here to find this power, and I am going to take it."

A strong, steady hand touched her elbow. Reyna twisted up to meet Lorcan's eyes. Concern flickered in his deep irises. "Are you certain you want to do this?"

"I am," she said firmly.

With a nod, he stepped back and watched her remove her boots and her light leather armor, dropping it all into a scattered pile a few meters away from the edge of the pool. Lorcan handed her a rope when she was down to her tunic and trousers. She wrapped it around her waist and cinched it tight.

"Nollaig," Reyna said, twisting to the hooded fae. "Wingallock can swim, but not too low beneath the surface. This pool looks deeper than any I've ever seen before. Can you..?"

"Look after him? Of course, Shieldmaiden. It would be my honor."

Reyna reached up and gave her familiar a scratch beneath his chin, and then her owl took off to settle onto Nollaig's shoulder. She hadn't brought her own familiar along. Reyna had noticed that Holas never joined her on quests, even ones that led far from the castle. How she could do that, Reyna did not know. It was another question about the strange fae that had no answer.

Lorcan gave Reyna a grim smile. "If you get into any trouble—"

"Tug six times," she said, heart tumbling. "I know."

With a grunt, he wrenched her against his chest and kissed her as fiercely as he had ever kissed her before. When he pulled back, she was left breathless and all too aware of the audience to their right.

Nollaig cleared her throat. "Be careful down there, Shieldmaiden. If anything looks off, at least try to let go of your stubborn nature long enough to swim away from it."

Tarrah strode over to her and clasped her arms. "You will be fine. All you have to do is listen to what the power says. It will give you a choice. Choose the right thing, and it will fill your bones with light."

"Light...and not darkness?" Reyna could not help but ask. Despite her determination to go through with her plan, she could feel the strangeness of the power, the danger in the hum beneath her feet.

Tarrah nodded. "As long as you choose correctly."

Reyna pressed her lips together and turned toward the pool. With a deep breath, she jumped. Her body went weightless as she soared through the air. She slid into the waters, but she did not feel a flicker of the same soothing chill she'd felt from the river. Instead, she felt a strange nothingness surround her as if she had jumped into an empty pit instead of a pool.

She fell. The pool stretched wide like an open maw as she hurtled past stone after stone after stone. Her heart flailed wildly inside of her as a scream built up in her throat. Time became meaningless as the darkness deepened into an impenetrable black. She could no longer see the hole above her. No light speared this terrible darkness. Suddenly, something yanked on her waist. The rope, slowing her fall.

She came to a sudden stop, her body jerked like a rag-doll. For a moment, she just hung there, swinging back and forth in the darkness. It was quiet down here. Too quiet. So quiet that she could hear nothing but the trembling breath on her own lips.

A voice boomed, making her lurch in the rope. "Reyna Darragh."

The voice was endlessly deep and loud. It burned with power, every word dripping with pain and fear and death. She trembled, her hand twisting up to grab the rope. This was wrong. She shouldn't have come here. Whatever this was, it wasn't good. She could feel the darkness whisper across her skin.

"You came here for power, did you not? The power to stop the plague spreading across your kingdom's dying lands."

She stilled, her breath frosting before her. Suddenly, it was very cold. As cold as ice. Never before had she feared ice, but it terrified her now.

"I came here to find a power great enough to stop the Ruin," she whispered to the voice.

"The Ruin?"

Fear stole through Reyna's heart. The power did not know of the Ruin. And if it didn't know, then it would not know how to fight it. She needed to get out of here.

But she tried one more time. "Yes, the Ruin. It's a powerful dark magic destroying the kingdoms of Tir Na Nog. Ash falls from the skies, and—"

"The Ruin is what *you* call it."

Reyna's heart pounded. "Does it have another name?"

"Many have seen the Ruin but few know the truth of it. Some have called it the Great Ash. Others have named it the Dionadair."

"Then, you do know what it is," she whispered, breathless.

"All of us in Inishfall know your Ruin. The Dionadair of Tir Na Nog."

"Tell me," Reyna said. "Please tell me how to stop it."

"Only *you* can stop it, Reyna Darragh," the voice rumbled. "But only if you choose well."

*Choose.* Just like Tarrah had said.

"How?"

The rope at her waist suddenly unravelled. She broke free, and the pit beneath her stretched its maw wide. A scream ripped from her throat as she tumbled into darkness. She flailed, reaching up for the frayed edges of the rope, but her fingers found nothing but air.

Her heart thudded in her chest, and the scream died on her lips. The wind rushed up around her, death beckoning her further into the pit of the world. She had never been more scared in her life. The terror was the heartbeat racing in her chest, the frantic grasping for breath by her lungs. Reyna was going to die here. She would never get out. The power would swallow her whole.

The winds began to slow, and her feet hit the ground. Gently, she fell to her knees on moss as black as night. Another pool lay a few steps away, glistening from an indigo glow that came from within. She pressed her hand to her heart, trying and failing to catch her breath.

She reached for her dagger, but the voice broke through her thoughts. "You will not sow violence here."

With a gasp, she dropped her hand. "Where am I?"

"You are in Inishfall, the birthplace of the gods."

She swallowed hard, pushing up to her feet. "Are you a god?"

"Look into the pool. You will see two reflections before you. Two paths for your life. Two powers you may claim. Choose wisely, Reyna Darragh."

"What am I choosing?" she whispered, taking a slow, timid step toward the pool.

"A power and a path." The voice paused. "Inishfall has deemed you worthy. You may have what you seek. But you must *choose*."

Reyna could not help but notice that this invisible voice was stubbornly refusing to chat about anything other than the choosing business. She wanted to know so much more. What the Ruin was and how these powers would help her stop it. And what would happen when she made her choice. She wanted to know it all, but when she tried voicing her questions aloud, the voice went silent.

"All right," she said, whispering to herself. "Step up to the pool and look inside. Nothing terrifying about that, right?"

Squaring her shoulders, she knelt beside the cool, slick water. It was a beautiful blue. The color of the sky after a fresh snowfall when the clouds had blown so far away that nothing was left but an endless expanse of cerulean. She pressed her hands against the edge of the rock and leaned forward, gazing into the very depths of the pool.

Reyna saw her own face. Her silver hair was wet through, hanging in clumps around her shoulders. Her eyes were hollow and full of fear, but there was strength in them, too. Rosy lips, long slender neck. Her mother's ice glass ring dangling to her chest from a chain.

"I only see myself," she said.

The pool began to shimmer, transforming Reyna's face

into blurred ripples. A featureless face. When the waters stilled, she was still there, but she was different. Older, stronger, wiser. A crown perched on her head, and a glorious golden light filled the sky behind her.

The voice was back again, speaking in an insistent tone. It sounded as though it were behind her, lurking in the shadows. "If you choose this power, you may have everything you want and more. There will be a crown on your head and fae will kiss your feet. The powers of the fae will fill your mortal form, blessing you with immortality. The elements will bow to your will. Your wings will take flight. You will be unconquerable."

Reyna's heart thundered. "Will I be able to defeat the Ruin?"

A small pause. "You will be able to defeat anything or anyone that you wish, Reyna Darragh."

A thrill went through her. This was it. The answer she had been searching for all this time. She imagined Eislyn's face when she finally told her. Glencora would awaken from her unending slumber. She would be able to see once again. Villages would be restored. Lives would be saved. So many lives. The Ice Court would be a great kingdom for centuries to come.

"But," the voice whispered, and her heart froze. "You must give something in return. A very, very small piece of your soul. You will give it up, and it will belong to me."

Reyna frowned. "A piece of my soul?"

"Oh yes. Only a tiny little piece. It is a small payment for such a great gift, is it not?"

Reyna's frown only deepened, though the reflection's smile never died. Her face began to shimmer once again, replaced by a very different version of herself. This one was older as well, and strong, but she looked sad. There was no crown or golden skies. Just Reyna, surrounded by a grey murkiness.

"This is your second choice. Much like the first, you will gain everything you might need to defeat your Ruin. Immortality, strength, power over the elements. You will become what the fae once were, before the terrible Fall that stole their strength. And you will keep all of your soul."

"What's the payment for this one?" she whispered, terrified to know the answer.

"You must give up your greatest desire."

Her blood churned hotly through her veins as she stared at the sad Reyna in the pool before her. "My greatest desire is to stop the Ruin."

"It is not," the voice replied sharply. "Inishfall can see into the very depths of your soul, Reyna Darragh, and you desire something else far more."

"What is it?" she asked, her voice cracking, knowing at once what he would say.

"Your greatest desire is to live a normal life with Lorcan Rothach."

Pain was a knife in her gut. She sucked in a sharp breath and pulled back from the pool. The vision of her sad eyes vanished into the blue, leaving nothing behind but a blank, unending darkness. Trembling, she stumbled back, desperate to get away from the voice, this strange power, and the choice that it demanded from her.

She could give up a piece of her soul. Or she could give up Lorcan.

"This isn't fair," she hissed, hot tears bubbling up in her eyes. Her chest felt on fire, as if her very soul was burning up inside.

"Power, Reyna Darragh. You will have the power to change the world. That cannot be given freely. You must *choose*."

It was an impossible choice. She new what the first power

would do. It would take a part of her, and it would use it for its own ends. Much like her vow to the shadow king, she would be trapped. Forever bound to it, for as long as the world continued to spin.

"You must make your decision *now,* Reyna Darragh," the voice whispered harshly in her ear. "*Now* or we will offer up our power to another soul. Someone else. Someone who is willing to make the choice that you resist. And then you must go and destroy the Ruin in the place where it began."

That first power, the one that wanted her soul, was Unseelie. She knew it in her bones, even as the voice whispered his own name into her ear. *I am Unseelie. I am that power,* it hissed.

But the second power was something else, a forgotten power that the fae of Tir Na Nog did not know. It wasn't the Dagda. Suddenly, memories of the world sparked to life in her mind as the powers washed knowledge through her like a storm.

The second power was Seelie.

If she chose Seelie's power, she would keep her soul but lose *him.* Great sobs shook through her as she stared at the pool. She could leave this all behind and walk away from it, she knew. But she would never again find a way to save her kingdom from certain death.

"I choose Seelie," she whispered, her shoulders sagging forward. All the happiness she'd felt during the past weeks with Lorcan got sucked out as the magic poured in.

## 41

### TARRAH

Tarrah stumbled back from the pool, gasping as the rope unravelled in Lorcan's hands. The prince roared in frustration, throwing the rope at the ground and shouting down at the pit. Suddenly, a soothing calm washed over her, and a familiar voice spoke into the very depths of her soul. She did not know if she should trust it, but it had been with her for so very long.

*It is all right, Tarrah Glas,* the deep, dark voice said into her mind. *Reyna Darragh is alive. She will return to you soon.*

Relieved, she stumbled toward Lorcan. "Reyna is fine. She'll be back soon."

"How can she be fine?" he said, pounding his fist against the ground. "The rope broke. She's down there, alone and trapped, and I have to go after her."

He started to throw off his clothes, but a strange rumble shook the ground. Nollaig stumbled back from the pit as the waters frothed, splashing white foam onto the banks. A face crested the waters, a face framed in silver hair.

Tarrah sagged in relief. Unseelie had been right. Reyna was here.

Coughing, Reyna swam to the bank. Lorcan rushed to her side, hauling her into his arms with a kind of ferocity that made Tarrah's heart ache. She would never experience love like that. Teutas had been taken away from her forever.

"Reyna," Lorcan said, pulling back to press the damp hair away from her face. "Reyna, are you all right? The rope broke. I thought you were..." His voice broke with emotion.

"I'm fine," she said stiffly, pulling out of his arms. "The gods broke the rope so I could reach the bottom of the birthplace, and then they sent me back."

"What in the name of the Dagda are you talking about?" Lorcan demanded. "What's wrong with you? Why won't you look at me?"

Reyna cringed away from him, and the smile slid from Tarrah's face.

"The Dagda isn't a god. He was a Fomorian," Reyna whispered with a haunted fear creeping into her silver eyes. "Those two powers down there are the ones that began this world, not him. I had to make a choice between them. The light or the darkness."

Lorcan just gaped at her, incredulous.

Tarrah's heart pounded in her ears. "What did you choose, Reyna?"

Reyna gave her a sad smile. "I chose light."

Tarrah let out an audible sigh, smiling. She knew Reyna would choose the right option, unlike her mother. "I knew you would. I knew it! My mother chose the wrong power, but you didn't."

Reyna stood and pushed the damp hair away from her face. She gazed at Tarrah almost...sadly. "You're right. Your mother chose Unseelie, Tarrah. She had to give up a part of her soul for his power, and some of that power got passed onto you through her blood. Not all of it, but some. Enough that it's been with you every day of your life. It's why you've been able to see his visions and hear his voice in your mind."

Tarrah hissed and stumbled back. "Unseelie's power isn't here. Stop it. You're full of lies now. Just like everyone else."

The voice began to rumble in her mind again.

*Reyna isn't lying. It is me, Unseelie, in that pit. I thought I could trust Reyna to make the right decision, but I was wrong. She chose the god of destruction instead of the god of light. You must kill Reyna, go into the pit, and take my power so that* you *can become the one to fight the Ruin. If you do not, Reyna will destroy the world. Seelie is the dark god. I am the god of light, don't you see?*

Tarrah hissed when Reyna got too close. Her mind was full of whispered words and fear.

"Tarrah, what are you doing?" Nollaig asked from where she stood firmly by Reyna's side. "This isn't like you. Reyna has shown you nothing but kindness."

*Has she shown you kindness? She punched you once, remember?*

"She punched me," Tarrah whispered.

"Tarrah, you tricked her into thinking the king had her sister." Nollaig gestured at the princess who had taken the darkest power in the world. "That was weeks ago besides. Calm down and get over here. We need to get Reyna dry and hear what happened down in that pit."

"I know what happened in that pit. She chose *Seelie*. She chose the dark god. Reyna Darragh will destroy the world."

A tiny part of Tarrah's mind wondered if she was wrong. Unseelie had given her so much truth, but he had also given her lies. Teutas was dead. Desperately, Tarrah tried to grasp onto that memory, even as it tried to slip through her fingers like sand.

Nollaig turned to Reyna. "I fear the power here is getting to her mind. She is not being herself."

"It's in her blood, and Unseelie gains strength through

blood," Reyna said softly. "But yes, the power is strong here, too."

*You must kill her,* Unseelie whispered into her ear, every word drenched in anger. *She chose the wrong god. The evil god. The one that twists minds and spreads lies about my power. I told you about him. You must kill her.*

Tarrah stared at Reyna, her heart in her throat.

"No," Tarrah mumbled. "No, I won't. Teutas—"

*Teutas was a test. One you failed. If you'd passed, I would have returned him to you.* The hiss grew louder in her mind, so loud that she had to clamp her hands over her ears. *I will give you one more chance because I am a gentle, kind god. Teutas will be returned to you if you kill Reyna Darragh. If you do not, she will destroy the world. And you will never see Teutas again.*

This was it, Tarrah realized as she gazed across the forest at Reyna. This was Tarrah's choice, her test. She had chosen wrong before. She had trusted those she shouldn't have. She had listened to sweet words and smiled at false smiles. She had been tricked and used and tempted to stray from the truth.

Unseelie whispered all of this into her ears, and Tarrah knew. Teutas would give her the seed for the babe who would cross the impassible sea and conquer the Fomorians. It would all happen just as Unseelie had said. But she had to prove her faith.

"You chose wrong!" she shouted at Reyna, trembling as she grabbed her bow and drew an arrow from her back. In an instant, she had her aim. Her arrow was pointed right at Reyna's heart.

"What the hell, Tarrah?" Nollaig asked, shocked.

"Reyna Darragh chose wrong. She chose Seelie. The god of blood and death."

## 42

### REYNA

Reyna stared down the center of the iron arrowhead. "Tarrah, you know I can dodge those. You've seen me do it."

"What are you doing, Tarrah?" Nollaig hissed angrily.

Tarrah shifted on her feet, swallowing hard. Reyna ought to be angry that the shadow fae was pointing an arrow at her heart, but she wasn't. Instead, she just felt sad for her. All these years, she'd been living with the constant hum of Unseelie in her blood. Tarrah's mother had given a part of her soul for his power. It had twisted her, and in turn, it had twisted Tarrah, too.

No one could survive that and come out whole.

"Tarrah," Reyna said softly. "If you want to shoot that arrow at me, then go on and do it. And then let's put down that bow and try to talk things through."

Lorcan let out a low growl, a verbal display of exactly how he felt about *that* plan. He'd seen her dodge plenty of arrows and yet he held onto his protective instinct like a shield. It had pained her to see his face when she'd climbed out of the pit. His dark eyes had sparked with love and concern. The strength of his arms around her had been so familiar and so wrong. She did not know how to tell him what she'd given up.

He would never forgive her.

The power of Seelie felt like lightning in her veins, filling her up with life. Everything was clearer now. Colors glowed brighter and deeper, and the sounds of the forest were loud in her ears. She swore she could hear the crackle of a branch from miles away. It felt as if she had been born anew.

"Go on then," Reyna said to Tarrah, knowing that nothing she could do would harm her.

Tarrah roared and loosed. Reyna ducked without even focusing on what she was doing, and the arrow splashed into the pool behind them. She distantly wondered what would happen to it now. Would the gods snatch it into their grasp and use it on an unsuspecting passerby? Would they stab it into someone else's heart?

Trembling, Tarrah nocked another arrow.

"Tarrah, honestly, this is ridiculous!" Nollaig threw up her hands and stalked toward Tarrah. "I'm going to put a stop to this right here and now."

Tarrah shifted her aim toward Nollaig's heart. Without hesitation, Reyna threw herself to the side, slamming Nollaig hard into the ground just as the arrow whizzed passed the cloaked fae's head. Reyna rolled off of her at once and jumped to her feet, leaping in front of Lorcan in case Tarrah decided to turn her attentions onto him.

But she was fumbling with the third arrow, clearly growing flustered. Tarrah had never been fond of battle.

Nollaig brushed off her cloak and stood. "Tarrah, I cannot believe what you have just done. After everything I have done for you. I am not your enemy, and neither is the princess. Stop this nonsense now!"

"She can't," Reyna whispered, watching Tarrah's every movement like a hawk and motioning for Wingallock to do the same. She'd finally gotten another arrow nocked, and Reyna did not doubt she would try to kill Nollaig again. She was past seeing reason now. "It's Unseelie. This isn't her fault."

"How can we stop this?" Lorcan asked in a low voice, pressing a firm, steady hand against her back. She wanted to lean into him, to give in to the strength she felt when he was near. But she couldn't. Not anymore. She had thrown their future away, and it wasn't right to let him believe that nothing had changed when everything had.

"We need to dig it out of her," Nollaig said. "Just like we dug the mark out of Lorcan's skin."

"Tarrah doesn't have a mark, and making her bleed out the poison will only leave her dead," Reyna said sadly, while still keeping her eye locked firmly on Tarrah's fingers.

Nollaig leaned in close and whispered into Reyna's ear, bringing with her a whiff of fire and smoke. "You said Unseelie's power is in her blood. But what's in *your* blood, Shieldmaiden? If you took Seelie's power, could you pass it onto her by giving her some of yours?"

Reyna cocked her head, considering.

"You cannot expect Reyna to cut herself open like that," Lorcan said in a low growl. "We're in the middle of a bloody forest with no help in sight. If we're unable to staunch the wound, she could die."

Reyna did not know how to tell him how very wrong he was. All she could say was, "That won't kill me. Few things can now." She turned to Nollaig to avoid the shock in Lorcan's eyes. "Even if we try this, there's no guarantee this will work, or if she'll even let me close enough to do it."

Nollaig spoke with enough strength to bring down an entire mountain. "We will *make* her take it. I don't care if she fights us or not. It is time to release this god's grip on her mind. Look at what it has done to her."

Reyna pressed her lips together. She did not disagree, but

she did not believe it would be as simple as that. Unseelie would not want to relinquish his hold on Tarrah. She'd been a loyal servant for years, always pushing his agenda one step forward. Unseelie wasn't done with her yet.

"I know what you're saying!" Tarrah trembled, the arrow quivering in her tense hands. "You're going to kill me. The three of you are plotting my death."

"We don't want to kill you, Tarrah," Nollaig said gently. "We want to help you."

"You don't. Your minds are being bent by the Seelie servant's whispered words." Tarrah swallowed thickly, her eyes darting from Reyna to Nollaig and back to Reyna again. "She wishes me dead. That way, you will never know the truth about her power."

Reyna's heart twinged. In truth, Tarrah was partly right. She *didn't* want the others to know what she'd been forced to give up. It was just as she'd guessed. There was always an undercurrent of truth in Unseelie's lies. He'd done it to Tarrah over the years, showing her visions that would come to pass so that lies were less noticeable when he needed to use them. Now, when it mattered the most, his words were impossible to resist.

"How should we do this, Shieldmaiden?" Nollaig murmured. "She seems to be growing more frantic by the moment."

"We need to disarm her first. Otherwise, I fear she will turn the both of you into pincushions with her arrows."

"You paint quite the pretty portrait," Nollaig said dryly.

Lorcan lowered his lips to her ear, his breath hot on her skin. "I don't like this."

"Neither do I. But I'm not going to fight her, and Unseelie will not let her give up until I'm dead." Reyna finally drew her eyes up to meet Lorcan's. He gazed at her with such fierce devotion that it made hidden tears burn her eyes. Why had

Seelie made her give him up? Why did the sacrifice have to be so astronomical?

*Because the power you now yield is even greater than yourself, and so is the kingdom you wish to save.*

Reyna let out a shuddering sigh and pulled away. Perhaps one day she would find the words to explain what she had done, but right now, they had a murderous shadow fae ready to kill them all.

Taking a slow and steady step toward Tarrah, she drew her dagger and slashed it across her arm. The pain was nothing compared to the ache in her heart, the loss she felt from letting go of her future life with Lorcan. And it would heal soon enough, within moments now that she had the power of Seelie singing through her veins. She doubted her heart would ever heal.

"What are you doing?" Tarrah hissed, flicking her eyes from side to side as Reyna drew closer. "Stay back. I'll shoot you with this arrow."

"I'll just dodge it, Tarrah." Reyna spread her arms wide. "If you wish to fight me, then face me with your sword."

Tarrah swallowed, her knuckles white from her death grip on her bow. "Only if they stay back. I want to fight you and you alone."

"They'll stay back," Reyna said.

"All right." Tarrah nodded, still trembling, and slowly lowered her bow to the ground. She dropped the arrow and reached for her sword, but Reyna was on her before she could draw it.

Reyna raced forward at an impossible speed, drawing from the strength of the newfound power in her blood. She knocked Tarrah off her feet, pinning her to the ground. Tarrah screamed and writhed beneath her with murder in her eyes.

"I have her!" Reyna shouted.

Lorcan and Nollaig were right behind. They dropped to either side of her and each grabbed an arm, holding down the shadow fae. Tarrah screamed, loosing an inhuman shriek that pounded against their ears. Wincing, Reyna shifted her weight to Tarrah's thighs, holding down her bucking body.

"For the love of the gods, what is this?" Nollaig asked in shock.

"You know what it is," Reyna answered grimly.

Narrowing her eyes, she leaned over Tarrah's shrieking face and pressed her open wound against her lips. Suddenly, Tarrah went deathly still. Reyna's blood dripped into the shadow fae's open mouth, and with it, the power of Seelie, she hoped.

After several silent seconds ticked by, Reyna pulled her arm back to her side and wrapped the wound with a torn scrap of her tunic. She would heal soon enough, but she did not wish to leave her blood in this place.

Tarrah remained still. Her vacant eyes stared up at the dense rainforest canopy. The only sign of life was the shallow rise and fall of her chest.

Lorcan frowned and sank back onto his heels. "She's stopped fighting. Perhaps it worked."

The steady hum of the forest rose up around them as they waited for Tarrah to wake from the slumber that had wrapped her in such a tight embrace. Lizards scuttled past on the blanket of moss, their scales flickering from green to brown to red. Crickets chirped, joining together in a song that warned of the impending darkness of the night. And all around them, birds began to sing. Those strange hidden creatures who knew the songs of the ice.

Nollaig let out a heavy sigh that spoke of relief. "It really has stopped. Your blood must be healing hers. She needs to rest for awhile, I'm sure. We should set up a camp and get a fire started. It will not be long until nightfall."

Reyna's heart thudded. She placed her palm against Tarrah's cheek, trying to feel the power inside of her.

Suddenly, Tarrah's eyes flipped open. Her body jerked with a force so strong that it knocked every last one of them aside. Reyna hit the ground, twisting just in time to see a terrible darkness stream out of Tarrah's widened mouth. It looked like a writhing snake of shadows.

"What's happening?" Nollaig desperately tried to grab Tarrah's arm, but the shadow fae writhed out of her grasp, and then kicked her in the face.

"Fucking hell!" Nollaig stumbled back, pressing her palm against her hood. When she pulled her fingers away, they were drenched in blood.

"Tarrah." Reyna grasped the shadow fae's wrists, finally pinning her back onto the ground. Tarrah screamed, and her eyes rolled back in her head.

"Poison, it's poison. Your blood is poison," Tarrah gasped, teeth chattering. "Unseelie hates it."

"Tarrah, can you ignore Unseelie for now? Focus on the Seelie power. Draw upon that. Find strength in it."

With a shuddering sob, Tarrah whipped her head from left to right. "I can't. I can't, I can't, I can't."

"Try, Tarrah," Reyna said fiercely, fear and worry twisting in her gut. "You need to find a way to fight against this."

The tremors began to subside, and her breathing went shallow. Tears poured from Tarrah's blood-streaked eyes. "It doesn't work that way, Reyna. Only Unseelie can spread his power through blood."

Reyna frowned. "Tell me how to give you Seelie power then. If it isn't blood, it must be something else. I'll do whatever it takes. Just tell me now."

Tarrah sobbed. "It's too late. He has me, and he's never letting go. Just like he wouldn't let go of my mother." Her eyes slid shut, and she gasped. "I see everything so clearly now. He isn't what I thought he was, and his goal is—" The shaking resumed, hurtling through Tarrah's body with a violent force.

"Tarrah," Reyna whispered, holding Tarrah's trembling body in her arms. She hugged her close, trying to hold her still, but it was no use. "Tarrah, shhh, it's okay, it's okay."

But it wasn't okay. Unseelie was wrenching the life out of Tarrah. And there was nothing to be done.

"You were right," Tarrah suddenly said with a gasp. "He is in my blood, and he is boiling it. Everything's on fire. Reyna, help me. Please."

Reyna wanted to shout at the gods. She had been given a great power, but there was little she could do to stop this horrible torment.

Tarrah stilled. Blood bubbled up from her mouth, spilling onto her chin.

"You've been tricked," the shadow fae whispered with her dying breath.

# 43

## LORCAN

They buried Tarrah's body in Inishfall, not far from the pool that held the power that had claimed her life. It was a somber affair. They poured the fresh dirt over her broken body, silent but for the occasional sniffle from Nollaig's cloak. Lorcan had a heavy heart. He'd felt nothing but disdain toward Tarrah when she'd first arrived at court. He'd thought her cruel and weak-willed. A fae with a twisted plan to ruin a dying kingdom.

In the end, he had been wrong about Tarrah. But he'd been right about the thing controlling her mind.

Reyna seemed distant and haunted, though he could scarcely blame her. He could not imagine what she had seen in that pool, nor could he know how she'd felt when she'd returned, only to be attacked by a fae she'd come to trust. He couldn't help but wonder if it had reopened a wound he thought they'd healed. Had Tarrah's betrayal reminded her of his?

He hoped not. But if it had, then he would once again prove his devotion to her. He would go to the ends of the world if that was what it took.

As they journeyed back to the portal, Reyna filled them in on what had happened in the pool. The pit, she called it. The birthplace of the gods. Lorcan listened to her every word in shock and awe. The Dagda was not a god but a Fomorian. He'd been a follower of Seelie himself, and he'd taken the power from the pit. He'd never intended to create a religion of devoted fae to worship at his feet. But the fae had been amazed by his powers. They'd declared him a god. So, he had left Tir Na Nog behind to get away from it all.

Reyna had learned all of this in the pit, but there was still much she didn't know. Where had the power come from? Could it be returned to Tir Na Nog? And why had Unseelie been so desperate to kill her?

"You said you were given a choice," Lorcan said quietly when they were half a day's march from the waterfall. "Unseelie's power in exchange for a piece of your soul. Did Seelie demand anything in return?"

Reyna gave him a sad, haunted smile. "He asked me to prove my selflessness."

"And how did you do that?" he asked as a terrible unease swirled through his gut. This muted, downcast Reyna was nothing like the fae he knew and loved. Something had hurt her down in that pit, and he had a mind to turn back and rip that power apart, piece by piece, seam by seam, until it gave her happiness back. Even Wingallock seemed forlorn, flapping his wings mournfully in the skies above.

"There is nothing you can do, Lorcan," she said, as if reading his mind. "It is done."

"*What* is done?" he asked, his voice rising in frustration.

Reyna stopped and pressed her palms against his chest. She gazed up at him with those silver eyes. Once, they had stared at him with hope. Now, her irises churned with something else. He wanted to make her see that everything would be all right. He wanted to hold her tight to his chest and tell her that nothing else mattered. They had each other. He'd never leave her side. But something stopped him. Something in the way she held back.

"When we return to Tir Na Nog, I will explain everything. After we've found a way out of Findius, so that I can go home and save my kingdom. I have to fight the Ruin where it began, and it began north." She sighed and glanced around her. "But I do not wish to speak of it here. The forest is inviting, but I do not trust the trees. There are eyes and ears we cannot see."

Lorcan frowned. "What does that mean?"

"There are others here," Nollaig whispered. "Some prisoners who have survived all these years, no doubt. They are very curious about what we are doing here."

Lorcan stiffened and rested his hand on the hilt of his sword, thumbing the gold. He gazed at the trees, searching for any sign of life. But there wasn't even a whisper of movement in the thick of it all.

"We ought to hurry," Nollaig added. "Some of the prisoners here were convicted of cannibalism. I would prefer not to get eaten this day."

Despite Nollaig's worries, they made it to the waterfall without incident, and Reyna's newfound power prevented them from being trapped in Inishfall. Soon, they were back on familiar lands, standing on the rocky outcropping of the Shadow Court's jagged mountains.

Night had fallen, and the harsh winds swept through the rocks. They made camp for the night, holding off any forward trek until they'd decided what to do. Findius was full of treachery and mad minds. But the realm's low fae needed him, perhaps now more than ever.

"What do you wish to do, Lorcan?" Reyna asked, poking a stick into the fire as she stared into the flames. He frowned, watching her. She'd never before seemed keen on fire. In fact, she avoided it like the plague. Now, she seemed enthralled by it.

"My father sent assassins to kill me," he said as if that answered everything, but it didn't, and they both knew it.

"He is a wicked, cruel king."

"Tarrah said he sacrificed eight thousand lives because of a vision he thinks he received from Unseelie." A hot fire licked down his spine just at the thought of it. He had always thought his father cruel, but this was far past anything he would have expected, even from him.

"And he would likely sacrifice many more if he believed it would give him the power he craves." She glanced up from the fire. The flames danced along her ice-kissed skin.

"You should stop him, Lorcan." Nollaig suddenly spoke up from where she'd quietly been listening to the exchange. "You're free now. You can."

An ache formed in the middle of Lorcan's chest. "And then what? This will still be an exiled kingdom with no hope of survival past half a dozen years, if that. They will have no ruler. Any lord that rose up to take his place would no doubt be just as cruel as him. Maybe less mad but just as cruel."

"You are the prince. You would take the throne."

"What?" He laughed around a sickening lump in his throat. "I could never do that. I—"

*I only want to be with Reyna.* She would never be happy if she stayed in the shadow realm. She needed fresh air and ice and cold. Hair tumbling down her back, her horse charging through a snow-drenched woods. He could not imagine her truly happy anywhere else.

And beyond all that, there was the Ruin. It had begun in the ice kingdom. So, that was where she needed to go.

If he stayed in Findius, he would have to watch her leave. He would have to endure the shattering of his heart. The people of the Shadow Court needed a steady ruler. Someone to right Bolg Rothach's wrongs. But if Lorcan was the one to do it, he would have to...

Selflessly sacrifice his own happiness.

Realization slammed into his gut like an iron fist. Slowly, he stood, clenching and unclenching his hands and desperately trying to hold on to the last bit of composure he had.

"Reyna," he said in a deep, rumbling voice as he stalked toward her. Her words echoed ominously in his mind.

*I had to prove my selflessness.* She had looked *so sad,* so defeated. Like the power had broken her heart. Now he knew why.

She stiffened, the stick stilling in the flames. He felt Nollaig watching him, clearly confused, but she had not been inside his thoughts, piecing the puzzle together and understanding everything all at once.

"Reyna, what did you give up?" he said in a low voice he knew was edged in danger.

She pressed her lips together, and the color fled from her cheeks. "Judging by your expression, you've figured it out."

Anger clawed up his throat, slashing it raw. "I need you to tell me. I need to know I'm not going mad. Because I cannot believe that you would do what it is I think you've done."

Sighing, she twisted away from the fire and stood. Her face was a storm of emotion. "You do believe it. Because it was the only choice I had."

A feral roar ripped from his throat as the truth crashed down all around him. She had done it. His heart pounded. She had really given him up to the gods.

"How could you?" he asked, his fisted hands trembling. "How could you give us up so easily? Have I meant *nothing* to you?"

"You mean everything," she whispered, tears filling her eyes. "That's why *you* were it. For the power of Seelie, I had to sacrifice my greatest desire."

Taken aback, Lorcan stared. *He* was her greatest desire? A storm of emotions shook his body. Happiness, that she cared for him so much. Pain and fury, that she had thrown it away like an old, dirty rag.

Nollaig cleared her throat, stood, and then vanished into the cavern. He didn't blame her. He didn't want to be here either, faced with the truth of such terrible agony.

"I gave you my heart," he said bitterly.

"And I gave you mine. This doesn't change how I feel about you, Lorcan. Nothing could ever change that. This doesn't mean my love for you is gone."

He shook his head, speechless. She had never spoken those words, and now they hung between them like daggers of ice, ready to pierce every part of him.

"What it does mean is that we will be ripped apart."

She flinched, nodding. "It has already started. You have your task. I have mine. Soon, we will be on opposite ends of the world."

"It doesn't have to be this way."

"We don't have a choice." With a trembling chin, she reached out, but then let her hand drop to her side again. "We can try to fight against it. We can try to stay together as long as we can. But you would have to leave your kingdom behind. I have to go north, Lorcan, to where the Ruin began. The power is a part of me now, and I took it for a reason."

"The power," he said in a growl. "You could have walked away from it. You didn't have to take any of it at all!"

"Yes, I did," she whispered, tears pouring down her flushed face. "I had to take it, Lorcan. *I have to save them.*"

He whirled on her, his body brimming with all-consuming pain. "What about us though, Reyna? Who saves us?"

She shook her head, and her eyes were drenched in sadness. "We don't get to be saved."

"I don't accept it," he shouted, pointing a finger at the

cavern. "Return to the pit and tell Seelie to take it back."

"I can't. And I won't."

He stormed off, leaving the camp behind to find somewhere he could think. Her face was emblazoned in his mind. He couldn't bear to see it anymore. Not knowing what she'd given up.

He stopped at the edge of a cliff and gazed out at the dreary, mist-enshrouded expanse. The odds that he and Reyna would have ever met were alarmingly small. They were from opposite ends of a continent that had been ravaged by war for a hundred years. In truth, it was a miracle they had ever stumbled upon each other. And even more of a miracle that they'd survived everything the world had thrown at them, to find themselves in each other's arms.

For a fleeting moment in time, they had been happy.

How could she have given it up? How could she have tossed away her own happiness, and his, for a chance to save her kingdom?

*Because she is Reyna Darragh.*

Lorcan closed his eyes and sagged against the rock. This was what he loved about her. Her bullheaded, single-minded determination to protect her people. Her ferocity toward anyone who threatened their safety. She would do anything for them. She never would have chosen any other way.

Letting out a great, shuddering sigh, he suddenly knew what must be done. His entire life had tunnelled into this very moment. When he had lost his mother to the Fomorians. When his father had forced him to become his legitimized son. The years he spent as a spy, standing beside Thane Selkirk and learning the ways of the courts.

And now, losing Reyna and any hope he'd ever had of living a normal life.

Lorcan would return to Findius, and he would become the next king.

## 44
### EISLYN

Eislyn had never been happier to see Snowport in her life. The small city sat on the northwestern edge of the Ice Court's frozen lands, its shores edged by the glittering Sea of Fomor. The city itself was much smaller than Falias, and the fae who called it home were the sturdiest of them all. Temperatures often dropped so low that the citizens tended to snack on ice when they were thirsty rather than bother with finding water.

And despite its size, Snowport was a booming city. The trade route with the Empire of Fomor meant that merchants from all over the realm would travel far to the weekly market set inside the castle walls. The castle itself had been carved from gleaming white stone, and its windows had been crafted from some of the earliest ice glass mined from the nearby caves. Two towers rose from opposite ends of the sturdy structure, identical in height. It had been built in a way to honor the link between the two continents, forever bound by their centuries-long trade.

From the top of the western tower, you could see Tuath Isle on a clear day. When Eislyn had visited in years past, she'd often peered out the glistening windows in search of foreign ships. Not once had she ever been lucky enough to see a Fomorian.

She wondered if today would be her day.

Vreis shivered as he stared up at the icy city. "It's beautiful, Eislyn. I've never seen anything quite like it."

"You'll like Falias more. There is nowhere in this world better than Falias. Everything is such a crystal, clear blue. The castle itself looks like it was built from ice."

Vreis lifted a brow. "Snowport looks pretty icy itself. In fact...where's the smoke? Where are the fires?"

Eislyn smiled. "We only use fire to cook, and you'll find ice fae are a superstitious lot. Many avoid fire when they can."

"I am going to freeze to death."

"There will be fur, and there are some hot springs just north of the castle. We don't use them for bathing—we prefer the cold—but the fae here like to use them to cook their meats."

"So, I would be bathing in your ovens," he said flatly.

She couldn't help but laugh and hook her arm through his. "You're reminding me of Reyna, you know. When we first arrived at the Air Court, she couldn't stop complaining about all that wind. You would have thought she'd been dropped into a vat of molten iron."

At the sound of her sister's name on her tongue, her smile dropped like a stone into the churning sea. *Oh, Reyna.* She fought back her tears. Even when Reyna had been a Shieldmaiden, Eislyn had seen her almost every day. They'd never gone more than a week apart. It felt like one of her arms had been chopped off and buried somewhere in the ground.

She did not even know if Reyna was safe, let alone alive. And Reyna would have no idea where Eislyn had gone either. She could picture her sister's face now, screwed up in tormented rage. If anyone was going to kill Aengus, it would be Reyna Darragh.

"You've disappeared on me again," Vreis said quietly, a gentle hand on her back.

She flushed from his touch. "I'm sorry. I'm just—"

"Worried about your sister," he finished for her. He could always do that, read her thoughts so easily. Despite herself, Eislyn had begun to feel certain things for Vreis that she knew she mustn't. But he was warm and he was kind and he was good. He saw her for who she was, and he cared for her in spite of it all. She did not know if it went deeper than that for him, but even if it didn't, she knew she'd found a true friend for life.

Not a shield. A friend.

She nodded. "Come. Let's go see my cousin."

They strode through the open city gates, smiling up at the guards that manned the wall, passing fae who were bustling to and from the market square. For once, it felt nice to come and go as she pleased. It had been so long since her every action had not been watched, where she was safe enough to stride down a street without worry.

Tairngire had been a beautiful place. But it was a dangerous one. The fae hid behind their city walls, terrified to leave for fear the enemy might sprout from the very ground itself and kill them instantly.

The Ice Court had not avoided war either, but the battles never made it this far north. Here, peace was an ever-present calming presence, and the city knew it. Few fae were carrying weapons, and their faces were unlined, free from worry.

Eislyn could not help but be envious of every last one of them.

When they reached the castle gates, one of the guards recognized Eislyn and welcomed her inside. He jumped down from his post, his long white hair twisted up into a knot on top of his head. The Ice Court armor fit him well, and his hoarfrost cloak rippled in the light breeze.

"Princess Eislyn, we weren't aware you were paying a visit," he said. "Lord Morcant will be exceedingly pleased to see you. How long has it been since you were last in Snowport?"

Eislyn wasn't certain. The years were all jumbled up in her head.

"A few," she said tightly. "Too long."

"Aye, you mustn't stay away too long next time." He grinned. "Or does your southern king demand too much of your attention?"

A snake of unease hissed through her gut. She glanced at Vreis and caught his frown. "I'm not certain what you mean."

"Don't be so bashful," the guard said. "All of Tir Na Nog is abuzz with the news. The youngest princess of the Ice Court has caught the eye of none other than the air king."

Her cheeks flared beneath his knowing stare. "I'm afraid it has been a long journey, and I need to see my cousin at once."

The guard caught the change in her tone, his own grin dying. "Suit yourself. I'll escort you inside."

"That's hardly necessary," she said with an exasperated sigh. "I've been here a dozen times before. I know the way."

"Lord Morcant wouldn't want you to be wandering around by yourself. The north isn't as safe as it once was."

At his ominous words, Eislyn snapped her mouth shut and followed him through the cerulean square. He led them into the looming doors of the main hall and into a study where she found her uncle bent over his desk, scribbling furiously on a sheet of rolled parchment.

The guard cleared his throat. "My lord."

Lord Morcant jumped halfway out of his rickety chair and whirled toward them with an accusatory glare. When his eyes landed on Eislyn, they widened in shock. He wet his lips, and then glanced at Vreis, before twisting his face into an expression of familiar kindness.

"Princess Eislyn." He pushed up from his chair. "I daresay you have given me quite a shock! Come in. Come in. And your friend. Are you quite all right? Everyone is worried about you. Your father is about to tear out his hair, what's left of it."

At once, she relaxed. It felt so good to see her cousin's familiar face and hear his voice, the one that sounded so much like her father's. She edged inside the study and perched on a leather armchair that sat beneath rows of packed shelves. Vreis stood just to the side of her, choosing to stand rather than sit. Her cousin noticed, but he did not say a word.

"My dear, Eislyn." He clasped his hands, leaning toward her. "I don't know quite where to start. Perhaps with the obvious question. Are you all right, my dear?"

"I am fine," she said, nodding to Vreis. "Thanks to him, of course. He smuggled me out of the Air Court and sailed me all the way north."

"All the way north?" Her cousin frowned. "To Margaidh?"

She nodded.

"Oh dear." Lord Morcant twisted his clasped hands into a knot. "There has been quite the rumbling going on in Margaidh. They're unhappy with the alliance. There's been talk of war. I assume if you're here then you didn't get caught up in all of that?"

Eislyn filled her cousin in on everything that had happened since leaving Tairngire. It was a long tale, and by the time she was done, night had cast a heavy blanket on the sky. The stars were out in full force this night, thousands of brilliant suns gazing at them from far above. An ache formed in Eislyn's chest. She had missed home so very much.

If only she could stay. If only the answers to the Ruin did not lie across the sea.

When Eislyn had finished with her very long and scattered tale, her uncle sat back in his chair, chin rested on his fist. "So, no one has any idea where you are?"

She shook her head. "We must send word to my father at once. He needs to know what we've encountered, and what's happening in the Air Court."

"Because of this Grand Alderman, Aengus?"

"My father will take his army to the city gates and forced Aengus to abandon the throne. Then, it will be Thane Selkirk's once again."

*If they can ever find the missing king.*

Lord Morcant sighed and shook his head. "No, he won't do that, child. We cannot tell your father any of this."

Confusion ripped through her. "Why ever not? Aengus has stolen the throne from Thane, the rightful ruler. *Our ally.*"

"Your Thane has run away, Eislyn. A king who would abandon his people, for whatever reason, does not deserve his title, his people's loyalty, and especially not that seat. It's either that or he's dead." Lord Morcant leaned forward, his eyes sparking. "Your father will feel the same, I'm afraid. And, as none of his daughters actually ended up marrying into that court, they are certainly not our allies now."

Eislyn gasped, shaking her head in disbelief. Vreis placed a comforting hand on her shoulder and squeezed tight. His touch emboldened her. "I can't believe what you're saying. What Aengus has done is *wrong.*"

"Oh, he's in the wrong but for not the reasons you think." Her uncle tapped his chin. "You see, part of the reason we're all so shocked to see you, my dear, is...well, it appears Aengus has been pretending to *have you.*"

"What?" Shock hit her like a slap on the cheek.

"It seems he has a pretender by his side. A girl with silver hair. All this time, we've thought he had you trapped inside that castle. A prisoner in a gilded cage, forced to convince the air fae lords to join his side." Lord Morcant sat back in his chair. "And it's working. Many have already taken their armies to Tairngire. They're preparing for more war. War against us."

Anger charging through her, she stood. "Well then surely you see why he must be stopped at once! How can you possibly believe my father wouldn't agree?"

"Your father is tired of war, child. He wants peace. As soon as he finds you safe, he will hole up inside that castle of his until the day he dies."

"No, he won't," she said, her voice rising. "He'll do something. Maybe not war, but he'll do something."

"But *something* is not why you came here, is it, child?" he asked, eyebrows winging upward. "You want to see your lover avenged."

"He is not my lover," she said, her voice trembling. "And there is nothing to avenge. Thane has gone somewhere safe, I'm certain of it. And he will return to take his crown and then—"

"Guards." Lord Morcant stood and flicked his fingers at a dark figure lurking in the doorframe. "Take Eislyn to the secure chambers at the top of Frost Tower. Take the other one to the dungeons."

Eislyn jumped to her feet, her heart jumping wildly in her chest. Shock and fear battled for dominance, chasing away the hope and relief she'd felt only moments before.

"Cousin, what—" The guards clasped her arms just as two others bustled into the room and dragged a stone-faced Vreis away. Her guard, her companion, her friend...he didn't make a sound. He merely stared at her, a haunted goodbye flashing in his mis-matched eyes.

"What are you doing?" she screamed, yanking at the terrible grip on her arms.

"Don't worry, child. I'm not going to hurt a hair on that

pretty silver head of yours. Once all of this is over, I'll send you on home, safely to Cos."

"My father will never forgive you for this," she hissed.

He gave her a blank stare. "He's forgiven me for far worse. The Air Court is our enemy, and we don't need a bloody alliance to make things right. With the Selkirks gone and near forgotten, now is the time to take the kingdom as our own. Cos will make a good emperor once he snaps out of this anti-war business. I daresay those air fae will likely love him far more than Sloane Selkirk, that terrible creature they used to call their king."

"You can't do this," she whispered, tears blurring her vision.

"I can. And I will," he said evenly. "Settle in, Your Highness. You're going to be here a good long while."

## 45

### REYNA

They approached Findius from the west. If the High King had scouts searching the wastes for any sign of his son—or the missing assassins—they would expect to find him striding through the ashen fields just south of the city. West meant journeying the long way around, and it took twice as long. They were forced to cross another patch of mountains and wade through a thick swamp. Its stench clogged Reyna's nose with rot.

The tension was just as thick. Lorcan's anger simmered beneath the surface, but it was nothing more than a blanket on top of his pain. Reyna had hurt him, the last thing she'd ever wanted to do, but he'd seemed to accept her choice.

He'd stopped questioning her about her decision, and he was no longer demanding that she return to the pit so that she could undo it. But, of course, he'd scarcely said a word to her at all. The only conversation involved Nollaig, but only with one of them at a time. If Reyna was talking to the cloaked fae, Lorcan kept his mouth shut. Reyna tended to do the same if it was the other way around. All of her words had left her. There was nothing else she could say.

As they crept through the barren fields, they spotted smoke on the distant, hazy red horizon. The king had lit the fire pits again, it seemed. What was he anticipating now? But as they drew ever closer, they began to see that it did not look like the fire pits at all. Findius itself was on fire.

"What in the name of the gods is happening now?" Nollaig muttered, her voice holding the same weariness that Reyna felt in her very bones. It had been a very long and draining journey, and chaos was not what she had hoped to see upon their return.

Her gaze drifted toward the eastern harbor. There were a cluster of ships there. She needed to grab one and flee before the king spotted her.

"Look." Nollaig pointed at a flicker of green at the edge of the city wall. "Wood Court banners."

Lorcan pressed his lips together. "They're attacking the city. Hundreds of low fae will be trapped inside. And the wood king knows it."

A terrible ache surrounded Reyna's heart. This was it. The moment they were parted. "They need your help. Only two thousand warriors survived the Ruin, and there is no telling how many the wood king has brought with him. Your father is likely holed up in his fortress. He won't come out, not for anything. You need to go to your people."

"And you, Shieldmaiden," Nollaig said. "These low fae need your help, too."

Reyna clenched her hands. "You know what I must do. I have to go home to my kingdom and stop the Ruin."

"And you shall do it," Nollaig said firmly. "But there are innocents inside Findius, likely dying. You have the power of Seelie rushing through your veins." She grasped Reyna's arm, shaking her gently. "The shadow fae are greatly outnumbered. Even if Lorcan and I rush into the fight, this city will fall. You have seen the wood king's atrocities. You know what he will do to them all."

Reyna swallowed around a hard, hot lump in her throat.

"You gave up your heart for that power." Nollaig shook her harder. "Use it."

Her throat closed up as she fought for breath. Nollaig was right. Findius would fall, and the wood king would begin a reign of terror over anyone who survived. They would be tortured, flayed, consumed raw. Trembling, she gazed across the black stone that rose up from the fiery ground. Her heightened senses sharpened, zooming in on the fight.

Bodies already littered the ground. Some were warriors but many others wore the simple linen of innocent civilians. Orange light flared in cottage homes. Roofs had been consumed by flames. Low fae screamed as they raced from attackers, donned in the unmistakable green-tinted armor of the Wood Court.

Reyna pulled back within herself, pressing a palm against the ache in her stomach. She was not accustomed to this power, and it made her nauseous. The sight of the battle haunted her mind. As much as she needed to get home, she could not turn her back on this. Bolg Rothach was cruel and wicked, but the innocents of the city were not. She couldn't leave them here to die.

She set her jaw, turning to Nollaig. "You're right. I'll do whatever I can to help."

They huddled together for a moment, exchanging ideas. In the end, there was only one answer. Most of the activity appeared to be at the gates that led deep into the hidden caverns and tunnels beneath Findius. The wood fae had discovered the way inside, and they were swarming out of the ground like ants.

They would converge on those gates. Lorcan and Nollaig would fight while Reyna drew the focus of the wood fae away.

And then she would unleash the power of Seelie onto them all.

Just before they set off, Lorcan grasped her elbow. "Look at me," he said in a low and dangerous voice. He had been so angry when he'd found out what she'd done. That anger lingered in his voice even now, but she knew it was the gods he hated. Not her.

She dropped back her head, swallowing hard beneath the weight of his familiar dark eyes. "I don't want to argue, Lorcan. Not now. Not when we're about to rush into a fight."

"I don't want to argue with you. I—" His jaw clenched in frustration, and he dropped a fierce kiss onto her mouth. She leaned into it, breathing the scent of him deep into her mind. Leather, smoke, steel. A scent she would never forget.

He pulled back, chest heaving. "This power you have, it's dangerous and raw and new. Be careful, Reyna. Promise me you will not die in this fight."

Tears welled in her eyes. "Only if you promise you won't die either."

"I promise you." He tucked his finger beneath her chin, a move so achingly familiar that her bones throbbed. "And I promise you that we will figure out a way through this. You can help me lead this kingdom, and I can help you defeat the Ruin. We can do this together, Reyna."

"I don't think we can," she whispered, wanting nothing more than for him to be right.

"At least promise me you won't leave without saying goodbye."

"All right. I will promise you that." She did not think Lorcan was right, that they could find a way past a deal she'd made with a god. But she would keep this promise. She would fight this battle, and then say her goodbyes. She would gaze into his eyes one last time and memorize the light within the dark.

But first, there was a battle to be won and a king to defeat. Together, they raced to Findius.

Chaos had consumed the black stone city. As they huddled at the base of the towering, impenetrable city walls, they could hear the screams of fae dying.

"How will we get in?" Nollaig asked, her cloak fluttering around her hidden face. "The gates are shut. And no one is there to open them."

"I have an idea, but I don't think either of you will like it," Reyna said, glancing up at where her owl swooped overhead. It reminded her of the last time she'd faced a battle in a city. She remembered what Wingallock had done then.

Lorcan scowled. "I don't even want to hear it."

Reyna ignored him. She was yet to understand the full extent of her new Seelie powers, but there was one thing she knew she could do. Something the Dagda had done, and something fae could do before the Fall. With a deep breath, she closed her eyes and focused on the light thrum of power charging through her body. She thought of what she wanted and pictured it in her mind's eye.

Her back began to stretch. Bones and flesh snapped, pain flickering through her shoulder blades. With a trembling growl, she bent at the waist and grasped her knees, digging the nails into her thin trousers. More bones snapped. Her body shuddered as if it had been thrown into a tempest sea. A horrible, excruciating *snick* ripped her flesh open wide.

Nollaig gasped. Lorcan took Reyna's hand, holding her steady as the magic twisted her body into a terrible, wrangled mess.

And then the torment suddenly stopped. A fresh buzz of power flared through her shoulder blades. With a gasp, she glanced behind her. A pair of silver wings stretched wide on either side of her, the glittering feathers impossibly large. She reached out and traced a finger down one feather. A shiver of sensation stormed through her, and she gasped.

Long ago, the fae of Tir Na Nog could fly. Losing that power had been one of their greatest losses. Reyna had never known flight herself. She'd been born years after the Fall. But she felt a fierce sense of completeness as she stared at her newfound wings. A piece of her had always been missing, and she'd never known it. Wingallock hooted happily from above.

She smiled up at her owl, understanding at once. Now, she could fly.

"You mean to fly us over the top of the gates, don't you, princess?" Nollaig asked, her voice flat. She did not sound particularly impressed by Reyna's newfound wings.

"It will get us inside." Reyna grinned. "Why? Are you scared?"

Nollaig snorted. "Nothing scares me."

"Then, you should go first." Before Nollaig could object, Reyna wrapped her arms around the cloaked fae and pushed off. The ground vanished beneath them at a dizzying speed. Nollaig let out a strained choke. A gloved hand snapped tight around Reyna's wrist, the rough material digging into her skin.

"Careful, Shieldmaiden. You've never done this before."

Reyna smiled and flapped her wings once. They spun forward, lurching over the top of the wall. Nollaig let out an uneasy moan.

"This is fun," Reyna said.

She could have sworn she heard Nollaig mutter something close to, "Goddamned ice fae."

Soon, they were over the side of the gates, and Reyna gently lowered them to the ground. When she released Nollaig, the shadow fae coughed, clearly disoriented by the flight. Reyna pushed off again, landing on the other side where Lorcan was waiting.

"Your turn," she said chirpily.

He scowled, large arms crossed over his taut chest. "I'll find another way inside."

"Don't be ridiculous. The city needs our help, and this is the fastest way inside."

"I don't want you scooping me up into the air as if I'm a princess in need of a rescue."

Reyna arched a brow. "There's nothing wrong with being a princess."

A pause. "No. I don't suppose there is."

"Come on." She stepped behind him and wrapped her arms around his waist. Her breasts pushed against his back, and memories of his body over hers flashed in her mind, peaking her nipples. She shivered.

"Are you certain you'll be able to hold my weight?"

But she was off, throwing them both up into the misty skies. Her wings beat heavily at the air, pushing them toward the top of the gates. Lorcan was much heavier than Nollaig, and she had to push hard to hurtle them over the edge.

When they finally landed on the other side, she held on for a moment too long, pressing her cheek to his back.

"That was mortifying," he muttered, unsheathing his sword as if that would somehow bring back his masculinity.

Reyna had to admit, he did fit the part of a dangerous, vicious Prince of Shadows. With his raven hair that framed an angular face and those hooded eyes that seemed to see everything, he was all shadows and darkness. He towered over them all, his strength evidenced by his corded shoulders and his taut chest visible beneath his patchwork leather armor. His sharp jawline was set in anger, and the glimmer of his steel beneath the reddish sun made it look as though it was drenched in blood.

"Nollaig? Reyna?" A voice called out as a form hurried toward them. "Prince Lorcan?"

Segonax darted through the buildings on the opposite side of the street, flanked by half a dozen armed warriors. He rushed across the dirt path and ducked into an alley beside them. His eyes were wide as he took them in, and even wider still when he noted Reyna's wings.

Quietly, she pulled the wings back inside of her, hiding them from view.

"The king said you'd all died in an accident," the commander said in a hush. "You don't know how relieved I am to see you. Where's Tarrah?"

"She's dead," Nollaig said flatly.

Segonax winced. "I...the poor thing."

"What has happened here?" Lorcan asked, taking charge of the conversation. "Exactly how many wood fae are we looking at?"

"Fewer than you think. The wood king did not send his entire army," Segonax replied, glancing over his shoulder as a screaming shadow fae ran by, arms engulfed in flames. "Perhaps three thousand in total. Under normal circumstances, we would have easily fought them back."

"But they came in through the tunnels," Lorcan said with a frown. "How?"

"They must have seen us flee there when the Ruin attacked."

"Or Unseelie could have told them," Reyna interjected.

Every pair of shadow fae eyes turned her way.

"The wood king is an Unseelie worshipper. He's likely been getting visions, just like Tarrah."

Segonax rose a granite brow. "So, during this quest of yours, you've not only gained a pair of wings—glorious ones, I might add—but also a new faith in the death god?"

"I believe he's real. I've seen evidence of him with my own

two eyes." She pressed her lips together. "But I doubt I'd call it faith when I'd love nothing more than to meet him on the battlefield and stab him with my blade a thousand times."

"Ah. Well then." Segonax cleared his throat, turning his eyes back to his prince.

"She likes to stab things," Lorcan murmured. "How many have we lost?"

"Several hundred warriors and just as many low fae. Our losses would be higher but we have a thousand warriors stationed by the gate that leads into the caverns. They're holding back the wood fae as best they can." Segonax sighed. "But the press is relentless, and there are enough wood fae already inside that we might lose this city. What we truly need is more warriors, more fighters. Even five hundred more and we'd have hope. For this battle, anyway."

Lorcan's eyes landed on Reyna. "Reyna is worth five hundred."

Segonax let out a chuckle, but it quickly died when he realized that Lorcan was not deadly serious. "She is a formidable Shieldmaiden, Your Highness, but she is only one sword against many. I do not think that will be enough."

"During our journey, Reyna picked up more than just a pair of wings." Lorcan rested a steadying hand on her shoulder. "Imagine she is five hundred warriors. Where would you send her to save this city?"

For a moment, Segonax did not reply. He seemed too stunned to do anything but stare.

"Answer your prince, Seg," Nollaig said. "He's asked you a question."

"I would send her to Fomorian Square where the statues are. It's only a few streets away from the gate. There's a group of about five hundred wood fae there. If they approach our warriors from behind, we'll be surrounded. The city will have no hope."

Lorcan gave a firm nod. "Then, that is our task. We will get Reyna to Fomorian Square and form a barrier around her while she fights. She can stop the wood fae from taking our army down from behind."

"What's she going to do, Lorcan?" Seg asked, his firm and unyielding frown a sign that he was not convinced.

"Whatever it is, the wood fae will not stand a chance against it."

# 46

## REYNA

They pushed forward down the thin city streets that wound through the black stone huts of Findius. Lorcan took the lead, his loyal commander by his side. Nollaig and Reyna moved just behind them while the warriors took the rear. In total, there were ten of them, scarcely enough to face down a thousand well-trained wood fae and win.

But Lorcan had faith in her and in her powers. Far more faith than she had in herself. She did not yet know the full extent of what she could do or how to harness the magic in her veins. How could she use it to fight the battle that was looming before them? Would she even be able to control it? Or would it control her?

As they rounded a corner, a large company of wood fae blocked their path to the square. There were at least a hundred of them, and they had corralled a large group of trembling, sobbing shadow fae. The glittering green of the armor was dulled by the misty red light of the skies, their boiled leather weak and dull contrasted to the grey scales and embossed breastplates of the warriors who called this city home.

The wood fae turned when they heard Lorcan's company storm into the streets. Several of them laughed, clearly unconcerned. Lorcan's company was few in number, and Reyna was armed with nothing more than a slender ice dagger she hadn't even bothered to draw. She didn't even have her familiar. She'd told him to wait far out of sight, fearful that a wood fae arrow would strike him in the heart.

"Fan out!" Lorcan commanded, taking charge. The shadow fae cast nervous glances amongst themselves, but they followed the orders of their liege.

*They are loyal to him,* Reyna thought with a tight smile. *Good. He will need them when I leave.*

As the shadow fae fanned out and the wood fae drew their arrows, Lorcan grabbed her one last time, his fingers digging into her shoulders. "Can you do this?"

Swallowing a hard lump, she nodded.

"I'm trusting you," he said hoarsely. "I'm trusting you to not get yourself killed. Please, for the love of the Dagda, don't let me down."

He stormed off, motioning for the others to lift their shields. A volley of arrows soon followed, a storm of feathers and iron and wood. Reyna focused on the path of the arrows, dodging each one and then snatching a few from the air. The front line of the wood fae fell back. Some shouted, waving ahead another volley of arrows.

With a sigh, she ducked and spun and dodged. She heard the thunk of iron slamming into wood as the shadow fae did their best to stand their ground.

"What the hell is she?" one of the wood fae shouted.

"A Shieldmaiden," another replied.

"Is she a Fomorian or something?"

"No. She's just an ice fae. They can dodge arrows, but they can't dodge swords. Send in the melee team."

Reyna smiled and curled her hands into fists. This was what she had been waiting for. A real challenge. She could dodge arrows all day, but *this*. This was new.

The archers parted, and a rush of sword-wielders charged toward Reyna and her group. Smiling, she raced forward to meet them. She leapt into the air, calling upon the one element she knew would never fail her. In her mind's eye, she imagined her kingdom back home. She thought of the ice-peaked mountains and the snow that blanketed the woods. The hoarfrost worms and their whispers, their urging her to go on.

Suddenly, her body filled with strength. Her mind felt clearer than it ever had before. She slammed onto the ground before the wood fae, and the ground transformed to ice beneath her feet. Fingers of ice stretched out from where she knelt, crawling up the wood fae forms and freezing them into place.

Reyna gaped, her heart a somersault of emotion.

She hadn't meant to do *that*, but...it would work.

Curses exploded from the remaining wood fae as their line stumbled back even more. She quickly scanned the street. About twenty had frozen, leaving at least seventy more. The archers had fallen back to lurk in the buildings behind them, and only the melee warriors were left.

They sized her up, watching and waiting.

"Too scared?" she called out.

A few of them chuckled, but she saw the fear in their eyes. There was no hiding it.

"How do you have magic?" one shouted. She turned, zeroing in on the speaker. She was a tall, strong fae with willowy hair and gleaming turquoise eyes. Her armor was made up of thin scales made from bark, and her feet were bare. A Dryad then. Reyna was surprised they would be willing to fight for the wood king.

Reyna gave her a wide smile. "Because I feast on the flesh of my enemies."

The wood fae mumbled amongst themselves, alarmed, and Reyna laughed. "That was a lie. I've never eaten flesh in my life. Your king, on the other hand..."

The mumbling grew louder.

Reyna glanced at Lorcan. He stood only a few feet away, watching her every move with sharp and focused eyes. They hadn't really discussed what to do if they came upon a group like this. A group who stopped fighting. She hoped he wouldn't mind what she said next.

She rose her voice so that it could be heard at the very back of their group. "Your king is a cruel beast who feasts on his own people. Put down your weapons and surrender, and Prince Lorcan will show you mercy."

The Dryad let out a tense laugh. "You are greatly outnumbered, Shieldmaiden."

Reyna arched a brow. "Are we? I just took out twenty of your warriors by myself. It would be little effort to kill the rest of you, but I'd rather not. Yield."

"We heard the shadow king is as mad as our own!" another wood fae shouted.

Several screamed in agreement, raising their swords once more. The throng rushed forward, barely giving Reyna time to think. Startled, she reached for the first thing she could find. All she thought was *power*.

A rush of wind exploded from her body, storming out of her flesh like a violent exhale. The wind hit the wood fae head on. It threw them off their feet, carrying them away and slamming others into the stone buildings at the back of the street. That was all it took. The wood fae scattered like ants, running into the streets to flee from Reyna's attack.

Relief shook through her. She had no idea what she was doing, but it was working. Of course, they had not even reached the square yet.

"Well done, Shieldmaiden," Nollaig said as she approached from behind. "Remind me to never get on your bad side though."

Reyna grinned and turned to Lorcan. He was gathering the warriors in close again and pointing down the street to highlight the path they would take to the square. They all listened with rapt attention, respect in their eyes. A hot ache clawed its way through her gut. She loved seeing him this way, strong and in command. These fae looked to him as their prince. She had never before seen any of them look at their king the same way.

They needed Lorcan. They needed a ruler who would not let them down, one who would *never* be willing to sacrifice them because of the madness in his mind.

Lorcan motioned them forward, and they began the trek into the next pocket of the city. Ahead, Reyna could hear the distinct turmoil of terrified screams and clanging steel. Lorcan heard it, too. The hardness in his eyes, and the grim set to his jaw was evidence enough that he knew exactly what lay around the next corner.

Suddenly, a familiar sensation skittered along Reyna's skin. Unease slid gnarled fingers along her neck, teasing her hair so that every single one stood on end. With a shuddering breath, she stopped suddenly in the center of the street. Several of the warriors thumped into her, frowning as they came to a stop by her side.

Reyna dropped back her head to stare up at the sky. Thick storm clouds had rolled across the city, blocking the reddish light of the sun. It drenched everything in shadows, and the pulse of dark magic echoed with every crack of thunder.

"The Ruin," Reyna whispered. "It's here."

Lorcan looked up and cursed beneath his breath. "We need to get everyone inside."

"No, buildings won't save them" she said, a strange calmness suddenly coming over her. "Take the others far ahead. I can draw the Ruin away from you and give you time to push forward."

Nollaig was by her side in an instant. "We need you with us, Reyna. We can't do this without you."

"And I'll be there with you," she said. "But I have to take care of the Ruin first. Otherwise, the city will fall regardless of how well we fight."

"Reyna," Lorcan said. "You can't stay here and face this alone."

"Go," she said. "I'm the only one who can stop it. It won't even take very long. Just go. Continue pushing forward. In no time, I'll be right back by your side."

She could feel Lorcan frowning in her direction, but Reyna continued to stare up at the sky, her skin buzzing in anticipation. She had planned to leave this place to find the Ruin, but instead, it had found her. It *always* found her, she realized. Every time she called upon her powers, even before she'd known what they were, and even before she'd gone into the birthplace of the gods, the Ruin was there.

It was almost as though it could sense her.

The sky crackled, and the clouds opened up. Black flecks stormed out like a hundred angry locusts.

"Your immunity will save you, Lorcan, but it won't save them." She yanked her gaze away from the Ruin and gave him a fierce smile. "Go!"

## 47

## LORCAN

Lorcan wanted to beat his chest in rage. Reyna was screaming at him to go, but he could not bear the thought of leaving her to face the storm alone. He knew she could fight it. He'd never been so certain of anything in his life. But that did not stop him from wanting to throw her out of danger, to put himself in her place, to do anything he could to protect her from harm.

But his men were watching him and waiting for a command. They had put their trust in him. He could not let them down.

"Your Highness?" Segonax asked, enthralled by the storm cloud above him. His cheeks had blanched, and his lips trembled. The loyal, brave commander had faced death so many times, but the Ruin was the one thing that could make his soul quake.

He'd only barely survived it once. He likely thought he wouldn't survive it again.

Lorcan snapped his mind away from its singular focus on Reyna, and then turned to his men, despite the worm of pain tightening around his heart. "We need to continue forward and get everyone to safety. When Reyna has fought this thing and won, we will make our move to the square."

Their frightened eyes said it all, but Lorcan motioned them forward. Reyna was right. The warriors could not stay here. As soon as the black snow hit their skin, they would crumble into nothing more than piles of ashes. He needed to clear this street as quickly as he could. Once his warriors were out of the Ruin's path, he could return to Reyna's side and help her. He just needed to get the others to safety first.

As they rushed forward, Nollaig fell into step beside him, a glinting scythe in her right hand. "Your Highness, I think the plan to take the square might be folly now that the Ruin is here." She shook her head. "I cannot see how we survive this."

Lorcan frowned, every now and again casting a glance over his shoulder. Reyna stood in the middle of the street alone, glaring up at the churning sky.

"I don't see an alternative, Nollaig," he said, dragging his gaze back to the cloaked fae. "If we don't secure the square, the entire city will fall."

"*Reyna* will secure it. When she is done with the Ruin."

"Which is why we'll all go there with her once the Ruin is gone."

"Your Highness, *listen to me.*"

Lorcan had never heard Nollaig so insistent. Usually, she floated through life, commenting here and there but doing little more than making gentle suggestions. The intensity of her tone now stopped him short.

She grabbed his arm with her gloved hand and led him into a black stone hut just off of the street, outside of the Ruin's current path. It was empty inside, abandoned. Blood splashed the floor, turning Lorcan's stomach. Whoever had lived here had been caught up in the fight. They had likely died fleeing from the enemy.

He turned to the shadow warriors, motioning them inside. For now, this hut was safe, but it might not be for long.

He took the cloaked fae to the back corner of the room where they could speak privately without being overheard. "I'm listening, Nollaig, but I don't understand."

"The streets ahead are packed to the brim with enemies. As soon as we round that corner, we will be swarmed by wood fae. Two hundred, at least. Against nine. We will surely die."

Lorcan's heart roared in his ears. "Then, we'll stay here."

"We can't. The Ruin will come this way soon enough."

He shook his head, gazing at the path ahead. "What are you suggesting then? We can't just hide here like cowards until we die."

"I would not suggest anything of the kind." She pointed out the window, toward a distant alley. "Go right. We can get to the castle that way."

A slithering unease unfurled in his gut. "The castle."

"Where your father is hiding."

Lorcan clenched his fingers around the hilt of his sword. "And why would we go to the castle to see my father, Nollaig?"

"So that we can take the throne from him and end his terrible reign."

Lorcan's throat was thick. "Take it from him? How?"

"I think you know how. There is only one way to take down a mad king like that." She turned and nodded toward Segonax. "He will be locked up in the fortress, but he'll allow Segonax inside. And us along with him."

He shook his head. "I can't believe what I am hearing. You plan for me to abandon the fight so that I can kill my own father. I wanted to help this kingdom as best I could, Nollaig, but not like this."

"No, *I* will kill the king."

He took a step back. "*You?*"

"It is the only way to save the realm. You can't do it yourself. You'd be cursed."

"And you'd be cursed, too!" Frustration raged through him, hot like a knife drenched in blood. He did not know what worried him more. That Nollaig wanted to kill the king, or that Lorcan did not know if he could let her do it.

"I'm already cursed, Your Highness."

Mouth dry, he tried to speak. "How long have you been planning this?"

"For a very long time." A pause. "Once the battle is over, we will not get a chance like this again. His assassins missed us once, but they might not miss again. This might be our only chance. The city is in chaos. We can use that to our advantage."

"It sounds as though you've thought a lot about this."

"Oh, I have, Your Highness," she said, her voice sharp. "I have very much indeed."

Lorcan could only stare at the cloaked fae he had known for so many years...except had he ever truly known her? He had never seen her face or even her hands. She had hidden herself from the rest of the court for as long as he had known her. She had never once shared a thing about her past. Nollaig had always been an enigma.

A *harmless* enigma, he realized. Perhaps that had been the point all along.

"My father will have guards with him," Lorcan said.

"He will." She nodded toward the warriors who were waiting for his signal. "A few, but no more than what we have here."

"Segonax will never go along with it."

She chuckled. "Segonax might feel quite a bit differently than you'd expect."

"You two have been waiting for this moment for a long time."

"Biding our time."

"Are you even a shadow fae, Nollaig?"

She hissed. "I am more a shadow fae than anyone else here, and far more than your father ever was."

Lorcan did not know what that meant, but he did know that he couldn't spend any more time asking questions. The city was under attack on two fronts. Three, if he included his father. He needed to make a decision. There was no more time to think. He needed to act.

Nollaig cocked her head, listening. "The wood fae are coming, Your Highness."

Lorcan let out a growl. He hated this. Everything about it. It felt wrong. The city was burning because of his father's actions, and Bolg was only showing signs of getting worse. If someone did not step in and stop him, there would be nothing left of the shadow realm to save.

And yet...

"Your Highness, what is it you wish for us to do?"

"This is madness," he said, his stomach in turmoil.

"Madness is a king sending thousands of his people to die."

Lorcan winced. It was true, all of it. Nollaig had suddenly placed the future of the realm in his hands, and he did not know what to do. He'd never wanted this kind of power. His princedom had been forced upon him by a father he'd never even met. He'd gladly gone to the Air Court to spy, if only to escape these barren lands.

But he had made a vow back in the mountains. He'd promised himself that he would return to Findius, find a way to stop Bolg Rothach, and become the king himself. This was his chance to right his father's wrongs. To save the people of this crumbling kingdom.

Lorcan fisted his hands. "Fine. I will go to the castle to carry out your godforsaken plan. But I am *not* leaving Reyna here to fight the Ruin alone. First, I'm going to help her in any way I can, and then together we'll fight the wood fae threatening to tear this city apart. Then, and only then, we will go rip my father off his throne. *After* our enemies are defeated and not before."

Nollaig sighed in disappointment. "I truly am sorry about this, Your Highness."

He frowned. "Sorry about what?"

Pain flared through his head, and then the world went black.

# 48

## REYNA

The wind was harsh and brutally hot. Her hair was a storm of silver, slashing at her face and neck. Gritting her teeth, she flicked her gaze down the street. Lorcan and his warriors vanished around the bend, ducking out of the path of the Ruin. The storm above could grow and expand and consume the entire city whole. But for now, they were safe. The Ruin was nothing more than a bulbous cloud wide enough to destroy a single city street.

And so she could finally focus on her greatest enemy and keep it drawn to her side. She needed to give Lorcan a little more time to get his warriors to safety. The last thing she wanted was to get others caught up in this, particularly Nollaig and Segonax. Lorcan was immune, but they weren't. She couldn't bear the thought of losing anyone else.

She dropped back her head to glare up at this dark thing that had haunted her for so many years. It wanted *her,* she understood now. It had ravaged the ice kingdom, all in search of *her*. It had followed her to the Air Court. And now it was here. Little did it know, she was finally ready for it.

She opened her arms wide as the black flecks fell heavily onto her cheeks.

"What do you want with me?" she shouted into the storm.

But the storm was silent, save the whistle of the harsh wind and the drumbeat of near constant thunder. More ash rained from the pulsing cloud, a steady torrential downpour. Reyna stood still, closing her eyes against the onslaught. The wind tugged at her tunic, and black sand rushed against her legs. But she held her ground. There was nothing the Ruin could do to her now.

She reopened her eyes, smiling. "For dark magic, you certainly don't seem very smart. Haven't you figured it out yet? Your godforsaken ash doesn't do a damn thing to me! *I'm immune.*"

That certainly seemed to get its attention. She swore she heard a low growl rumble from deep within the pulsing storm cloud. The dark flecks ceased at once, and the wind vanished so quickly it was almost as though it had never even been there. A few lingering flakes fluttered to the ground, slowly, gently, softly.

Reyna stood in the middle of the ash, hands fisted. Around her, she could already see the devastation the Ruin had wrought. Buildings had been reduced to charred remains, smoking black pits of destruction. There was no sign of bodies, though it would be difficult to tell if anyone had died in this place. There would be no bones or flesh left behind when this storm was done with them.

The Ruin reduced everything to ash.

Reyna called upon the power deep within her, gently testing the strands of each one. There were six in total, all unique and far different than the magic she'd felt from the wings she'd sprouted on her back. These six, these were the elements. She felt ice, as familiar as breath. Beside that was air, powerful winds that would knock her off her feet. Next was sea, followed by wood. She was not certain what those would do. Finally, fire and shadow pulsed quietly together. Darker elements but just as powerful as the others. She held all of that inside of her and more.

And she had no idea how to use any of it to destroy the Ruin.

Perhaps she could conjure up every last one of them and blast it all at the storm in one mighty explosion. But that was just as likely to tear apart the entire city, she realized. The power was strong and electric. If she used it all at once, with no idea how to control it all, there was no guessing what it might do.

*Ice,* she thought. The most familiar of elements. The one she could best control and command. She could fly up into the center of the clouds and freeze the very depths of the storm. Then, once every last inch of it was frozen, she could shatter it with a single blow of her dagger. Right in its heart.

*That* was how she would defeat the Ruin. With ice.

With a deep breath, she *pushed* the wings from her back once more, stumbling forward as the pain sliced and popped through her skin. As the wings grew, so did the Ruin. The clouds churned once again, and the black flakes appeared anew, crashing down all around her.

"I told you I'm immune," she shouted as she took to the skies.

But no matter. If it wanted to waste its energy trying to kill her with the ash, then so be it.

The sky was a storm of wind. It battered her wings as she rose up to meet the Ruin above the city. Heavy gusts slashed at her body, knocking her off course. Gritting her teeth, she beat her powerful wings and set her sights on the center of the cloud where a flash of light split through the black. She pushed against it with all her might. Determination clawed through her, mixed in with sheer desperation. No matter how much wind this godforsaken storm threw at her, she would not let it win.

In fact...perhaps she should use wind herself.

She took a deep breath and called upon the element of air, reaching for the strand of magic she had used against the wood fae. As she found it, she thought of wind and—

A hurricane gust slammed into her body, twisting her wings up behind her and throwing her into a spin. She cried out and reached for an anchor that was not even there. Anything. A rock, a rope, Lorcan's hand. But she was far above ground, lost in a sea of vengeful air. It threw her halfway across the city. The black stone buildings were a blur beneath her, and the warriors were ants scurrying beneath the shadow of a heavy boot.

Finally, she found the strength to flare her wings and caught herself mid-air. Another blast of wind slammed onto her from above, throwing her down. Terror gripped her heart as the ground rushed up. She flailed in the air, desperately calling upon her wings to work.

A sound as loud as thunder exploded as she slammed into the dirt. Pain lashed through her bones. Her shoulder screamed, and her head thundered from where her teeth had knocked violently together.

Shuddering, she slowly pushed up to her knees, shaking her head to throw the ringing out of her ears. The world swam before her. She blinked, trying to clear the fog out of her head.

Reyna would heal, she knew. Seelie's powers would make certain of that. But it was not instantaneous. It would take time and rest to allow the healing magic to fill her body with its life, mend her broken bone—her shoulder was definitely broken again—and soothe any other wounds she might have.

It was impossible to tell what those wounds were. Everything hurt.

The storm clouds crackled overhead just as the thunder of footsteps filled the air. Frowning, she blinked again, and the fog finally began to clear. Palms flattened on the black dirt, she peered up toward the sound. Throngs of wood fae pressed in all around her. Several had arrows aimed at her head, and many others held spears at the ready. Fear poked up from deep inside of her, pulsing out a heavy drumbeat in the veins of her neck.

Her eyes caught on the marble statue in the center of it all. A tall winged figure, dipped in paint of gold. A Fomorian statue, one of six scattered all throughout the square. She had landed right in the midst of the enemy, right where Segonax had said they needed to go to protect the city from being sacked. They were all here. Five hundred of them. And she had no one to stand by her side in the fight. She was strong, but was she *that strong*?

Reyna glanced up to see the storm cloud ripple and crackle and pop.

Then, it went silent and still, waiting.

Reyna understood at once. The Ruin could not kill her with its ash, so it had to kill her some other way. And it was going to try this. A courtyard teeming with enemies. It had picked her up by her wings and tossed her straight into hell.

*Smart,* she thought grimly. And then she pushed to her feet, calling upon the magic within her. She would not let the Ruin win this way. It was cowardice, this game it played. Instead of facing her head on, it was hiding behind five hundred fae. It was hiding *from her*.

*That means I can win.*

Determination a storm within her, she turned to face the wood fae and shot forth a blast of ice.

# 49

## EISLYN

She did not know what day it was, nor did she care. When the guards had first thrown her into the tower, a strange, eerie numbness had stolen across her body and mind. Days passed in a blur. Nothing much ever happened. Vaguely, she wondered if they had already gone to war.

She asked for Vreis a couple of times when the guards dropped off food. It was the only time she ever bothered to rouse herself from the numbness in her mind. They never answered.

One day, things were different. The guards came by at first light as they normally did, but they had no food for her. Instead, they dragged her out of the room. Her entire body was limp like a doll, and her feet scuffed along the stone floor, leaving behind trails of ice down the corridor. She didn't care enough to consider what that meant.

They took her to her cousin's study. He was at his desk again, scribbling another letter. She wondered what twisted truths he wrote down and if her father had any idea of the treachery of his own family.

Who would Cos Darragh choose if he did know, she wondered vaguely? She had never been his favorite, nor even liked much at all. Perhaps he wouldn't even care that his own cousin had taken his daughter captive.

Her cousin snapped his fingers before her eyes. "You really are messed up in the head, aren't you? The rumors are true."

She pressed her lips together.

Rolling his eyes, he sat down hard in the chair across from her. "There's something I need you to tell me."

"What do you wish to know? How to betray your own family?"

Anger flashed in his eyes.

"We need to know about the Prince of the Shadow Court," he said in a calm yet dangerous voice.

The Prince of the Shadow Court? How...odd. She had not thought of the exiled royals in ages, nor did she think anyone else had. They were a distant memory in the history of Tir Na Nog. Gone *and* forgotten. Much like she would be soon, no doubt.

She frowned. "I don't know anything about the prince of shadows."

He arched a brow. "Don't you?"

"Why would I know anything about him? The Shadow Court has been exiled for years. Aren't they all dead?"

"You didn't answer my question," he pointed out.

"I did," she said through gritted teeth. "I said I don't know anything about him."

Why was he being so insistent about this? Clearly, she wouldn't know a damn thing about an exiled court, nor their prince. She'd read their histories, of course, but she knew nothing about their present nobility.

He leaned back into his chair, considering her. "I find it very curious that you are capable of lying to me."

Exasperated, she tried to push up from her chair, but the

guard slammed her right back down again. Her teeth knocked together from the force. Terror melted her insides.

"I'm not lying to you, Lord Morcant," she said quietly, her heart thrumming like hummingbird wings.

"One wonders...if you can lie, what else can you do?"

Tears filled her eyes, as hot as lava. "I can't do *anything*. Because I'm not lying to you. I don't know why you're so convinced I am. I don't know anything at all about the Shadow Court! Please, just send me back to the tower and leave me alone. You've already done enough by capturing me. Stop shouting at me about things I know nothing about!"

He leaned forward, ice in his eyes. Her pleas had clearly landed on deaf ears. "So, the name *Lorcan* does not ring a bell?"

She stiffened, her heart in her throat. Slowly, she swallowed around the lump. "Lorcan?"

He nodded, his keen eyes watching her every move. "Lorcan Rothach, the son of High King Bolg Rothach. *The Prince.*"

Her mind began to race. Lorcan was the *prince* of the shadow kingdom? How in the name of the Dagda could that be true? He was Thane's closest guard, one of his oldest friends. The Selkirks *hated* the shadow fae.

Did her sister know? She couldn't. Or could she? The two had spent weeks sneaking around the city together, all secretive, hiding from everyone else.

They'd gone in search of Thane together. Her sister was with the prince right now. Did that mean her cousin knew where they were? Did he know where *Thane* was? She had so many questions to ask, but she didn't want to give anything away.

If Lord Morcant, her cousin *who had captured her,* wanted to know about Lorcan, then she wasn't going to tell him a damn thing.

"Why are you asking me about the Shadow Court?" she tried instead. "They haven't been involved in the war for decades."

"Never you mind about that. What I want to know is—"

"Are they causing trouble?" she quickly interrupted.

His eyes narrowed. "You aren't answering my question, Eislyn."

"I *did* answer it," she insisted. "And you keep ignoring my answer and branding me as a liar. I don't know what else you want me to say."

His lips flatlined. "I can see you aren't going to let us do this the easy way."

Standing, he motioned for the guards behind her, and a bound and gagged Vreis tumbled onto the floor. His mismatched eyes were swollen shut by fist-sized bruises, and blood caked his chin. Slashes ran along his arms, deep cuts that spoke of torture and pain. He could not even hold up his own head to look at her. Horror churned through Eislyn's gut. She pressed a hand to her lips, biting back a scream.

"What have you done to him?" she hissed.

"Nothing he couldn't survive. Though I can't say the same about this." Lord Morcant nodded to the guards.

The guard fisted Vreis's hair, yanked back his head, and sliced an ice glass dagger across his neck. Blood shot from the gruesome wound, coating the floor with a sickening crimson. Eislyn choked. A terrible, excruciating pain carved a hole into the very last remnants of her broken soul. Her body trembled as great shaking sobs tore through her. But she didn't cry. She just shook. Shook like the very world itself was ending.

"How could you?" she whispered. "How could you do that to him? He was a good male. He did more for me than you ever will, and you're my father's own flesh and blood!"

"I did it to prove a point, Eislyn," her cousin said with ice in his voice. "I'm not asking for your insight. I'm demanding it. I need you to tell me everything you know about Lorcan Rothach and his relationship with your sister, or I will find someone else you care about, and I'll be forced to have them killed, too."

"You're a monster," she hissed. "I thought the ice fae were good."

"I am not the enemy here, Eislyn. The shadow fae are. The air fae are. And, it appears, your sister is." He leaned forward, fire dancing in his silver eyes. "What do you know about the Prince of the Shadow Court?"

Eislyn gaped at him, her heart bursting out of her chest. She pushed up from the chair, this time knocking aside the guard's hand with a strength she did not know she had. "Did you just threaten my sister?"

Eyebrows raised, Lord Morcant drew himself up tall so that he towered over Eislyn's frail form. "She is working with the enemy. She must be stopped."

"And what do you plan to do?" Her lips trembled as she spoke. "Kill her, too?"

"If I must."

Eislyn's soul rattled inside of her.

Reyna, who loved her. Reyna, who had never judged her darkness. Reyna, who had thrown herself into danger to save her, time and time again. Her shield, her heart, her sister. Reyna had sacrificed so much for Eislyn. She'd even given up the only life she'd ever wanted to lead, as a Shieldmaiden, all to keep Eislyn safe.

And now her own cousin plotted her death after he'd murdered Vreis, one of the best fae she had ever met in her miserable life.

Fury rose up within her like a vicious storm. The kind that capsized powerful ships. The kind that ripped trees from the ground. Eislyn had never before felt anger quite like this. Like she wanted to kill the male standing before her.

Curling her hands into fists, she narrowed her eyes. "I'm not telling you anything! I won't let you harm my sister!"

A knife of pain stabbed her gut as the ground beneath her feet began to shake. Her body convulsed, teeth slamming together. Her arms snapped wide on either side of her as a strange, eerie chill swept through her body. Everything was cold. So cold. So brutally, horribly cold.

Ice shot out from her outstretched palms. Great, gleaming spikes of it that exploded out of her body like a mirror shattering from a terrible blow. Shards soared into her cousin's shocked face and buried themselves deep in his gut.

Blood sprayed the room. Flecks landed on her face and on her neck.

From behind her, she heard the thud of heavy bodies thundering to the floor.

Eislyn stumbled back, jaw slack. She stared down at the body, at the blood. Her cousin was dead.

She had killed him.

"Oh, Dagda," she whispered. "Oh god, oh god, oh god."

She whirled on her feet, panic a hollow ache in her heart. The guards were dead, too. They gazed up at her with vacant eyes. Their bodies were littered with ice shards.

She had killed them all. Five fae.

Five *ice* fae.

At any moment, more guards would come, and they would find her here like this, surrounded by bodies and blood. They would execute her at once. She was their princess, but they'd happily held her captive, so they clearly didn't care about her title or her father.

She had to get out of here. Whirling on her feet, she grabbed her uncle's sword and wrapped the sheath belt around her waist, hands trembling. Then, she grabbed some coin from the dead guards and took one of their daggers for good measure. At long last, she glanced at Vreis.

Her heart ached so horribly that she swore it would never beat normally again. Once more, she had to run, but she did not have Vreis to run beside her this time.

She didn't know how she would survive without him.

Kneeling by his side, she took his necklace, a glowing amber jewel that hung from a leather cord. It was a symbol to remember him always. And then Eislyn Darragh ran.

## 50

### REYNA

The wood fae began to scatter as soon as the first blast of ice hit. At least a quarter of them froze instantaneously, forming an icy barrier between Reyna and the rest of the army. She sucked in deep breaths, fighting through the pain in her shoulder and her head, but smiled all the same.

The wood fae would struggle to reach her like this, if they even wanted to after seeing a large contingent of their fellow warriors turned to frost. She dropped back her head once again, glaring up at the Ruin.

"Nice try, but you failed. You'll have to do better than that."

The storm cloud rippled in anger.

Reyna curled her hand and threw a blast of ice upward. It hit the clouds but bounced off, shattering into the wind. Reyna frowned, fingers of dread creeping down her spine. She tried again, but it only had the same result. The ice did nothing to harm the Ruin.

She shook her head, not understanding. Seelie had given her this magic. He'd said the power would be enough to destroy the Ruin.

Or had he?

Her heart began to pound. Seelie had never spoken a word to her in the birthplace of the gods. That voice had belonged to Unseelie and no one else. Had this all been nothing more than a trick? A lie? Her mind flashed back to Tarrah's last words. *You've been tricked.* At the time, Reyna had thought Tarrah had been referring to their fight, to the twisting of Tarrah's mind.

But had it been more than that? Reyna's body trembled, terror and anger uniting to create a spear right through her soul. Had she given up Lorcan *for nothing*?

*No,* she thought, fisting her hands. She refused to believe it. She had been given this power for a reason, and it wasn't to let the Ruin win.

A speck of ash drifted down from above and sizzled against her skin. It melted, absorbed by her body. Reyna stared down at it, and then glanced back up at the sky. The ash had brought a spark of life to her throbbing arm. It was soothing and almost as if she'd...*consumed* part of the Ruin, as if she'd pulled it into herself.

Her eyes widened as she thought back to the fight at Feurach Fortress. It had been the same there, too, she realized. As the storm had raged around her, she'd grown in strength and power. She'd fought with abilities she'd never had before, all because the ash and the snow formed a perfect storm over her head.

Suddenly, she knew what she must do, but a snake of fear sank its fangs into her heart. If she did this, if she pulled this power into herself, what would it do to her?

Kill her, she realized. If she didn't have Seelie's powers, it would kill her. The journey to Inishfall had never been about giving her the elemental gifts to shatter the Ruin into a thousand pieces. It had been about making her strong enough to withstand pulling the darkness into herself.

It would make her dangerous. Far more dangerous than any other being in the world. If she ever lost control of it...if she ever used it for her own gain...

That was why Seelie had demanded what he had. *Selflessness.*

She'd had to prove what kind of fae she truly was.

For a moment, she stood trembling beneath the weight of it all. Only someone good and pure and true could be trusted with a power as destructive as this. But *was* she good? Was she pure? She did not think so. Reckless, wild, impulsive, and stubborn, that was what she was. Bloodthirsty, at times. Quick to anger when it came to those she thought wronged her.

Several arrows swirled through the air as she stood there, standing on the edge of a future she did not think she could withstand. She was Reyna Darragh, a princess who had walked away from her duty. A princess who had plotted murder against another royal family. She was not good and pure.

But she was all the world had.

If she did not consume the Ruin, it would continue to rain down devastation on the world. Countless lives would be lost. Seelie had chosen her, for better or for worse. This was her duty, her curse. She'd thrown everything away for it. She could not walk away right when it mattered the most.

A few more arrows soared toward her. She dodged them easily, knocking them aside. The wood fae had gathered a small contingent of their archers behind the wall of frozen warriors, just close enough that she was within their sights.

With a growl, she shot some more ice in their direction. They shouted, ducking down behind the wall to dodge her blast. Frost crackled through the air, shattering out in a dozen directions. Several fae got hit, and their eyes went wide with shock as the ice consumed them whole.

She opened her arms wide as the storm whipped a frenzy

of ash through the square. More fae got hit by the flecks. Their screams were drowned out by the whistle of the wind. Thunder shook through the entire city, rattling the ground.

Gritting her teeth, Reyna focused on the clouds, pulling with all her might. Her breathing grew ragged; sweat beaded on her brow. The wind suddenly whipped toward her and slammed into her shoulder. Pain ricocheted through her body like an arrow. A scream ripped from her raw throat, but she stood her ground.

She *tugged* at the wind, welcoming it inside of her.

A cloud of ash hit her square in the face. It stung her eyes, blinding her momentarily. The black flecks clung to her skin, and then they melted against her. The Ruin filled her flesh and her veins, and suddenly, a new strength rushed through her.

She sucked in a lungful of ashen air and *pulled* again with her mind, her body, and her soul. More Ruin whipped toward her and away from the wood fae cowering behind the icy wall. The ash surrounded her like a tornado, spinning in vicious circles as it tried to rip free of her grip on it.

She tugged again, screaming and dropping to her knees from the sheer, unbridled effort of it all. Her wound was throbbing now with so much torment that she could barely think around it. Her head had gone numb, and tears or blood or both streaked down her face.

The ash consumed her as she consumed the ash. It was everything around her, so thick that it formed a blanket over her trembling body. Another scream clawed its way up her throat, ripping free from her in a violent release of sound. She dug her fingers into the ground like claws. She drew strength from the feel of the dirt beneath her hands.

And then she yanked at the Ruin with all the strength left in her broken body.

It flew into her. Ash poured into her open mouth, filled

her nostrils, and crawled into her eyes. It sank into her skin, filled her veins, and stormed through her stomach. It pushed its way into her throbbing heart, spreading out to her every limb, her every toe, her every finger.

Silence fell like a hammer on the courtyard. Reyna gasped for breath, heaving as she curled over the ground. Everything hurt, even as her body buzzed with new life. Electricity crackled through her veins, sparking as it collided with her new Seelie magic.

*It's over,* she thought, sagging, or had she whispered it out loud? She could scarcely even remember where she was, let alone hear anything other than the echo of her painful screams as the Ruin had stormed inside of her.

With a deep and shuddering breath, she pushed up from the ground and leaned back on her heels. It was over. It was done. She had faced down the Ruin, and she'd won.

Her relief was so overwhelming that she almost tumbled face-first into the dirt.

*It is not over,* a voice suddenly whispered into her mind.

She straightened, alarm slicing through her like a knife.

*This is the beginning of everything they feared,* the same voice spoke.

Her heart thundered. Was this Unseelie? Had he followed her from the pits only to taunt her here? But no. This voice was nothing like the chilling, dark tone of Unseelie. This was something else. Something...sad.

Suddenly, a barrage of images flashed through her mind. She cried out, holding her throbbing head as a whirlwind of sensations crashed into her. The image of a silver princess standing on a blackened hill, a snow owl perched on her shoulder. Another flash. Another image. Ash pouring down from a dark sky.

The images continued to flash, growing darker with every passing one. Blood and destruction. Death and gore. Tir Na

Nog gone. And then a sea...a new land, one inhabited by giant fae with gold-tipped black wings. The Fomorians on majestic horses cresting a hill backlit by a brilliant, blazing sun.

And then darkness. More blood. And then a princess on a throne, commanding an army of twisted, shattered minds.

The images stopped. Reyna's mind went black. Slowly, she opened her eyes to stare down at the charred soil. Her heart thrummed an uneasy beat. Tears of horror left wet trails down her cheeks.

She could not explain how she understood what she saw, but she did. The Ruin, perhaps, filling her mind with everything it knew about the world. And what would come of it. She shook as understanding gave way to a horrible, aching regret.

Reyna had made a *terrible* mistake.

"You are not called the Ruin," she whispered to the thing inside of her.

*No.*

It was the *Dionadair,* just as Unseelie had said. But he had never explained what that meant. He'd never translated from the ancient language of the Fomorians. Eislyn might have known, from all her studying and reading ancient texts, but Reyna didn't. Not until now.

*Protector.*

She squeezed her eyes shut.

*The Dagda created me,* the voice said softly, *when he first arrived in Tir Na Nog through the portal in Cinder Ridge. He saw a vision in the birthplace of the gods. It spoke of an ice princess, one who would one day draw upon the might of Unseelie and destroy this world, beginning with Tir Na Nog.*

A hot ache clogged Reyna's throat.

"And I am that princess," she whispered, eyes burning.

There was a name for her, too. The Namhaid. The enemy.

The Dagda had sent word to the Fomorians across the sea.

They had spoken of her in hushed tones for centuries, hoping that the Ruin would stop her, hoping that Unseelie would never get his claws into the fae who would one day kill them all.

And she was that fae. She had to be. Everything fit. Deep, shuddering fear shook through her.

It all made horrible, brutal sense. The Ruin had not begun to destroy her kingdom until she was born, and it had always seemed to strike when she was nearby. It wasn't all-knowing and it wasn't all-seeing, and the power of it was so dark and so great that it stormed through the world, destroying everything. It had only one command: kill the ice princess and her owl. It did not care about keeping anyone else alive.

"He accidentally created a monster," she whispered.

*I am not a monster. I am the Dionadair. And now you control me, just as he feared. You will bring destruction to them all. You are the Keeper of Storms.*

## 51

### REYNA

Reyna stood, her aching body as bruised and battered as her heart. She scanned Fomorian Square, bracing herself for another onslaught of arrows, not knowing if she would have the strength to dodge this time.

A harsh fire had settled in her chest, burning her up from the inside out. Unseelie had used her. She'd been tricked. He'd *wanted* her to destroy the Ruin...the Dionadair. She could not bear to think about what she'd done. Not now. She was still in the midst of a battle-ravaged city. Distantly, she could hear the clash of steel on steel. She needed to find Lorcan and help him fight the wood fae...just so long as she could stay standing long enough to swing her blade.

As soon as it was all over, she would press her cheek against his chest and breathe him in. She would tell him everything, at once. He would know what to do, even if there was nothing they *could* do. This could not be her fate. Together, they would fight against it, tooth and nail.

She needed him, she realized, that painful ache spreading through the rest of her limbs. And nothing would stop them from staying together now. She hadn't needed to return to the ice lands to find the Ruin. It hadn't begun in the north at all. It had begun here, in Findius. She clenched her hands, shaking her head. She could not think of the Ruin anymore. Not until she'd found Lorcan.

As she stepped through the broken courtyard, she saw nothing but frozen bodies and piles of ash. The stench of death was overwhelming. The ice wall blocked her path to most of the streets.

She had no idea where to find him. The Ruin had knocked her off course, and she did not know this city well. Taking in a ragged breath to steady her racing heart, she reached deep into her soul for the power that Seelie had bestowed upon her. Instantly, she bumped up against the Dionadair. The powers curled together in a strange, twisting embrace.

Reyna hissed and drew back.

*I am not the dark thing inside of you. You are.*

She ground her teeth together. "I'm not going to use you," she said aloud, not even caring how demented she looked to the fae cowering inside the few nearby buildings that had not crumbled beneath the magic of the ash.

*I am born of Seelie magic. The Dagda created me, for the good of the world.*

"Yeah, well," she muttered and shielded her eyes against the red light of the sun to find a better path forward. "He did a terrible job of controlling you. Do you know how many fae you've killed?"

*Because he left these lands. Now,* you *control me, Keeper of Storms.*

"I don't want to," she snapped.

*You have no other choice.*

She really wished she could shut this voice up. It had only been a few moments since she'd consumed the Dionadair, and it was already annoying the hell out of her.

"Well, then I command you to be silent."

No reply.

"Good."

In the moments since the fight, the magic had infused her bones with a small amount of strength. It would be hours yet before she was whole again. Days even, perhaps. Her shoulder was still very much broken, her arm dangling at an odd angle by her side.

But she would be able to fly.

Squeezing her fingernails into her palms, she cried out as she pushed her wings through the throbbing skin at her back. She had to pause to catch her breath when it was over. If she was going to do this flight thing on a regular basis, she needed to find a way to do it that wasn't so painful.

It felt like someone had lit her back on fire.

She pushed up into the air, gently flapping her wings to test her balance. When she didn't immediately plummet to the ground, she pushed higher into the sky, wings flaring. She rose above the charred buildings. The maze of city streets stretched out before her. Some were on fire. Others were dark and silent and dead. Some were still alive with the battle. The wood fae had yet to be defeated.

Her feathers rippled in the soft breeze. Now that the Dionadair was no longer tossing her about, she could feel the fragile strength in the silver-tipped wings. She felt like an unstoppable force, even if the rest of her was still ripped raw from the fight against the storm.

Soaring over the buildings, she swooped down to spin close to the streets. Eyes darting, she sought a very familiar head of sable hair. He would have it pulled back for battle, tied away from his face with a black band. In his boiled leather, he would be stalking through the streets, ferocity pulsing from his body like the feral warrior he was. His muscles would contract and ripple as he swung his sword, the red light glinting off the impressive Tamaris steel blade.

She could picture him so well in her mind's eye that she swore she saw him running through the Findian streets, a whirlwind of leather, smoke, and steel. But when she dipped closer to the ground, she saw that it had been nothing more than a shadow. A trick of the eye. He was not here.

Frustrated, she pushed back up into the clouds, spinning so that she could gaze across the entire expanse of the black stone city. Her chest ached, raw with need. Where was he? Why couldn't she find him? She'd seen no sign of Segonax or Nollaig either. She did not dare consider what that might mean.

She closed her eyes.

Surely, Lorcan had found safety. Surely the Ruin—the Dionadair—had not fallen upon them all as it tossed Reyna through the clouds above the square.

Lorcan could not have died in the Ruin. She knew he couldn't. He was immune. She'd seen it herself. But the storm could have disintegrated the rest of his party, leaving him to face an insurmountable number of wood fae alone.

Blinking back the tears, she swooped down once again, spinning through street after street after street. She passed burnt-out husks of buildings—remnants of fires left by the attacking wood fae. She passed blood-plastered walls and street corners piled high with the dead. She passed mountains of ash, the frozen wall she'd created herself.

She passed the living, the crying, the afraid. They huddled beneath the weight of the battle, trying to gather their wits after so much death had stared them in the face.

And then she passed shadow fae warriors shouting in victory as they shut the gate tight on the encroaching enemy. They'd won. The shadow fae had beaten back the wood fae. For now, at least. But the victory felt hollow to Reyna.

They had won, but where was their prince?

*Where is Lorcan?*

There was one last place she had yet to look. She turned her sights on the harbor where a small cluster of shadow fae warriors stood beside a ship that held the flickering banner of the Sea Court. Curious, Reyna flared her wings and pushed through the air. She called upon the magic within her, begging for enough strength to sharpen the sight of her eyes.

The magic flared to life, filling her up with power. Her body felt weak; her mind was numb. But she could see so clearly that the distant specks solidified into fully-formed fae. Three shadow warriors stood blocking the wooden path that led from the docks to the winding stairs up toward the castle and the city beyond. Before them stood two sea fae. Reyna recognized neither, though one wore a glimmering turquoise circlet, and her matching gown was spun from rich silks and embroidered with golden thread.

Reyna frowned, slowing as she approached the docks. What in the name of the Dagda was this? Why was sea fae royalty here, docking at the Shadow Court, *especially* while a battle raged on in the distance?

As much as she yearned for answers, something inside of her warned her to hold back. Something was wrong about this. She could feel it in her gut. With a frustrated sigh, she twisted back to the city, wings beating the thick, humid air.

*Where is Lorcan?*

The clouds shifted in the sky, parting so that the red sun now glinted across the black stone of the castle.

*The castle,* Reyna thought, understanding at once. Lorcan had taken the others to the safety of the castle. Relief surged through her. *Of course* he would have gone to the castle. There, he could take down his father and end his cruel reign. She could have kicked herself for not realizing it sooner.

Flaring her wings wide, she took off through the clouds.

Her eyes zeroed in on the twisting black mass of towers in the distance. Suddenly, a sharp *rip* tore through her left wing. A pain as great as any she'd ever felt burned through her feathers like molten iron.

She screamed, reaching behind her to claw at the pain. Her fingers curled around an arrow. A pit of shock tumbled into her belly. She'd been so focused on the castle, and finding Lorcan, that she hadn't bothered to look below…at the wood fae who had yet to be killed or captured, wreaking as much havoc as they could before they were caught.

Her vision clouded as the poison charged through her wings. She tried to hold on to the world around her. Distantly, she heard herself screaming, knowing that if she did not stay lucid, her body would plummet to the ground. Seelie had gifted her with immortality, but that did not mean she *couldn't* be killed. She would never die of old age, and she could survive most things. She did not know if she could survive slamming into a rock from a thousand feet in the air.

Before she could find out, darkness consumed her.

# 52

## THANE

"What is that?" Thane pointed up at the sky at a whirlwind of feathers and flesh. He had never seen anything like it before. Bright silver glistened even beneath the strange reddish haze of the shadow realm.

He shielded his eyes from the glow, frowning. The bird-like creature seemed to be hurt, and it was tumbling to the ground. Tumbling right toward them.

"Get out of here, sea fae," one of the warriors blocking their path growled out in a tone that reminded Thane so much of Lorcan. "Come any closer, and we'll slice off your heads."

"Your prince will want to see us. All you have to tell him is that we're here," his aunt said, her tone sinking into irritation.

They had been trying to get off the docks for at least an hour, but the shadow fae would not let them enter the city, regardless of what Thane told them about Lorcan and the letter they'd received. It had been an inquiry as to his safety, to ask if he'd gone home to his mother's old court. Thane had considered penning a letter back but then thought better of it.

His aunt wanted to make an alliance with the shadow fae, to strengthen their army against Aengus. So, they came for a visit, for a parley. And they'd stumbled upon a war.

At first, Thane had understood why the shadow fae would not let them leave the docks. The city was in the middle of a battle with an invading army of wood fae. There was no reason for these warriors to believe they had come in peace. Except that they had not come with a legion of ships, they were not attacking, and they were politely requesting to see an old friend.

But they were as stubborn as his old betrothed was.

"Aunt, I think you might want to take cover. Something is coming right at us," Thane said grimly as the hurtling bird thundered through the skies. He ducked into the captain's bridge, along with his aunt and uncle. They made it just as the bird fell with a loud *thrack* on the dock.

Thane's throat tightened when he saw it was not a bird at all.

"*Who* is that?" his aunt asked, stumbling back with her palm at her throat.

Thane pulled in a sharp breath. He should have known. The silver, the whirlwind, the pure chaos of it all. "That is Reyna Darragh."

His uncle gasped and jerked toward him. "*That* is the female you were to marry?"

She looked a mess, he thought fondly. Her hair was a wild tumble, all jumbled up in knots. Her clothes were ripped and bloodied, and the set of her jaw was a fierce one, even with her eyes shut tight against the world. He glanced at a very large pair of wings that had sprouted from her back. And the arrow sticking out of it, slick with blood.

"She's hurt." He whirled to the captain. "We need an alchemist and several strong males. And some bandages at once!"

"What are you doing, Thane?" his uncle asked as he hurried back onto the docks to kneel by Reyna's side. "What is happening, where did she come from, and *why does she have wings*, for god's sake?"

Thane gently pressed his hands to Reyna's wing. It was impossibly strong, corded in powerful muscles that could pound a fae to death with very little effort. "I don't know the answers to any of those questions. All I know is Reyna has fallen to our feet, and she's hurt. Badly. If we don't get this arrow out of her...wing, then she could die."

"She won't die," his aunt said quietly from behind him.

Frowning, Thane glanced up, just for a moment, before turning his attention back on Reyna. "She's unconscious, and she's barely breathing."

"Thane, if the girl has wings, then she's far more powerful than you think she is. The Dagda has blessed her with magic. He's undone the Fall. If she has wings, then she has the means to heal. It may take several days, but soon that wound will be a tiny scar and nothing more."

"That's impossible," Thane muttered. No one had the magic of the Dagda, not anymore. But he could not deny her wings. They were monstrously large and glistening silver. Fae wings only came from one place. Magic.

"We need to get her onto the ship and return home," his uncle said excitedly. "Think what we can accomplish with her on our side. No army will stand a chance."

Thane's frown deepened. "We came here to parley with my old friend, to make allies with the Shadow Court."

"Look at the Shadow Court, Thane." His uncle gestured at the ruin that stretched out before them. "If this city hasn't fallen already, it will soon. If we'd brought our army with us, we could save them. But we didn't, and it would be far too late by the time we returned." His lips pressed firmly together. "In truth, Thane, it is dangerous for us to stay here much longer. You know what the wood king is like. He will slaughter us all."

"I hate to agree with my brother, but for once I do," his aunt said with a sigh. "I came here wanting to make an ally with the shadows, but I don't see how we can now."

"And leave Lorcan to face this alone?" Thane gestured wildly at the castle, his heart pounding thunder in his ears.

"You're the High King of the Air Court, Thane, and you need to save your kingdom from your enemy. Go on into that city and get yourself killed, if you'd like, but it will only solidify Aengus's rule at your court."

Thane growled and punched the dock, the wood splintering. Sharp slivers dug into his flesh, but he didn't care. He hated this. He hated all of it. Nothing was ever easy. It was always so damn hard.

"And you just want us to steal Reyna?" he shouted up at his uncle.

"Lorcan is the one who stole her. I see this as more of a rescue."

Thane was not so certain his uncle was right. Reyna loved Lorcan. He'd seen it in her eyes. Would her love have survived his betrayal? He glanced down at her broken body, the wings. She'd been flying toward them when she'd been hit. Perhaps she'd seen him, and she was trying to get away.

They had come here for an ally, and they had found one. Just not the way they had expected.

He stood and turned toward the alchemist who was waiting for a command. Thane pointed at the princess, steadying his racing heart. "Bring her on board and make her as comfortable as you can." He turned toward the captain. "Raise the anchor and prepare the crew. We're sailing back to the seas."

## 53

## LORCAN

"We're here to see the High King," Segonax announced to the two guards stationed on either side of the midnight black throne room doors. The shadow fae sigil had long ago been carved deep into the wood. Twisting antlers stretching wide like wings. The symbol of Lorcan's father. The symbol of *him*.

Lorcan had awoken only moments earlier, a whirlwind of anger. Segonax and Nollaig had teamed up against him. They'd knocked him out and dragged him to the castle, forcing him to face down his father. If they had been anyone else in the world, he would have sliced their heads clean off. But he couldn't bring himself to kill two of his oldest friends.

The warriors they'd collected on the way were heavily armed. They weren't letting him do anything but walk through that damn door. He would have fought them all, too, to get back to Reyna's side, but the battle was long done. Reyna had fought the Ruin. She'd won. And she'd taken down the wood fae army, too. She was on her way to the castle now.

The guard on the left frowned. "The king said the prince died in an accident on the mountains."

"And as you can see, he is fine," Segonax said with a tight smile. "The king will be very pleased to see him indeed."

The guard grunted but then nodded, stepping aside. "As you wish, Commander."

The doors swung wide, and the trio strode tall into the throne room, flanked by two dozen warriors. They filled the small space beneath the dais, staring up at a king who was half-asleep, wine-stained lips puckered out, eyes half-lidded. He was drunk. Again. While his city burned down. A serving girl sat on his lap, stuck in place by stubby arms wrapped around her waist.

"Father," Lorcan said quietly.

The king jerked up, only just realizing they were there. Shock flittered through his eyes as he took in his son and the company of warriors he'd brought with him.

"Thought you might come. I hear your little princess has made quite an impression on the city. Heh." Bolg grunted, grabbing at the poor serving girl's arse as she scurried away. "She took out that blasted Ruin, and she helped our army push the Wood Court back into the tunnels."

A wave of pride rippled through Lorcan's heart. "It seems you underestimated her."

Bolg grunted again. "And you. You're harder to kill than you look."

Lorcan froze, hands half-clenched by his sides. His fingers itched to draw his sword, but he held himself as still as a rat under the gaze of an owl.

"That's right. No need to dance around it. You're not loyal to me." The High King's beady eyes flicked toward Lorcan's bare arm, scabbed over from where Reyna had dug the mark out of his skin. "I've known it for awhile." His eyes flicked to Nollaig. "And neither are you. Traitors, the both of you. Guards. Take them. They'll both be executed on the 'morn."

But the guards stayed rooted to the spot.

Bolg growled and stood from his throne before stumbling sideways half a step. Everyone watched him, silent. Shaking his head, he plopped right back down. "What's the meaning of this? I said *take them*."

"We will not be taking them," Seg said with a steely glint in his granite eyes. "Prince Lorcan is our liege. No harm will come to him."

Bolg stared, and then he let out a great snorting laugh that echoed off the lofted stone ceiling. "He's a bloody bastard is what he is. And I'm done looking at his traitorous face. Guards, I said seize him. Obey the command of your High King!"

No one moved. No one even blinked.

When someone did finally step forward, it was Nollaig.

"You," the king spat when he saw her. "I knew I never should have trusted you. You're just like the rest of them. A liar. A traitor. A sneaky little thief."

"You're right," she said in a dangerously calm voice, taking another step toward Bolg Rothach. "You never should have trusted me. You see, the shadow fae are not so different from the rest of the realms, *Your Grace*. The low fae of the Air Court don't want to be ruled by a wicked, demented king, and neither do we. The only different between us and them is...well, we are brazen enough to end a king's reign when he has not been kind to us."

Nollaig whipped a dagger out from the depths of her cloak and launched it at the king. It landed with a sickening crunch in his throat. Lorcan winced, grinding his jaw as he watched the blood gurgle from his father's lips. It only took moments for him to die. The wine goblet tumbled to the ground, cracking on the stone floor, just as the High King slumped in his seat, the tormented life dying in his eyes.

The warriors sprang into action, rushing forward and lifting him from the stone chair. Several more followed just behind, quickly wiping up the blood and the wine, scrubbing away the crimson as if it had never been there. None of them said a word. They simply cleaned and vanished. Only Segonax and Nollaig were left in the throne room when all was said and done.

Lorcan still hadn't spoken. He did not quite know what to say. His father had just died, yet he felt nothing. Not angry. Not sad. But…not happy either. He just felt...empty. Ripped raw.

It had been a very long past few days. He needed Reyna.

"Well, Nollaig, we have finally done it, "Segonax announced with a weary sigh as he sagged against the wall, head in his hands. "It has taken us over ten damn years, but here we are."

"A decade." The cloaked fae shook her head. "If only we'd known then how long it would take, I fear we would have forgone the plot completely. I'm glad we didn't, now that it is done. The realm will finally have a chance to heal."

Lorcan's frown deepened with every passing second. "I am going to need you two to explain to me exactly what you mean."

Segonax tapped his finger against his chin, taking his time. Finally, he relented. "I suppose it does no good to hide it from you anymore. You're the king now. We don't want to start off on a path full of lies."

"You knock me out and force me to come here, and now you speak in riddles?" Lorcan's hands fisted. "*What are you talking about, Segonax?*"

"Nollaig and I...well, we were not as loyal to the former king as he thought. In the end, he seemed to realize that Nollaig was against him, but I daresay I got away with it right up until his dying breath. Otherwise, he never would have let me into the throne room today, especially not with the both of you."

Lorcan clenched and unclenched his hands, staring in horrified awe. "It's true then. You've been planning to kill the king for years."

"Oh yes, but we needed a suitable replacement to take the throne in his stead. We were very lucky when we found a bastard who appeared to be a good male. Strong and steady, good with a sword. You're a bit moody at times, but moody is better than mad."

"Wait...*you* found me? I thought my father sought me out."

"Your mother was never your father's favorite. That was another one of his lies. In fact, I'm not entirely convinced he ever knew who she was." Segonax's granite eyes flickered with remorse. "I am sorry about that, Your Majesty. It was not our intention to hurt you. Your father could be very cruel."

"What are you saying?" Lorcan demanded.

"It was not Bolg Rothach's idea to bring you to the Shadow Court."

Segonax's words hit Lorcan like an iron fist. He stumbled back, mouth dropped wide. All this time, and he had not once questioned why his father decided to send for him. Lorcan had believed the king just wanted another plaything, a toy.

But *Segonax* had brought him to the Shadow Court. Lorcan did not know if that made it better or worse.

"And the mark?" Lorcan asked dangerously.

"That, unfortunately, was not our idea. Bolg was worried a bastard prince would someday try to kill him, and he wanted the mark to prevent you from doing him harm. It wasn't until later that he decided to use it to make you spy on another court."

Lorcan stared, trying—and failing—to grasp the full meaning of Segonax's words. He had not been brought to this dreadful place because his father wanted to use him. Someone else had. Someone he had trusted.

Nollaig stepped forward. "We only did all this so that we might one day put a better ruler on his throne."

He let out a bitter laugh. "And instead, you ended up with me. Someone with half his loyalty devoted to the Air Court. Someone in love with an ice princess."

"We did worry that your father's insistence on capturing your lover would prove to be the final nail in the coffin of our hopes. At first, you seemed very distracted by it all." They exchanged a glance. "Of course, it also seems to have made you see just how much the realm needs a ruler like you. Instead of one like him."

"I only see it that way because this entire time you've been plotting against me."

"No, Lorcan," Nollaig said with a ferocity in her voice. "We've been plotting *for* you."

He shook his head. "You should have told me."

"We couldn't. That mark in your skin. We feared it would somehow know, and then reveal the truth to your father."

They were right to fear that. Lorcan had often feared it himself. He did not truly understand the extent of the power that had once lived inside his skin, but it had been terrible indeed. He didn't think his father had ever been able to read his mind, not fully, but he'd known some things he never should have. Some things Unseelie must have whispered into his mind.

"What if I don't want to sit on the damn throne?" Lorcan asked, hands hanging heavily by his sides. "Look at it. It's a bloody terrible seat, and everyone who sits there dies."

"Then, you'll be an even better High King than we hoped."

"Reyna," he said, shaking his head. "I need to speak with Reyna."

He knew what his kingdom needed from him, and he would not turn his back on them, even if outside plots had put him there. But he needed to see her, to ask her to stay with him. She'd defeated the Ruin. She did not have to go. He knew it would be tough. She would miss the ice and the snow, but they could journey north once it was safe. Once the kingdoms were settled. Once peace found them once again.

The war had lasted one hundred years. It would not last forever.

"Reyna has already gone," Segonax said quietly.

Lorcan's heart dropped into his boots. "What? You said she was on the way to the castle."

"I didn't want to tell you she was gone until after we'd confronted your father. I was afraid you'd rush after her and forget about the throne." He pressed his lips into a thin, white line. "We sent a scout to find her, and the warriors on the ground said they saw her board a ship sailing north."

A sharp pain sliced through his gut. He almost fell to his knees from the force of it. Everything ached. His soul, his heart, his body itself. One moment his arms had been around her, and then the next...he'd been here, in the shadow of his father's blood, staring at a cursed throne he did not want. Alone. Even though he'd known she'd planned to leave, it still felt as though she'd shoved her ice blade deep into his heart and then wrenched it to the side, destroying him completely.

"She wouldn't do that," he whispered. "She promised she would say goodbye before she left."

"Unfortunately, Your Majesty, it seems she lied."

Lorcan flinched at the sound of the title on the commander's lips. "I am not your majesty yet."

"With the death of your father, you very much are. We will call for your coronation by the week's end. The kingdom will be pleased. After the recent turmoil, they will enjoy having something to celebrate."

Lorcan growled, glaring at the luminous stone seat for which so much blood had been spilled. "I don't want it, and I don't have to take it. I could walk away from this right now and never look back."

"You can," Nollaig said quietly. "But you won't."

He whirled on Nollaig, heart thundering. "You did all this for the realm. You've plotted it for decades. Why don't you sit on the damn thing yourself, Nollaig? Why don't *you* become the High Queen?"

She was silent for a long while before answering. "Because I am a cursed monster, and this kingdom needs better than me."

Lorcan turned his glare onto Segonax. The old commander lifted his hands in surrender.

"Do not look at me. If I wanted it for myself, I would have killed him a long damn time ago."

"I am just a bastard," Lorcan said, his hands hanging heavily by his sides. "A village bastard, raised in an enemy court. A spy who betrayed his lover. A son who watched his drunk of a father bleed out on his throne."

"It will make a great tale for a bard," Segonax said with a slight smile. "The Bastard Prince of Rothach."

"No," Nollaig whispered, striding forward with the twisting antler crown. "The King of Shadows."

## 54

### MARIEL

"Grand Alderman." Lord Neil dipped low as if he were addressing a king rather than a weedy male who had tried to steal the title for himself. He held up a rolled parchment, tied together with green string. "A letter arrived for you."

Aengus frowned and snatched the parchment from where he sat at the head of the strategy table, pushing pieces around. He'd been doing this for days, distracted by the news that the Wood Court and the Shadow Court had engaged in battle.

"Who's it from?" he asked, tossing it onto the table.

"There is a green tie on it, my lord," Lord Neil said with a tight smile. "The color of the Wood Court, as I'm sure you know."

Mariel bit back a smile at the dig. Of course Aengus would know. The majority of his army was with the wood king, and Aengus had yet to get them back.

"Why would the wood king be sending me a message?" Aengus snapped. "Think he's finally decided to relent? Too scared to keep ahold of my army any longer, is he?"

Lord Neil pressed his lips together. "Of all topics this letter might cover, that is certainly an option."

"Your niceties are sickening, Lord Neil." Aengus snatched the letter from the table and unrolled the parchment. Mariel watched him hold the letter extremely close to his narrow eyes as he scanned the words. His expression went from angry to incredulous to intrigued. When he finally slammed the letter on the table, he was full on delighted.

"What does the letter say?" Mariel asked innocently.

"He wants to make an alliance," Aengus said triumphantly. "I knew he would! Now that I have the entirety of the realm on my side, he's terrified of me. He wants me to come at once and join the army down south. We're to lay siege to the Shadow Court."

Mariel exchanged a glance with Lord Neil. "Well then, it certainly does seem you were right all along. And once the rest of the realms see two great powers come together, they will surely fall in line as well."

"I shall leave at once." Aengus stood eagerly, his eyes wild with anticipation. Mariel had guessed he would react this way. She'd long suspected that he did not agree with Imogen's decision to fight the Wood Court. The king was a terrible, cruel creature who inflicted monstrosities upon his own fae. Exactly the sort of fae that Aengus would be drawn to.

"Wait, my liege," Lord Neil cut in as Aengus scurried toward the door. "Is this wise?"

"Why ever not?" Aengus snapped. "Or do you not wish to see our great kingdom rise to something even greater? We can finally become the empire we've long deserved to be." His chest puffed. "*I* could become an emperor."

"What I mean to say is that your absence will be surely...noted, my liege." Lord Neil cleared his throat. "You are the Grand Alderman and the voice of our missing king. With you gone as well, who will rule us? Who will keep this court running smoothly in your absence? I worry we risk everything falling apart. Lords revolting. City uprisings."

Aengus frowned as if this thought had not even occurred to him.

Of course it hadn't. One mention of the wood king, and he had gone scurrying away like the rat he was.

"Quite right," Aengus said, rubbing his chin. "We will need someone who is trusted, particularly amongst you lords and ladies of the court." His eyes slid to Mariel. "You. I need you to take charge of this castle in my stead."

Her lips twitched. "Of course. I won't let you down."

Aengus left at first light with a company of guards. The entire court saw him off, waving and smiling and tossing golden handkerchiefs in the air. Celebrating his great victory in allying with the wood king, of course. But as soon as he was out of sight, Lady Regan turned to Mariel with a scowl.

"Gods, am I glad to get his weaselly face out of my sight. I thought he'd never go!"

Lord Neil strode closer, beaming. "He's like a fungus. Hard to scrub out."

Mariel crossed her arms over her chest. "Why *did* it take so long? Frankly, I thought one of you would kill him. Did you not get my letter?"

Lord Neil and Lady Regan exchanged a glance. "We weren't certain it was true until we saw you with our own eyes. And, truthfully, we were worried about that curse. You saw what happened to the Selkirks when they murdered a king."

Mariel frowned. "Aengus is the Grand Alderman. He doesn't hold the Seat of Power."

"Then, why didn't you kill him? You had plenty of chances yourself."

"It isn't the curse. It's the principle," she said. "My father always taught me that if you need to kill someone to gain power, then you shouldn't have that power."

Lady Regan's eyes softened. "Ah, your father. He was a good king."

"Unlike Sloane Selkirk," Mariel said through gritted teeth. "The fae who killed him."

"Well, my dear, he got his due in the end. He's gone and so is the rest of his dreadful family. And you're here. The throne is yours for the taking."

"Except it isn't. Not truly. Thane Selkirk still holds it, wherever he is. And Aengus is the Grand Alderman. He can claim it upon his return, and it is rightfully his. In name, only. But his."

They exchanged a glance again. "We will never allow him to have it. Besides, he won't be coming back."

Mariel raised her brows. "Don't tell me you sent assassins after him."

Lady Regan smiled. "Not at all. As I'm sure you've guessed, the wood king did not write that letter. He didn't extend a hand to Aengus. And when Aengus trots into the Wood Court on that high horse of his..."

"High King Ulaid Molt will chew him up and spit him out."

"Perhaps literally."

A shiver went down Mariel's spine. She had known the lords and ladies were conspiring, but she had not guessed quite how much. It was clever, she would give them that.

"But how did you do it?" she asked. "We can't lie. Not even in a letter."

Lady Regan shrugged. "We had a human write it for us. Turns out, there are far more of them on this continent than you'd think."

Mariel smiled.

So, Aengus truly was gone. He would not survive the Wood Court, no matter how cunning he was. Hopefully, Thane would never return either. He had been a decent lad. He'd tried to do the right thing until he'd abandoned his people. In the end, the Selkirks had torn the realm apart. The kingdom of air needed a fresh start. A new ruler. Someone stronger. Someone fairer. Someone not tied to a cursed family.

They needed Mariel Dalais.

It was her court now. Her throne. Her city. Her rule.

And she would never allow anyone to take it from her again. The Bloody Dagger was finally home.

# 55

## EISLYN

It was easier to find smugglers when one knew what one was doing. Eislyn Darragh hunkered behind some barrels at the edge of Snowport's docks, watching the crews come and go from their ships. There were three that looked to be the right size with crews much more varied and wild than the others. Ones with fae who had glints in their eyes.

Squaring her shoulders, she pushed up from her hiding place and approached the nearest ship. It was a large black thing with a mast decorated with sigils from each of the six courts. *Bold,* Eislyn could not help but think.

"Excuse me," she said to the female whose back was turned toward her. The fae shot a quick glance over her shoulder, a ginger-haired female with a smattering of freckles across her nose and cheeks.

Her deep green eyes slightly widened when she caught sight of Eislyn. "I don't want any trouble, love."

"Good," Eislyn said. "Neither do I."

"Then, you'll need to do a better job with that disguise of yours." She gestured vaguely at Eislyn's face. She'd hidden her hair beneath a hoarfrost cloak hood, and she'd thought the shadows would hide most of her features. Many ice fae had silver hair. She was not unusual in that.

"Maybe I'm not who you think I am."

The female fully turned to her, crossing her arms over her beige linen tunic. "Aren't you?"

Eislyn pressed her lips together. "What gave me away?"

"Well, for one, everyone in the city is talking about you, and I'm the kind of fae interested in what kind of coin I could get in exchange for handing you over to Lord Morcant's angry sons." The fae gave Eislyn a pointed look that made her skin crawl. "And two, you look like a damn princess, love. You're pretty and shiny, and that cloak of yours is worth more than everything I've got on this ship combined."

"What do you have on this ship? And by that, I mean your hatch," Eislyn asked with a small smile.

The fae started, and then laughed. "Clever. What gave me away?"

"None of your crew is from around here," Eislyn answered. "Your accents are from all over the place, and you don't have the silver hair of the north. That might not stand out in Falias, but it stands out here. These fae rarely venture further south than Hoarfrost Forest. There's also your mast with all the sigils. That could work for some merchant ships, but not here. Not in Snowport."

"And here I thought princesses were dumb."

"Are you still going to try to sell me to my cousins? Because I'll just tell them what you're doing here."

"Sure, you might. Unless I cut out your tongue."

Eislyn fisted her hands and stalked closer to the fae. "Listen. I have had a really bad month, and I need to get the hell out of this city. Where are you going?"

The smuggler arched a brow. "Tuath Island."

"Good," Eislyn snapped. "I want to go with you."

She laughed. "You're going to have to do better than that, love. If you want passage on my ship, I'll need something in return."

"And what's that?" Eislyn demanded.

"You have coin?"

"A little.

"How much?"

Eislyn scowled. "A hundred airgead."

The smuggler shook her head, still chuckling. "You know what that'll buy you? I can take you as far as that rock over there, and then I'll have to toss you overboard."

Irritation bubbled up in Eislyn like a hot spring about to blow. "Can't you, I don't know, just do something *nice* for someone? People want me dead. If I stay here, they're just going to kill me."

"That's not my problem, princess." The fae turned back to her ship, readying the anchor.

"Just...tell me what you want, and I'll give it to you, all right?" Eislyn's voice cracked, desperation falling out of her mouth before she could stop it. The last thing she wanted to do was cry in front of this heartless fae, but this might be her only chance to escape, and she couldn't let it pass her by. Not without trying her damnedest. She was done giving up when things got hard.

The smuggler sighed and turned back. "All right, listen. I'll let you on board, but you can't just float around all princess-like and expect us to dote on you. You've got to take care of yourself, and you've got to chip in with the work. And if there's trouble, it's every fae for himself. You know how to use that sword you're hiding under that cloak of yours?"

"Actually, I do."

She smiled. "Good. Now hurry and get on board before I change my mind or people start getting curious about you.

And get rid of that damn cloak. No, stop. Don't throw it away, for Dagda's sake. Give it here. We can sell that for good coin."

With a hopeful nod, Eislyn tossed the smuggler her hoar-frost cloak and climbed on board. Only moments later, they pushed off from the docks, and the ship turned north for the path up to Tuath Isle. Eislyn stood on the stern, watching Snowport vanish into a distant speck on the horizon.

Against all odds, she had survived. So far. But she still had a very long way to go. First stop, Tuath Isle. And then, on to the Empire of Fomor.

# 56

## REYNA

Reyna had the vague notion that something in her world had just changed irrevocably. Light speared her eyes as she pushed sleep from her addled mind. The scent of brine clogged her nostrils, and the sound of crashing waves drew her thoughts away from the dull ache in her shoulder.

Suddenly, panic choked her throat. She sat up fast, blinking against the blinding light.

An alarming sense of deja vu rushed through her as she tried to make sense of her surroundings. The sound of the waves. The scent of brine. It was all too achingly familiar.

It was just as it had been on the ship when the poison had rushed through her veins. Back when Lorcan had taken her to the shadow lands. That could mean only one thing. She'd been taken captive. Again. Some new horror had rushed into her life, and she'd been taken against her will. Again. What would she have to endure to get out of *this* gilded cage?

But there was no scarlet light slanting through the open window with its gauzy turquoise curtains fluttering in the salty breeze. Shadows did not lurk in every corner. Instead, the room was blindingly bright. The silk bedsheets were pearly white, and a patchwork rug wound with blues and greens stretched across the grey stone floor. Turquoise stones dotted the walls.

She clutched at her neck. Her ice glass ring still clung to her throat, and she spotted her dagger on a table beside the bed. There was even an owl perch in the corner where Wingallock rested quietly, calmly. He seemed happy enough, which doused her worried heart with some measure of relief. That still did not explain where she was, however.

Suddenly, the door creaked open, and a familiar head of golden hair edged around the doorframe. A forehead came into view, one tattooed with the limbs of a hawthorn tree.

"I told you, she is not awake. Leave her be for now," a soft voice said.

And then Thane Selkirk popped into the room. Reyna let out a shriek and dove beneath the covers, more from the shock of it all than anything else. Thane tensed. He held himself still in the doorframe, his familiar golden eyes darting around the room, and then he relaxed and strode inside.

Reyna peeked over the covers, heart hammering. "What in the name of the Dagda are *you* doing here?"

Not that she had any idea where *here* was. But it clearly wasn't the Air Court. Or the Shadow Court. It especially wasn't the Ice Court. There was a chill in the air, but it was still far too warm for that.

"It's nice to see you, too, Reyna," he said, grinning. "You haven't changed at all."

"Where am I, Thane? What's going on?"

She dully remembered soaring through the skies above Findius, desperately trying to find Lorcan before being shot down by an arrow. She'd tumbled to the ground, and then...nothing. Everything was a blank slate after that.

"You're in the Sea Court," he said gently. "We found you

half-dead on the docks of Findius, and we brought you back here so you could heal."

Her heart thumped. Once, then twice, and then it froze. "I'm in the Sea Court?"

Thane nodded, warily taking a step back, clearly reading the danger in her eyes. "We were just trying to help you. You had an arrow sticking out of your, um, wing. And you'd lost a lot of blood."

"Where's Lorcan, Thane?" She swung her legs over the side of the bed and stood, a surge of power rushing through her veins.

He blanched.

*"Where is Lorcan, Thane?"* Every word was louder than the last.

"He's in the Shadow Court. They've crowned him High King."

A tormenting cascade of emotions crashed over her. Relief that he was alive. Pride that he had saved his kingdom and had risen so far. But there was also sadness there, and regret. Horrible, terrible regret. She curled her fists around the bedsheets and swallowed down a feral roar. Reyna had done this to them both. *All* of this was her fault. If she hadn't taken the power of Seelie, they would be together even now.

Instead...she would likely never see his face again. Anguish pulled her down, holding her there for so long that she thought she might drown in it.

"Why am I *here* instead of there with him?" she asked, her voice breaking.

"When we found you, we thought the city had fallen, and Lorcan along with it." His deep golden eyebrows slammed down. "It was not my intention to separate you two. I was just trying to save your life, Reyna."

Thane could not lie, and she could hear the earnestness in his every word. With a sigh, she sagged back against the bed, head in her hands. "It's all right. You didn't know. Thank you, Thane. It means a lot that you would try."

"You may not be my betrothed anymore, Reyna, but I do care for you."

At that, Reyna's head jerked up. "Eislyn, have you had word from her?"

A dark storm cloud rolled across his golden face. "No. Last I heard, she escaped Tairngire to return home, but that's all I know. I'm having trouble finding out what is happening at court. No one is answering my letters."

Relief shuddered through her. North. Home. Eislyn truly was safe, after all. "And Lorcan? Does he know I'm here?"

Thane winced. "He does, and I'll daresay Reyna, I think he wants to chop off my head for taking you away."

She couldn't help but laugh. "Oh my gods, Thane. You have no idea what I thought when I woke up and found myself here. I thought I'd been taken captive again. You don't know how glad I am that I've found myself amongst friends for once." Sighing, she smiled. "I know it's a lot to ask after everything you've done for me, but do you have a ship to spare? I need to return to the Shadow Court as soon as possible."

Thane's face was a mask of stone. His jaw slightly rippled, but that was it. The only indication that something was wrong.

Her heart twitched. "What is it, Thane? What aren't you telling me?"

"You cannot return to the Shadow Court," he said, turning away so that she could only see the long, sharp profile of his solemn face.

"Why?" She shoved up from the bed and stalked toward him. "So, you *are* keeping me captive after all!"

"No, Reyna, I'm not. You're free to go whenever you want," he said through gritted teeth. "But you cannot return to the

Shadow Court. You'd never make it. You can survive falls from the sky, apparently, but you would not survive that."

Fear had a tight, choking hold on her heart when she whispered, "Why?"

"It might be best if you sit down. You've been through quite the ordeal, and the alchemists say it'll be days yet before you're fully back to normal. It's a miracle you even survived."

"What is wrong with Lorcan?" she thundered. Ice crackled as it shot from her open mouth, surging up to the ceiling and then shattering when it hit stone. Shards rained down all around them, a cascade of sharp and jagged pieces. A reflection of her heart. Reyna's breath stilled in her throat.

Thane arched a perfectly-sculpted brow. "Another new trick of yours?"

"I swear to the Dagda, Thane, if you do not tell me what's going on, I will—"

"The city is under siege. At least...we think it is."

Confusion rippled through her. "You *think*? Are the reports inconsistent? Why not send Lorcan a bird, and he can tell you himself."

Thane's lips flatlined. "We've sent him birds. Every last one has been shot down. We were in contact with him when we were sailing back. We'd made it about halfway before his letter arrived. He demanded your return, and I was of the mind to turn our ship around and do exactly what he asked."

"And then?" she prodded.

"We sent another message, to tell him our plan, and I saw the bird get shot down with my own two eyes. Only...I didn't see a damn ship to shoot her down. There was nothing there, Reyna. Not even a tiny boat. The arrow appeared out of nowhere, punched through her gut, and she fell."

Reyna swore, fisting her hands. "The wood king is using Unseelie magic to hide his ships. It's an illusion."

"And they turned one of those ships on us. The arrows

came our way and kept on coming until we sailed further away from Findius." Thane dragged a hand down his face, and suddenly, Reyna could see the vague hints of exhaustion on the golden prince. A slight tint of purple lined his eyes. Stubble dotted his chin. Two firm lines had deepened between his brow where he had furrowed them so often.

"And so you believe they've put Findius under siege," she finished for him. "But you aren't certain because you can't get word to Lorcan and he can't get word to you. And you can't see an army either, I'm guessing?"

He shook his head. "No army that we can see, though there are signs of a camp on the northern side of the Findius city walls."

"Well, then let's go help him." Reyna pushed away from the wall to stalk toward the open window. She gazed out at the seas below, watching the boats bob in the water. There were hundreds of them, all shiny and glistening and new. "You have the ships. And you have the warriors. This court hasn't been involved in battles for years."

"I don't have a thing, Reyna," he said quietly.

She whirled on him, gesturing out the window. "You have far more here than any other court!"

"This is not my court." He pointed at the turquoise stones that made up the walls, and then raised his finger toward the glittering sea. "Those are not my ships."

Her heart sank as the meaning of his words were made clear. "But this is your mother's court. Her family. That makes them your family, too."

Thane shook his head, a bitter laugh bubbling up in his throat. "You have no idea how right you are, Reyna. Aengus had my mother killed. My aunt and uncle refuse to sail to Lorcan's aide not because he's a shadow fae. That doesn't seem to concern them at all. They even wanted to ally with him before all this."

Thane had been right. Reyna needed to sit down. Instead, she held on tight to the window ledge, trying to understand how it had come down to this. Lorcan was surrounded by enemies, and there was nothing she could do.

He continued. "I've sent letters to all the lords who have been loyal to the Selkirks, but they have ignored my pleas. Aengus must have found loyalty in them instead. I have no doubt he plans to fight against my return."

Reyna could only stare, open-mouthed.

"I'd have half a mind to let him have it all. The kingdom, the crown, that horrible bloody throne. I don't want to see my city fall, and after everything that has happened, I'm not even certain I want to rule. But...my mother's family does not feel quite so generous." He laughed bitterly and shook his head.

"They're sailing for Tairngire. They plan to sack my city. And they've asked your father to join them. Ice and Sea will join together to end Air once and for all."

# EPILOGUE

## GLENCORA

A pair of unseen fingers *snapped,* and Glencora awoke at once. Sucking in great lungfuls of air, she threw herself up from the bed and launched across the room, clutching her nightdress in terror.

She remembered every moment of the attack. The fear. The pain. The ruin of it all. It flashed through her as fresh as the day it had occurred. Every emotion was heightened, real, and raw. It was as if she was reliving it all over again.

Gasping, she stumbled toward the door and wrenched it open. A guard stood just outside, bathed in the silver light of the orbs that hung along the castle walls. He let out a curse when he saw her, and then took off down the corridor at once.

She waited, sagging in the doorway, her back facing the bed where she'd laid for so very long. It had been months, she knew. Perhaps even a year. The time had stretched on tortuously. She'd been aware of every moment, every whisper, every hush of the door opening and closing. She'd heard the fear in her sisters' voices.

All that time, she'd been unable to do anything but lie

there prone and still. Sometimes, great tremors had stormed through her, lighting up her body with pain. But mostly, she'd been forced to remain still.

Every moment that passed had felt like her last.

And yet she had lived on. She never should have survived.

Footsteps thundered down the hallway, and her father suddenly appeared before her. He looked older than the last time she'd seen him. Ragged. Tired. Worn. The glistening silver crown perched atop his white hair, and his ever-present armor gleamed still. But the past year had taken its toll on him. She could not blame him. It had taken a toll on them all.

"Glencora," he shouted, rushing toward her and wrapping his strong arms around her. She sighed and closed her eyes, breathing in the scent of snow and pine. It had been so long since she had felt someone's touch. For awhile, her father had come to see her daily. But soon, those daily visits had turned to weekly. And then longer. By her count, he had not come to see her in well over a month.

"Father," she said stiffly. "There is news I must tell you at once."

He pulled back, concern flickering across his tired face. "News? Glencora, do you remember what happened to you?"

She nodded.

"Good," he said with a sigh. "Come. We will have the alchemist take a good look at you and make certain you're well enough to be out of bed. Oh, Glencora, you do not know how relieved I am to see you." His voice cracked. "I didn't think you were ever going to return to us."

"Reyna and Eislyn are in danger."

Her father pulled back with a sharp gasp, and his grip tightened on her arm. "Your sisters are..."

"In danger," she said again.

His eyes darkened. "Glencora, I fear you've woken quite

unwell. I think it might be best if we get you back into bed at once."

"They've been captured."

A moment passed, and then Cos Darragh drew himself up to his kingly height. "By whom?"

"By everyone."

Her father stared at her for a good long while before he let out a shuddering sigh. "Glencora, you have been in a coma for a very long time. It makes sense you would be confused. We need to get you back in bed where you can rest. I'm certain you'll be well enough to walk around soon enough."

"I'm not confused, Father," she said insistently. "Reyna and Eislyn are on a terrible path. One of them will bring the end of everything. She will start the Cleaving of the World where realms burn and minds twist. And the other...she will try to stop it. One will kill the other, but the gods have yet to decide which sister will win."

The High King of the Ice Court stared at her in shock. "You're mad. The Ruin has driven you mad."

"No, Father, I'm afraid I'm not. I came so close to death that the Dionadair showed me everything." She paused. "It even showed me that you've been exchanging letters with the Sea Court."

He took a step back, staring at her as if he didn't know her, as if she'd been transformed into a beast. "You overheard a servant talking."

"You have not spoken of this to anyone. In fact, I believe you ripped up the letters and burnt the scraps."

"Your sisters, they would never do such a thing," he said in a rush of words. "Eislyn would never hurt a fly, and Reyna...she would do anything to protect her people. She would never do this thing you speak of, this cleaving of the world. And she would certainly never lay a hand on Eislyn. She would rather die."

"For now, you may be right, but not for long." Glencora took his hands in hers and whispered fiercely. "She is the Keeper of Storms, Father. Do you know what that means? Reyna will kill her sister. Or she will destroy the world."

***The Fallen Fae* continues in...**
*Keeper of Storms*
*(The Fallen Fae, Book Three)*
Available for Preorder Now

**Join Jenna's reader newsletter** to be notified on release day and to receive exclusive free stories not found anywhere else.

**The World of Tir Na Nog:** Find extra information about the books, including a larger version of the map, a Spotify playlist, upcoming release dates, and more at www.thefallenfae.com

**Jenna's Court of Books and Readers** is a Facebook group with early access to cover reveals and sneak peek chapters.

## GLOSSARY OF TERMS

**Adhradh** - a building of worship for followers of the Dagda

**Airgead** - the coin of the six kingdoms in Tir Na Nog

**Alchemist** - a healer in Tir Na Nog who specializes in herbal treatments

**Alder** - a tree found within the Wood Court lands that turns to an orange red when cut

**Animal familiar** - an animal whose soul is linked to the soul of a fae

**Beltane** - the yearly celebration that takes place at the beginning of summer

**Brigantu** - one of the two moons

**Buntata** - a strong drink brewed from spirits, potatoes, sugar, pink coloring and egg whites

**Court of Death** - the mysterious home of the Dagda

**Dagda** - the god worshipped by all of those in Tir Na Nog, other than the shadow fae

**Danu** - one of the two moons

**The Dionadair** - the true name of the magic plaguing the lands of Tir Na Nog, created to protect the world from Unseelie

**Dryads** - tree nymphs who live in the wood fae lands, who tend to avoid courtly politics so that they might live in peace

**Druid** - a religious leader in the faith of the Dagda

**Elemental Arts** - the powers that were once available to fae based on their lineage

**The Fall** - the event where every fae upon Tir Na Nog fell to the ground, losing the magic given to them by the Dagda

**Fomorians** - the mysterious people of the Empire of Fomor, found across the impassable sea

**Ghaisgeach** - a hero spoken of in the lore of the sea fae

**Grand Alderman** - the right hand of the High King and the second most powerful position in a kingdom

**High King** - the highest ranking noble in the kingdom who controls the Seat of Power

**High Queen** - the highest ranking noble if there is no High King

**Hoarfrost silk** - expensive, valuable silk obtained from the hoarfrost worms only found in icy terrain

**Ice glass** - a strong, sturdy glass found in the mines of the Ice Court that can be used to create jewellery and weapons

**Ifrinn** - the fae underworld where damned souls are forced to live for eternity

**The Namhaid** - the enemy of the Fomorians, according to an ancient prophecy

**Priest** - a religious leader for the followers of the Unseelie god

**Rowan** - a tree found in the north yielding berries that can intoxicate

**The Ruin** - a terrible magic that falls from the sky, destroying everything it touches

**Seat of Power** - the coronation seat in each of the six kingdoms that bestows power and strength

**Seelie** - the god of light who has long been forgotten by the fae of Tir Na Nog

**Sgail** - the dead coin of the shadow fae, no longer accepted in any market in Tir Na Nog

**Shadowsteel** - a powerful steel forged from metals only found within the Shadow Court lands

**Shieldmaiden** - a female warrior who vows to spend her entire life protecting her people no matter the cost

**Tamaris steel** - a strong, sturdy steel forged within the Fire Court lands

**Tir Na Nog** - the continent of the six fae kingdoms

**Unseelie** - the dark magic god that bestows powerful gifts, but requires sacrifice in return

**The Wild Hunt** - the rumored hunt by Fomorians every Beltane where they kill every fae they see

**Winter Solstice** - the yearly celebration during mid-winter

**Yew** - a poisonous tree found throughout the continent

## ALSO BY JENNA WOLFHART

**The Fallen Fae**

Court of Ruins

Prince of Shadows (A Novella)

Kingdom in Exile

Keeper of Storms

**The Paranormal PI Files**

Live Fae or Die Trying

Dead Fae Walking

Bad Fae Rising

One Fae in the Grave

Innocent Until Proven Fae

All's Fae in Love and War

**The Supernatural Spy Files**

Confessions of a Dangerous Fae

Confessions of a Wicked Fae

**The Bone Coven Chronicles**

Witch's Curse

Witch's Storm

Witch's Blade

Witch's Fury

**Protectors of Magic**

Wings of Stone

Carved in Stone

Bound by Stone

Shadows of Stone

**Otherworld Academy**

A Dance with Darkness

A Song of Shadows

A Touch of Starlight

A Cage of Moonlight

A Heart of Midnight

**Order of the Fallen**

Ruinous

Nebulous

# ABOUT THE AUTHOR

Jenna Wolfhart spends her days tucked away in her writing shed. When she's not writing, she loves to deadlift, rewatch Game of Thrones, and drink copious amounts of coffee.

Born and raised in America, Jenna now lives in England with her husband, her two dogs, and her mischief of rats.

www.jennawolfhart.com
jenna@jennawolfhart.com

www.ingramcontent.com/pod-product-compliance
Lightning Source LLC
Chambersburg PA
CBHW020556310726
48979CB00008B/1238/J
*9781916383715*